D1806492

About the Author

Cathryn Chapman nearly gave up her writing career when her eighth grade English teacher refused to believe her sensual poem could have been written by somebody so young. Two years later, when Cathryn was fourteen, that same English teacher declared she should start writing for *Mills & Boon*, and a women's fiction writer was born. Cathryn graduated from university with a business degree and has spent seven years travelling the world — working on cruise ships and living in London, New York, Paris, and South America. In her thirties, she left a successful marketing and public relations career to pursue her dream of gracing the stages in London's West End. When this failed dismally, Cathryn settled down in Brisbane with her husband and baby boy, and finally stayed in one country long enough to write her first novel, SEX, LIES, AND CRUISING.

Cathryn is currently working on the second and third books in this series... LOVE, DRUGS, AND NEW YORK is due for release in October 2015.

Sex, Lies, and Cruising

CATHRYN CHAPMAN

SEX, LIES, AND CRUISING

Author's note: All characters, cruise lines, and companies appearing in this work are fictitious. Any resemblance to real persons, living or dead, or cruise lines/companies, is purely coincidental.

Copyright © 2015 Cathryn Chapman
All rights reserved.
ISBN: 978-0-9943143-0-7
Cover design: Jo Kuipers Design
Photo Manipulation: Wasfi Hfaidhia

Hey Dad, I hope you'd be proud of me for doing something this significant. Of course, you wouldn't like the sexy content, but don't worry—I've never done any of these things. It's fiction…mostly.
I love and miss you every day. xxx

Chapter One

Twenty-four hours on board the ship and I've already shagged someone.

It's the first time in four years I've been to bed with someone who isn't my fiancé. Not exactly what I expected to happen when I started this job, but not as bad as it might sound. I'm not some completely heartless cow who left her lovely man in England for a cruise ship job in the Caribbean and then embarked upon an illustrious affair within hours. I needed to get as far away from London as possible…

It was big. Enormous, really. I craned my neck back as far as it would go and stared up, speechless. I'd googled cruise ships, read countless forums, and pored over the ports and the passenger photos, but nothing had prepared me for the real thing. The *Galene*, one of the ships with Celestial Cruise Line, was quite possibly the most amazing thing I had ever seen— and I got to live on board for six months. She had at least fifteen decks above the waterline, and the orange lifeboats were bright against the shining, snowy expanse of the hull.

Wow. I had never seen anything quite so big or impressive since the summer I spent working in a Turkish steamroom.

I was definitely excited, but it was all so new and overwhelming; a momentary wave of panic about leaving my safe and familiar life back in England washed over me and was promptly quashed.

Onwards and upwards, I said to myself, following the signs to the crew purser's office. *This is the new, exciting life you deserve.*

Dan can get stuffed.

I was told a colleague had been allocated to show me around on my first day, so I stood outside the office, scanning the scores of faces swarming around me and waiting to be rescued. Languages and accents from every corner of the globe tickled my ears, and the sea of smiling faces was a treat for my eyes. It was truly a cultural melting pot and I loved it already. The flight from London, via Madrid and Miami, had left me exhausted, but I felt my energy picking up as I looked around, my heart pulsating with excitement and anticipation.

A blonde girl appeared out of nowhere and grabbed my arm. "Oh, my God, Ellie?" She squealed with excitement and pulled me into a hug. The girl had the tiniest waist I'd ever seen. "I'm Caitlin, your new roomie! It's *so* good to meet you! Welcome!" She spoke in exclamation marks and sounded American, but you can never be too careful about offending a Canadian who might crash tackle you while educating you about the Canucks, so I erred on the side of not asking, and instead just squeaked, "Hello."

"I'm going to show you around the ship and get you settled in," she said cheerfully, catching my hand and towing me along behind her. "There are about a million things you need to know. Just stick with me and you'll be fine."

As she led me through a maze of corridors, I immediately got lost; everything looked the same, and as we moved down into the ship, below the waterline, the lack of windows made everything just a little scarier than I'd anticipated.

"You know the itinerary, right?" she asked over her shoulder. Before I could reply, she barrelled on. "It's pretty boring… Playing pool in San Juan on Sunday, cocktails in St Thomas on Monday, sleeping-in for Martinique on Tuesday, private beach in Barbados on Wednesday, 365 beautiful beaches in Antigua on Thursday, dual French and Dutch culture in St Martin on Friday, and a looooong, boring day at sea on Saturday." She glanced back at me and grinned. "The cruise line likes to squeeze out every last dollar from passengers during their last day on board the ship."

I was feeling more than a little overwhelmed. "Gosh," I said intelligently.

"Pretty boring, right? Don't worry, we find plenty to do!" She winked.

"Oh, good," I said. My trademark loquacity was completely failing me. I sounded like an idiot.

"So I heard you were English, yeah?" she said, pointing out the crew quarters and sailing on. "We're super international on these ships, you know. Think I've worked my way around half of Europe by now with the guys I've dated." She laughed wickedly and carried on down the corridor at breakneck speed. "So have you ever been to Canada? Spent my whole life in the same little town in Alberta. Cruise ships are waaaay more fun." My Canadian warning bells had been correct.

We passed the staff quarters and a dining area, Caitlin rattling away the whole time. "Cleaners, waiters, bartenders, security—they're all 'crew'. Photographers, entertainment staff, casino staff—all 'staff'. We members of staff are a bit higher in the pecking order, so we get better cabins and a better dining room." We walked past another dining room with white tablecloths, napkins, and several glasses at each setting. "This is the officer's mess," Caitlin said, walking backwards so she could see me. "They're mostly the guys who drive the ship, or other senior crew, and they have their own areas altogether."

I wasn't sure how I felt about the ranking system; it seemed a bit unfair, but it seemed that as a photographer I'd still have access to really good facilities.

Caitlin showed me to the crew bar, a huge room split in two; at the moment, vacant, it was dark and rather dingy, and I tried to imagine what it would look like full of people. It had the standard bar set-up: bar, tables, dance floor (with a mirror ball, in case we felt like reliving the seventies with disco), and a sad bunch of Fourth of July decorations that had clearly been left over from months earlier.

"This is where all the action happens..." Caitlin said, twirling in the empty space. She came to a stop and added, "Or at least where it normally starts." She winked. "Ooh, speaking of which, do you have a boyfriend at home?"

I was temporarily thrown by the change of topic. I'd thought it would come up eventually, but I hadn't expected to be asked about things so soon. "Oh," I said. "Erm. Yes. Well, I mean, no, not anymore." I hesitated, but Caitlin was waiting eagerly for further details. "I had a fiancé, actually. His name was Dan." As I said his name, a small wave of emotion surged through me. I'd avoided talking about him to anyone since we'd broken up, including my parents, and now all of my insecurities and frustration bubbled up and spewed forth like an emotional volcano. I couldn't be stopped. "I met him at university and we were together for four years," I said. "We moved in together, got engaged…and then everything turned to shit." I took a deep breath, trying to banish the tears at the corners of my eyes. "All we ever did was watch telly and order in take-away. Dan always said he was tired from working all day, so he never wanted to cook and he never wanted to go out. I couldn't tell you the last time we had a proper night out—oh, no, wait." I laughed bitterly. "I remember. He dragged me to a bloody One Direction concert, was super keen on it, and you want to know why?" Caitlin nodded mutely, eyes wide, waiting for me to go on. I half laughed, half choked, and continued, "Turns out he was shagging some bloody twenty-year-old bint from the office. Laura. Turns out One Direction is Laura's favourite band. He wanted to have something to talk to her about at work on Monday!" My voice had become loud and shrill, leaving the last word to echo in the otherwise silent room.

Caitlin was still staring at me, her mouth hanging open. "Oh, God, dude, fucking One Direction?" She shook her head and wrinkled her nose. "That's just wrong."

"She was thin and pretty and exciting," I said. "According to Dan, I'm fat and boring and frumpy." I poked dismally at my tummy.

"He's an idiot," Caitlin said promptly. I liked her more every minute. "So, did he leave you for her?"

I thought back to the conversation we'd had after Dan had

finally came clean about his affair, and snorted. "No," I said. "Can you believe he actually begged me to stay? Turned out that despite my many, *many* flaws, he wasn't quite ready to let me go, just in case his bit on the side fell through. Nothing like being someone's backup to put your life in perspective." I sighed. "So I left him."

"Good for you, girl," she said, giving me a thumbs up. "What a complete fucker."

"Yep," I said. That pretty much summed him up. "Total wanker. You know, I'm actually rather glad he turned out to be such an arse."

"No kidding?"

"Gave me a chance to come here and pursue my dreams, instead of focusing on his. I have to tell you, playing the dutiful housewife gets terribly boring after a while!" I smiled. "I like to think that the whole end of that relationship was just fate's way of telling me I was in the wrong place."

"Well, Ellie, if your dream is to meet some damn fine men, you've come to the right place," Caitlin said, grinning. "There's someone for everyone here, and they're all up for a good time—though not necessarily for a long time. We like to say that life on ships goes at four times the speed of real life. Because we live together in such close quarters, everything is really intense and things happen much more quickly than they do at home. Relationships start and finish and tend to be real fast and furious." She sighed.

I was single for the first time in four years, which was both a terrifying and exhilarating thought. I was eager to dive back in, but I had to admit I had more than one reservation. My love life with Dan had been pretty boring for years and, to be honest, before I'd met Dan my love life could have been summed up in about five minutes. Now that I was here, I was determined to get out and explore what real men had to offer. I didn't want to rush into anything serious with anyone; I was more interested in having the chance to play and explore, something I'd never really been able to do before. From Caitlin's description, the relationships aboard ship sounded like just the kind of thing I was looking for.

I looked around the room, feeling slightly delirious from jetlag, but terribly excited all the same. "This is so brilliant. I can't believe I'm finally here," I said.

"And trust me, we are going to have a fucking great time," Caitlin said as she led me out of the bar. "Starting tonight."

When we reached the photographer's cabins, the area was deserted, something Caitlin had been expecting. "Everyone will be down shooting embarks," she explained. "That's where we take photos of all the passengers as they arrive, before the stupid Americans all ask 'Where's the buffet?'" She smiled. "Let's dump your stuff and grab something to eat. Then we'll go and do all the formalities."

When Caitlin opened the door to our cabin, I was shocked at how small it was. Two bunk beds, both neatly made, a TV/DVD hanging off the opposite wall, a desk with a bar fridge underneath. On the back wall there was a tiny wardrobe with drawers underneath, and a bathroom which had the shower almost on top of the toilet.

"It's not much," she said, "but it's home. There's a cabin steward who comes every day to clean the room. He changes the towels, makes our beds, empties the bin, and does a general tidy up. He changes the sheets once a week, but if you mess them up earlier" she grinned and winked "he'll change them for five dollars."

The way Caitlin was looking at me made me laugh nervously. I had a niggling feeling Caitlin was probably a lot more adventurous than I was, and while on the one hand this provided me with an immediate, friendly, and knowledgeable resource for my goal of self-exploration, on the other I was a bit anxious that I was going to end up seeming judgmental. I'd just have to change my way of thinking, that was all. This whole job was for me to have fun and experiment, I reminded myself. I was sure there was a lot I could learn from Caitlin.

Still, it was a funny conversation to have with someone you'd just met.

Standing in the room, staring at the bathroom, I suddenly

realised how disgusting I felt. I'd been awake for most of the preceding thirty-six hours and was desperate for a shower.

"I really need to rest for a bit," I said, sinking down at the desk before my legs collapsed beneath me.

"No problem," she said. "Bet you want a shower. I've got some stuff to do, so I'll come back in a bit."

Fifteen minutes later, I stepped out of the shower feeling like an entirely new woman. I'd managed to shove the fatigue into a tiny corner of my brain and was ready to dive back into the world of the ship.

Caitlin had laid out my uniform on the bed for me before buggering off; I held it up before putting it on and sighed. I'd requested a size smaller than I actually wore as a weight loss incentive, but for the time being it was a bit of a struggle to get into.

Uniform on, I looked at my reflection and poked at my muffin top. Pale skin, lank hair, and more than my fair share of squishy flesh. Disheartening. Not quite the sexy babe I wished I was. As much as I hoped that I'd find my sexy fling on the ship, the mirror was telling me that I paled in comparison to the beautiful, tanned, leggy women on board. *Just eat less and move more*, I told myself. Dan had said I could serve to lose thirty pounds, but it was really more like twenty. Okay, twenty-five.

Irritated at myself for thinking about Dan again already, I pushed him out of my head and half-heartedly started to unpack. I was interrupted by Caitlin's return, and was more than happy to abandon my suitcase for the sandwich she handed me and follow her to the photo manager's office.

A really tall guy was leaning at the desk, chewing his thumbnail. "You're Ellie, then," he said. His accent was British—hooray, a commonality with a member of the crew! He looked me up and down quickly and then just sat there, and I had a sinking feeling that nationality wasn't going to help me here. An awkward silence filled the room.

I stuck my hand out awkwardly. "Yes, that's me. It's Justin, right? Really pleased to meet you."

"Yeah, great. Same here," he said in a decidedly uninterested tone. "The girl you replaced got appendicitis and had to be airlifted out after three weeks on board. Hope you'll last longer."

That was a hell of a vote of confidence.

"Fill out these forms and drop them back later." He slapped a stack of papers into my hand. "You start in the shop tonight. Seth will explain what to do."

Caitlin gave him a scowl and ushered me out of the room. "Ignore him," she whispered. "He's got, like, no personality."

Well, that was something. Maybe it wasn't just me. I'd been expecting a manager more like Caitlin, to be honest—welcoming and eager to get to know their team. Obviously not.

Caitlin skipped to a lift with a plastic 'CREW ONLY' sign on it, and got in, pressing level five. "Are you ready?" She squeezed my arm reassuringly.

The glass lift rose above the crew levels, and I found myself looking out across a large open area.

"Welcome to the Atrium," Caitlin said, stepping off the lift.

I had seen it online, but nothing had really prepared me for the incredible expanse of light and space we'd just entered. A huge atrium towered high above us. Shops, restaurants, and bars were visible around the edges, a haze of gleaming windows and twinkling lights. Everywhere I looked was a luxurious display of gleaming surfaces. Directly ahead of us was a small dance floor flanked by intimate clusters of chairs; huge potted palms surrounded a grand piano sitting on a platform.

"Bloody hell—this is incredible!" I exclaimed. My voice bounced around the open area.

"I know, right?" she agreed. "Trust me, you won't even notice after a while."

She led me to a tiny shop with a window display of cameras, memory cards, and souvenir digital photo frames.

"Welcome to your new home," Caitlin said, laughing as she opened the door. "The *Pic Stop*. Don't you just love a play on words?" She smiled wryly as I slid into the shop behind her, and then said, "Ellie, meet Seth."

The guy who had been bending down behind the counter straightened up and came towards us with his hand extended, smiling and watching me from behind a flutter of long, black eyelashes. Crazy perfect chiselled jaw, tall, tanned, a muscled chest barely concealed by his regulation polo. Bloody hell. I loved hot countries. Men like that shouldn't ever be wrapped up under layers of winter woollies. I had to stop myself from sighing out loud.

"Hey, Ellie, how ya doin'?"

A sexy Texan. Lord, help me. All my teenage Mills & Boon fantasies came flooding back.

"Oh, right, yes," I said, suddenly realising I'd been staring. "Hi! I'm Ellie." I took his hand and then never wanted to let it go; warmth spread up my arm from the contact with his fingers. "Oh, you already knew that. Yes. Absolutely smashing to meet you." I was babbling. Ah, the return of my tendency to fill awkward silences. Hooray.

He turned my hand over and pressed it to his lips. They were warm and soft.

Be cool, Ellie.

Telling myself to be cool when quite frankly I'd never been cool a day in my life was a bit of a lost cause. I felt giddy, like I had an excess of hormones swirling around my body. I was going to get paid to work with this guy. I snuck another look at him and supressed a dreamy sigh. This guy could have been a Grecian god, he was so perfect. I suddenly wondered why I'd wasted the last four years with a man who'd greeted me with little more than a grunt most mornings.

Caitlin disappeared to get on with her own duties, leaving us alone. It was slightly surreal, getting straight to work after hours of flying and only a few hours of sleep on the plane…but I had a feeling that as tired as I was, working with Seth would make everything just a little more bearable.

"So, tell me, Ellie, have you worked in a shop before?" he asked, looking at me intently.

"Um, yes, I spent four years as a retail assistant in a really unfashionable boutique," I said, cringing as I remembered the horrid old lady clothes I'd had to sell to pay the bills. I'd hated that job, and it had only been made worse because Dan spent his money on lads' weekends away and season passes to the football. "My real passion is photography, though. I've got a BA in Photography, but this is the first time in years I've had a job remotely related to taking pictures." Which was true. I very much wanted Seth to know I wasn't just a salesgirl. I had *depth*, dammit.

"Wow," he said, smiling. "You're even more impressive than I first thought. We need someone like you around here."

I felt my cheeks burn, and tried my best to concentrate as Seth went on to explain the shop operations. Despite my best efforts, I kept getting distracted by the long lock of hair that repeatedly fell into his eyes as he spoke. Every time it happened, I had to bite my lip to keep from dribbling. He really was ridiculously good looking.

To make concentration more difficult, Seth regularly stopped speaking and gave me a very slow, sexy smile. More than once he followed that smile up by asking, "Are ya with me there, Miss Ellie?"

I just giggled in response. I was acting like a pathetic schoolgirl, and failing miserably at projecting a cool image. But in my defence, I'd been living with a soulless twat for four years and had become completely starved of attention. And Seth had complimented me, so obviously he saw *something* in me!

Also, a woman is never at her best when suffering jetlag. Yes, now I mention it, jetlag was definitely the biggest contributor in my inability to focus on his instructions. Probably.

Despite my wandering thoughts, running the shop didn't seem like a difficult task. The Pic Stop would only open when the ship was sailing, as customs regulations meant I couldn't open while we were in port, but it would close at 11pm so guests could focus on drinking and gambling.

"So I'll only be open from 5pm till 11pm, with a break from eight till nine?" It didn't seem long, but I wasn't about to complain. More time for me to have fun.

"Yep," Seth said. "Except in Martinique; we don't dock till after 11am, so you'll be open in the morning. Saturday's pretty long and dreary—the shop is open all day."

Gosh, his accent was dreamy.

He grinned. "So most days, you can party all night and sleep late…"

"Sleeping in has always been one of my favourite hobbies," I said, smiling.

"Well, I bet a pretty girl like you will have all kinds of attention on this here boat," Seth said, raising his eyebrows. "You'll be glad of a little sleep-in come mornin'." One of those sexy smiles spread across his face. "If I'm lucky, maybe I'll be a-sleepin' next to you."

Oh, Lord. A sexy, confident man I'd known for less than an hour was flirting with me in a completely obvious way. And he was sober. I'd never experienced anything like it. Dan hadn't bothered to flirt with me in years, and I'd completely forgotten how it felt to be sexy and attractive. And I liked it.

"What will I do the rest of the time?" I asked. Despite being completely thrown by Seth's flirting, I was genuinely intrigued by the stipulations of my job. It seemed crazy to work so few hours and get paid over $2000 a month, cash in hand, tax free, and with no living expenses. I kept waiting for the catch.

"Whatever you like," he said. Putting on a bad Jamaican accent, he added, "Hang out with me, maaaan… Dance a little…" He grabbed my hand again, pulling me into a dance hold for a moment.

"Oh, right, sounds cool." I giggled again. He was really quite full-on. I'd read about this kind of thing on a crew forum back at home; the guys had to get in quick to call dibs on the new girls. I'd just never imagined I'd actually be one of those girls. I thought I'd be out of sight behind scores of gorgeous, leggy blondes with exotic accents.

I heard a long, loud horn, and Seth opened the doors. "The ship's setting sail. Time to open shop. You got out of the safety drill today, but you'll be expected to do it next week." He slid back behind the counter, pulling me with him. "I'll help out in the shop tonight, but you'll be on your own tomorrow."

I said a little prayer for the evening to pass slowly.

Despite my wishes, the night passed by in a blur of friendly and inquisitive faces. I lost track of the number of times I was asked where I was from. My name badge said 'Ellie – England' in bold black type, but I realised pretty quickly that nobody actually read name badges.

Seth was lovely, helpful, and friendly to everyone. The men laughed and the ladies twittered and blushed. He certainly had a very special magnetism, and it became rapidly apparent that I wasn't the only one taken in by his charms.

At the end of the night, as we closed up shop to leave for the crew bar, Seth reached over and cupped my face in his hands.

"You did real good here tonight, Ellie," he said. "You're going to fit in here just fine." He looked deeply into my eyes for a moment, and I breathed in sharply.

The magnetism between us was totally electric. I could feel the energy coursing through his hands, sending a lovely tingling feeling zipping from my head to my toes. I felt such a connection with him—okay, it was mostly physical, but it was a connection all the same—but I couldn't believe how fast we'd clicked. A whispered "Thanks," was all I could manage in my completely failed state of nonchalance.

Seth gazed at me for a moment longer, and then dropped his hands from my face, breaking the connection. "Righto, let's go," he said. "I'm fixin' for a drink."

I trailed after him like a puppy to the crew bar. The music was loud and the mirror ball reflected dozens of tiny sparkling flecks around the room and across its inhabitants—a far cry from what it had looked like earlier in the day. Most of the people on the dance floor looked like they'd been there for a while.

Seth leaned over and said, directly in my ear, "Let's get you drunk, new girl." He winked and grabbed my hand again, dragging me to the bar.

The barman greeted me with a lovely, Scottish lilt.

"You must be new," he said, brushing his hair off his forehead and smiling. "Unless you've never been here before, but I think I'd've remembered you." He chuckled, and his blue eyes crinkled up at the corners. He looked like he was around thirty; I couldn't tell for sure because of the lighting, but I thought I saw a few flecks of grey in his dark blond hair.

"I'm Jock," he said, extending his hand.

He had a really warm spirit, and I liked him immediately. Nothing at all like my connection with Seth, but I felt immediately comfortable with him.

"Hi," I said, moving to take his hand, "I'm—"

"This is Ellie," Seth interrupted, grabbing a napkin off the bar and knocking my hand away from Jock's in the process. "Can I get a couple of rum and Cokes?"

Jock said nothing, just looked at Seth with a blank expression. There was some kind of unspoken tension between the two and it made me feel uncomfortable, though I'd no idea what it was about.

A couple of guys came up to Seth, greeting him loudly and interrupting the awkward moment. Seth turned to them to answer a question about a recent surfing trip, leaving me looking sheepishly at Jock across the bar.

"Sorry," I said, feeling a bit embarrassed.

"Nothing to worry about, lass," he said, shrugging it off and pouring our drinks. "I've had much worse in this gig." He slid one of the glasses across to me. "So you must be the new photog, then?"

"I'm in the Pic Stop, actually," I said. "I want to be a photographer, so obviously being in the shop's not as glamourous as it could be, but it's a start, right?"

"Glamorous, you say?" Jock chuckled. "I hate to disappoint you, Ellie, but there's not a lot of glamorous activity going on here at all."

He was obviously joking. Seth alone qualified for the Most Glamorous Man of the Year award.

"Come on, Jock," I protested, "we get paid to see beautiful islands, meet new people, and have a good time!"

He snorted and held my gaze for a few moments before smiling and moving away to his next customer. Then, as though he had a sudden thought, he turned back to me and said, "Just be careful, lass. It's not all it's cracked up to be. Get to know your way around before you do anything crazy."

I followed his line of sight and found Seth. I returned my attention to Jock as he slid Seth's drink over to me.

"This one's on me," he added, gesturing towards our drinks. "See you around soon, I hope."

And then he trotted off to the other end of the bar.

I didn't have a chance to ponder Jock's words, as Seth reappeared by my side and threw his arm around my shoulder.

"C'mon, you," he said, leading me towards a dark corner.

I glanced back at Jock, but he was busy at the other end of the bar with a group of men who'd just come in.

"Well, Ellie, I'm real glad you joined us," Seth said in my ear as we sat down. I put Jock out of my mind and focused on the very sexy man I was sitting next to. He'd appeared a bit rude at the bar, but thinking about it, I figured he'd probably just been showing off. Alpha males are all alike.

Now, I've…had…the time of my life…

My ears pricked up at the opening strains of the most classic boy-girl anthem of all time, certainly rather apt in this very 'Dirty Dancing at Sea' environment. My first instinct was to jump out of my seat, link arms with the closest girl, and sing at the top of my voice while waving my drink in the air. Key dance moves were optional, but when drunk they were always my favourite part.

I didn't have to restrain myself for long. Seth caught my controlled reaction and, laughing, launched into the chorus.

"I've had the time of my life; no, I've never felt like this before…" He sang with unabashed enthusiasm.

A rum and Coke for courage? Three dollars. A man who

was brave enough to sing with me, especially in a room full of other men? Priceless.

We sang, drank, flirted, and laughed our way through the night. I was surprised how much I had in common with a football-playing, horse-loving, rum-chugging Texan—and even more surprised at how freely the conversation flowed. Almost everything I was into, Seth enjoyed too, and every story I told, he laughed until his abs hurt. And when I thought about what those abs looked like...

After being with Dan for so many years, I'd stopped telling stories. Dan never listened; he was bored and disinterested, and if he paid any attention at all it was only to complain that I wasn't any fun anymore. As I met Seth's eyes yet again, and felt his hand resting on my knee, I was pleased to think that I was proving Dan wrong already. I knew how to have fun and, even better, real, live men actually found me attractive. And interesting. Maybe I'd just been fishing in the wrong pond all these years.

I blushed, laughed, and giggled my way through several drinks rather quickly, certainly more quickly than I was used to. The atmosphere was as intoxicating as the alcohol; I only had to look around to see that everyone was enjoying themselves. The lights were festive, the music was loud, and it was way too easy to swipe a crew key card at the bar for another round. I offered to buy a couple of times, but Seth wouldn't allow it.

"Your money's no good here," he said, playfully swatting my hand away.

In the middle of a story about a drinking game gone horribly wrong, a small but noisy group took over the booth next to us. As I carried on my conversation with Seth, I couldn't help but keep catching the eye of one of the guys at the other table. He kept chatting with his friends, but his attention clearly wasn't on the discussion; his eyes kept darting back towards me. Finally, he smiled widely and stood up.

"G'day," he said as he approached, extending his hand to me and completely ignoring Seth. "You must be new. I'm Mike. Can I buy you a drink?"

Hello, Australian accent. This place was like the bloody United Nations.

I looked down at the drink Seth had just bought me. "Erm, thank you, that's ever so kind of you…but, erm, I've already got one for now." I glanced at Seth, who didn't look too happy, then back at Mike. "Thanks," I said again for emphasis, adding a smile to soften the blow.

"Yeah, buddy," Seth said, puffing out his chest. The alpha male asserting his dominance. "She already has a drink, okay?" He placed a protective hand on my knee. My skin tingled at his touch.

Mike shrugged. "Let me know if you change your mind," he said, completely ignoring Seth and giving me an exaggerated eyebrow raise before returning to his mates.

It was truly bizarre. My online research meant that I'd expected the guys to compete for the new girls, but I'd hardly anticipated being in the middle of a pissing contest on my first night. Of the first three men I'd met, two of them had been clearly interested. I contemplated my brief chat with Jock, and decided that though he'd been charming, his warning had felt more friendly than anything else. It was becoming rapidly evident that I'd have plenty of options available to me, so there was no sense in being interested in someone who belonged in the 'friend' category.

No, my focus for now was Seth, as he'd made his interest clear; males marking their territory is more or less the same the world over. It wasn't like I thought I'd be interested in everyone—I'm reasonably picky—but it was certainly good to feel desirable for the first time in many years, muffin top and all. It had been a very long time since Dan had last made me feel good about myself.

And anyway, I was here to have fun! And, you know, further my photography career in the process. There was that, too.

"So, Miss Ellie," Seth said, abandoning the macho display and moving straight back into sexy mode, "the other photographers have been up in the gallery, selling embarkation photos. There's not much point waiting for them here. We'll catch them later...or in the morning." He moved his hand a little further up my leg.

I hadn't played the flirtation game in years, but four or five—or was it six?—drinks into the evening, I was really getting into it, leaning into Seth, laughing at his jokes, enjoying every time we touched...

A few drinks later, I suddenly felt a little giddy and sick, and wondered how much I'd actually had to drink; I never usually drank this much. On top of only a sandwich to eat and way too many hours awake, the alcohol had hit me hard.

"Can we go back to the cabins now?" I asked. My stomach gurgled, and I fervently hoped that Seth hadn't heard it.

He stood up, pulling me with him; I caught my foot under the table and tripped, but Seth caught me before I fell. The room still seemed to be tilted a bit, and then I remembered that I was on a ship, so that must be normal.

As we headed out, I glanced at the bar to see if Jock was still on duty, but a different guy was behind the bar. Oh well, I'd check in with him tomorrow—just to thank him for the drink.

As we walked back to our little area below the water line, the ship's tilting felt much worse, like the whole thing was lurching from side to side. Surely that wasn't normal?

Oh, bollocks, I thought, I'm drunker than I thought.

With that in mind, I concentrated hard on walking as straight as possible, which proved to be an incredibly difficult thing to do given how much my head was spinning.

Ooh, gosh, I thought, squinting down the corridor, I've drunk too much. Hope Seth doesn't mind I'm a bit squiffy...

The hallway seemed to run on forever, and I had a momentary mental panic that I was never going to find my way around. If the ship would just stop moving... I tipped slightly and knocked against the wall, and for a moment thought I was going to topple over. And then I felt Seth's firm hand beneath my elbow, steadying me. *Look at that,* I thought fuzzily. *Found myself a man who's funny, strong, chivalrous, sexy...*

When we reached the photographer's area, Seth opened his cabin door and ushered me in. "Just come in for a drink of water and take a load off," he said. "We don't want Caitlin thinking you're a lush."

I hesitated for a moment before stepping into his cabin. Should I go in? I needed time to think.

Okay, time's up. Yes...yes, I should. I mean, it was probably just as well I try to sober up a bit before going in to sleep; Caitlin had been lovely earlier in the day, but I didn't really want to embarrass myself by turning up absolutely plastered on my first night.

I tried to focus on Seth's cabin. It was pretty much the same as ours, but the top bunk was folded up against the wall.

"Uneven numbers," he explained, seeing the focus of my attention. "I don't have to share." He flipped a switch above the desk and the room sparkled in a wash of fairy lights and added, "Leftover from the previous occupant."

"Great," I said, easing myself onto the edge of the bed. Sitting down was definitely a good idea. The fairy lights made everything look soft and romantic, and given that my face tended to go a bit shiny when I'd been drinking, this was a definite plus for me. I looked up at Seth and a silly smile spread across my face. He was so lovely, and he lived right next door. How perfect was that? And it was only the first day.

Seth didn't seem to notice I wasn't speaking much, probably because he was putting on music. As a Latin rhythm filled the cabin, he pulled me to my feet and grabbed me around the waist. "I spent a summer in Cuba and learned to salsa," he said, swivelling his hips like a pro. "Let me teach you."

I relaxed into his hold, feeling lovely and warm and happy. His arms wrapped around me, like he was protecting me, and then slid a little lower.

"Swing your butt. That's right."

As I did as he instructed, I felt sexy and free. I'd needed this. It was exactly the Caribbean fantasy I had envisioned; I should have done it years ago.

Seth and I twirled around the cramped space like experts—or at least it felt like it. We were a swirl of tousled brown hair, sparkling lights, and white cotton polo shirts.

"Time for a turn!" he announced, and lifted my arm to push me awkwardly in a circle. Then, just like a tacky teen movie, he pulled me from the turn into his arms. I was breathing heavily; Seth wiped his forehead with the back of his hand.

I was still laughing when he grabbed my face with both hands and kissed me square on the mouth.

"I've been wanting to do that all night," he confessed. "You're amazing, you know. I liked you from the moment I saw you." His face was inches from mine.

"Really?" My battered self-esteem perked up.

"Totally. You're awesome." He stroked my arm and then ran his hand up until his fingers were tangled in my hair. My head was spinning, and as Seth leant in to kiss me again, I felt like I was melting in his arms. After years of kissing Dan, I finally discovered what a sexy kiss actually felt like. His lips were warm and soft, and the way he was tracing the outline of my lips with his tongue and nibbling on my bottom lip was very, very erotic. My lady bits fired up with the sweet burn of lust, and my heart was pumping furiously.

On reflection, Dan had kissed like a sucker fish. No wonder I hadn't felt like sex very often; I'd had to put up with his poor excuse for foreplay first.

The music had become slow and sultry, and I knew what was coming next. Seth pulled off his polo and tossed it aside, revealing a perfectly tanned and athletic torso. Oh, Lordy. My mouth was suddenly dry and I nervously licked my lips, having an eleventh hour panic about whether I still remembered how to do this whole sex thing with someone who wasn't Dan. Ooh, was that guilt I was feeling? I shoved the feeling away; I'd left Dan. I needed to remember that. I'd nothing to feel guilty about.

Jock's warning flitted through my mind, but I ignored it, shoving it into a corner of my brain. After all, I wasn't made of stone.

And on the bright side, I'd had a wax before coming aboard. Just in case.

"Oh Ellie," Seth murmured, nuzzling my neck, "you're so beautiful." He kissed me again and tugged at my shirt.

Wow. Guys like him didn't fall for girls like me. I'd got so used to seeing myself as a frumpy housewife that it really hadn't occurred to me that someone like Seth could want me. But there was definitely no doubt about it.

He unzipped my skirt, his hands running all over my body. "Don't you know how beautiful you are?" he asked. His kisses were getting deeper and I could feel my body responding. My heart was beating like it wanted to leap out of my chest, I was breathing heavily, and my lips were tingling.

My God, thought the one tiny part of my brain that was still capable of rational thought, *did I only just leave England yesterday?* It felt like a million miles away.

His slow gentle moves became more feverish, and I wound my arms around his neck and pulled him closer. He smiled and buried his face in my neck. I closed my eyes and tried to stifle an overly enthusiastic moan. *Oh, Seth…*

I was ready for my high seas adventure to really begin.

Chapter Two

A phone was ringing, waking me with a start from a deep sleep. I sat bolt upright and smacked my head. "Ow, ow, fucking owwwwwwww!" My head was pounding and my mouth felt fuzzy, and on top of that I was coming up blank about where I was. Why was it so dark?

Panicked, I stared into the dark until my eyes adjusted, instinctively drawing the sheet up to my chest. And then I remembered. Oh, my God. I was on the cruise ship. In Seth's cabin. I lifted the sheet and peeked beneath it. Apart from a striped vest, which wasn't mine, I was naked.

"Shit." The events of last night started flooding back to me. The phone kept ringing.

"All riiiiigggghhhhht!" shouted a voice from above me. A light came on as Seth jumped from the top bunk and landed heavily on the floor. He grabbed a phone from the wall, and thank God, the ringing stopped. "Yeah, yeah, yeah. *All right.* I'm a-comin'." He hung up the phone and turned around to look at me. "Hey there, Miss Ellie. Thought we'd all be more comfortable if I pulled down the top bunk and camped out there."

I hesitated for a moment. Who knew what to say in this sort of situation? It had been years since I'd spent the night with someone new.

"I hope my snoring didn't scare you off," I teased, trying to lighten the moment. He looked away awkwardly. I snored? Shit. I had been kidding!

"Well, uh, I have to go to work. I was supposed to be

ɔting gangway this morning." He ran his hands through his ᴧir, looking dishevelled and gorgeous. "Please don't feel you need to rush out of bed. You don't have to be at work till tonight."

The pain in my head was turning into more of a throbbing sensation, but memories of the previous night were determined to take centre stage. Basically, I'd been on board for about five minutes, downed drinks like a university student, and jumped right into bed with a virtual stranger. The fact that he also happened to be a colleague I'd see daily for the next six months only made things worse. Flashbacks of sloppy kissing and loud exclamations of pleasure—I mentally cringed. I'd a bad feeling I must have come across as terribly out of practice in the bedroom. I felt like a bit of a twit, really, because the whole thing was so unlike me. And then I thought about getting out of bed and going to work, and immediately started to panic about what people would think of me if they knew what had happened. Arg, I should have known I wasn't going to be very good at this!

"Should we keep this secret?" I asked abruptly. "It's a bit weird, right, that I only got here and yesterday and we've already…you know…"

"I wouldn't worry about it," he said with a shrug. "This is a cruise ship, little lady, not a convent."

Our night of passion had been one of my exotic cruise fantasies, and he was being refreshingly nonchalant about it, but I still felt awkward as arse. It had been a long time since I'd had to deal with the walk of shame. But before I could skulk back to my own cabin, there was something I needed. I felt around under the covers and quickly scanned the floor. Damn, they were about three feet away, curled up in a little ball right near Seth's left foot. Bollocks.

"Can you, um, please pass me my pants?" I felt my cheeks go hot. This was embarrassing.

He looked around in confusion. "I thought you were wearing a skirt?"

I suddenly remembered the difference in vocabulary across

the pond. Cringing, I said, "My...underpants." Excruciating.

He looked down and spotted them. As he handed over my pants, uniform, and thankfully, my bra, our hands met and I felt a little jolt of electricity. His hand lingered...then he leaned over and kissed me quickly on the lips. "Thanks for last night, Miss Ellie. I had a jolly ol' good time," he said, mocking my accent embarrassingly badly.

"Oh, no problem at all. I'm not normally so...forward...but it was fun." I reached under the sheet, trying to struggle into my pants. Where was last night's carefree Ellie when I needed her?

"Well, we should do this again," he said over his shoulder as he disappeared into the bathroom. I heard the toilet flush, followed by the shower being turned on full blast. I swung my feet onto the floor, straightened myself out, and looked for a mirror to check how scary my hair and makeup looked after last night. I couldn't find one, so I rubbed a finger under my eye and groaned when it came away black. I gingerly patted my hair and quickly discovered it was sticking up at the back. "Ugh." Not the best look. Then again, if someone like Seth wanted to spend the night with me, again, I must have been doing something right...

I looked around Seth's cabin as I squeezed myself back into my wrinkled uniform. It was the same size as mine, obviously, but surprisingly neat for a guy's room. The desk held a laptop, iPod docking station, and a few books. At the back of the room were a couple of little chairs and a small, round table, where Seth's crumpled uniform lay in a little heap.

I really couldn't believe I'd slept with him. I hadn't been with anyone other than Dan for years, and while I *was* looking for fun, I hadn't intended to play 'How's Your Father' with someone quite so soon. Mind you, I wasn't complaining. Seth had the accent, face, and body of most girls' secret (and not-so-secret) fantasies.

A knock at the door interrupted my thoughts. "Seth? Please hurry up!" It was a woman with an unidentifiable accent. "We were supposed to be on gangway five minutes ago. Justin is going to kill us!" Knock, knock, knock. "Seth!"

The door flew open and a short girl with wavy black hair burst into the cabin. "Oh, it's unlocked. I hope—" She saw me and stopped short, staring. "Oh. You must be that new girl."

Damn. So much for getting out of there before anyone discovered me and started labelling me as some wanton whorebag. I'd thought these doors automatically locked from the inside…

Naturally, I had to play cool. "Oh, hello, I'm Ellie. Really lovely to meet you." I stuck my hand out.

She just looked at my hand without shaking it, and then looked back up at me. "You seem to have settled in." There was no trace of a smile on her heart-shaped face. I figured she was South American, or maybe Spanish; either way, she was astonishingly beautiful, and I suspected I might hate her already.

The sound of the shower stopped. "Hey, Maria, how many times have I told ya not to come into my cabin without being invited?" Seth called from the bathroom. "I really need to get that lock fixed," he added, almost, but not quite, under his breath.

"Sorry, Mr Big Shot," she said sarcastically, watching me with narrowed eyes.

"What was that?" He stuck his head out the bathroom door.

"I said sorry, I forgot," she said, smiling with total insincerity. "I see you have a guest."

"Ellie, this is Maria. Maria's a fellow photographer, from Brazil. Maria, Ellie is our new Pic Stop girl from England." Seth came out of the bathroom, drying his hair, a towel casually slung around his waist.

Maria and I caught each other eyeing his toned torso. "We've met," she mumbled, and swung around so that her back was to me. Her curvaceous figure was barely contained by her tight work skirt. I'd inherited my mum's flat bum and cursed the fact I'd never look that good in mine. I was hoping eventually I'd fit into my uniform and look stunning, but right now I just felt like a cow in a skirt too tight for me. Far cry from Maria's glamourous figure.

The tension in the room was very uncomfortable. I wondered if Maria was not the type to have fallen into a fling so quickly. According to Seth we didn't have anything to hide, but I didn't want to get a colleague offside so quickly, either.

"I just popped over to find out from Seth if, um, I could come and help today." I stumbled over the lie and felt my cheeks going red.

"Oh yes, obviously that is what you were doing." Already halfway out the door, she said over her shoulder, "Do not bother. We do not need help." Then she was gone.

"Sorry about her," Seth said, touching my shoulder. "She's not very nice to other girls…" He kissed me. "I have to get going. Oh, I've been thinking. I know I said we don't need to keep this a secret, but you know, Justin is actually pretty weird about photographers getting together because it can cause too many problems. So it might be best if we keep things on the down low after all." Oh. It was a rather significant change of heart since his breezy response prior to Maria's arrival. I narrowed my eyes, wondering if seeing her was the reason he changed tack, but wanting to appear relaxed and unflappable, I didn't say anything. He didn't seem to notice my response as he was already halfway out the door himself. "Anyway, see you later on," he said over his shoulder before disappearing down the hall.

Once he was gone, I waited a few moments before I slipped out and paused outside my cabin, just next door. Thank God Caitlin was cool. The last thing I needed was to worry about my roomie judging me. On the bright side, even if Seth and I couldn't have a relationship out in the open—I'd still met someone! Despite the embarrassing morning-after and the lack of sleep, my spirits were high; I couldn't wait to see Seth again.

I came down to earth abruptly as I found myself staring at my door, and realised I'd no idea where my key card was. Had I seriously lost it already?

Sighing, I knocked timidly at the door, and hardly had to wait before Caitlin flung it open.

"Hiya," I said sheepishly, slinking into the cabin. "So... I guess you were right about the gorgeous men who were up for a good time. Am I a complete embarrassment to newbie photographers everywhere?"

Caitlin let out a gorgeous peal of laughter. "Oh, my dear Ellie, you are fucking hilarious! I totally don't care what you get up to, and if needs be, I've got your back." She shut the door and turned back to me. "Anyway, sounds like you had a damn fine welcome last night."

"Ummm, you heard?" I was okay with her knowing everything, but hearing everything was another story entirely. I felt myself blush yet again, and cursed my pale complexion.

"Dude, don't be embarrassed," Caitlin said, slapping me on the back. "These walls are pretty thin. We've heard it all, believe me. Besides, you're talking to a woman with one hell of a history with men on ships. In fact, first night sex is a lucky charm. If I don't get lucky my first night on board, I feel like a complete failure." She laughed so hard that she snorted. "Just remember to keep it light and never get too emotionally involved."

"Oh, no chance of that," I said, sitting down on the bottom bunk. "He is gorgeous and, well, you know, sexy..." We both giggled. "But it's clearly just going to be fun."

"Not to mention a great distraction after leaving that shithead fiancé of yours," she said. "As I always say, to get over an old relationship, you've got to get under someone new." She snickered, and then said, "My mom never approved of that philosophy, as she's dying for me to tie the knot, but it's always got me through the dark moments." Caitlin looked very serious for a moment, and then continued, "But let's not focus on that now. We can save that for a sad night of story swapping over a lot of wine. What I want to know right now is how you ended up in the sack with Seth. I want all the details."

Not one for sharing my playbook with a stranger, I faltered for a moment. Then again, I'd just had the most exciting night in years, and possibly of my entire adult existence. I really needed to offload at least a few of the gory details.

Unfortunately, my stomach had other plans. Until that moment, my mouth had felt like cotton wool, but suddenly, I felt the saliva building up in my mouth, and the nausea hit me like a slap in the face. I lurched into the bathroom and threw up.

Outside the door, Caitlin was laughing again. "Oh, Ellie. You're well and truly one of us now!"

I knew I should be laughing at myself, but I was way too embarrassed. "Sorry, Caitlin, I'm feeling pretty rough."

She fussed around me like a mother hen, handing me a bottle of water from our fridge and pushing me into the shower. "You just get freshened up and we'll go to breakfast. Nobody will know anything." I was grateful for her help and breezy lack of judgement.

A shower made me feel almost human again, and I was gagging for something to eat by the time we got to the staff mess. We arrived at the same time as a thin-faced girl with a long nose and lanky brown hair, and before either Caitlin or I had a chance to speak she'd put out her hand, a smile on her face.

"It's Ellie, right? I'm Jacoline," she said. She had a strong South African accent. I took the proffered hand and was treated to a firm handshake. "I'm one of your fellow photographers. We're so excited you could join us. Welcome to the team." She released my hand, sniffed the air, and then said, "Let's go in and grab some breakfast."

The buffet spread was impressive. Caitlin explained we essentially had the same food as the passengers, but that down in the crew mess, they got whatever the cooks felt like making that day.

"Trust me," she said, "you don't want to be on the receiving end of a chef with a hangover and a taste for braised dog." She stuck out her tongue. "Blech."

I blocked out the mental picture of cooked canines and

chose a traditional English breakfast. I was hoping the grease would settle the queasy feeling still lurking in the pit of my stomach.

Caitlin and Jacoline were already nattering at a million miles an hour when I joined them.

"Oh, Ellie, you have just GOT to meet the man in my life," Caitlin said excitedly, pulling me into the seat next to her.

She hadn't mentioned a current man the night before or this morning, so I was intrigued and wondered what fine specimen of manhood she was loved up with—no doubt a gorgeous man with broad shoulders and a devastating smile.

Something caught her eye and she squealed. "Here he is now!"

I turned to see a guy making a beeline for our table with open arms. Chinese, or maybe Filipino, I wasn't quite sure, he had bleached blond hair, was wearing a skin-tight mesh top and was swinging a pink feather boa. Perhaps not quite the winsome beau I'd envisioned.

"Ellie," Caitlin said, "meet my very best friend in all the world, Nick Canlas." She pulled him into a very long cuddle. They air-kissed, cooed, and preened.

"Oh, my God, Ellie, hi!" Nick said. His accent, surprisingly, was American. He released Caitlin and seized me instead. "You are simply gorgeous, darling!"

Every woman needs an amazing gay man in their life. I loved him immediately.

"Are you a photographer, too?" I asked, already imagining the fun we'd get up to.

"Me? God no," he said, shaking his head. "I'm a senior dancer in the Production Cast." He bowed his head before curtsying gracefully. "Soon to be on Broadway—as soon as I save enough clams to haul ass to the Big Apple."

Nick seemed as fun and over-the-top as Caitlin—these were exactly the friends I needed to break me out of my shell on this whole adventure. I felt butterflies in my stomach at the excitement of the whole scenario. This was definitely going to be fun!

"Sooooo, ladies," Caitlin said, motioning for us to sit down and huddle up. "What's the latest with your skeeze roommate?" She directed the question at Nick, but then turned to me to explain. "See that black guy over there, with the incredible biceps? That's Tyrone—Nick's roommate. His girlfriend works on the Shore Excursion desk." She leaned forward, speaking in a dramatic stage whisper. "Anyway, he's constantly cheating on her when she's working or sleeping, and last night he asked Jacoline to leave a crew party with him... When she told him to fuck off, he disappeared, and one of the other Shories slipped out right after." She turned back to Nick. "Did they come back to the cabin?"

"Well, Princess, let's just say that when I got back from the gym last night—when the rest of you were partying—the sock was on the door handle for quite a while...and I didn't even recognise the girl who came out." Nick wiped imaginary crumbs from the corners of his pursed lips, obviously enjoying divulging juicy gossip. "She looked pretty damn dishevelled. I thought she might have been a passenger."

Jacoline shook her head and lowered her eyes, making one of those tsk-tsk-it's-so-terrible faces.

"To make it worse," Caitlin said, "he already slept with me a few weeks ago!"

I was surprised, but a bit confused. "Wait, so...the bad part is that he tried to sleep with Jacoline? Or that he slept with you? Or that he slept with a passenger? Or is it that he has a girlfriend?" Actually, it all sounded pretty dodgy.

"Oh, gawd, everybody sleeps around on ships," Caitlin said, "but we draw the line at friends... Well, colleagues, at least." The way she casually shrugged off the cheating surprised me. Cheating had been the nail in the coffin of the life I'd thought I had.

"Chicks before dicks," Jacoline chimed in, and they high-fived.

I had just found the only two women in the world who actually used that expression.

"And yes, the passenger part is bad, but it depends who you

are," Caitlin said, looking suddenly serious. "It's officially against the rules, but staff higher up on the pecking order sometimes get away with it. It's easier if you have a cabin on a higher floor, though—getting a passenger below the water line can be tricky."

Nick and Jacoline nodded in agreement, and then Nick launched into a story about waiters and bar staff who'd been caught with passengers and fired on the spot.

"Darling," he said, "they literally got dropped off in the next port and had to find their own way home." he said. It seemed like a harsh punishment, but he explained that a cruise line could potentially face legal battles of nightmare proportions if a passenger later called foul play. "Not that it's ever stopped me, of course," he added, sniggering, and the girls both giggled.

That story led to another, and another, as they entertained me with tales of passengers and the crazy things they did and said. "Do these stairs go down?" was an obvious favourite and had us creasing up. Caitlin relayed the cruise ship urban legend of a passenger who phoned the Guest Purser's Desk for help because they were stuck in their room with two doors—a bathroom and one with a 'do not disturb' sign hanging on the doorknob. "They said 'I can't get out!'" she yelped, wiping away tears of laughter.

As breakfast came to an end, Jacoline got up from the table and said her goodbyes. "I'm going back for a sleep," she said. "I'm completely fucked today. And not in a good way." We all smiled and waved her off.

Nick stood up too. "I hate to love you and leave you, but I'm off to do a stretching session," he said, air kissing us both. "But I'll see you later, promise?"

I turned to Caitlin to ask what she suggested I do for the day, but before I could say anything Seth walked into the mess. He'd obviously finished shooting gangway already. There was a guy with him who looked to be a bit older than Seth, maybe in his late thirties. Possibly Italian or Greek, he was really tanned with jet black hair, and very handsome.

"This is Luciano, the ship's Senior Engineer," Seth said as they approached our table. "He thought he'd come and join me for breakfast instead of sufferin' through any more of that silly five star service they get up in the officer's mess."

Luciano nodded and smiled broadly. *"Ciao, belle,"* he said. Definitely Italian.

They loaded their plates up high at the buffet and then joined us. Seth sat down close to me and put his arm around the back of my chair; little hairs all over my body stood up in excitement. His leg was touching mine, and even though I had been considering getting up to get more coffee, I didn't want to move and break the energy field.

"You won't get a breakfast like this at crappy old Parsons," Seth said to Caitlin, raising his juice to her in a mock toast.

"Parsons?" I repeated, curious.

"I've applied for a scholarship to Parsons' School of Fashion to do a BA in Fashion Design. I'm just here killing time and saving money," Caitlin said, turning to me. She appeared a bit embarrassed, though it seemed to me she was playing down its importance. I was impressed—I'd incorrectly pegged her as a perennial party girl.

Caitlin and Seth led the conversation, rapidly leaving Caitlin's ambitions behind in the interest of getting me to talk about home, family, hobbies, and my past jobs. I avoided mentioning my ex. I didn't want to be 'that' girl, the one who went on about her previous relationship in front of her new man.

After a while, Caitlin noticed we all had empty mugs; when she got up to get refills, Seth offered to help. While they were gone, Luciano leaned in, his face serious.

"So, Ellie, you and Seth are together now?"

"Well, I guess so," I said, startled. I hadn't expected to get asked so directly and so hadn't really thought about what I'd say—especially in light of Seth's comment about keeping the relationship quiet. "I mean, I think he's great, and I don't know him that well yet; but we definitely…hit it off." How did you explain your involvement with someone you'd met yesterday but had already gone to bed with? How did I justify anything without spilling my long, boring history? And did I need to? These guys were a mixture of the party-people and the fun police.

"Ah yes, he's 'great', as you say," Luciano said. "We're very good friends, and I know him well." He paused to take a deep breath, running his fingers through his hair. "It doesn't bother you that he's also been with your colleague Maria? I assume you've met her already?"

The look on my face obviously spoke volumes and Luciano started to backpedal immediately. "Sorry, I thought you knew…well, they were not really, you know…um… She is really *pazza*." He wound his finger near his temple to indicate somebody crazy. Red-faced, he mumbled something else and walked over to join Seth at the coffee station. He started talking earnestly to Seth, prompting Caitlin to scamper back to our table.

"Oh darl, I'm so sorry I didn't get to warn you," she said apologetically as she set down our coffees. "The stuff I was saying this morning about people sleeping with friends and colleagues…well, I think Seth's kind of on a different page with that one." Caitlin was shaking her head, looking genuinely frustrated. "I was going to say something, but it had already happened, and everyone will know you didn't know…" She took my hand. "Seth and Maria were seeing each other for a while, but he broke it off with her and she's been pretty pissed at him ever since."

This last part gave me hope. "At least he broke it off with her, right? That means he's not pining after her."

Caitlin didn't look convinced. "Well, yeah…but I think Maria REALLY liked him, so while you might not have to worry about Seth still holding a torch for her, I think she's still holding one for him." Caitlin looked around to make sure we were still alone. "Babe, I'm not someone who backs down to bitches, but Maria isn't someone you want on your bad side." She took a deep breath and leaned closer. "On her last ship, Maria and this girl Katie from the beauty salon got in this huge spat. Same old story—boy meets girl, boy meets other girl, girls duke it out…" She flicked her hair over her shoulder and continued, "The guy was a passenger, some big shot sports agent, so they shouldn't have been messing with him anyway, but never mind. Rumour had it that Maria was so pissed about Katie getting involved with her man that she spiked Katie's drink one night in the nightclub, then took a bunch of half-naked photos of Katie once she'd passed out back in the cabin. If that wasn't bad enough, all of those photos got posted to Facebook where everyone could see them. Katie's parents tried to get her to come home, but in the end she took a demotion so she could be trans-shipped and just get away from the whole thing." She shrugged. "I guess no one could ever prove anything—even the photos were posted through Katie's account, so Maria never got in trouble. She just said she'd been worried about Katie and had helped her back to her cabin, and then left, but I wouldn't put it past her to have pulled such a shit stunt. I've seen her lose it, and man, it's not pretty… The bitch can be seriously vindictive." There was a pause, and then she added, "So…yeah. She's kind of used to getting what she wants. If I were you, I'd keep out of her way for a while. Lay low, you know?"

Great. I had unleashed a scorned, potentially violent woman. And it was only my second day.

Caitlin obviously saw the anxiety in my face, because she hastily added, "But don't worry, I've totally got your back. Just be careful; South American women are totally loco." She made the same crazy-in-the-head sign with her index finger.

I wasn't one for stereotyping, but it was a bit worrying to see Maria described that way twice in the space of minutes.

Seth and Luciano returned, and as Seth sat down he said, "So you heard about Maria?" I nodded, mutely. "Don't worry about it. It didn't last long. She's really not my type."

Did that mean I was? Hope fluttered in my stomach, but my masochistic side needed to know all the details, and so the questions began. "How long ago did you finish with her?" I prayed it was far in the past.

"Well, it's been quite a while…like, a week or so."

A week? I'd still been crying into my pillow a week after I'd broken it off with Dan. I knew cruise ship life is meant to move at four times the speed of real life, but in the real world, you didn't normally have to sleep in the room across from your lover's ex. Still, Seth's tone told me he was confident a week was long enough for bygones to be bygones.

"She's a little bit crazy," he continued, "but don't worry, as long as I'm around, she won't do anything." He smiled his winning smile and looked around the table. "Don't you think so, Caity?"

Caitlin shrugged and took a huge sip of her drink.

Seth turned his attention to Luciano. "Back me up here, man?"

Luciano also shrugged.

Great. I'd managed to get on the wrong side of my new man's ex already, and everyone pretty much agreed that she was not only a bitch, but a little crazy into the bargain.

Bollocks.

Chapter Three

As I opened the Pic Stop that evening, my mind again turned to the problem of Maria. In my single days, my friends and I had always followed the rule about not messing with each other's blokes—even if it had been years since the friend in question had been with him. If I'd known about Maria, I wouldn't have slept with Seth, although in my defence I hadn't actually met her until afterwards... Sigh. I probably wouldn't have done it if I'd been sober either; I would have waited a week. Or at least a few days. Still, the damage was done. Maria was clearly already pissed off at me. So there was no need to stop sleeping with him now, right? Single women all over the world would be very disappointed if I let the side down by letting such a fine-looking specimen get away.

It was hard to focus on sales and service when my thoughts were on Seth, and it didn't help that my head was slightly splitting with the remnants of a hangover that had only been temporarily dulled by the application of coffee. I was really going to need to sleep more during my contract. I had a feeling that the constant drinking and late nights would take their toll before long. I was definitely going to start going to bed earlier...next cruise.

I had fudged my way through two hours of forced smiling when Seth popped his head in through the doorway, just in time for my hour-long meal break. He was sporting a massive grin and holding out a huge bottle of water, which I knew was icy cold from the tell-tale drips of condensation running down the sides. Just what I wanted.

And the drink was a welcome sight too.

"Oh, you're a lifesaver," I exclaimed, and raced over to have a sip.

"Not without a kiss first," Seth said, hiding the bottle behind his back. As I leaned over to kiss him, he whispered in my ear, "Would you like to come for a ride?" He was looking at me with come-hither eyes and a white-toothed grin.

"A ride?" I looked at him quizzically. Then it clicked, and I felt my cheeks burning. "Oh. But what about dinner...?" I asked, not really caring if I never ate again.

"It can wait. I can't." Wow, the sign of a horny man. Or a pushy one. I settled on the former with a touch of the latter. "Now...let's go." He pulled me out of the shop with one hand, reaching back to lock the door with the other. I liked a man who could multitask.

We raced back to Seth's cabin and were barely through the door before he had my shirt halfway over my head. Hating to have my muffin-top on display, I reached over and turned off the light. It was pitch black. Damn, I kept forgetting about that. Reading my mind, Seth flicked on the fairy lights, which were much nicer and considerably more flattering to the complexion.

Seth didn't seem to mind my curves. If anything, he loved them. He kept murmuring, "you're so beautiful", over and over again as he kissed my face, my neck, my hair. I was completely under his spell. What girl doesn't like being told they're beautiful? This time we were totally sober and, amazingly, he was still completely into me. The fact Seth thought I was sexy was really flattering, if a little hard to believe, and it really turned me on.

He picked me up easily, placed me on the edge of the desk, and lifted my skirt. "Time is of the essence..." he whispered. "Much faster this way."

God, he was sexy...and efficient. Dan hadn't so much as touched my hand in months before I left, and here possibly the most beautiful man I'd ever seen devouring me like a feast in the desert. I melted in all the right places. I held my breath in anticipation of the foreplay that was sure to follow.

What felt like moments later, it was all over. For him, at least. I was still balancing on the edge of a rather pointy-cornered hardback by the time Seth was all zipped up. He ran his fingers through his hair and peered at himself in the little mirror on the wall.

"Sorry, Ellie, I'm starving. You're the best, though. I owe you one."

I felt a little stunned by his love-'em-and-leave-'em approach and must have looked a little hurt, because he leaned over and whispered in my ear, "You're gonna get it good later." He kissed me on the forehead.

Ah, I realised. The anticipation game… This guy was good.

I slid off the desk and bent down to pull myself together a bit. When I looked up, he was already halfway out the door. "Feel free to use the bathroom. Don't rush. See ya at the crew bar later." And he was gone.

I went back to my cabin for a shower. It just felt wrong to go back to work with the smell of a sexy Texan all over me; I was sure people would immediately know what I'd been up to.

The rest of my shift passed uneventfully. I kept standing at the door and furtively glancing around, hoping Seth would make an appearance. He didn't, but Caitlin swung by at closing time with a covered plate.

"Hi, darl, I noticed you weren't at dinner and thought you'd be hungry." She lifted the cover off the plate and revealed soggy looking nachos. "I know it's not the best, but hopefully it will fill the hole." She grinned. "Speaking of which, I saw you and Seth disappearing into his cabin at dinner time… You didn't see me because you were blinded by the passion." She laughed out loud. "Give me the gory details, lady."

As we closed the shop and rushed back to the cabin to change for the crew bar, I filled her in with all the bits I didn't feel too embarrassed to repeat out loud. We danced about to pop music as we got ready, and as one of her favourite old school tunes came on, Caitlin turned it up. "Rock this party, dance everybody, make it hot in this party...!" she sang loudly and out of tune, dancing around in her g-string. Caitlin wasn't conventionally beautiful, but her energy and enthusiasm definitely made her attractive. I loved her lack of inhibition and wished I had a tenth of her confidence.

I waited until she was dressed and then asked her how she kept in shape. She had a remarkably tiny waist and slender arms—both things I lacked, and longed for.

"Oh, I'm just lucky, I guess," she replied, shrugging it off. Trust her to be humble about it.

While we were doing our make-up, jiggling and dancing on the spot, Caitlin reached into the wardrobe and pulled out a bottle of Kahlua and two shot glasses. "To get us in the mood!" she yelled over the music. I wasn't sure how much more of a party mood she could be in, but I was happy to have a swig. I was actually feeling a bit nervous about seeing Seth again.

The liqueur was warm and sweet. As the alcohol kicked in, I got a bit of a head spin.

"Whoa," I said, grabbing onto the top bunk. "I better slow down, especially after last night!"

Caitlin just laughed and said, "It didn't seem to end too badly, so maybe you should have another." We clinked our tiny glasses and gulped them down. Caitlin poured another one. "To good times and new friends," she said, looking me in the eye and gulping hers down. I closed my eyes and poured the nip down my throat. "Ellie, don't you know the rule about looking someone in the eye when you toast and drink?" She sounded horrified. "It's seven years bad sex!"

"Sounds like complete rubbish," I laughed, feeling slightly giddy. "But then again, who'd want to take the risk?"

"My thoughts exactly," she said, pouring another. "Last one, then let's go."

We were laughing and dancing our way into the crew bar when a slight girl with stringy hair grabbed onto Caitlin's arm quite firmly. Her eyes were red and watery—it looked like she'd been crying. Caitlin immediately pulled her into a hug, patting her back. Clearly the story had a history, so I left them to it and popped inside.

The moment I walked in the door, I spotted Maria and regretted my decision to enter without backup. My first instinct was to turn tail and run—to be quite honest I found Maria a bit terrifying and the last thing I wanted to do was strike up a conversation with her. But I couldn't get rid of my father's advice, which echoed relentlessly in my head. "Always settle an argument, Ellie," he used to say. "Apologise first, regardless of whether or not you think the other person will. Be the bigger person."

Right, then. I took a deep breath and entered the fray. "Hey, Maria," I said, once I was close enough that she had to acknowledge I was there, "I think we got off to a bad start." She didn't say anything, so I tried again. "I had no idea about you and Seth, or I would never have even looked at him…"

Maria stood silently, her arms crossed and her mouth a thin line. She stared straight ahead, doing her best to ignore me, and I wobbled as I considered moving even closer. Rejecting the idea, I instead reached out and touched the wall to steady myself before continuing.

"I only just found out today that you guys were together," I explained, "so I feel really bad. I've always had a rule about getting involved with friends' exes, and so I just didn't know."

Dan used to say I just needed to give him breathing space, that it wasn't necessary to fill every silence in a conversation. I'd always disagreed. Nothing good could come from a half silent conversation—so naturally, I kept talking, despite the fact Maria was still mute, and apart from raising her eyebrows slightly at the mention of the word 'friend', remained completely expressionless.

"We had a few drinks at the crew bar, waiting for you guys to arrive, and well, you know… Sorry." I was definitely straying into babbling territory. I was starting to wonder if she would ever say anything, since it was becoming blatantly obvious that she wasn't going to come around so easily.

At last, my words received a reaction as Maria put her hands on her hips. "Well," she said, her voice icy, "maybe if you had been here for more than five minutes before getting into bed with him, you might have found out. I see that you are drunk again tonight. I wonder who you will sleep with next?" She sneered disdainfully.

My cheeks burned and tears threatened to well up in my eyes. Perhaps I had been just a tad optimistic to have expected Maria to respond positively to an apology. I had put myself out on a limb to apologise, and it had clearly been a big waste of time. Was I going to have a problem with her for my whole contract? Surely, with her looks, she could just move on. It was a big ship.

She wasn't finished. "I curse the stupid British *bardajonas* they hire for this job," she said, and then added, "Anyway, I do not care about you and Seth. He is leaving next San Juan." She zeroed in on my look of surprise, and a fleeting expression of triumph crossed her face. "I am not interested in being a one-week fling, but if that is what you want...you can have him." She spun on her heel and walked away.

Wait, what? I stared after Maria long after she'd disappeared, my thoughts a jumbled mess. I rapidly went over all of my interactions with Seth, and couldn't remember him ever mentioning that he was buggering off in a week. Surely Maria was wrong. He couldn't be leaving—I'd only just arrived! He was my cruise ship fantasy man; he couldn't leave just after I'd met him! Not to mention he'd slept with me, and he'd seemed so keen on me... I bit my lip, suddenly nervous. Despite thinking about Seth earlier in the day as the love-'em-and-leave-'em type, I hadn't ever thought he'd actually *leave*.

An unpleasant thought wormed its way through my mind—had Seth only been using me for sex? It hadn't seemed like it at the time, but now I couldn't help but wonder. With a sinking feeling in my stomach, I remembered earlier that day, when he'd dragged me off for a bout of sex in which only he'd got off. He'd said he'd return the favour later, but later hadn't actually happened yet. And now I was stuck thinking that maybe he hadn't actually liked me at all, that maybe I'd been the chubby girl so desperate for male attention that I'd been naively easy to get into bed…

I desperately wanted answers to the innumerable questions clamouring in my mind, but a quick look told me that Caitlin was still caught up outside, in what looked like a pretty involved conversation. Shit.

I wasn't in the mood for the crew bar anymore, but going back to a quiet, dark cabin without Caitlin probably wouldn't help much either. I'd just sit and overthink everything that had happened since I'd first come aboard. I contemplated leaving, if only for the sake of my poor gnawed-on lip, but then Jock caught my eye from behind the bar. He smiled warmly at me, his eyes bright, and waved me over.

Maybe I'd stay for one drink, after all. He was really very cute, and anyway it wasn't really fair to Caitlin to disappear.

I drifted over to the bar and mustered up a smile in return. "Hey, Jock. Can I get two glasses of house white, please?"

Years of bartending had, no doubt, honed Jock's awareness of customers' moods, including the ability to slice right through bullshit. He placed two glasses on the counter and got straight to the point. "Are you ok, lass? You look really down."

"Yeah, I'm fine," I said, watching him measure and pour the wine. "How are you?" I thought I sounded convincing, but the look on Jock's face as he slid the wine over told me that I wasn't doing a very good job. I took a sip of my drink, trying to think of what to say. It was difficult not to show how upset I was, especially with my mind spinning with Maria's Seth-related bombshell…but I really didn't want to explain everything and have Jock think I was a complete trollop, like Maria obviously did.

Jock studied me for a moment, polishing a glass, and then leant over. "I saw you talking to Maria a bit ago," he said quietly. "She has a habit of bringing people down. You might say it's her primary occupation. I wouldn't let her get to you."

Oh. Well, that was nice to hear. I took a deep breath,

wondering how much to say, and then opened with, "Well, yeah. She hasn't really taken a liking to me, unfortunately."

"Not sure she takes a liking to most other women," he offered, a crooked smile on his face.

I managed a laugh, but it ended up sounding more like a sob and I swallowed hard several times before saying, "We got off to a bad start because...well..." I shook my head. "Anyway, it doesn't matter. We just didn't hit it off. To be honest, it was just a shit first day, actually." They say that getting something off your chest is good for you, but as the words came out of my mouth, I rather felt like I was going to cry. Now that would be embarrassing. I stared straight ahead, focusing on one of the bottles behind Jock, digging my nails into my palms to keep back the tears. Perhaps I should have gone back to the cabin after all.

Jock's expression was as soft and kind as his words. "Ellie," he said gently, "your first couple of weeks are going to be hard. It's a different world. People come from all over to work here, and while that clash of cultures can be exciting, it can also make for a whole lot of misunderstandings." He reached over and placed his hand on top of mine. "You've probably heard that life on board flies pretty much at the speed of light, and while the good experiences build up quickly, so do the bad." He smiled and added, "If it helps, I don't think Maria's as crazy as everyone says." He squeezed my hand and then released me. I looked down at my hand, still feeling the warmth of his touch.

"Thank you," I said, dragging my gaze back up to his face. "I hope you're right. It's definitely a whole new world." Normally I would have broken into song at such an obvious Disney-expression—but I felt too deflated.

Before I could say anything else, arms slid around my shoulders and I was hugged from behind.

"Sorry I took so long," a familiar voice said in my ear. Caitlin rested her chin on my shoulder. "Dramas outside." She let go and leaned back against the bar, her elbows on the counter. "What did that bitch say to you?" she asked, looking worried. "She walked past me on her way out a few minutes ago."

I didn't want to have that conversation in front of Jock, so I snagged Caitlin's drink and handed it to her. Pushing her away from the bar, I glanced back and smiled at Jock, mouthing 'thank you' at him. He was so kind and warm, I didn't actually have to fake it that time. He winked and turned to serve his next customer.

I clung to Caitlin's arm and guided her to a space we could talk more privately, or more accurately, so I could blurt out the question I'd been burning to ask her. I collapsed into a seat and managed to squeak, "Seth's leaving on Sunday?" I took a few gulps of my wine.

"Oh," Caitlin said, her eyes searching my face. She knocked back half of her glass of wine, shrugged, and said, "Babe, it doesn't really matter. If he's leaving, it just means you can just go on to bigger and better things… He was your warm-up game." She grinned wickedly.

I knew everyone else was casual about sex, and it wasn't as if I'd planned to act like an angel, but I still felt like an idiot. Seth could have at least mentioned it. I felt like that was only the courteous thing to do, though I had a sinking feeling that maybe that was my naivety speaking. Even though I obviously hadn't gone into it thinking it would turn out to be a long term relationship, it would have been nice to think there might have been a tiny chance for it to be ongoing. Maybe I'd been unrealistic. I knew I'd sound like a wet blanket trying to explain it all to Caitlin, but I gave it a go anyway, reasoning that I couldn't feel worse than I already did.

"I just feel like a prize idiot," I said. "Everyone probably knew except me, and now I've pissed off Maria, basically for no reason."

A fan of getting straight to the point, Caitlin said, "Ellie, fuck her. She's a fucking bitch. You didn't do anything that any of us wouldn't have done. You've got nothing to be sorry about. He's leaving on Sunday; so what? Just move on, babe."

She was probably right, but it didn't really help. I still felt stupid and cheap. Hardly the way a liberated woman ought to think (hah), but I couldn't help the flickers of guilt from surging to the fore. I'd had a few partners before I met Dan, but no one night stands. Well, no, actually, that wasn't quite true. I'd once gone home with a bloke from TGIF bar, but that was due more to a misunderstanding regarding his celebrity status. In my drunken state I'd thought he was Marvin from JLS, but instead he'd turned out to be Mark who worked at the fish and chip shop. In my defence, they'd looked very similar...

In any event, that had only been once, and the rest of my romantic life had always progressed at a snail's pace. I'd had friends who'd hopped from one bed to another, and while I'd never thought it was wrong, it had never really been my style. I was always much better at accepting the liberal behaviour of others than I was at accepting my own. And so I'd always clung to the familiar. The thrill of the chase. The frisson of sexual tension that came from getting to know each other before jumping into bed. It was one of the things Dan had loved about me, actually. He'd said he liked the idea of an old-fashioned courtship. Except once we were properly together, sex suddenly dropped to the bottom of his list of priorities— with me, at least—and things in the bedroom had gone downhill almost overnight. Which was bizarre, thinking back on it; weren't men supposed to be keen on sex no matter what? Still, although I'd tried numerous times, in the end I'd just accepted that our relationship wasn't going to be very physical. And I'd been okay with that. As long as we loved each other, I'd reasoned, then I was happy. Sex *wasn't* nearly as important as honesty and communication. Of course, then it had turned out we didn't have those either...but I had been okay with minimal sex for years. Yet the moment I arrived on this ship, I jumped into bed with a guy I barely knew. What had I been thinking? That wasn't like me even *before* I was a scorned woman! Maybe I'd been so sex-starved from my years with Dan that my hormones had run riot upon being presented with a perfect specimen of the male half of the species. I quite liked that idea, actually, seeing as it more or less got me off the hook for my behaviour. Hah. Didn't really change the facts, though—just when I'd started a fantastic new job, with people I'd be trapped with for months on end, I had acted like the kind of woman you don't want to introduce to your male friends for fear she'll sleep with them. I thought about Laura and cringed. I hated those women.

I came out of my retrospective to see Caitlin staring at me. "Dude," she said. "Don't look now, but your loverboy is here."

Promptly ignoring her, I spun around and saw Seth and Luciano walking through the door. Seth smiled and waved when he saw me, looking unconcerned and clearly unaware of the storm about to descend upon his head. After a moment's conversation, Luciano peeled off towards the bar, while Seth continued in our direction.

"What's going on here?" Seth asked, pinching my bum in greeting. "Who died?"

Caitlin shot him a look and then said, furrowing her skinny brows, "Maria gave her an earful."

"Ahhhhh, okay," Seth said, softening. "Don't even worry about her, Ellie. She's just a bully." I obviously looked unconvinced, because he put his arm around me and continued, "She's jealous that you and I are having a good time together." He pulled away again, clearly worried someone would see.

Just as well—I wasn't really in the mood for canoodling. Between Maria's bitchiness and Seth apparently leaving, I was jittery and anxious and completely uninterested in anything but the truth.

"Can I talk to you, please?" I asked.

"Oh no, I'm in trouble now," Seth joked, nudging Caitlin's arm. She fixed him with a piercing glare and then stalked away to join Luciano at the bar.

Seth turned to me and said, "Now, Miss Ellie, nobody ever likes to hear the words 'Can we talk?' Especially after only knowing each other for two days…" He sighed.

Too worked up to acknowledge his tone, I got straight to the point. "Why didn't you tell me you were leaving on Sunday? I thought we had something good starting…"

Seth stood with his arms folded, tapping his foot. "Aw, come on, Ellie. We only met yesterday. I thought we were both on the same page here—that it was fun while it lasted. It wasn't exactly relationship-building material."

I shook my head, struggling to find the words to express what I was feeling and knowing I was completely failing. "Well, no, but it would have been nice to at least be aware…"

Seth opened his hands and shrugged. "It's just the way it works on ships. Nobody wants to get real about what's going to happen. It's part of the game. We just talk…say the right things…everybody's happy."

I wasn't. Quite frankly, the idea that Seth had just been 'saying the right things' made me feel incredibly uncomfortable, and made me wonder how much, if any, of our time together had involved any truth on his side. I'd thought he found me sexy and attractive and beautiful, and for a brief moment I'd believed it and my self-esteem had soared. And now I felt like it had all just been a façade, him saying the right things at the right time to get what he wanted. It was a depressing thought.

As much as I tried to stop it, my bottom lip quivered a little. I really didn't want to turn into a sobbing mess in front of Seth, but I felt overwhelmed with conflicting emotions. I'd come aboard the *Galene* with high spirits, intending to have a good time, and now I felt completely mortified. The strong, independent image I'd been hoping to encourage had slunk away, tail between her legs, and my awkward, self-conscious self had crept back out. Never mind jumping in bed with someone so soon; the worst bit there was letting Seth's compliments fool me into thinking I was actually desirable. That plus the outright hostility from people like Maria, who didn't care that I'd made a mistake, made me just want to jump ship at the next dock and run home again, taking refuge in my parents' familiar cosy house.

I raised my eyes, attempting to plaster on a neutral look, but Seth had already seen my emotions. He sighed again and said, patiently and more than a little condescendingly, "Look, Ellie, I'm sorry that you're upset, but I never imagined you would think anything of it. If you decide you'd like to keep having a good time until Sunday, let me know. If you don't, whatever; it's cool." He shrugged and turned away. I didn't have the energy to stop him, and instead just watched as he strolled back across the room to join Luciano at the bar.

Staring at his back, I thought about the forums I'd read online. They'd all warned about the party lifestyle, but I'd seen that as a good thing. I had come here for fun; I just hadn't imagined it could turn sour so quickly. My over-eager first moves were already proving to be rather embarrassing. Ugh.

It was clearly time to head back to the cabin. Caitlin had disappeared from the bar, so with a sigh I headed for the door. Before I reached it, Luciano came up behind me and tapped me on the shoulder. His liquid brown eyes looked dark and sad. "I'm so very sorry, Ellie," he said. "You deserve a good man."

"Yeah, right, thanks, Luciano," I said as I kept walking, unconvinced that good men actually existed in the moral vacuum of the cruise ship world. I'd hardly imagined Seth was going to be the love of my life—I wasn't the kind of girl to fall in love in the space of a day—but I'd been willing to go with the flow and see where it went. I'd just thought that the flow was going to last more than a week. And I'd thought we were both on the same page, too; turned out it was a different book altogether.

As I opened the door to our cabin, the bathroom door slammed shut. I heard Caitlin coughing, then something that definitely sounded like vomiting.

"I'll be out in a minute," she called. "It's my turn to be sick tonight!"

Oh yeah. The party was definitely non-stop here.

"Let me know if you need water," I called through the

crack in the door, trying to keep my voice steady. Alone at last, the emotions I'd been struggling to keep in check all evening began to wash over me, threatening to swamp me completely. I sat on the bottom bunk and put my head in my hands. I could feel the stress and tension building up inside and threatening to bubble over. I tried to control it, but a fat tear rolled down my cheek. I was homesick, tired, and my high seas adventure had got off to a terribly disappointing start. I really needed to turn things around.

Chapter Four

The next two days on board, despite being busy, were incredibly boring. Stocktaking the shop, putting new orders into storage, running through order sheets…all the crappy stuff the recruiters don't tell you about when you sign up for a life of professional cruising.

I called my parents to check in, and despite the fact it had been mere days since I saw them, the sound of their voices brought home just how sad and homesick I really was. My mother, no doubt relying on that sixth sense mothers have to tell when something's wrong, asked if everything was okay, and I promptly burst into tears.

"I really miss you," I said, sniffling. I couldn't quite bring myself to tell her what had really happened, and anyway I did miss my parents. The separation from friends and family had been harder than I'd expected.

I missed my mum's Sunday roast, her endless cups of tea, and even her funny habit of shoving gardening magazines under my nose every time she discovered a new flower she wanted for the garden. I missed the way Dad laughed hard at the old TV shows and then said "Oh dear" as he wiped away tears of laughter with a hanky.

They sounded chirpy, which was almost a little disappointing; I'd kind of been hoping that they might miss me so much that they'd beg me to come home. Then I'd have known that at least *someone* wanted me, even if I had no intention of abandoning ship at the next port. Even so, their enthusiasm helped to pump me up, and their reassurances that

I was bound to have a fabulous time reminded me of why I'd come aboard in the first place.

"Make sure to really get to know people," Mum advised.

If only she knew just how quickly I'd become intimate with one of my colleagues. Somehow I didn't think that was quite what she'd had in mind.

Despite being in and out of the Pic Stop, gallery, and photo lab, I didn't see Seth all week, except in passing. It wasn't that he was avoiding me, exactly…but he definitely didn't want to hang out with me, and that's pretty much the same thing.

At breakfast on Thursday, when we were docked in St Martin, Seth was conspicuously absent. So was Maria, although Caitlin and Nick assured me they weren't together. After breakfast, Caitlin boarded the tender boat to the island. Left to our own devices, Nick and I went up to the top deck for coffee.

"So, Princess," Nick said as we sat down at a small table out of the sun, "tell me more about you. Surely you're not here just for the men. I can see you're smarter than that."

I smiled sadly. "Well, I'm glad somebody can," I said. "I left a cheating fiancé for a new, exciting life on ships. I imagined myself sunning on the islands, meeting great friends, and building a photography portfolio that would actually get me somewhere." I sighed. "Maybe I was too naïve."

"You can have those things, Ellie," Nick said, sounding uncharacteristically serious. "You just have to be careful. There is fun to be had, money to be made, and friends to meet, but you have to choose wisely how you spend your time. Haven't you noticed I don't go to the crew bar much?" He was right; I hadn't seen him there all week. "I'm here for one reason only. My Broadway dream isn't just a pie-in-the-sky thing, you know. I practice my dance craft every day, even on top of the dancing I'm doing here. I rarely drink, and pretty much every decision I make is based on saving money." He shook his head and leaned back in his chair. "I guess I'm just like my parents in that way."

"How so?" I asked. I didn't want to intrude, but he was certainly turning out to be more three dimensional than first impressions would have had me believe.

"My parents are what some call 'New Money'," he said, crossing one leg over the other. "They emigrated from the Philippines to the US as newlyweds and have spent their lives totally obsessed with making coin. They have an import business, selling clothes and handbags, and have worked seven days a week for as long as I've been alive. Suffice it to say they've got a tidy sum tucked away, and so when they found out I wanted to dance on Broadway, I hoped they'd chip in. They certainly have enough to buy me an apartment, even in New York." His tone turned bitter. "They just don't agree with my choice of career, and we've been arguing about it for years." He sighed deeply. "They want me to join the family business and forget all about what they call 'dancing silliness'." He mimed quote marks. "But I'm determined to become dance captain when the current one leaves to get married next month. Big pay rise. More mon-ay for my Broadway adventure." He cackled, and the sudden change in tone startled me a bit. The camp Nick was back, his serious demeanour of moments before gone as fast as it had arrived.

"Anyway," he said with an exaggerated sigh. "Moving on. I've found a super cheap room in Brooklyn through an old friend, so I don't even need my parents' help now."

"Well, good for you," I said. "I can absolutely picture you on Broadway. I really hope you get the dance captain job."

"Oh, I will, Princess," he said, smiling confidently. "I will."

He bounded out of his chair and pranced across the deck to order our coffees. Momentarily left to myself, I looked around the pool deck. I'd been up here a few days earlier, but it was still spectacularly impressive.

Two long, sparkling pools glimmered down the centre of the deck, and hundreds of deck chairs surrounded them, on two split levels. On a sea day I'd been told it was positively heaving with guests, but as today was a port day the deck was comparatively empty. There were still numerous people around, though, laying in the sun and sipping on cold cocktails, even at this hour of the morning. With a fully-stocked bar at each end of the pool area and smiling drink-waiters roaming the deck, there were ample opportunities for guests to drink plenty and spend up big on their on board accounts.

It was surreal being here. I knew the jetlag had subsided, but the crazy excitement of the whole scenario was making my head spin. *You are seriously getting paid to do the most adventurous thing you've done in your entire life*, I reminded myself, not for the first time. *Unfuckingbelieveable.* I'd grasped the opportunity to take numerous photos of anything and everything, ensuring I would inflict the maximum groans from my friends and family back home in the UK. I'd been careful to not block Dan on Facebook, at least not yet. I was quite keen that he see as many photos as possible of me having a wild time, and realise that not all men found my muffin top so off-putting. I'd had some success, as he'd messaged me, after I'd posted a few sneaky photos of myself and Seth from the first night's crew bar shenanigans, to say it was clear that I'd managed to move on.

"What are you smiling at, Princess?" Nick asked, interrupting my thoughts.

"Oh, nothing... You know, thinking about how jealous my ex-fiancé will be when he sees all of my fabulous photos." I smiled wickedly and brushed away any feelings of guilt about leaving him behind.

"Ooh, an almost-marriage!" Nick exclaimed. He pushed a coffee towards me and pulled his chair closer. "Do tell." He leaned in, eyes wide with interest.

I couldn't resist such an attentive audience and told him the whole sad story, explaining that Dan and I had gradually faded into nothingness. Nick pressed me for more details, so I related all of the times Dan had rejected me and made me feel like a fat cow, and then topped it off by cheating on me with an almost-teenager.

"Well, he'd have to be blind, deaf, and dumb not to cherish you, darling," Nick gushed. Then in a normal, more masculine voice, he added, "Seriously, Ellie. If he was bored with you, he was a complete idiot. You're fucking amazing."

I adored him already, and patted his hand in silent thanks. Even so, I was feeling a little self-conscious, having aired all of my dirty laundry, so rather than dwell on my tales of woe, I wondered aloud where Caitlin might be.

"I shudder to think what she's been up to today. St Martin is known for two things… great food and Orient Beach," Nick said, and laughed. "They call it 'clothing optional', which is really code for being full of naked old men with wrinkly wieners nobody needs to see, even including our crazy Caitlin." We both grimaced at the mental image before Nick continued, "The cheeky broads down on the Shore Excursion desk get paid by tour operators to push poor, ignorant passengers to go there, and they've been doing so for years. Awful situation, Princess, but it means we can almost be alone on any one of the thirty-something other beaches on the island."

I liked the sound of that—a Caribbean beach all to ourselves. We sat there for nearly another hour, Nick answering my countless questions, before he suddenly noticed the time and realised he was late to rehearsal.

"Shit," he said, leaping to his feet and downing his coffee. "Must rush, Princess. We've had a run of replacement performers and so we have to do extra run throughs all damn week." He waved and was gone.

I spent the walk back to the cabin lost in thought, half-hoping to bump into Seth and half-hoping he'd fallen overboard. I was surprised to see Luciano waiting outside my cabin. He smiled his lovely, friendly smile and gave me what I interpreted as an apologetic shrug; I guessed he felt awkward and sorry for his mate having turned out to be such a genuine fuckwit.

"Ellie, you look so…sad," he said, a frown creasing his face. "Please show me that beautiful smile." I obediently gave him a weak smile. "Ahhhhh, *bellissima*. That's better…"

"I'm sorry, Luciano," I said, "but I'm really exhausted. Can I catch up with you later?" I didn't even need to pretend to look tired. I could feel my eyes drooping.

"Of course, Ellie, of course," he said quickly. "I just wanted to apologise for everything that happened." He clasped one of my hands in his and met my eyes. "I feel so terrible I didn't warn you about what men can be like on the ships. Seth is...well, typical in that way." He shrugged again.

Luciano was such a warm and sincere person that I felt myself relax a bit. He didn't need to apologise; Seth's behaviour had really had nothing to do with him, and so his apology was an especially thoughtful gesture. "Thanks, Luciano. I appreciate that, but it's not your fault. You didn't do anything wrong."

"I know I've said it already, Ellie, but you need to have more than that." He squeezed my hand. "You deserve a real man who treats you with respect. The first time I saw you, do you remember how I smiled? That's because you're so beautiful. You could have any man you want with that smile, and you don't need to choose one like him. I'll be your friend and help you choose better next time. Okay?" He stroked the back of my hand with his thumb and then released me.

I smiled again, grateful for the sentiment, and opened my cabin door. "I'll talk to you later," I said. "I really need to rest now." He nodded and walked away; as he reached the corner, he turned back and gave me a little salute before disappearing.

I shut the door behind me and leant against it, closing my eyes. I'd come here to break away from my sad little life, have a good time, and pursue a photography career. So far I was only partially succeeding. Granted, I'd had a good time with Seth, but I had kind of just fallen into it and then promptly back out, which hadn't been quite what I'd envisioned.

Now that he was leaving, perhaps I could just wipe the slate clean. The crew was so transient, I reasoned, so anyone who knew we'd been involved was bound to forget about it quickly, and I could move on. I vowed I'd be a bit more particular the next time I met anyone nice. There were loads of cute blokes on board, so I was hopeful it would turn out well. It was quite exciting, really. After the Seth fiasco I knew better than to get serious, so a bit of light-hearted fun would keep me occupied without getting in the way of my photography ambitions.

My freshly made bunk looked particularly inviting, so I climbed into it and snuggled down under the covers. I flipped the light switch behind the bunks and happily enjoyed the feeling of being in a dark cave. I breathed deeply and started to have a lovely snooze, but what felt like minutes later, the door banged open and the lights came on like a sheet of lightning in the night sky, rousing me from what had promised to be a wonderful nap.

"Ellieeeeeeeeeeeeeeeeeeeee!" Caitlin yelled in her unmistakable twang. "Where are you, roomieeeeeeeee?"

She tumbled into the room, falling over her own feet, laughing hysterically and wiping her face repeatedly with the inside of her upper arm. The smell of alcohol was overpowering and I suspected she might have been just a teensy bit over the allowable limit for staff members.

I slid down from my bunk and was greeted by an overly enthusiastic hug.

"Oh, Ellieeeeeeeeeeeeeeee," she said, her head resting on my shoulder, "I wish you had come today. God, we had fun, and fuck, we were naughty."

I couldn't help but smile at her unique way of expressing herself. Despite being only half-awake, I was intrigued. "Right, I need details…" I sat down and put on the most engaged expression I could muster in my zombified state.

She collapsed on the bed next to me and put her head in my lap. "I went ashore with Ruby. Don't think you've met her yet. She works in the perfume and make-up store. She's Irish and fucking hilarious." She beamed up at me. "We went to the Honky Tonk bar over on the Dutch side for lunch. And by lunch, I mean drinks!" At the mention of drinks, Caitlin jumped up and rummaged through her side of the wardrobe for the trusty bottle of Kahlua. I waved away her offer, determined I wasn't going to be drunk again this week.

Probably.

After downing a shot, she was ready to continue her story, though this time she sat cross-legged on the floor, the Kahlua next to her. "We were sitting on the deck, having a round of shots," she said, "when these two really cute guys walked past along the beach. One of them smiled and gave me a double eyebrow raise, and we ALL know what that means…" Given the stories I'd already heard about crew being offered drugs in every port, I wasn't one hundred percent sure but, with Caitlin, I was pretty sure it wasn't about weed.

Caitlin's arms flew about with wild abandon. "They turned around and came back, so we invited them to join us. They were so cute. One had dark hair, and the other looked just like Channing Tatum." At the mention of my dream man's name, I was suddenly wide awake, and felt the first pinpricks of jealousy. "Well, except that he was a bit chubby, and his hair was a bit longer, and kind of blonde…" Her voice trailed off, and then she quickly added, "But apart from that, he looked just like him!"

She twirled her hair around her finger, giggling, when she mentioned the Channing Tatum-not-exactly-look-alike guy. "Let's just call him Channing," she said. "I don't remember his name—it wasn't important! I did really like him. They bought us drinks and god, they were just so funny! Not that I can remember anything they said, but still… So funny. They work on the Carnival ship docked next to us today. They're pursers. Or waiters? Something like that…"

Distracted by her memory lapse, Caitlin stood up, wobbling a bit, and started stripping off her beach clothes, which were looking more than a bit damp and dirty.

"Come on, Caity," I complained, "tell me more about the cute boy!" If I was going to be a bit more conservative in my choices from then on, I could at least live vicariously through her adventures.

"Oh, yeah," she said, perching on the edge of the desk in her bikini, "so anyway, they had rented a topless jeep and asked us to go to the beach with them. I know that it's probably not the *best* idea to get into a car with guys we don't know, but it was totally obvious that we could tell they were good guys."

I nodded in agreement, though secretly I thought that some

of the worst decisions ever made by women involved a guy who'd seemed really nice.

"We went to this beautiful beach... Oh, God, Ellie, it was just amazing. Totally deserted...really white sand, really blue water. The guys had beers in the back of the jeep, so we cracked them open and drank them lying in the sun."

So far, so good, except the part about getting in a car with drunk strangers who took them somewhere deserted.

"Ruby and the dark-haired guy went for a walk along the beach," Caitlin continued. "I stayed with Channing, and in the middle of swapping funny stories about the ship, completely out of the blue, he kissed me. Wasn't, like, love at first sight or anything, but he definitely thought I was hot, because there were tonnes of beautiful girls back at the bar." She smiled and giggled again and took a huge swig of Kahlua—from the bottle.

She wiped her mouth and continued her story at a hundred miles an hour. "And he was so hot, Ellie, I can't even tell you. And, well..." She blushed for the first time. "I jumped his bones. It was just one of those things that happened on the spur of the moment... We were kissing, and then I was on top of him... And oh, shit, Ellie, we did it right there on the beach! I'm not gonna lie, dude. It was awesome!"

Caitlin clearly got lost in memory for a moment, before suddenly remembering she'd been in the middle of recounting her naughty adventure. "Aaaaanyway...when Ruby and her dude came back, she couldn't look me in the eye..." Caitlin's enthusiasm had returned with a vengeance. "Once the boys dropped us back at the ship, I turned to her and said, 'Dude, I have to tell you something... I had sex with him.' And she said, 'Oh, my God, so did I!' Which made me feel so much better, 'cuz I'm not the only one who's bad!"

She had certainly confirmed the meaning of the double eyebrow raise. I would once have been shocked, but given my recent escapades with Seth, it seemed I'd become more blasé about these things. I'd hardly been an angel in my past, but I'd been brought up Anglican, and, well... Even love scenes in films shocked me, though usually I couldn't tear my eyes away from them—the only exception being when one popped up unexpectedly when I was watching a movie with my parents and I had to pretend to be horrified.

Apparently, my curiosity wasn't limited to the movies. My interest had been piqued by Caitlin's story, and I couldn't help but wonder what it would be like to have sex out in the open like that—just the idea sent tingles up and down my body. Maybe I could add that to my Caribbean to-do list…

I sighed internally; thinking about sex unsurprisingly had led me to thinking about Seth. As humiliating as the whole thing had been, I didn't want to part on bad terms. I figured that even if he was kind of avoiding me, I could probably snag him for a quick chat before he jumped ship.

Caitlin prodded my knee, bringing my attention abruptly back to the present. "Ellie, are you still with me?"

"Sorry!" I said. "I was just daydreaming." I took a deep breath. "Caity, do you think Seth would have kept sleeping with me if he wasn't leaving? I feel most embarrassed he might have been faking his interest in me, and everyone is going to laugh at me behind my back for being so naïve."

"I don't know about Seth," she said, studying my face. Then she reached out and touched my arm. "Even if people aren't the nicest, the truth is that we've all done it, babe. We all do stupid things. Hell, I still do it all the time. It's just the way of ships. Just try to forget about it and have a good time."

She bounded to her feet and headed to the bathroom, taking off her bikini as she went. "Babe, I have to get in the shower. I've got sand in all sorts of awful places." She snickered. "Channing had a…what do you call it? When their dick gets covered in sand?"

"A crumbed sausage?" I offered helpfully.

"Exactly! A crumbed sausage," she repeated, giggling. She ripped across the plastic curtain and turned the shower on full. Then she poked her head out the door and said, "Shit, the guys said they'd Facebook us—but they didn't even ask for our last names! Hmmmph." She screwed up her face as she popped back into the bathroom and jumped in the shower. "Bastards!" she called out, gurgling through a mouthful of water.

The rest of the night was much less interesting. Later in the crew bar, I noticed Caitlin wasn't the only one who was breaking the non-drunk-on board rule. I couldn't imagine constantly going to work in the morning with the inevitable hangover, and the idea of trying to keep the cruise line from finding out just how much alcohol I was drinking made me far from inclined to over-imbibe. Caitlin had lectured me when I'd first come on board about the cruise line's firm stance on passenger safety, and it seemed like a day didn't go by without something or someone reminding me of it…but it seemed like most of the crew weren't as fussed about getting into trouble as I was.

Being the most sober person in a group full of people who are completely trolleyed gets quite tiring quite quickly. As I'd no intention of keeping up with the rabble-rousers, I wandered over to order a drink from Jock.

"Ah, Ellie, lass, you look lovely tonight," he said with a warm smile.

"Hah," I said.

"So do you miss it yet?" he asked.

"Miss what?"

"England," he said.

"I miss my parents," I admitted. "But not the rain. Or the cold."

"More of a warm weather person?"

"Guess you could say that," I said. I rested my elbows on the counter and propped my chin on my hand. "When I was fifteen, we went on holiday to Spain. My dad complained the whole time that it was too hot. I couldn't get enough of it. I cried when it was time to go home." I laughed a little and added, "Of course, the cold weather is better for covering up."

He raised an eyebrow. "Can't imagine why you'd be wanting to cover yourself up, lass."

I rolled my eyes and moved on. "So are you running from

the weather, too? Scotland's even worse than England, isn't it?"

"Oi," he said, "mind your tongue!" A crooked smile on his face, he continued, "I miss it. I'm much happier with the rain and the fog and the snow than with sun and sand."

"What the hell are you doing on a cruise ship, then?"

Before he had a chance to reply, a very loud group appeared at the other end of the bar and demanded his attention. He flashed me a quick smile and left me to serve them. I was a bit disappointed, as he was so easy to talk to and quite frankly I could have sat and chatted with him all night. He had a way of making me feel special. Given he was a bartender, I suspected that was a skill that he employed regularly, but it was nice all the same.

As I surveyed the scene, I marvelled at the transformation of the friendly, professional crew and staff into loud, crazy, debauched party-goers. If only the passengers could see them now, without their crisp uniforms and professional demeanours. If there was one thing I'd learned on the ship so far, it was how truly amazing the customer service was. The cruise line took their reputation very seriously; a lot of time and effort went into training and encouraging the staff to be perfect hosts.

An elbow whammed into my back, nearly knocking me over. I spun around, annoyed, to find an overweight guy with a neat schoolboy haircut standing there, red-faced and apologetic. "Sorry, miss," he said awkwardly.

His accent was really thick, but I'd no idea where he might be from. Maybe somewhere in Eastern Europe?

He shuffled his feet and stared at the ground as he said, "I did not mean to hit to you there. I am rocking with the waves tonight." He laughed nervously.

His downcast eyes and forlorn stance made me feel immediately sorry for him. Okay, maybe I was a bit of a pushover; I had a throbbing pain pulsating around my spine, and I was standing there feeling sorry for the guy who'd caused it.

Pasting a smile on my face, I reached out and touched his arm in a friendly gesture. "Don't worry about it. It was just an accident. I do things like that all the time." Feeling the need to smooth things over a bit more, I added, "My name's Ellie," and held out my hand.

He shook it gently, my small hand engulfed in his massive paws. "I'm George," he said, leaning really close. It was so loud in the crew bar that he was practically yelling in my ear. "I work in the casino."

I leaned in and shouted, "What? Sorry, I can't really hear you." For lack of anything better to say, I added, "Catch you another time?"

He smiled and nodded, then walked away to join some friends. As I turned back to the bar to buy another drink, I chided myself for being a grumpy cow—he seemed like a nice guy. Oh well. There were so many members of the crew and turnover was so high that trying to get to know every single person was bloody well impossible.

Jock poured my drink but there was such a crush at the bar that there was no chance to pick up our conversation. Left momentarily at loose ends, I scanned the crowd for Caitlin. I found her dancing with a good-looking blond guy to the pulsating beat of 'I Just Can't Get Enough'. Caitlin was burning up the dance floor with some 80s moves, including a very impressive robot. I started to wend my way towards her, and got to her just as she stepped off the dance floor for a break. When she spotted me, she flung her arms around me in an enthusiastic hug, almost knocking me over.

"Hey, roomie!" she shouted in my ear. "I've had about enough of the crew bar—want to go back to the cabin? I'll invite some of these guys for a party!"

I nodded enthusiastically. I wasn't in the mood for disco. The idea of sitting around in the cabin, getting to know some other people, sounded much more appealing.

When we got back to our hall, I spotted Seth coming around the corner from the opposite direction and froze. My brain seemed to come to a complete stop before sputtering back into life. This could be my chance! I could invite him to our cabin, and we could have the chat I had already practised in my head. And it would be perfect, because it couldn't get too emotional with everyone else around, so I'd be able to say what I wanted to say and have done with it. I hated how things had turned out, and even though I was feeling let down, he seemed like a decent guy. I just really wanted to smooth things over before he left. Anyway, if I stuck with the whole cruise ship gig, it was entirely possible I'd run into him again down the road; Caitlin had told me stories of people who'd never expected to see each other again unexpectedly turning up on the same ship. So who knew? It was certainly worth a conversation.

Seth caught my eye and a smile tugged at the corner of his mouth. Before I could respond in kind, a tall, lithe redhead came around the corner. She was laughing and stumbling, her hand gripping Seth's arm for balance.

Caitlin saw them at the same time I did. She was silent, though worry flickered across her face, and her body stilled. Her hand squeezed mine, and I was grateful for the tacit support.

The redhead spotted Caitlin moments after we'd seen them and gave a little shriek. "Hey, girl!" She pitched herself down the hall and threw herself into Caitlin's arms.

Caitlin gave her a quick, stiff embrace, which was really out of character for someone who usually put her heart and soul into hugging people. "Hey, Ruby," she said, her voice oddly flat. "This is my cabin mate, Ellie."

Ruby. The name echoed through my head, and I finally realised that she was the other girl from Caitlin's story. The one who'd buggered off for a beach shag with the dark-haired bloke while Caitlin went off with her Channing lookalike.

"Oh," I said, and my eyes flickered from her to Seth and back.

"Ellie, this is Ruby," Caitlin said to me. "I told you about her. She came with me to lunch today."

There was an odd tension in the hall, and it was only made

worse by the fact that Seth refused to meet my eyes or even look at me. Since Ruby was Caitlin's friend, I'd have thought she'd be friendlier, but then I realised what the problem was.

Me.

Caitlin was clearly unhappy with Ruby for being with Seth, given he'd so recently been with me. Ruby was clearly uncomfortable that I'd seen her with Seth, though I wasn't sure if that was because she saw me as a threat—which was laughable—or because she wished I'd not had to see them together. And Seth was clearly not thrilled to have run into me, full stop.

"Ruby, come on," Seth barked, urging her into the cabin. His eyes were on the floor, on Ruby, Caitlin…anywhere but looking at me.

Caitlin squeezed my arm as Ruby followed Seth into his cabin. As she stepped over the threshold, she turned around and gave us a double eyebrow raise that was clearly meant for Caitlin, not me. The door closed behind them.

Chapter Five

"So, Ellie," Jacoline said, grinning, "I heard you slept with George from the casino last night."

I nearly choked on my scrambled eggs. Jacoline was eagerly awaiting my reply, and though I knew she wasn't being malicious, I couldn't help but feel cross at her for lobbing gossip at me without any warning.

"You certainly don't waste time," Justin muttered, his eyes on his plate.

Great. This was just...great. I hastily swallowed the bits of egg I hadn't choked on and spluttered, "Excuse me, what? George?" It took me a minute to even remember who the hell he was. "Oh, for fuck's sake," I said, "do you mean that guy I met in the crew bar last night? I talked to him for maybe two minutes!" I didn't have to fake my incredulous tone.

Jacoline laughed. "Oh, Ellie, it's fantastic you're not wasting time. Why wait when there are so many options available?"

I opened my mouth to reply, but was cut off by Justin.

"Best be careful," he said snidely. "You wouldn't want everyone to think you're a slag."

This was ridiculous. I hadn't even recovered from seeing Seth and Ruby together, and now I'd slept with someone new? Didn't these people have any more salacious—and true!— gossip to talk about?

Next to me, Caitlin shook her head and rolled her eyes. "Guys, don't be ridiculous. Ellie just said hello to the guy. Are we seriously doing this shit again?"

"*Bom dia, meus amigos!*" Maria was almost singing as she

walked in. She made a beeline to me and said, "Hello, Ellie! I am so glad you are not sad about Seth leaving." A Cheshire cat grin spread across her face. "I did not think George was your type, but when I saw you together in the crew bar, you seemed very cosy together."

I knew we had our culprit.

I took a deep breath. "Maria, I didn't sleep with George. I talked to him for two minutes, and that's all."

She patted my shoulder, an insincere sympathetic smile on her face. "It is okay, *chica*, you are a grown up woman. You can be with anybody you choose."

I wasn't normally a violent person, but I wanted to slap the smile right off her face.

My cheeks burning from the implication that I was, as Justin had said, a slag, and my hands were actually shaking. I hadn't slept with him and Maria knew it. It had nothing to do with George—I was sure he was lovely. It was about my reputation, which, if I was honest, had already been hanging tenuously by a thread before everyone thought I'd hopped into bed with George. If I'd any chance of retaining any kind of reputation whatsoever, I couldn't let them believe this rubbish.

Trying to keep my voice even, I said, deliberately calmly, "I didn't sleep with George. He literally bumped into me and tried to apologise. End of story."

Jacoline's gaze flicked between me and Maria; the smile had faded from her face and she seemed uncertain who to believe. The scowl on Justin's face, on the other hand, had only deepened. Caitlin rubbed my arm soothingly and mumbled something about not worrying what people say.

At that moment, because my life really needed to get more complicated, Ruby appeared in the doorway, spotted us, and practically waltzed over. She had what was almost certainly a post-coital glow, and I was tempted to chuck the salt shaker at her pretty face.

"What's going on, guys?" she inquired.

"Ellie slept with George from the casino last night," Maria announced, wasting no time in jumping in to spread the rumour.

Caitlin rushed to defend me. "'Maria, shut up. Ruby, it's not like that at all. Maria saw them talking in the crew bar, and well, you know how ships are…and *Maria*" she cast a burning glance at the Brazilian rumourmonger, "should know better."

I shot her a grateful look.

Ruby shrugged. "No big deal," she said. "We're all here to have fun, right?"

I didn't really want to think about the kind of fun she'd been having…

Nodding, Jacoline added, "It's okay, Ellie. We all know what ships are like!"

Fuuuuuuuuuuuuuuck! I wished they would actually listen to me.

Maria obviously wasn't finished and kicked the boot in a little harder. "You know, Ellie, I was a little bit sad when you and Seth were together while he and I were trying to work things out—" Ruby's head came up but she wisely said nothing "—but now I can see you do not like to spend the night alone. I am sure you left him no choice. Men are simple, yes?" She sat back and folded her arms, smiling at everyone. "If you offer them a warm body, they do not say no. Not on a ship, anyway." Laughing, she added, "We all know where to send the new guys for a good time, yes?"

Caitlin stayed silent and Jacoline looked uncomfortably down at the table. Justin snorted. Ruby took advantage of the awkward moment to escape to the buffet. On the upside, at least nobody actually agreed with Maria. Not out loud, anyway.

No one but Caitlin had bothered to defend me, either, and as I sat there, feeling desperately alone and friendless, tears began to well up and threatened to spill over. Not wanting anyone to see me cry, I quickly got up to race back to the darkness of the cabin. Caitlin wasn't far behind.

Grabbing my arm as we walked, she said, "Ellie, please don't worry about them. There's no point trying to convince them. People on ships will always believe what they want, and getting all upset about it won't really help. They'll forget all about it by next cruise, I guarantee you."

Rather unsurprisingly, this didn't actually make me feel any better. "But Caitlin," I wailed, "I didn't sleep with him, and I don't want them to think I did! I don't want everyone to think I'm a bloody slag!" Was this really what ships were like? It was worse than secondary school. Here, I'd slipped up once and had pretty much been branded a scarlet woman. I wasn't about to look for another man, but if I did meet a good guy there was no way he'd want a girl he believed had slept with two guys in less than a week.

I vowed to never speak to anyone in the crew bar ever again. And I definitely wasn't sleeping with anybody else on this contract. I would just focus on my photography and hang out with Caitlin. And watch lots of DVDs.

I was just about to share my thoughts with Caitlin when we passed the officer's mess and saw Luciano talking to a tall blond officer. If there was anything guaranteed to stop Caitlin in her tracks, it was two men in white uniforms with shoulder stripes.

Caitlin immediately veered into the officer's mess. "Well, hello, gentlemen," she said, turning on the charm. "How are we on this fine Barbadian day?"

In the craziness of the morning, I'd completely forgotten we were docked in Barbados. I'd been looking forward to it all week.

Luciano gave us a huge, warm smile and leaned over to give us double cheek-kisses. "*Ciao belle*, it's so good to see you." He gestured to the other officer. "This is my friend, Thomas. He's another engineer, from Norway."

Thomas had blue eyes and high, flat cheekbones that looked as though they'd been carved out of smooth, expensive stone. He nodded politely. "Hello, ladies. It's lovely to meet you. Would you like to join us on the beach today?"

It was certainly a better idea than hanging out in the dark cabin all day. The promise I'd just made to myself flitted through my mind, but I dismissed it. I wasn't going to sleep with them, and it wasn't the crew bar, so it was fine. Talking on a beach was surely allowed.

Caitlin and I dashed back to the cabin, where we snagged our swimsuits, cameras, and sunscreen, and I cursed my substantial pale thighs in the mirror. The guys were waiting for us when we finally arrived.

Barbados's only city, Bridgetown, was on the harbour, and it was full of beautiful, crumbling colonial buildings. In stark contrast to the characterful architecture, enthusiastic street vendors selling tacky wares lined the streets we passed. Cruise ship tourism, Luciano explained, had made tiny islands like this thrive all over the Caribbean and Bahamas. Barbados, apparently, was one of the most developed.

Caitlin and I held hands to avoid losing each other in the heaving crowd. "I forgot there's a festival on today," she yelled in my ear. "What a pain in the ass."

The island was full of tourists, but Caitlin's bright blonde hair still got a fair share of wolf whistles and attention. Normally she loved attention, but today I could tell it was making her a bit uncomfortable.

The boys ushered us away from Swan Street to find a taxi. As we walked down the side streets, shady-looking men with beady eyes repeatedly approached us. Well, maybe they didn't actually have beady eyes, but they were definitely of questionable character; every single one of them offered to sell us drugs.

"The salesmen get really damn annoying," Caitlin said. "It really takes the shine off the island paradise myth when you're continually offered a multitude of crap every time you come ashore." She gave an exaggerated sigh. "A few of us hatched a plan one night to screen-print t-shirts that say 'I don't want braids, t-shirts, drugs, or a taxi…I'M CREW!'"

We all laughed, though after only a brief sojourn on the island, I could already see why you would want such a shirt. That being said, one of the savvy salesmen would almost certainly try to score some and try to sell them back to you, totally missing the irony.

We managed to flag down a taxi, which took us to a flashy hotel about twenty minutes away. After tipping like a rock star, Luciano had a quick word with the concierge and then led us through a stunning marble-floored lobby onto a private beach complete with beach volleyball, sun lounges, water sports, and waistcoat-wearing waiters. An array of women in string bikinis lazed in the sun and sipped on colourful cocktails, while oily-chested men drank beers and eyed up the women.

"So this is where the beautiful people go..." I mused, feeling extremely self-conscious in my Marks & Spencers get-up.

"Yes, and on this day we too are the beautiful ones," answered Luciano, his Italian accent making the line sound more poetic than corny.

We found a group of sun lounges towards the back of the beach, partially under the shade of tropical palms that lined the edge of the sand. I might have been British, but I wasn't going to fry myself today. Previous beach holidays had taught me that a gradual tan was the way to go. Steamed lobster isn't a good look on anyone.

Caitlin stripped down to her bikini immediately. I was incredibly envious of her tiny waist, and even more jealous that she was able to eat so much junk and still stay so trim. I wasn't exactly a fast food lover, but I struggled even to stay the somewhat well-rounded shape I was. My bikini was still stashed away in the bottom of my suitcase; for the time being, a one-piece and a sarong were my best friends.

The guys were both tanned and seemed confident in their swimming attire. Luciano had a hairy chest that would have made a Roman God proud, and the way he looked in his tight white swimming trunks showed he had time to visit the gym. The fact Seth would look incredibly sexy in those swimming trunks briefly crossed my mind, but I waved it away before I got too wistful. Seth obviously wasn't that into me, and thanks to Maria, I sincerely doubted anybody else would be either.

I was just digging into my beach bag for sunscreen when Thomas asked the inevitable question: "Anybody want a drink?"

We agreed upon wine, and Thomas beckoned to a waiter, who returned with four huge wine glasses and an ice cold bottle of Pinot Grigio in a silver bucket. He pushed its stand down firmly into the sand and left with a nod and a bow. Did people actually live like this? If I'd been in a children's storybook, I would have pinched myself to see if I was dreaming.

Luciano pulled out a small digital camera to record the moment for Facebook; we all smiled, toasted for the camera, and squinted against the bright Caribbean sun.

After draining their glasses, Caitlin and Thomas disappeared, leaving Luciano and I to sip ours in a more cultivated fashion. They returned shortly after, wearing orange and black life vests; they'd rented a double-seater jet-ski for two hours.

Luciano and I watched them speed across the waves, laughing and shouting over the noise of the engine. Luciano poured the remaining wine into my glass, and as I sipped I noticed how happy and relaxed Caitlin looked as she clung onto Thomas, who was extremely competent at driving the speedy little machine.

I had been watching them for a while when I realised that Luciano and I had been sitting in silence for some time. There were very few people I felt comfortable enough to sit with without needing to fill the silence with idle chitchat. That had got me into trouble more than once. When I'd been little, Mum had been a master at standing silently, waiting for me to break down and confess to stealing biscuits or ruining her favourite top or breaking into her emergency chocolate stash. And I always broke down. I'd make a terrible spy. I'd never hold up under torture. They'd just have to look at me and I'd tell them everything I knew.

Somewhat depressingly, my big mouth had got the best of me yet again when I'd tried to apologise to Maria.

In any case, I'd already found ship life quite overwhelming, and my tendency to rattle on without pause wasn't really helping. So it was nice to discover in Luciano a friend who didn't make me feel like I had to fill the silence.

Of course, as soon as I noticed the comfortable silence, I felt self-conscious and needed to talk. "So Luciano," I said, "tell me about your family."

He smiled as he told me about his large family back in Italy. "My parents are getting a bit older, but they're wise and kind," he said, looking a little bit wistful. "My mother is a very good woman. She taught me to respect women and always be a good friend to them. I hope I've always followed her advice."

He drained his glass before he continued. "I have two brothers and two sisters—I'm the middle child. My parents both have several brothers and sisters, and everyone has children, so I have many cousins, nieces, and nephews. Easter and Christmas are big and wonderful celebrations, but it's very sad I don't get to attend all of them because of working here."

No mention of a wife or girlfriend. Not that I was paying attention to such things, of course, seeing as I was on a self-imposed ban on men. So instead of admiring the lines of his muscles, I nodded and smiled and listened to his stories about his family's antics. It was interesting, actually, as I was an only child, as was my mother, and my father only had one brother we didn't see very often. I'd never been part of a big family like Luciano's, so our celebrations were very different. Luciano spoke with such passion and tenderness about his family; it was really sweet, but it made me feel a little sad. I'd always wished I had a large family to throw big parties with.

As I listened, I wondered why he had never married or mentioned any serious relationships. Obviously this was great news for all the single ladies out there, but I couldn't understand how a handsome, kind, well-dressed man in his thirties who was extremely close to his mother hadn't managed to find someone... Oh! It suddenly dawned on me I should introduce him to Nick! I nearly laughed out loud as I wondered why it hadn't occurred to me before. It wasn't that Luciano was at all effeminate—he was actually quite masculine and attractive—but when I thought about it, I guess he did have a certain *je ne sais quoi.*

Of course, it wasn't the kind of thing you just come out and ask, because as extroverted as I could be at times, I was still British. I'd found that people tended to volunteer the things they wanted you to know, and I was sure the topic would arise at the right moment.

I'd always had a knack for finding the gay men in a crowd. Maybe Luciano was just who we needed to round out the posse. I already knew Nick would sometimes be in rehearsals and performing other dancer duties, Caitlin often had to shoot gangway or process film, and Luciano only had random half and full days off each fortnight; between the three of them, there should always be someone to hang out with. I could keep busy with friends and avoid getting into any further man-trouble.

Having kept me entertained with stories of his family, Luciano politely asked about mine. I had only just started the short story of my own family when Caitlin and Thomas returned. They ran right up to our seats and shook their wet hair like dogs, and then Thomas grabbed the ice bucket and dumped its contents over the both of us.

I jumped up and shrieked. "Nooooooo, stop!"

The water felt icy cold as it hit my warm skin. Luciano shouted something about Thomas being a bastard and laughed at me as I removed my sopping t-shirt. I noticed my feelings of self-consciousness about my body had disappeared; knowing that Luciano wouldn't be looking at me in 'that' way had made me feel a lot freer.

Though they'd successfully managed to interrupt our relaxed reverie, Caitlin and Thomas had actually returned to give us the life vests and keys to the jet-ski. The second hour of rental was ours.

I chased Luciano down to the beach, feeling like an excited child. My first lunge into the water was a shock—it was freezing. I screamed with surprise, and screamed again when Luciano splashed me. Any feelings of light-headedness I might have had from the wine were banished by the succession of cold water assaults.

Luciano jumped on the jet-ski first and then helped me up onto the seat behind him. Another confident operator, he jumped over waves and turned it in tight circles, spraying water everywhere and making me feel again and again like we were on the verge of tipping over.

"Hey, don't kill me!" I yelped, holding on for dear life.

"Don't worry, I've done this many times!" he shouted, laughing like a maniac, and then added, "Ellie, it's much better if you hold on here." He tapped the outside of my knees. I gripped his thighs with my knees, suddenly feeling slightly more stable. Then I tried to relax and loosened the death grip of my arms from around his waist.

The time flew by quickly and I felt a bit disappointed when Luciano tapped his chunky diving watch to announce we had to go back in. Back on the sand, my legs felt shaky, and I realised I was actually quite tired. Having an early night after work suddenly sound incredibly appealing.

In the taxi back to the ship, Caitlin put her head on my shoulder and closed her eyes. Thomas chatted with the taxi driver, while Luciano watched the township flash by, occasionally turning around to smile at us. I realised Seth hadn't been mentioned once during our conversation on the beach. I could have pumped Luciano for information, but truthfully, it hadn't occurred to me, and even if it had, I wouldn't have wanted to spoil the moment.

We got caught in a bit of passenger traffic back on the dock and I barely had time for a quick shower before I had to race up to the Pic Stop. Justin was outside with his eyes on his watch, frowning as usual, and walked away in a huff when I opened the door bang on opening time.

The night dragged on. I was dreading the following long day at sea, when I would be stuck in the shop all day. After less than a week on board, it already felt like I had been there forever, not least because I'd answered the same questions from guests a hundred times over. It was already apparent many of the crew were there for the fun and the money; passengers were something tolerated as a necessary, if sometimes annoying, part of the job.

I was more than a little surprised when Luciano appeared at the shop just before closing.

"Come join us in the crew bar tonight," he pleaded. I protested that I'd intended to go to bed early. "You can sleep on the plane," he said, laughing. It was an expression I'd hear many times during my contract.

My objections overruled, I trailed after Luciano after I'd locked up. The crew bar was thick with sweaty, fine-looking men speaking a plethora of languages at the top of their voices. I stopped in the door, stunned by the higher than average presence of the male half of the species. There were dark haired, tanned guys with white teeth and neat clothing speaking Italian; tall, blonde-haired, blue-eyed, Aryan-type specimens, the tell-tale sing-song in their voices giving away the fact they hailed from Norway and Sweden; and drinking vodka in the corner were a cavalry of hulking men with bulging biceps, speaking something I guessed was probably Russian. The testosterone level was so high, I felt like I'd walked into an episode of *The Bachelorette* on speed.

"The officers' bar is closed tonight," Luciano explained, his mouth close to my ear. His breath tickled my neck. "Fire hazard. Everyone has come here instead. Mostly you are seeing officers."

I hadn't even known there *was* an officers' bar, but given how spectacular some of them looked, I wondered if I had been too hasty in writing off the possibility of meeting Mr Right. Or, hell, even Mr. Right Now.

If I was going to be honest with myself, I knew I'd just decided to cut men out of my life because I was hurt and afraid. And that was stupid. I wasn't going to let Seth, Maria, or anybody else ruin my cruise ship experience. I was here for fun, dammit. I could advance my career and sample the international man-cuisine at the same time. That was entirely doable. Anyway, what was the point in wasting this opportunity? As my father had always said, "You're only young once, my darling." I was quite sure he hadn't been talking about men, but the intent was surely the same.

"*Bella*, do you see anything you like?" asked Luciano, sounding a bit hesitant. I imagined he was cautious about introducing me to someone new, in case he turned out to be one of the bastards he had described earlier.

I looked around eagerly, like a tourist in Rome's Gelateria del Teatro...what flavour should I choose? "That one," I said, a little too loudly, pointing at one of the blonds drinking white beer. He'd been the first one I'd noticed when we'd walked in. His horn-rimmed glasses and rolled-up trousers gave him a sexy nerd look, which I'd always been a sucker for. "He looks nice. Smart. And a bit quieter than the rest," I said, feeling a bit excited. My vow to take it slow had sailed out the window without a second thought.

Luciano paused, the corner of his mouth twisting into a slight frown. "Hmmmmmmm. I'm not so sure, Ellie. I know him a little, and now that I know you better, I don't think he's your type. I could have told you that about Seth, too, if I knew you before."

I mock-pouted in disappointment at his first comment and ignored the second one. "Hmmmmm," was about all I could muster. I knew how stupid I sounded. One minute I was shocked at Seth's departure and the next I was salivating over a Ken doll. Caitlin was right that ship life moves fast; I already felt like I'd been here for weeks rather than a matter of days.

Luciano was staring at me, studying my reaction. I must have looked a bit pathetic, because his stance weakened a little. "If you really want to meet him," he said at last, "I can introduce you. We'll talk to him and see what you think."

I held back my applause and tried to look cool.

On the walk over to his group, I had an attack of nerves. Had I suddenly developed a toned midsection and thighs that didn't resemble cauliflower sausages? That would be a no. Shit. A fit guy like the sexy nerd I'd singled out wasn't going to fancy me. I grabbed Luciano's arm. "Let's get a drink first."

At the bar, Jock's face lit up when he saw me. "What can I get for you, lass?" he asked. "Wine?"

"Something that will give me nerves of steel, please," I said, aware of how ridiculous I sounded.

"Och, got your eye on somebody, hey?" Jock asked with a laugh, cocking an eyebrow like a cartoon character. "Don't tell me it's one of them officers." His light-hearted expression slid away as he directed his next comment at Luciano. "I've often wondered why you come into this bar so much when you have a perfectly grand one of your own." His jaw clenched. "Tonight you brought all your mates, I see."

"*Sì*, only because you are the best bartender on the ship." Luciano said, winking at Jock. Jock narrowed his eyes and looked away.

"I'm just socialising," I blurted out, interrupting the awkward situation. I didn't want Jock to think I was easy, too. So far he didn't seem to know, or care, about my rapidly disintegrating reputation, and quite frankly I was happy to keep it that way. With that in mind, I was keen to keep him out of the loop with regard to my romantic endeavours.

Jock slid a glass across the bar to me. "Rum and Coke," he said. "Guaranteed nerves of steel. Just mind you be careful, lass." He glanced at Luciano and added, "I'd hate to see you get hurt."

"You never answered my question," I said, suddenly remembering our conversation from the night before.

"When you're not so busy," he said.

Sensing that was all I was going to get out of him, at least while Luciano was around, I thanked Jock and steered Luciano back to the group of hot men. Entrance into the group was as easy as Luciano walking into the centre and saying, "Eh, can we join you?" The group responded with a roar, which I took to be an affirmative. One of them patted the seat next to him and smiled at me. He was a bit tubbier than the rest, who were all even fitter up close, but he had a lovely smile. Still, I hesitated, hoping to snag the empty space next to the nerdy guy. Luciano plonked himself down in it before I could get anywhere close. He smiled and nodded at me, then patted his knee.

I cocked my head to the side, trying to work out what he wanted. Did Luciano fancy the sexy nerd, too? Was it going to be a competition? Our new best buddies stance was going to get old fast if this kind of thing was going to happen.

Luciano patted his knee again. "Sit, sit, Ellie," he crooned. "Come talk with us."

I shook my head and opened my mouth to reply, but at that moment, noise erupted at the entrance to the bar. I looked around to see that the rest of the photographers had arrived, obviously already drunk. Seth was leading the group, with Maria hanging off him. Seth looked around, surveying his audience. Spotting Luciano, he shouted, "Hey, Luca, come have a drink with me!"

Luciano shifted in his seat, looking rather uncomfortable. He nodded at Seth in acknowledgement, then looked back at me and shrugged. He rose from his seat slowly and muttered something under his breath.

"This is my friend Ellie," he said to the group. "Please take care of her." Then he went to join Seth, who greeted him with a bear hug.

I stood awkwardly at the edge of the group, clutching my glass and wondering what to do. The nerdy blond looked at me, clearly confused, and with no more idea of what to do now that Luciano had buggered off than I did. He shook his head, and then, with a big breath and a swig of rum, I lunged for the seat.

"Hi, I'm Ellie," I blurted, feeling the rush of rum giving me confidence. "I love your glasses. They give you that really hot nerd look." I smiled like a crazy person, cursing my habit of saying the first thing that popped into my head. I stared at him beseechingly, hoping he'd say something and end my misery.

"Hello, Ellie," he said, taking my hand in a firm but not overly-assertive handshake. Excellent. "I'm Axel. Very pleased to meet you."

He pushed his glasses up on his nose, actually looking a bit nervous. "Thanks for your compliment about my glasses. Sometimes I'm not too sure if they're very fashionable, but I need them to see." He flashed a brilliant smile and gave an embarrassed-sounding little chuckle. So far, so good.

I glanced up to see Luciano standing with Seth near the entrance to the internet room. Both of them were staring at me, although Seth was obviously trying to pretend he wasn't. I felt as though I had done something wrong, but then reminded myself it was Seth who had led me on. Feeling vindicated, I returned my focus to Axel. Well, mostly. I stole the occasional glance to see if they were still watching me. They always were.

Axel was still talking. "It's a very nice crew bar. We officers have our own bar, but it's very boring. There are always the same people there, and they're the people I work with all day on the bridge. I don't need to see them in the evenings as well! I've only been here for two weeks and didn't realise there were so many beautiful girls on this ship." He smiled and took a long drink of his beer. This was really weird; I was supposed to be the one who was nervous because he was so good looking, yet *he* was the one acting nervous!

We chatted for a few minutes, yelling over the music, and I thought it was going well, given he hadn't made a dash for the bathroom and 'forgotten' to come back. That's usually a pretty tell-tale sign someone isn't that into you.

Just as the music changed to a 90s James Bond theme, Axel leaned in to say something; his hand accidentally brushed my knee. He did that double-take you do when you've touched somebody you fancy and aren't sure if you should move your hand or not, and decided on the bolder course of action: his hand stayed where it was. It wasn't actually on my knee as such, but sort of hovering to the side, enough to make contact.

Somewhat depressingly, I didn't feel much of a connection despite how good-looking he was; I didn't feel compelled to accidentally graze him back.

A few of the guys made "woohoo" noises, and I quickly sat up straight, thinking they'd noticed Axel's smooth move and were teasing us. I was getting ready to pull my knee away and make a joke when I realised their attention was not focussed on us at all. They were staring at the dance floor, mouths hanging open, and I saw more than one crotch rearrangement.

I turned around slowly to find Maria alone on the dance floor, gyrating her hips and pulsating her whole body to the aching, dramatic melody. She was wearing tiny shorts with high heels and a loose top that hung enticingly off one shoulder. The most annoying thing was that she didn't look stupid or self-conscious. Dancing alone was not something I could ever do, but Maria made it look like a sexy foreplay scene straight out of a Bond film. Never mind the fact that she would have been the romantic interest who tried to kill Bond at the end of the movie...

Until the world falls away...

Maria flicked her hair dramatically and drew a circle on the floor with her stilettoed foot. Damn you, Sheryl Crow. Something by Mumford and Sons would have been considerably less alluring.

Beside me, Axel was transfixed. His stray hand had dropped back to his side, and though I didn't want to look too closely, it looked like he might have been dribbling beer from the corner of his mouth.

Maria caught my eye and slowly raised her eyebrows. She smiled at the same time, baiting me with every move she made. Then her eyes locked solely on Axel. In what I thought was an overly obvious stripper move, she bent at the waist to touch her ankle and then slid her hand all the way up to her thigh; then she trailed it up her side until she flicked her hair again. I couldn't understand how she still managed to look beautiful and classy when she looked like she ought to be dancing around a pole with cash sticking out of her waistband. If I'd tried to dance the way she was dancing, it would have been much less *Showgirls* and much more *Scary Movie*. How depressing.

My head started to spin with the need to distract Axel from the floor show. I didn't feel any connection with him, but that didn't mean I wanted Maria to steal him away. The guy had only been here for a couple of weeks; he couldn't possibly have been prepared for an encounter like Maria. But before I had a chance to plan my next move, Maria reached out her left hand and beckoned to him. Surely he wouldn't fall for that...

Axel got up from his seat. "Um, sorry, Ellie," was about all he could muster before he walked, just a little too fast, towards the dance floor.

Were men really that easy?

Maria grabbed him as soon as he was within reach and kissed him with urgency. Axel wasn't shy in responding, and his glasses nearly fell off as he nuzzled the side of her face and neck.

Yep, they were that easy.

I sat in stunned silence for a minute before being motivated into action. I stood up, making weak excuses to the group around me; they probably wouldn't have noticed if I were on fire. I took one last look at the dance floor, and Maria smiled at me over Axel's shoulder. She rubbed her hand up and down his back, then pulled it away to make the V for victory sign.

I wondered about the enemy I had made. In less than a week, I'd managed to piss off a passionate and angry woman, and it was becoming increasingly obvious that she was going to do whatever she could to cut me off at every pass, not to mention making absurd hand gestures that only belonged in tacky 90s teen movies.

I thought about the guy in the *Godfather Part II* who'd said, 'Keep your friends close and your enemies closer'. I didn't think I could be close to Maria without getting burned. This wasn't what I'd wanted, but it was clearly game on.

Chapter Six

"Obviously, Princess, we have to slap that bitch up."

Caitlin and I were sitting in Nick's cabin, munching on crackers and cream cheese. Nick's suggestion was not especially helpful. Supportive, but not terribly realistic.

"Babe," he added, swiping a cracker from my hand, "I have *seeeen* the guy you're talking about, and he is worth a lawsuit."

"I beg to differ, Nick," I said around a mouthful of cheese. "If he was that easily swayed, I doubt he's worth anything." The fact I hadn't been interested was beside the point. "Axel isn't even the issue, anyway. The problem is Maria. I tried explaining things and being nice, but didn't get anywhere." I reached for some pastrami and said, "I guess I've got to get her at her own game." Being with the two of them was already relaxing. Nick had put on disco music and called one of his waiter friends for an emergency food delivery.

Caitlin was quite chuffed by this, as crew weren't allowed room service under any circumstances unless you happened to come down with the dreaded Norovirus, which called for immediate quarantine. Nick said that many staff and officers got away with it, probably because they tipped quite well and were a good long term investment for the room service crew. Nick's friend had hooked us up with an Italian-inspired platter, which went remarkably well with plotting the demise of the Brazilian Bitch, as we'd started calling her.

"Well, I do have one suggestion," said Caitlin in her trademark dramatic stage whisper. "I just found out Maria actually has a boyfriend at home. You'll never guess what he's like."

"Rich?" I guessed.

"Gorgeous" was Nick's suggestion.

"Half points to Ellie!" Caitlin said, giggling. "Apparently he's some sad, overweight loser who comes from a rich polo family. She doesn't give a shit about him, but she's holding onto him until she finds another rich guy—and that's what she's here to do." Nick and Caitlin both guffawed at this, although I wasn't sure what was so funny. Before I could ask, Caitlin said "Fuck, I'm Starvin' Marvin. I'm gonna order some more food. This stuff is just the warm up."

As she dialled room service, she asked, "Does anybody want anything?" I was already stuffed and shook my head, as did Nick. Caitlin ordered an absolutely ridiculous amount of food, including a burger, fries, onion rings, and more cheese and pastrami. And some fresh fruit, just for good measure.

"I like to at least pretend I'm healthy," she said with a grin.

When she got off the phone, Nick said, "Right, girls, let's find out what Maria has been up to. Then we can work out how to use that information against her." He grinned evilly. "What do you think?"

I'd not been on board long enough to pick up any dirt on Maria aside from what I'd just learnt from Caitlin, but couldn't wait to hear more about what Maria had been up to. I didn't think it would be too hard; people generally exposed themselves soon enough, and given how fast gossip spread on the ship…

When Caitlin's food arrived, I was shocked at the size of the platter. She'd ordered enough for two people. Two really hungry people. I looked at the platter and then at Caitlin; however big her appetite, I had difficulty believing someone as tiny as her could eat all of the food she'd ordered.

She tucked into a burger with a huge bite that left sauce dribbling down her chin. Wiping it away with her arm, she started in on a story about some of her shipboard antics. "A few months ago, we were all playing the 'Have you ever?' drinking game in the Senior Engineer's cabin on Deck 12, and

I was losing." She took another bite and said around the mouthful, "That is to say, I was drunk... And then we played strip poker and I was losing."

"Meaning you were naked," I filled in.

She grinned. "Anyway, we started to play Truth or Dare, and one of the guys dared me to run naked down the passenger hallway—you know the one that you can see from the atrium and the area outside the restaurants? It has a crew door at either end."

We both nodded mutely, and I snitched a fry from her plate.

"I really didn't want to, but I thought, 'It's the middle of the night, nobody's gonna be around'. Makes sense, yeah?" She rolled her eyes dramatically and continued, "So I opened the door and started running, and as I was running, I heard music and I saw people, and then I looked to the side, into the open atrium, and saw people on every level...and then I realised it was dinner time. I was so drunk I'd forgotten we'd started drinking after lunch!" Caitlin broke into loud gales of laughter.

Caitlin's enthusiasm for telling stories of her escapades was hilarious and contagious. Nick and I were both doubled over laughing, and we all looked so ridiculous that it didn't take long before we were laughing at each other laughing, and then we were all crying and hyperventilating and holding onto each other for dear life. Caitlin was laughing loudest of all; they probably could have heard her on the other end of the ship.

Nick finally pulled himself together and asked, "And you're still working here?"

Caitlin took a few breaths, dried her tears, and said in a low voice, "Well, I got disciplined by the cruise line, and by Justin, but it all blew over within a couple of weeks."

Lucky her. I had a feeling if I'd been caught running through the ship starkers, Justin would have pitched me over the side himself.

'Hot Stuff' came on and Caitlin bounced over to turn it up a bit, yelling, "I LOVE this song! Right, I've got to pee, but when I come back, we're totally dancing to it!" She disappeared into the bathroom and closed the door with a dramatic bang and a laugh.

A few minutes later, as Caitlin came out of the bathroom, the cabin door flung open and Nick's roommate walked in. "Hey," he said to nobody in particular.

Ah, this was the guy we'd seen in the mess a few days earlier, who had slept with Caitlin and unsuccessfully come onto Jacoline. Caitlin clearly had no interest in spending time with him. She barely even glanced in his direction as she reached over to flick off the music, and then stood up with a bored sounding sigh.

"Well," she said, "thanks for your hospitality, but I think there's a bottle of Kahlua calling our names back in the cabin." She smiled and began to pack up the food. "Anyway, we need something to wash down all of this food!"

She caught my hand and pulled me out, waving goodbye to Nick, and towed me down the hallways until we reached our cabin.

As we settled on the floor amidst the remains of the food, Caitlin caught me watching her. "Something on your mind?" she inquired, popping a fry into her mouth.

I hesitated, and then said, "I'm so jealous of how svelte you look." I nibbled at a fry of my own and added, "I can tell you right now that this fry is going to turn into a nice lump of fat on my thighs. How on *earth* do you manage to eat the way you do and still look so amazing? Tell me your secret, please, so I can finally lose weight!"

"You don't need to lose weight, sweetie," Caitlin said, smiling at me. "You're beautiful just the way you are."

I appreciated the sentiment, but knew it wasn't strictly true—she was just being nice. Everyone knows that girls are bound by the girl code to boost their friends' self-esteem. "Awww, thanks," I said, "but seriously, I've really put on the pounds over the last few years." I rolled my eyes and said, "Dan never let me forget it. I just want to lose a bit. Particularly on these thighs." I grabbed a chunk of thigh and gave it a slap, "See, just here."

Caitlin got to her feet and drifted over to the desk. She took a deep breath, appearing to chew over her thoughts, and began to re-arrange books and wipe away invisible crumbs. "Well…" she said finally, sounding rather unlike her usual confident self, "sometimes, but not always, I kind of make myself vomit." She kept her back to me as she said, "Ellie, you're not going to tell anyone, are you?" There was a note of anxiety in her voice that I wasn't used to hearing from her. "Justin would freak out about this sort of shit."

Some small part of me wasn't surprised; there were too many times she'd waltzed off to the bathroom right after a meal—including earlier that evening. Also she had such a tiny waist and slender arms, even though she never seemed to eat anything other than junk food.

At the same time, I was horrified, and instantly regretted putting so much emphasis on her appearance. I hated to think that'd been contributing to making her feel like she needed to go to extreme measures to look a certain way!

I went and put my arm around her, for once playing the role of comforter. "Oh, Caity," I said, "you are brilliant, and I already think of you as a close friend. I hope you know I'm here for you if you ever want to talk."

She put her head on my shoulder. "Thanks, dude," she said, sounding rather small and vulnerable. "I think I'm okay. I mean, I hardly ever do it anymore anyway."

I didn't really know what to say. I didn't know a lot about bulimia, but the last thing I wanted to do was pressure or judge Caitlin. I didn't want to alienate her, but what was I supposed to say? For once in my life, I didn't have the words to fill the silence that had fallen, and the worst part was it was the first time I'd desperately wanted to say something.

Caitlin filled the silence for me. "My dad left when I was nine," she said, her head still on my shoulder. I absently started to stroke her hair, figuring that if it had always made me feel better when Mum did it to me, it couldn't hurt. "My mom was convinced that if she'd only been thinner, more beautiful, more perfect, Dad wouldn't have left."

"That's terrible," I said. "I'm so sorry."

She lifted her head and sighed. "Mom starved herself, pretty much, until she finally got back the 21-inch waist she'd had when she first met Dad. She was convinced that if she made herself back into the person she'd been, Dad would come running back."

I thought of Dan and said, "I'm not sure that really works. I think they either like you or they don't, and if they don't like the way you look then they'll just find someone they like more." Lordy, look at me coming out with profound relationship advice. Where had that come from?

"You're probably right," Caitlin said. "Not that Mom would have believed it. Dad never came back, but Mom just blamed herself for not trying hard enough. She always told me that if I just tried hard enough, I'd always be able to keep a man. Nice clothes, nice hair, tiny waist, blow jobs. The keys to relationship success, you know. First time a boyfriend broke up with me, she raked me over the coals about how I should have tried harder!" She shook her head and sighed. "Sometimes I wonder if it's really true, or even if it is true—is it really worth it? Guess it doesn't matter, though; I keep trying anyway." She smiled bitterly.

She'd only mentioned her mother once before, and I couldn't help but wonder what their relationship was like. "Does she know about…you know…the throwing up?" I tried to be delicate.

"Yeah," she said with a shrug. "She does it too. She's totally disciplined with her diet, but not long after my first break-up, I discovered her vomiting after dinner, and she admitted it was a good compliment to regular diet and exercise. 'Just shifts those last few pounds, honey,' she said, before helpfully suggesting I try it. But the way I see it, though, instead of using it to just lose the last few pounds, I can eat and drink what I want, and just get rid of the first few pounds too, without all the deprivation my mom goes through." She caught my expression and added, "Dude, you'd do it too if you knew how easy it makes losing weight."

It was tempting for about a millisecond, and I was thankful for my mum, who whinged about her weight as much as the next woman but had never obsessed over it. I might not like my weight, and I might think my thighs were a travesty the world didn't need to see, but the idea of going to extreme measures was just frightening. But this wasn't the time to pass judgement, so I gave Caitlin a hug and said, "I'm here for you, roomie."

She hugged me back, but it was clear she'd decided the conversation was over. I just couldn't tell if it was because she was worried about what I thought.

With a complete change of tone, she pulled away and said quickly, "Ellie, seriously, it's no biggie. I hardly ever do it these days, I swear. Before I came here, I promised myself I'd stop. I intend on hitting the gym intensely very soon." She smiled almost-convincingly and changed the subject. "Soooooooooooooo, what's the story with you and Luciano?"

Making a note to do some research on bulimia later, I let her change the topic. I wrinkled my nose at her question and asked, "What do you mean? We're just friends, of course."

Caitlin laughed incredulously. "Awwww, come on, Ellie, what do you mean 'of course'? Don't play coy with me, girl! You should totally tap that. It's not because you're worried about Seth, is it? Because he is sooooooooooo gone on Sunday."

Really confused, I said, "Wait, what? Luciano's gay, right?"

"He's not gay!" she shrieked. "What *are* you talking about, woman?"

I tried to remember all of the things that had, to me, made his sexuality blindingly obvious. "He's so put together, you know? He's handsome and he dresses soooo neatly and properly, he's close to his mother, he wears those tiny, tight, white swimming shorts…" In retrospect, it was fairly weak evidence.

"Dude, he's *Italian!*" Caitlin was laughing so loudly I thought the passengers up on the promenade deck would hear her. "Luciano is a total ladies' man, like all the Italians I know, and most men on this ship!"

I thought about the Italian men I'd known over the years, trying to rethink Luciano in that context, and wondered if she was right. Italians did tend to have a certain way about them, caring about clothes, so smooth and charming, definitely Mama's boys.

Was my gaydar so completely off all of a sudden? Maybe it was the change of time zone.

Still, he wasn't sleazy and over-the-top like the ones I'd met through Dan's football club, which seemed to have more than its fair share of Italian stallions, so I wasn't totally convinced. From what I'd heard at our countless post-game nights out, I knew that being gay was horribly frowned upon in most Italian families, and maybe he just wasn't out because he was afraid of upsetting his mother. Either way, he had proven to be a good friend to me and I felt the need to defend his honour.

"He's nothing like the other men on this ship, Caity," I protested. "He's been really supportive and kind, and helped me a lot with the Seth situation."

"Uh huh. Or just maybe he's just trying to get into your pants." She was still chuckling away like one of the Three Stooges and obviously wasn't listening, which made me smile. I loved the easy relationship we were developing. It was something I missed about Dan; we'd had such an easy relationship before it all went to shit.

The cabin phone rang loudly and Caitlin jumped up to answer it.

"Well, helloooooooooooooooooo, Luciano," she said, grinning at me. "Fancy hearing from *you*. Ellie was just telling me how fabulous and handsome you are." She was smiling and laughing silently, pulling the phone away as I tried to swipe it from her. I suddenly felt like I was thirteen again, at the slumber party where Virginia Mason had dared me to ring up my crush and then had embarrassed me when I'd chickened out.

"Caitlin!" I hissed.

She ignored me. "Uh huuuuuh, uh huuuuuh, I know, I

know…" she said in to the phone, twirling a strand of hair around her finger. "Oh, yes, I'm sure she'd be very glad to talk to you. Here you go." She handed me the phone.

I shook my head at her as I tucked the phone between my shoulder and ear. "Hey, Luciano, sorry. Ignore Caitlin. She's just being funny."

I could hear the smile in his voice as he replied, "So you don't think I'm handsome, *bella*? I'm disappointed."

I felt a bit confused at the whole thing, but then gay men were always searching for compliments, so… "Well, no. I mean, yes, you're…an Italian Ricky Martin," I stammered, throwing out the first name that came to mind. He was just as handsome, just as lovely, and I imagined his reaction to the reference would confirm things.

"Who?" asked Luciano.

So much for that idea. "Never mind," I said, shaking my head and smiling. "How are you, anyway?"

"Very excellent, Ellie. I need to ask you a favour. Your very handsome friend is hoping you can help him…me."

He explained that he needed help with a report that had to be completed in English and wanted to know if I could come by to help him the next day, after I closed the shop. I was happy to help, and since I enjoyed Luciano's company, it was hardly a chore. We made plans to meet up after work Saturday night, after our day at sea, where he would apparently spend ten hours in the engine room. Ten at night seemed late to be working on a report, but then what did I know? Nothing seemed normal on a cruise ship.

It seems Caitlin had been right to dread a day at sea; Saturday was incredibly long and mind-numbingly boring. I had the shop open all day long, with only a lunch break to escape the constant questions about my life. I found especially funny when people would ask what part of England I was from, and when I told them, would confess to having no idea where anywhere was, and to also knowing nothing about England, except that we had a Queen. And David Beckham,

Harry Potter, and poor dental hygiene, of course. "Beckham's wife is really skinny," one woman said, looking me up and down as though I was letting the side down. Another asked me if magic was really real, and the number of times people complimented me on my teeth made me incredibly self-conscious.

I was absent-mindedly poking my fat rolls, wondering if it was better to be chubby with good teeth or skinny with bad teeth, when Nick popped his head in the door of the Pic Stop.

"Hey, Princess, you coming to watch me dance in the special late show tonight?" he said, finishing his question with a little leap in the air. "I'm going to be fabulous, you know."

I had no doubt, but explained I was going to help Luciano with his report. "Sorry, Nick, he'll be in trouble otherwise."

"Uh huh…" Nick said. "A *report*… No better time than late on a Saturday to work on a *report*…" He winked.

This lot had sex on the brain. "You sound just like Caitlin!" I rolled my eyes. "We're just friends, and anyway I'm pretty sure he plays for your team."

Nick snorted. "Princess, I *wish* he played for my team!" He pouted and added, "Sadly for we fabulous male-fancying men, your Italian engineer is definitely a ladies' man."

"Really?" I said. Both he and Caitlin had been here longer than I had, so presumably they'd had ample opportunities to observe Luciano in action… Hmm. "I'm still not sure I'm convinced," I said, though I was starting to think I was wrong.

Nick grinned and said, "You go along and help Luciano with your report, and if in the morning you still think he's gay… Well. Then we can revisit this conversation." Laughing, he blew me a kiss and waltzed out of the shop.

By the time Luciano came by at closing time, I was exhausted and not particularly in the mood for report writing and editing. Still, once I committed to something or someone, I always saw it through, so I went with Luciano back to his cabin, keeping up a cheerful patter of conversation.

Papers were strewn across Luciano's bed and desk and a

tell-tale pile of dirty plates and glasses sat guiltily beside the laptop.

"Wow, someone's been busy," I commented, taking in the rest of the cabin. It was about six times the size of ours, with a queen-sized bed and bedside tables, various pieces of modern artwork, a long sideboard, and a desk. I was obviously in the wrong job, as my cabin was a sad and tiny space by comparison.

"Yes, I finished work in the engine room at four today, and I've been working non-stop since then," Luciano said, looking deep into my eyes as he spoke. I always found it weird when people did that, so I shifted around uncomfortably and avoided his gaze.

"Let's get to work," I said brightly, and sat down to look at the screen. All business, that's me.

Just as I started on the second paragraph, Luciano touched my shoulder.

"Ellie, I need to talk to you," he murmured.

About six different things ran through my head instantaneously, and I squirmed in my seat. Was he in trouble? Was he sick? Did he have a secret confession regarding his sexuality? I'd already heard Caitlin's secret; I wasn't sure I could deal with any more.

Luciano wiped his forehead with the back of his hand, as though he was very nervous. "From the first day I saw you in the corridor, I knew that we would sleep together."

That had not been what I'd expected to come out of his mouth. I sat very still, my mouth hanging slightly open as I silently sucked in air. I could feel the tension and expectation in the room building as my head spun and my heartbeat quickened.

For starters, I'd been with his friend, Seth—wasn't there some kind of bro code that made that a bad idea? Not to mention that he'd acted like a gay best mate and offered to help me find another man, which had lulled me into an apparently false sense of security, seeing as he now wanted to sleep with me.

Caitlin and Nick were totally right; I was clueless. I was shocked, flattered, and definitely intrigued by Luciano's statement, but that didn't mean I had a clue what to do next. He was gorgeous, caring, fun...and, apparently, straight. This put a whole different spin on things.

With all those thoughts running through my head, it felt like we'd been sitting there for ages when in reality it had only been a minute or two. Luciano, clearly impatient, spun my chair around, sat down on the bed, and reached out to take my hands in his.

"You are so... so...*bellissimo* and...sorry, I can't think in English when I'm nervous..." He smiled shyly. "Hmmm, yes... You're funny and intelligent and charming." He stroked my hand, very slowly and gently; he kept his eyes on mine and his voice low.

Another man telling me how wonderful I was. It could have been lovely, but it came so soon after Seth's glowing words, which had turned out to be bullshit, that it was hard to take him seriously. I was sure there was a distinctly cynical look on my face as I listened to the words flowing out of Luciano's mouth.

"You deserved so much better than Seth." He hesitated, then said, "Well, he is my friend, but, well... He didn't treat you right." He shook his head solemnly. "No, he wasn't good for you, Ellie. He doesn't know you like I know you. He does not know the wonderful and...and sincere woman I see in front of me. You and I are a good match, I think."

The words of flattery made me feel a bit uncomfortable, and to be fair, we hadn't known each other for *that* long, even in cruise ship time. Besides the fool I'd made of myself with Seth, I knew my strengths, and beauty wasn't one of them, yet these guys kept using it as admittedly effective bait. Perhaps the funny, intelligent, and charming part was a little bit more on the money... At least, those had always been the things I hoped men would notice, because while I'd always been doubtful about my looks, I *knew* I was funny and smart and, despite my mouth's tendency to run away with me, generally pretty good with people, too.

Luciano appeared to be holding his breath, and I guessed he wanted me to say something. Most men would, probably, if they'd just lavished you with compliments.

"I thought you were gay," I blurted out, and then felt my cheeks going hot. I definitely had a way with words sometimes.

"What?" Luciano jumped up, emphatic gestures accompanying the word. I couldn't say that the motions particularly helped his straight-man argument. "Ellie, why would you think that?"

I had to stop and think before answering, to make sure I didn't offend. Never mind that he'd already obviously not been impressed by what I was now convinced was an erroneous assumption. "You're always so well groomed," I said, feeling incredibly awkward, "and you're close to your mother, and you wear those tiny white swimming trunks…and… Well, you're always so nice and friendly to me…" I trailed off, realising I sounded ridiculous. *Note to self: get gaydar checked.*

"Ellie, *bella*, I was trying to…what do you call it in English?…court you." He sat back down, looking defeated.

"Oh." I was suddenly lost for words, which was probably a blessing, really. He was actually taking it slow and making sure we clicked, rather than jumping into bed like I had with Seth, and then having to awkwardly avoid each other in the halls… My mind raced with ideas of how to take back what I had said. Maybe I could claim some sort of language barrier problem? "But just one thing," I said, thinking back to my last experience. "You aren't leaving next San Juan, are you?"

Luciano laughed, obviously aware of my worries, and said, "No, I'm here for you to enjoy for many months to come." He rose slowly from his chair, slid his hand around the back of my neck, and started to play with my hair, twirling it around his fingers and stroking the side of my neck with light, feathery touches of his thumb. He leant over and whispered in my ear in Italian. It was a language I didn't know, but his seductive tone was all I needed to understand. As his hands wandered lower and his whispering became more intense, I suspected that those romantic words had become just a little more urgent.

God, that feels good.

I went from wondering what was going on to desperately wanting him to kiss me. It was my first experience of a drawn-out seduction dance, and I liked it. A lot. His body had become really hot to the touch and he had developed a faint sweat. Combined with the intoxicating smell of his aftershave, I was starting to feel more than a bit woozy.

Wait, don't fall for this again.

I swallowed with a conspicuous, nervous gulp. My mouth had become completely dry and I kept licking my lips and swallowing again and again. I could hear the pounding of my own heart inside my head. Every inch of my body was getting sucked into the Luciano vortex, and he hadn't even kissed me yet.

Then his lips touched the delicate skin at the base of my neck.

Damn it, I'm not made of stone.

The build-up of anticipation had been fast and furious, and I almost cried out with relief. He moved his mouth up, millimetres at a time, placing countless tiny, soft kisses along the front of my throat; and when the kiss-trail made it up to my mouth, I actually did let out a little whimper. Luciano pulled away for a moment and broke out in a huge grin, looking extremely pleased with himself. I reached around and grabbed the back of his head, pulling him back towards me.

He kissed me with the deep, intense longing of a hungry man. The idea of him being gay and us being friends was completely obliterated in the space of about two minutes. I kissed him back with an almost indecent amount of wild abandon. Italians were full of life and gusto, and I felt quite safe my enthusiasm would be well received.

In response, Luciano leant over and whispered into my hair, which made his words muffled and hard to hear. It almost sounded like he said he wanted to eat me, which I was sure I misheard...and then he shuffled down until he was kneeling on the floor with his head in my lap. It seemed I had heard him correctly.

After a few minutes of gripping the edge of the chair so hard I had cramps in my hands, Luciano popped his head up, patted the bed, and whispered hoarsely "Come here. I need you now." I just nodded. Right then I'd do anything he said. Men who were talented and willing in that department were worth their weight in chocolate chip cookies.

Apparently a cunning undresser, Luciano was naked by the time we hit the bed. Now, this was the kind of cruise ship adventure I'd been after. We already had a friendship, and I trusted him, so I wasn't even afraid what he'd think when he saw my naked body.

"Oh, Ellie... We must be a bit careful," Luciano whispered. "The captain and chief engineer are near to my cabin, and they would be very unhappy with me for being here with you. I am really on duty again tonight, to supervise some maintenance in the engine room..." He chuckled, looking a bit guilty. "But the guys down there know what they are doing. They really do not need me... But you... You need me...down here."

I hesitated for a moment at the familiar phrase. Seth had warned me that Justin didn't want his team sleeping together. I thought everyone was lackadaisical on ships, and yet these guys were apparently quite worried about being seen with me...

My thoughts were interrupted by Luciano tugging more urgently on my skirt. I heard an unmistakable ripping sound in the zipper region. Shit, my theory of going with a slightly-too tight skirt because I'd lose weight had backfired. Still, I had done a fair bit of sewing back in senior school, so I'd be able to fix it with a few carefully placed stitches... I caught myself mid-thought; was I seriously thinking about Home Economics at a time like this?

My top came off next and joined my skirt in a heap on the floor. Then Luciano flicked off the cabin light from a switch near the bed, turned on the lamp, and pulled a condom out of the bedside table all in one, fluid movement. He was an impressive man.

"Ellie, I have been waiting for this," he said, already breathless. "It's so wonderful we found each other."

The cynic in me knew it was just his pillow talk, but the romantic in me sighed in happiness, unable to get the grin off my face.

Without warning, he caught up both of my wrists in one hand and pinned them to the pillows over my head. His unexpected aggression sent a bolt of heat through my body, heat that only intensified as I realised that with my arms caught and my legs pinned beneath his weight, I could barely move. It should have frightened me, but instead I felt more turned on than ever before. Was this what I'd been missing?

Luciano breathed heavily into my ear as he concentrated on drawing little circles around my neck with his tongue. He traced a line up to my mouth and sucked on my bottom lip. With my head thrown back, I could feel my pulse pounding through my neck, down into my chest, where my heart was beating furiously. I squirmed as he kissed down my neck again, and arched beneath him as his free hand trailed along my neck and down to my breasts. He caught one of my nipples between his fingers and twisted, and I writhed in pleasure, wrapping my legs around him to feel closer. I could feel him, hard against my stomach, and pressed up against him, trying to convey the urgency I felt.

"Not like this, Ellie," he said, his voice hoarse. He released my wrists and slid to the side. "Turn over."

His words momentarily broke the spell. I silently hoped he wasn't going to try and go up my arse; I might be keen on sexual exploration, but I was definitely drawing the line there. Dan and I had only ever tried that once, plied with alcohol, and it had ended in embarrassing disaster. "It's like trying to shove a marshmallow into a letterbox," he'd moaned, destroying any shred of fun or romance there may have been left in the moment. No, it was definitely not something I wanted to try again.

"Ummmmm… I'm not really sure I want to do that," I said, snapping back into the present. I tried to sound casual and light, rather than boring or frightened; the last thing I wanted was for him to decide I wasn't exciting enough!

"No problem, *bella*," he said, clearly unperturbed. "There are many things I can do back here."

Somewhat reassured, I rolled over onto my stomach. Luciano caught my hips and drew them upwards, until I was kneeling, and then captured my wrists again, pressing them against the bed. In this position, I was completely vulnerable, and yet I still felt safe. I also felt like I was doing some sort of weird yoga pose, albeit an R-rated, nude yoga.

Gone was the sensitive soul I'd written off as preferring men. Confident, masculine, rough, shooting more than once glance at himself in the narrow mirror beside the bathroom. He held me still beneath him, his free hand busy at my breasts. I buried my face in his bed, trying not to make any noise; I was mostly successful, though a few stray moans slipped out.

The experience was easily the best sex I'd ever had. By comparison, Dan had been totally vanilla; I'd no idea what I'd been thinking all those years. And while Seth was skilled, I realised, as Luciano was making me squirm, he'd been much more interested in himself than in me. No one had ever brought me anywhere close to the heaven Luciano did.

I finally collapsed, Luciano just a moment behind me. I was just cosying up for a snuggle, looking forward to relaxing, when Luciano's beeper started buzzing and vibrating on the bedside table. He grabbed it and we could both see the message, which said *#911*. He punched the air and cursed loudly. "*Vaffanculo!*"

This was clearly my cue to exit. From what he'd said, I knew we'd have many more nights on this contract. I grabbed my uniform off the floor and tried to step into it as I stumbled towards the door.

Luciano was rifling through his wardrobe. He looked up and said, "Ellie, I'm sorry. Please let me find a way to make you happy later."

Even happier than he'd already made me? Sold. I raced over and kissed his cheek. He grabbed my face between his hands and snogged me passionately. Despite the fact that my skirt wouldn't stay up and my unbuttoned polo was exposing my matronly comfort-bra, I felt sexy and desirable. Hooray! I returned his kiss with enthusiasm, and reached around to squeeze his very tight arse. Then I pulled away and kissed his nose quickly, hoping for a light, sexy exit. I could sort myself out back at my cabin.

I gently closed his door behind me and took a couple of steps down the hall, clutching at my skirt to keep it from hitting the floor. I heard male voices, and as I turned the corner, I smacked straight into someone coming in the other direction. I was looking down and saw two pairs of shiny black shoes and trousers. I looked up just in time to see two older men in white shirts staring at me, and I noticed their four stripes on either shoulder. Shit.

"Good evening, Captain. Good evening, Chief," I said, bobbing my head in respect and flashing them a brilliant smile. I wondered what the odds were they wouldn't notice I wasn't exactly perfectly put together, or if they did, what the odds were that they wouldn't connect me to the Senior Engineer's cabin.

"It would seem Luciano is in his quarters," the Captain said, curling his lip in disapproval.

Bollocks. So much for no one noticing. I really hoped Luciano wouldn't be in trouble. Trust me to go running half naked into the hall at the wrong time and bump into exactly the people I needed to avoid. I'd give him a call in the morning and see if everything was okay.

Back in the cabin, Caitlin was already asleep, which was highly unusual, but possibly a good thing. I wasn't sure if I should tell anyone about Luciano yet.

I knew that she and Nick wouldn't judge...well, I was confident Caitlin wouldn't judge, but it did feel a bit weird to have slept with two guys in one week, especially two that also happened to be friends, so there was a small chance that Nick would have a field day with any potential future fallout. It was just that Luciano had been so lovely. He knew I'd been with

Seth, and had been upset that Seth had got to me first, knowing that Seth wasn't good for me. He hadn't pushed me; the things he'd said had felt really good and really natural, and I was suddenly looking forward to the rest of the contract again. With Luciano to play around with, I was sure to have a fabulous time…and even get a chance to explore the more exciting side of sex. I'd known coming aboard that I wasn't likely to find my soulmate. Didn't mean I couldn't dream, but I knew it would happen when it was the right time—no doubt far in the future. At the moment, having a good time was more important. I deserved it after so many years of boredom with Dan.

Although Luciano had been extravagant with his compliments, there was no pretence about a future relationship. I knew this was going to be a contract-length romance, pure and simple. When our vacations came, we'd smile and go our separate ways. No misunderstandings, no hard feelings. I wasn't going to make another mistake like Seth.

Chapter Seven

I smiled as soon as my eyes opened the next morning. After a shaky start, things had finally fallen into place for me on board 'The Lust Boat'. It might not develop into anything truly meaningful, but I was okay with things being short-term and drama-free.

I needed someone to share the sordid details with. And really, for me they were sordid…though I expected that Caitlin, at least, would still think the experience was pretty tame. From the darkness of my bunk I whispered, "Roomie…" No response. "Roomie… Roomie?" I flicked on my reading light and poked my head up to the top bunk. It was empty.

I jumped up to check the roster on the desk and saw that Caitlin was shooting gangway that morning. Damn, just when I had some fresh gory details—her favourite part!

A jiggling of the door handle interrupted the vivid images flooding my mind. She was back already? I'd thought she'd be gone at least another hour. A timid knock followed.

"Lost your key, roomie?!" I called out, laughing.

"No, *bella*, I do not have your key card…yet."

Shit, Luciano. I looked down at the comfy old lady pyjamas I was wearing; Mum had stealthily hidden them in my suitcase, and while they were my favourite go-to bedwear, I wasn't sure I really wanted Luciano to see me wearing them. I grabbed Caitlin's robe off the back of the door and slipped it on as I opened the door.

A moment of confusion washed over me when the

doorway was empty…until a beautiful red rose was thrust under my nose. Luciano stepped in and gave me a long, gentle, probing kiss that made my toes curl under in excitement and anticipation. I hoped he didn't mind morning breath.

"Ellie, I couldn't stop thinking about you all night," he murmured. "I had to come and see you straight away." He threw the rose aside and grasped my hands, pulling me closer. The moment I got close enough, I could feel exactly why he was in such a desperate hurry. I resisted the urge to start singing Oasis's 'What's the Story, Morning Glory?' and focussed on the serious business of surreptitiously trying to slip out of my unflattering pjs without attracting any attention to them.

Turned out I needn't have bothered. Luciano wouldn't have noticed if I was wearing a Halloween costume—he was a man on a mission. It was unlike the marathon session of the previous night—about five minutes of sweaty, grunting shagging on the edge of the rather flimsy desk easily resulted in a mutual, shuddering climax.

"Give me a minute and I want to give you more," he said, breathless. We clung onto each other for a moment before Luciano practically collapsed on the floor. I tried to pick him up, laughing; the laughter died abruptly as the doorknob rattled.

"Roomie!" yelled Caitlin as she opened the door.

I jumped over Luciano's languishing body and dashed to the door.

"Noooooo!" I screamed, pushing the door closed and basically slamming it in her face. "Just give me a minute… I'm just…cleaning up." I flicked the lock, preventing her from opening it with her key card.

"Ellie, what the fuck is going on?" Caitlin asked through the door. "Let me in. I've seen the cabin, dude—it's fine."

Luciano was already on his feet, pulling on his clothes; I struggled back into my pjs and robe, mortified, my heart pounding uncontrollably.

His clothes more or less back where they had been,

Luciano casually flicked open the door, announcing, "Caitlin, how are you?" He leaned over to kiss her on both cheeks. Cool as a cucumber.

A huge smile spread across Caitlin's face. "Well, hello, you two lovers." She nudged Luciano in the ribs. "I heard whispers about a beautiful woman leaving your cabin last night, you sly dog." Smiling, she pushed past him and walked into the cabin. My cheeks were still burning with embarrassment. I'd forgotten how fast word travelled on a ship.

Without acknowledging Caitlin's jibe, Luciano brushed a kiss against my cheek and headed out the door. "*Bella*, I'll see you later, my darling," he called over his shoulder.

Luciano was barely gone before Caitlin was on the phone to Nick. "Get over here," she said excitedly. "Ellie slept with Luciano and we need details!" I could hear Nick's squeal from two yards away. I rolled my eyes in mock disgust and headed for the shower.

By the time I got out, Caitlin and Nick were sitting on my bed, eager-eyed, cups of tea in hand. When I got to the part about Luciano turning me around and bending me over, Nick squealed again, "Oh, I love straight men. They're so dirty!"

Caitlin giggled, and then looked at me seriously. "I don't want to be a buzz-kill, dude, I totally don't...but just remember to be careful. Luciano is just like all other men on this ship. Don't have any expectations, and you won't get hurt." I knew she wasn't being a pessimist, she was just being kind.

"I know," I said, picking up the steaming cup of tea they'd made for me. "He's just the fun I need right now. Nothing serious." They both appeared relieved.

"Well, I for one am so sick of cruise ship boys," Nick said, fluttering his eyelashes. "I can't wait to get to New York. There's *so* many more beautiful men to choose from in the Big Apple."

Caitlin reached over and poked Nick in the arm playfully. "You better not bring a whole bunch of hot men back to our apartment every week. I'll be way too jealous!"

I looked at them both, momentarily lost. Then I remembered they both had Big Apple ambitions. "Are you two going to live together in New York?" I asked.

"Of course, lovey," Nick said, smiling and flicking his feather boa. "And I can't wait to get there and leave all this shit behind." Caitlin nodded in agreement.

From there, the conversation quickly steered off to men with questionable sexuality thanks to Caitlin teasing me for thinking Luciano was gay, and from there to the kinds of men Caitlin and Nick were likely to meet in the Big Apple. They were both so excited about living together and following their dreams that I felt a bit wistful, wondering if maybe I should rethink my dreams and go to New York, too.

At work that night, I felt myself falling asleep on multiple occasions, but a quick visit to Luciano's cabin that night definitely woke me up. His schedule that week sometimes made it tricky to hook up, but when I was willing and able for a passionate rendezvous, I paged him. We met up in his cabin, storage rooms, my cabin when Caitlin was working... Luciano was very energetic and liked to talk dirty. Sex with Luciano was fun and freeing, and as he introduced me to new ways of enjoying myself, I began to realise what I'd been missing. When we had more than a few minutes, he'd play with me, blindfolding me so that every sensation was heightened; his fingers would dance along my body, his breath sweeping across my skin. The first time he tied my wrists together—gently, with a silk scarf I could get out of at any time—and went down on me, it felt like my world exploded into millions of fireworks. And it only got better from there.

I developed a newfound respect for the Italian way— boundless passion, enviable energy, and a fascination with the female form. Luciano constantly praised and admired every inch of my feminine and fabulous body. I was still wary after Seth, but I certainly enjoyed Luciano trying to convince me.

After a particularly exhausting session, I rolled over to grab a tissue. In the soft glow of the bedside lamp, I spied a photo of a woman and two children conspicuously in the place he normally kept his pager and badges. My heart skipped a beat as I picked it up, hoping it was his sister and nephews.

"Who's this?" I was proud that my voice didn't betray how hard my heart was pounding.

"Oh, that's my wife and children," he answered, tucking his hands behind his head. "They're coming on board next week."

"Are you serious?" I spluttered. He had to be kidding. This was ridiculous. Confusion and anger and shock and betrayal crowded into my mind, each clamouring for my attention. "You gave me that big speech about how Seth didn't appreciate me and I deserved better!" This seriously couldn't be happening. Was anybody on board this ship capable of telling the truth? Of being genuine? Furious, I started gathering my clothes, desperate to get out of the cabin and away from Luciano as fast as possible.

"Ellie, *bambina*," he said, completely unmoved, "surely you know how it works on the ships… Everybody has fun, nobody talks about real life, everybody is happy."

Again he sounded like a Seth-clone. Did they practice this shit? Worse than that, it was possibly the most horrible description of life I'd ever heard. Life on board was happy because everyone lied. Truth was a rare and apparently not very valuable commodity.

"I do like you," he added. "Very much. But we're not married, and we're both here to have fun. The other girls don't have a problem with this."

This brought me up short, and I paused with one shoe in hand. "The *other* girls? Are you fucking kidding me?" Just when I thought it couldn't get any worse. At least Seth had apparently only been sleeping with me. I clutched my shoe to my chest in a protective stance and said, "You're sleeping with other girls? For fuck's sake, how many others?"

"Five," he said with a little shrug, "or maybe six. You never asked me, so I thought you didn't mind what I did when we're not together." He sat up and rolled off the bed, grabbing his top from where it had been draped over his chair.

I was fuming, but Luciano seemed completely unflustered by my anger. *How* could I have been so stupid? Again? Luciano hadn't thought I deserved a better man—he'd just wanted to shag me! It was a desperately humiliating realisation, especially coming on the heels of the Seth debacle.

"Ellie," he said calmly, "I am happy to have fun whenever you want. I'll be here for you, we'll have sex; we'll have good times, hey?" He actually had the nerve to smile suggestively, and I considered clobbering him to death with my shoe. "If you're not okay with that, it's okay, I understand. You just leave now and we'll just be friends, okay?" He smiled, obviously pleased with ending things so calmly. "But please follow the rules, Ellie, and don't say anything to my wife next week. She doesn't need to know all this information. It's much better for her to not know how the ships work. I send her money. Everybody's happy."

Erm, no. I wasn't happy. I was so far from being happy that I couldn't even begin to express how very, very unhappy I was. How could I follow rules I didn't know or understand? Every step I made seemed to be wrong; I didn't understand the rules of the game on this ship, but everyone expected me to pick it up instantly. And I couldn't.

I felt like bursting into tears, but instead jammed my foot into my shoe, tugged my top straight, and walked out of the cabin. I was proud of myself; I wanted to slam the door, but managed not to. I wanted desperately to throw a tantrum, but I managed to hold myself together until I got back to my cabin.

Caitlin was out, so for the time being I was spared the need to explain. I plonked myself down on the bottom bunk. The urge to cry had vanished; I was just floored, really. I couldn't understand how my life had changed so much in a matter of months. I had spent years living with Dan in London, creating our happy future together and completely missing the fact that the relationship was withering into a very dead mess following Dan's complete lack of respect for me, not to mention his lack of interest.

I had moved on, picked myself up, and run away to sea to fulfil my photography dreams. At least, that had been the plan. But now I was on this bloody crazy cruise ship and I was starting to wonder if maybe Dan had just been the symptom of a bigger problem. Or maybe the problem was me; maybe I was just somehow a magnet for men who were unequivocally prone to deception. I wasn't sure what was worse, indifference or infidelity...not that it really mattered, since I managed to find men who were both. Was I completely incapable of recognising a useless, lying bastard?

The real problem, I knew, was that I was struggling with the fact that, seemingly overnight, I'd become a girl who jumped into bed with a guy as soon as he showed the slightest hint of wooing me. As much as I'd tried not to judge Caitlin's actions, I'd felt somehow slightly morally superior—at least I didn't sleep with anything that moved. And yet I'd just done it twice in a row.

Pot, meet kettle.

Over the years, I'd comforted many single friends over a broken heart. I had smiled at them sympathetically, glad I was in a committed relationship and not making the same silly mistakes.

I suddenly found myself on the other end, making mistakes of my own.

I was shaking my head at my own stupidity when Caitlin burst into the room. "Roomie!" she said. "I just saw Luciano up at the officers' bar. He told me you would be here. What did that motherfucker do?"

"There are several other women... Oh, and a wife." I was guessing she already knew.

Caitlin nodded knowingly. "Dude, I think we need to talk about how relationships work on board ships," she said, sitting down. She reached out and put a gentle hand on my arm. "We're not in the real world. People come and go all the time. Everybody has lives at home, and they treat their time on board like it's a completely different life altogether."

She sighed and continued, her voice soft and kind.

"Luciano, Seth, and all the other guys probably have women at home who they say they love—and maybe they even do love them—and someone on board who they just have fun with." Her mouth twisted as she added, "Nobody wants to be alone, and ships can be lonely places." She looked down, wistful and sad at the same time, and I wondered how much of her confident persona was just a facade.

"Luciano must find it especially lonely," I said, "given how many women he's got on the go."

"Hah," she said. "Unfortunately, dude, he's an officer *and* an Italian—baaaad combination."

"I know, right?" I said. "I wonder when he had time for all these babes? Did he run a schedule, and keep it next to his work roster? Go door-to-door throughout the night? Sleep with two girls in one cabin to save time?"

I suspected that at least one of those was true. It was all so absurd that we couldn't help but laugh. It was either laugh or cry, so on balance I rather thought I preferred to laugh.

"Come on, don't let the bastards bring you down," Caitlin said, pulling me to my feet. "Let's go dance!"

I allowed her to drag me up to the crew bar. Loud music was pumping and ship life was going on as normal. People were drinking, dancing, kissing. Caitlin was right; I needed to grow up and move on. It was time for me to have fun—no more men, no more sad stories. I was going to drink, dance, and enjoy the Caribbean sun.

Starting with a drink.

I rocked up to the bar. "Jock, give me a Cuba Libre, please."

Jock smiled warmly. The light caught his eyes, and I wondered how I'd never noticed how dark his eyebrows were.

"How's my favourite photog?" he asked, pulling out a glass.

"Couldn't be better," I said, smiling. I didn't want to bother Jock with my tales of woe, not again. He'd been supportive about the Maria thing, but this was just downright embarrassing. I knew I'd look like a right fool. Instead, I said, "You never did answer that question."

"You're right," he said. "You really want to know?"

"Of course," I said, leaning on the bar and batting my eyelashes. "You're fascinating. I want to know everything about you."

A funny expression flitted across his face, so fleeting that I thought maybe I'd imagined it, and then he rolled his eyes. "Yes, I'm sure. Tell you what, I've been thinking about getting a group together to go ashore one of these days. Why don't you come along?" He grinned. "It'll give you the opportunity to learn more about me than you ever wanted to know."

Jock was lovely. Kind and not sleazy—I'd never heard about Jock sleeping around or breaking any hearts. I studied him as he reached up and pulled down a bottle of booze, watched the muscles move beneath his top, and wondered why I couldn't fall for someone as nice as Jock. And then his words rang in my ears again, and I sighed inwardly. He wanted me to join a group. The tried and tested statement of someone who wants to keep things on a strictly friends basis. This was why I never fell for blokes like Jock; they were never interested in me.

Oh, well. That was fine with me. I certainly wasn't going to ruin the friendship we'd been building.

That settled, my mind returned to the present, and my eyes fell on a girl a couple of feet away, standing with her back to me. She turned around, and I flinched. Maria.

Her eyes met mine, and that insincere sympathetic smile appeared on her face as she moved nearer. "Oh, Ellie, I heard that you and Luciano have finished your little fun already," she said, somehow managing to look both sad and smug. "What a shame you did not ask me about him. Did you not think there would be a reason he was with you, and not me? We were together for a while, but I did not want to deal with his wife. He begged me to come back, because I was the best lover he ever had, but he eventually gave up when he saw I was serious. I see he did not need to pursue you too much." Still smiling, she picked up my drink off the bar and turned to go, adding, "But I am so glad you can have fun with my cast-offs."

The Brazilian Bitch had struck again. And she'd stolen my drink.

Jock frowned after Maria and then made me up another drink before I had a chance to ask. "I see things are going well in that area," he said dryly, sliding the glass across to me.

I downed half the glass in one gulp. "Oh, quite," I said. "We tell each other all our secrets." I sighed and looked around the room for Caitlin. I finally found her pinning a guy I didn't recognise against the wall, her tongue down his throat. I didn't particularly want to interrupt—and realised, as she grabbed him by the hand and pulled him towards the door, that I was stuck here for probably at least an hour.

With my room about to be occupied and nowhere else to go, I settled in at the bar for the long haul. Jock gave me a sad smile and made me another drink.

"Cheers," I said. I thought about introducing myself around and meeting some new people, to open my social horizons, but I was tired, and quite frankly, I knew that Jock at least wouldn't let me down.

I looked out over the room. Socialising, schmocialising.

I'll start tomorrow.

Chapter Eight

It's funny how quickly life moves on when you're working and living on a ship. It had been weeks since I'd ended things with Luciano, and I'd had time to settle in and observe things a bit more. Nobody really tolerated you being sad and miserable, and they certainly didn't expect you to mope about a lost fuck-buddy. I soon learned one of the most widely used expressions on ships: 'It sucks to be you.' It was useful in all kinds of situations.

If you were extremely tired, and your boss asked you to work extra hours, and you actually complained to someone, expecting sympathy, they'd generally respond with 'It sucks to be you.' Same went for pretty much any problem, sickness, or minor catastrophe. In short, I soon worked out that people on ships were, well, kind of heartless. I think it's the nature of cruise contracts, especially on the big cruise lines with a fleet of vessels. You might never see your colleagues again, as they move from ship to ship, so why get too close, too involved? It just made it harder when it was time to say goodbye. It was harsh, but it was worth keeping in mind, lest you ever take anything too personally.

In taking no notice of any men for a couple of weeks (again), I finally had time to focus on myself. As the weeks went by, I managed to get ashore in every port, lugging along the fantastic camera I'd brought aboard and then forgotten about because of all of my romantic entanglements. It was lovely, really; I'd been able to explore to my heart's content, and was rapidly amassing a portfolio that I hoped I'd be able to use to further my photography career when I finally left the cruise ships.

I was sitting in the cabin, scanning through a series of photos of doors, when Caitlin appeared carrying beer, Nick in tow. I set my camera aside and took the beer Caitlin offered me as Nick launched into a bit of a rant about his roommate, Tyrone.

Caitlin nodded in agreement as Nick talked, but she'd rested her chin on her hand and was staring off into the distance, her eyes soft and dreamy. She was clearly miles away.

"What's his name?" I joked.

"Gabriel," she said, breathing his name out slowly. "He's the new…"

"Singer in our show," Nick blurted out, cutting her off. "Seriously, Caity? That guy is such a jerk."

Caitlin wasn't in the least perturbed; not that I expected she would be. She took a big swig of her beer and said, "He is super sexy and funny, actually." Laughing, she added, "You just don't like him because he doesn't play on your team, and you're jell-y."

Nick spoke seriously. "Caitlin, he's not a good guy… And I'm not saying that just to be a bitch."

"Oh come on, Nick, you know I can handle him," Caitlin said, nudging him playfully. "I want him immediately, and I'm going to put my naughty plan into action tonight."

Nick shrugged. "Don't say I didn't warn you."

After work that night, Caitlin was putting her man-scoring skills to work on Gabriel. I didn't expect to see her anytime soon, and was pleased for the opportunity to have time alone in my room. If Caitlin came back with Gabriel, I would leave, but until then, I needed a night in. I was tired of socialising; watching a DVD in my granny pyjamas and going through my photos again was a sure-fire way to avoid all men and stick to my revised plan of spending time on my own to focus on my goals. I picked out *The Hunger Games* to watch; tension and death was rather more appealing than something romantic and fluffy. I had good intentions of having a movie marathon, but fell asleep before the end of the movie. I woke up several hours later, the pattern of the camera strap imprinted on my cheek, and properly crawled into bed.

In the morning, Caitlin's bed was still untouched, although her early morning alarm woke me up rather earlier than I'd have liked. I assumed she was in Gabriel's room, and was grateful I hadn't got kicked out the night before. When she still hadn't returned by the time I was out of the shower, I started to wonder if she was okay; she was meant to be shooting gangway.

It wasn't long before Justin was banging on our door. "Where is she?" he spat. "I haven't got time for this shite."

Caitlin and I hadn't discussed what should happen in this situation, but I wasn't about to rat out my roomie. "She was here earlier," I said, shrugging, "but she wasn't feeling well, so maybe she's gone down to the medical centre or something?" I was actually rather pleased I'd thought of a good excuse for her if she happened to have a raging hangover.

"Really?" he said disbelievingly, raising his eyebrows at Caitlin's perfectly made bed. "She was just here?" I managed to keep a pleasant smile on my face and shrugged again. "I have a photo department to run, I can't deal with this bollocks. Just tell her to hurry the fuck up." He walked out and slammed the door.

Shit. Despite the early hour, I called Nick's room in desperation, hoping he'd be able to nip down the hall and get Caitlin up and out of Gabriel's cabin.

Ten minutes later, my bleary-eyed cabin-mate fell in the door, mumbling, "Fuck, roomie, I haven't had any sleep. I've been up fucking Gabriel all night. Fuck." I snorted, amused by her directness. "He's so not like the other guys, you know. Much more serious… He's just awesome." She smiled dreamily.

I was sorry to break her mood. "Justin was in here looking for you," I said, watching her carefully. "I told him you weren't feeling well and might have been at the doctor." I hadn't totally lied to Justin—she clearly wasn't feeling well.

"Thanks, roomie," she said. "I appreciate you not telling him." Caitlin brewed up a quick coffee in our little kettle and raced around the cabin like a hurricane for the next few minutes.

Once she was safely at work, I packed my little daypack and set out on an Antiguan photo shoot adventure.

Antigua's main township, St John's, was a bustling little trade centre full of shouting Americans in Bermuda shorts. The main street was lined with cute multi-coloured shops, many with white glossy trims on their doors and windows; judging from the foot traffic, most appeared to do an impressive trade.

Local women carrying armfuls of brightly coloured threads offered me braids, while T-shirt sellers came out of nowhere to show me shirts with slogans like 'I did it 365 ways in Antigua'. "One for every day of the year," I was told more than once—for the alleged 365 beaches on Antigua.

The enthusiastic traders of Antigua made me feel a bit ill at ease in a way that the business of London never had. Somewhere deep down, I was a little worried that if I didn't buy anything, they might drag me into a dark alley and rough me up. There were always stories about those kinds of things happening, and even though I'd been going out on my own with my camera for weeks now, I was still always acutely conscious of the fact that I was a woman alone.

Getting great photos of the little town wasn't difficult. There was an abundance of colour, texture, and life on display as I wandered around the local streets and Heritage Quay. I discovered an array of little huts like a jumble of candy coloured gems—mint green, aqua blue, and lots of sunny yellow, burnt orange, and dusky pink. Along with a plethora of dust-collecting souvenirs at every turn, Antigua made a quirky photo essay, and I took hundreds of photos in a matter of hours.

Taking a swig of my water, I flagged down a taxi to take me to Fort James Bay. I'd heard a few crew talking about the beauty of that particular beach, and was looking forward to getting the postcard shots I'd come all the way to the Caribbean for.

Pale, creamy sand hugged the coastline in both directions. Palm trees, fat, leafy bushes, and spidery bunches of long, spiky grass lined its edges, covering sand dunes and boulders, creating countless nooks and hidey holes. Without going more than twenty yards, I was overwhelmed with *National Geographic*-worthy photo opportunities.

The clear aqua blue beauty of the water was ridiculous. I mean, who lived in grey, cold, damp places like London by choice? Surely it was only the millions of people who didn't think places like this even existed outside of postcards and travel shows on the BBC.

It wasn't totally idyllic, of course. Capitalism ensured that windsurfing operators, souvenir huts, and horse riding tours were dotted right along the beach. Loud, Hawaiian-shirted Americans and sunburnt Swedes were laughing, drinking beers, and yelling into their video cameras, while dreadlocked locals said, "Ya, ya, okay, no problem," and pocketed fistfuls of cash.

Approaching some of the vendors for some 'real Antigua' shots, I was surprised how many of them were perfectly amenable to being snapped from every angle, enabling me to expand my portrait series. They smiled, nodded, and looked wistful while staring at the sea, all without prompting.

Later, in my cabin, I flicked through the few hundred shots I'd taken, marvelling at the beauty, colour, and rich flavours of Antigua. I couldn't believe I'd be lucky enough to visit once a week. I was so glad I'd decided to abandon men and lust and pursue photographic fulfilment instead.

I spent that evening's shift on a natural high, chatting with customers and brimming with confidence. I'd obviously caught a bit of sun, because people kept commenting on how 'healthy' and 'glowing' I looked.

When I arrived for my dinner break, I spotted Maria and Jacoline huddled at the end of the table, deep in conversation. Subtly eavesdropping, I was fascinated to hear about Maria's latest drama. It seemed a handsome, eligible bachelor had come aboard and Maria was eagerly employing her plethora of feminine wiles to get his attention.

"I even did a very sexy dance up in the disco," she whined to Jacoline, "but he did not take any notice of me."

I muttered "hmmph" under my breath, and realised almost immediately that Maria had heard; her head came up and her eyes narrowed as she saw me.

"Why are you listening to us, *gringa*?" spat Maria. "You do not have any friends to have dinner with?"

I kept looking at my plate, feeling my eyes welling up with tears. I hated confrontation; I didn't have the nasty streak necessary to fight back.

"She's got me, biatch," said Caitlin, slamming her plate down on the table. "Stop being a bully."

I smiled at her gratefully, but still felt a little on edge. Jacoline, looking decidedly uncomfortable, got up to get something else to eat.

"So, I hear you've been chasing after some guy," said Caitlin, pointing her fork at Maria. "Are you still on your quest to find a rich passenger?"

Maria glared at her with venom in her eyes but didn't say anything.

"Good luck with that," Caitlin said, laughing. Shaking her head, she changed the subject, effectively turning her back on Maria.

"So, roomie, you wanna come to the officers' bar later? Gabriel and I are meeting for drinks after we both finish work."

Glad of the diversion, I happily agreed, and it was hours and several rounds of drinks later that I finally stumbled back to the cabin. Caitlin had buggered off with Gabriel, leaving me with an empty cabin yet again.

I'd barely made it through my bedtime routine when the unlocked door banged open and Nick stormed into the room.

"Princess, you are not fucking going to believe what I just found out," he said, a furious expression on his face. He sank down onto my bed and patted the mattress beside him. "Sit."

No good sentence ever started with somebody telling you to sit down...so I sat down and took a deep breath.

Chapter Nine

"My asshole friend in New York decided to give the room to his brother at the end of the semester. I have nowhere to live and can't afford anything else." Nick banged his fist against the wall, which took me by surprise; I'd been on board for over a month and never seen him angry.

"Oh, shit, Nick, that's total bollocks," I said. Nick pretty much defined himself by his Broadway ambitions and this was a huge blow to his plans.

"Now my parents will want me to come home," Nick wailed, "and I'll be stuck packing clothes and bags into shipping cartons every day for the rest of eternity." He dragged me into a desperate bear hug. "I'll kill myself before I let that happen."

I knew what it felt like to have awful news, but I also tried to be pragmatic in a hopeless situation, or at least I was quite good at doing that when it was somebody else's problem rather than my own. "Shall I help you look online for another flat to share? Surely there's cheap rooms all over the place, or at least if you're willing to live in the Bronx or Queens..."

Nick pulled away from me and punched me playfully in the arm. "Now, I'm not that desperate, Princess," he said. I saw the beginning of a smile twitch at the corner of Nick's mouth. Perhaps there was light at the end of the tunnel.

"Come on, sweetie, we'll work something out," I said. "Don't whip out the sleeping pills just yet. We'll get you to New York."

"Okay," he said, steeling himself with a deep breath and a

117

flick of his hair. "I guess I'm off to search Craigslist, then. Maybe I can find something else. Nothing quite as fabulous, I'm sure...but I'll see what's out there." Nick excused himself as quickly as he had arrived.

I crawled into bed and fell asleep almost immediately. It seemed like moments later I woke up to Caitlin tickling my foot, looking extremely cheeky and very pleased with herself.

"Geez, Caitlin, I've only been asleep five minutes," I groaned, turning over and burying my face in the pillow.

"It's morning, woman!" she said.

It was so hard to tell in these windowless cabins. I was still foggy from being woken up, but Caitlin was too impatient to wait for me to wake up properly and ploughed on with her story. "I've just had another all-night bonk fest with Gabriel," she said happily. "Well, nearly all night. We decided to fit in some sleep this time...we spooned." A blissful look spread across her face. "It was so awesome."

As she explained the finer details of their escapades, I rapidly woke up. Complex descriptions of positions I didn't think anybody actually tried, kinky role play, bondage, and the sticking of things in places that should never be entered... just Caitlin's way of warming up. If there was anything she hadn't tried, I'd have been shocked. She made my experimentation and exploration seem tame.

"Oh, and dude," Caitlin said, prodding me to get my attention, "Borys is finishing up this San Juan, and the new guy's name is Cooper. Ruby did a contract with him before and said he's awesome... Really helpful, lovely, and hard-working, apparently. Most senior photogs are drunks, sleazes, or money-hungry bastards, so it'll be nice to have a good guy for a change!"

I nodded in agreement as she started undressing for the shower, though I wasn't sure I really wanted to take Ruby's recommendation of anyone. It would be nice to have a nice new team member on board. A new photog, especially a nice one, might be able to help me with my photography portfolio—maybe I could ask him to look over my photos, give his professional opinion. I thought I'd ask him once he'd settled in.

I didn't have too long to wait. The new senior photographer waltzed onto the ship next San Juan. Most of the team were busy on a Sunday, shooting embarkations, so I was sent to meet him. I was reminded of my own first day, except this time I was the all-knowing veteran.

"How you doin'?" he said, shaking my hand gently. "I'm Cooper."

Average height, thick glasses, and a mop of unruly sandy hair: he certainly looked harmless. Almost boring, really. Certainly not lady-killer material, which was a relief, and despite my distrust of Ruby, Cooper made a good first impression. I gave him the same tour Caitlin had given me; as Cooper wasn't interested in spending time in his cabin yet, I took him on a tour of the upper levels. Conversation flowed easily. He introduced himself to nearly every member of staff and crew we passed. He was friendly to everybody and had equal time and enthusiasm for both men and women. He didn't seem remotely sleazy, and, despite his friendliness, he was never inappropriate or flirtatious.

Cooper told me his main interest on this cruise was seeing the Caribbean islands. "It's one of the few places I haven't been yet. My life is all about travel and photography," he said. "I love cruise ship work, because it pays me to do both. Very different from my previous job," he added.

Before I could ask him about it, we encountered an elderly group of passengers, and Cooper stopped to chat.

One of the men took Cooper's hand and shook it vigorously. "And where are you from, young man?"

"I'm from Vancouver, Canada, sir," Cooper said respectfully.

I watched as Cooper transformed from friendly to truly charismatic, answering questions, making witty comments, and allowing the old men to slap him on the back and the women to cling to his arm. A smile remained on his face throughout, and whenever someone spoke, he'd lean in to hear better, for all intents and purposes appearing entirely engrossed in what they were saying.

I stood off to the side, feeling like a bit of a gooseberry. I knew I should have made an effort and joined in, but apart from being suddenly worried they wouldn't notice me, I was also in awe of the effect Cooper was having on the group, and wanted to watch. It was really interesting how such an ordinary-looking young guy could be equally popular with men and women, young and old. It was a rare skill. He reminded me of a politician: smooth, savvy, always coming out with the right thing at the right moment, and gently deflecting when he'd prefer not to answer a question.

Cooper caught my eye and winked, and then made his goodbyes to the group, carefully extracting himself from the grip of a particularly wizened woman.

"Nice people," he commented as we headed off again.

"You were impressive with them," I said, nudging him with my elbow.

"Aw, thanks," he said, looking embarrassed. "I think it's ingrained from my days in the military."

The mysterious former occupation, no doubt. He really was full of surprises. I tilted my head, encouraging him to elaborate.

"Well actually, it wasn't exactly the military," he said. "It was the Protective Policing Service. It's part of the Canadian Mounted Police. We provided security details for the Canadian Royal Family, the Governor General, the Prime Minister, and a bunch of other Canadian and visiting politicians." He casually looked out to sea, as though protecting the heads of country was really nothing special.

"Wow, really?" I was impressed. I had never even heard of such a job and I never would have pegged him as part of a security force. His build didn't exactly scream 'ex-police'. Perhaps that was why he'd left.

Cooper explained further. "I mostly looked after the Governor General," he said, "but sometimes we also had to take care of the Prime Minister. I had to travel with them overseas all the time, always on government aircraft."

No wonder he'd reminded me of a politician; he must have got particularly skilled at schmoozing with all of those years of close contact with people like that.

We had reached the buffet, and Cooper motioned to a small table near the wall of windows overlooking the docks. I sat down and then promptly leaned forward, eager to hear more. I'd never met anybody with such an exciting past. It was very intriguing.

"Why on earth are you here now?" I said, wondering why someone would give up all that excitement and prestige. Cruise ships were definitely exciting to me, but the job certainly didn't compare to being responsible for the safety of national dignitaries.

"It just got so tiring, you know, flying around all the time," he said. "We always had to be prepared to take a bullet for your man." He shrugged. "Besides, I wanted to see a bit more of the world, without worrying about His Excellency." He gave a mock salute and took a little bow in his seat.

"Who is the Governor General these days anyway?" I asked hesitantly, a bit embarrassed by my lack of political knowledge.

Cooper laughed and said, "It's okay, Ellie, you don't need to pretend to be interested in all that boring stuff. Let's talk about you."

I hesitated, still taking in his story. One would imagine that getting into such a special branch of police would take years of training and preparation. It was probably a highly desirable position; very competitive, you would think. And yet, here he was on a cruise ship, throwing away years of service. Why not take a military desk job? It didn't make any sense. But why would he lie? Did he think his life wasn't exciting enough as it was? I would err on the side of believing him, but my bullshit radar was on high alert.

I stared at him intently—he had such an innocent face. Maybe I was wrong.

I breezed through a brief history of my life, including my

love of photography. "It's been a passion of mine since I was a kid—I used to snap pictures of my dad slow dancing with my mum when they thought I wasn't around. I spent hours with my Nan in her damp darkroom, developing grainy black and white images of her fluffy black dog with three legs... I was even one of those embarrassing people who ripped pages out of photography magazines and Herb Ritts' books and stuck them on the back of the toilet door." Cooper laughed. "I'm hoping to have a career in professional photography, anyway. I'd love to shoot for *National Geographic*...or anyone, really. I've been working on my portfolio since I've been on the ship."

"Really? That's awesome," Cooper said. "I'd love to see your work sometime."

Hooray! I didn't even have to ask. "That would be great," I said. "It would be great to get your opinion."

"A good buddy of mine shoots for *National Geographic* sometimes," he added. "I should totally hook you up with him." My heart did a little leap. Maybe my doubts had been wrong—Cooper was definitely the man to know.

"That would be absolutely brilliant," I said. "I'm still working on my portfolio, but I'd love to chat to your mate."

"It's a done deal, my friend," Cooper said, smiling. "You just let me know when you're ready and I'll make it happen."

I'd already been feeling pretty positive about my portfolio, and the extra encouragement made me extra determined to keep working on it in my spare time. I'd have to do more exploring at every port—find places off the beaten path. And then, maybe... *National Geographic*! I could hardly believe it.

My head was spinning as I finished giving Cooper the tour. A few decks later, I dropped him at his cabin and headed back to my own room for a break.

After a lovely Sunday afternoon sleep, I was laying in my bunk, enjoying the solitude, when Caitlin burst in and flicked on the light. I sat up straight and stared, alarmed; her eyes were wide and desperate.

She crumped into a heap on the floor. "Gabriel slept with a

passenger."

"What? Today?" Was everyone sleeping with more than one person on this ship?

"No, yesterday, while I was working," she said, clearly distraught. I slid off my bunk and sat next to her on the floor. "We were walking through the atrium together this morning, and this middle aged Botox queen, apparently doing back-to-back cruises, started fawning all over him." She sounded on the verge of tears, which was more alarming than anything else; Caitlin didn't cry. "The motherfucker didn't even try to pretend nothing had happened."

"What did you do?" I asked. I could have throttled the bastard for betraying Caitlin. I'd realised pretty quickly he wasn't just another shag for her, and I was sure he knew it.

"When I tried to talk about it, he told me not to overreact," she said dismally. "That we were both as bad as each other." She shook her head. "I know that's normally true, dude, but you know how much I like him. He might even have been The One."

Well, shit. I'd known she was really into him, but I hadn't quite realised how much. She normally held onto new men for as long as the loan period of a new release DVD, so announcing she'd thought he might be The One was worrying.

"Caitlin, tell me what I can do, sweetie. Do you want me to come and talk to him with you?"

She sat silently for a moment, pondering the idea. Then she shook her head slowly. "No, dude, thanks for the offer, but I don't think I should. It won't really help anyway."

I suspected that was probably true, remembering Nick's warning about Gabriel. Now was not the time to remind her of this, however, and in any case I was hardly in a position to advise anybody about their love life.

Caitlin took a deep breath, let it out, and launched into a new subject. "Let's hire Harleys in St Martin this week!"

"Brilliant idea," I said. I'd always been jealous at how quickly she'd been able to bounce back from disappointment, but this time I was still a little worried. At the moment, though, it seemed the best thing I could do was go along with her plans. St Martin motorbike hire was legendary, and a day trip cruising around the island with the wind in my hair was definitely the best way to enjoy the sights of the island.

There was only one problem. "Caity, I don't know how to ride a motorbike."

"Ah, yes, my friend," she said, mimicking Yoda. "This is why we need some men. Do you have anyone you want to ask?"

I remembered Jock's suggestion about meeting up. "I'll ask Jock to round up a few of his mates," I said. "He was saying we should get a group together."

Caitlin smiled suggestively, and I hit her in the arm. "It's not like that," I objected. "He's just a really lovely guy. Maybe in another situation there could be something…but not here. Anyway, I'm not interested." Which was mostly true. Jock had all the hallmarks of a great boyfriend, but even if he had shown any interest in me—which he hadn't—he was the kind of serious, steady man I'd want in about five years, when it was time to settle down.

Jock was more than receptive to the idea and promised to not only round up a few of his mates, but to book the bikes as well. Sadly, it was five days away. Luckily, I had started to settle into the groove of things. First night of the cruise, everybody was excited, exploring the ship and asking a million questions. The next morning, they lined up at security to disembark in St Thomas, eager to see the island, drink cocktails, and buy a fridge magnet for their collection.

Martinique was always a challenge, because we didn't arrive until nearly midday, and I had to work in the morning. The first couple of weeks I'd forgotten and stayed up later than was ideal the night before, and the next morning had been a nightmare. A never-ending stream of customers keen to see their first digital prints and stock up on memory cards for the ensuing week was hard enough to deal with without being hung over and short on sleep.

By Barbados and Antigua, passengers swanned around the

ship with confidence. It was always a blessing when St Martin rolled around.

And this week had been long indeed. Monday started out with a hand slamming down on the Pic Stop's glass service counter. The hand belonged to a hefty middle-aged woman breathing so heavily I thought she was going to start spewing flames.

"Excuse me, young lady," she said, leaning in until she was about six inches from my face, "didn't you hear me say I wanted DOUBLE prints last night?" She glared and added, with the distinct punch of a New York accent, "It's not rocket science, you know."

Case in point.

I took a deep breath in what I hoped was a subtle manner and flicked to the back of the envelope she'd handed me, where the second set of prints were cleverly hiding.

Not at all flummoxed, she immediately bellowed, "Well, that's a stupid damn place for you to put them. Here, give them to me!" She snatched them from my hands and walked out of the shop.

The rest of the week got worse from there.

Friday did finally arrive, despite the week crawling along more slowly than a fat-bellied iguana.

Jock had rounded up a group of bleary-eyed bartenders to be our companions for the day. Since he was the only one I knew, we decided to ride together. Nick had begged off coming with us. "Not really my thing," he'd said.

At the rental place, Jock allowed me to choose our Harley. I didn't know anything about motorbikes, so naturally, I chose based on looks. The only non-black bike in the bunch, it was a big, silver, hulking beast with shiny double exhaust pipes and a very sexy name—V-Rod. Like all their bikes, the rental manager explained, it had been fitted with a backrest on the passenger seat. It didn't look exactly comfortable or supportive or substantial, but I figured I'd be leaning forward in excitement the whole time anyway.

"What a monster!" exclaimed Jock. "It looks a bit like a

bull, don't you think, Ellie?"

Getting a bit nervous by that stage, I just nodded and smiled. Jock noticed my trepidation and squeezed my arm. "You'll be right, lass," he said reassuringly.

Jock, in a very gentlemanly move, paid my share of the rental, waving away my protests. It was sweet of him, especially as I still hadn't accumulated much cash.

Although helmets were mandatory on the island, nobody appeared to be bothered about wearing protective clothing. I'd worn jeans and long sleeves, but I'd assumed there'd be other clothing on offer, like jackets and boots, but that turned out not to be the case. I said a little prayer for our safety and jumped on behind Jock, who was revving the engine impatiently.

After the first few terrifying minutes, the scenery distracted me enough to take my mind off my fear. Besides, Jock felt strong and confident in his riding. Caitlin, optimistically attired in a bikini top and shorts, was whooping and yelling with her usual lovely style of enthusiasm.

Between the distinct roar of the Harley engines and the thick, padded helmets, it was impossible to carry on a conversation, so I just leaned into Jock and enjoyed the journey.

The weather was truly sublime in its non-London perfection. The sun beat down with the intensity of a bonfire and the skin on my arms felt warm through the thin fabric of my peasant top. I rolled up my sleeves to soak up more vitamin D.

The sky was a remarkable blue, and I leaned my head way back until the smattering of fluffy clouds seemed to spin overhead. Peering around Jock at the front riders, I saw Caitlin perched upon a tiny pillion seat, waving her arms, dancing and gyrating. She had no fear.

"Are you enjoying the ride?!" Jock yelled over his shoulder.

I nodded enthusiastically, or at least as much as my massive helmet would allow. "Brilliant!" I shouted back.

It really was superb. The bikes were a blast, but the

stunning surroundings added a new dimension to the experience and distracted me from my fear of flying off the back like a paper bag in the wind. I closed my eyes and smiled to myself. It was near impossible to feel depressed in the Caribbean.

Riding in a group was also thrilling. The collective noise we made and the attention we got as we roared past groups of tourists gave me a real high. We were just like The Wild Ones, albeit a little less cool and intimidating.

Up ahead, Caitlin was gesturing and yelling at her rider, who waved and motioned to a group of colourful shacks before slowing down to a stop in front of one. A small café, it housed a motley collection of tables and chairs made out of recycled wood and building materials. The haphazard décor created a warm, inviting ambience, and wafting out the serving window was an even more inviting smell. My stomach had been rumbling as loud as the bikes; thank god it was lunchtime.

Jock and I grabbed a table, bravely allowing Caitlin to order for us. Thinking about the children we'd seen while riding through the villages, I asked Jock about his family and childhood. He took a deep breath and removed his sunglasses, the filtered sunlight intensifying the incredible shade of his blue eyes. They distracted me for a moment as he started telling me about his early years in Scotland.

It wasn't exactly the happy tales of hopscotch and roast dinners I had experienced; his father had left them for a family friend when Jock was two, leaving his heartbroken mother to bring up four children on her own. Jock had three sisters; the youngest, Bonnie, was diagnosed with quite severe autistic disorder at the age of four, placing considerable extra strain on his mother.

"She was such a brave and strong woman, my mother," Jock said, smiling fondly. "You wouldn't have known how hard her life was. Aye, it was really hard; but she kept fighting and smiling and looking after us like it was the most natural thing in the world to raise a family on your own." He shook his head in disbelief. "I don't know how she did it, Ellie. She held down two jobs and still managed to keep a clean house and put food on the table." He smiled again as he added, "My sisters were grand too. They helped with Bonnie and with me— making me do my homework, when all I wanted was to kick the football outside with the lads. We drank lots of tea; 'cures all kinds of ills', my mother used to say."

"She sounds wonderful, Jock, and so do your sisters," I said. Growing up with so many strong women was no doubt what made Jock the sensitive and respectful man he was today.

"I'm really quite lucky, you know. We had an arsehole for a father, and nought in terms of money and clothes and games, but we had a real strength and security, just the five of us. Not many people can say that. And when I'm a dad, I'll be the best there is… I won't shack up with anyone until I've found the right woman," he said. "I don't believe in divorce and bringing up children without both parents."

His confidence and gratitude were lovely.

"Let's not talk about me anymore, Ellie," he said, his eyes shining. "Tell me about your family and friends back home."

Jock was genuinely interested in my background. He laughed at my stories about my parents' silly antics, smiled at stories of their lovely, sweet relationship, and demanded to hear more of the scrapes I'd got into in my childhood. "Cheers to your parents, lass," Jock said, clinking his can of Coke with my water. "I hope we can both be like them some day."

As we headed back to the bikes with the others, I asked him if he'd met Cooper yet. He hadn't, so I told him about Cooper's amazing background, expecting that Jock would be as impressed as I'd been.

"Well, that's mighty interesting," Jock said when I finished. The corner of his mouth twisted. "Unbelievable, even." He sighed and then smiled, saying, "Bring the lad to the bar tonight. If he comes with your recommendation, I'm sure he's brilliant."

Later, in our cabin, Caitlin had undressed and was wandering about with only a g-string on as though it was the most natural thing in the world. "You know, dude," she said, "I've been thinking about it, and the only way to get Gabriel back for porking that ancient bitch is to fuck someone else. The new Golf Pro, Alex, is hot. He and Gabriel used to be best friends, but they had some big fight last contract and are now sworn enemies. Might give him a call." She smiled mischievously and slapped her own arse.

As much as I loved her, she was definitely a troublemaker. I grabbed our Kahlua bottle and poured two shots. With Caitlin about to shag up a storm with Gabriel's arch enemy—we were sure as hell going to need them.

Chapter Ten

"Fuck, Cooper is hot," Jacoline stage-whispered to Caitlin over breakfast a few days later. Caitlin snorted and stuffed a huge pancake into her mouth. "Well, you know, he's not actually 'hot', but he's really funny and charming," Jacoline amended.

Caitlin swallowed her massive mouthful and held up her hands in protest. "No, no, Jac, I'm not judging. Each to her own, I always say." She raised her eyebrows with mock cynicism and looked down at her plate. Jacoline elbowed her and Caitlin laughed and said playfully, "Okay, okay, whatever you say. He's awesome. Don't hurt me!"

"Sssshhhhhhhh," Jacoline whispered. "I don't want everyone to hear. You know what these bastards are like."

It was interesting how someone like Cooper could be the subject of such female fancy. If I were honest, he wasn't exactly a looker, but his friendly, open demeanour was clearly held in high esteem by Jacoline. She'd declared herself completely finished with 'bad boys' a few weeks earlier.

While I couldn't say I was as enamoured of Cooper as Jacoline, I had liked the way he'd opened up to me on his first day. It was always nice to click with someone and have that immediate rapport. I hadn't seen him much since he'd first come aboard; I'd meant to invite him for a social drink with my mates and introduce him around, but hadn't got around to it yet.

Before I could launch myself into the girls' conversation, Maria entered the mess, drawing all eyes, including mine. She was wearing a bikini and very little else, which wasn't permitted in staff eating areas. Not that any of our waiters were about to complain. They all loved Maria and openly worshipped her tanned, curvaceous body. She fed them compliments like little dogs, keeping them sweet for when she needed something.

"Good morning, *chicas*," she purred, slinking into the mess and slipping into a seat. Two waiters were on their way before she could beckon, one elbowing the other out of the way. She crossed one long leg over the other and turned her attention towards Jacoline. "Soooo, Jacoline," she said, fluttering her eyelashes, "I saw that you and Cooper were getting very cosy in the crew bar last night."

Here we go again.

"Fuuuuck off, Maria," Jacoline said angrily. "It was just one drink with a new colleague, and you know it. Stop trying to cause trouble!" She stood up. "I'm so sick of not being able to have a conversation with someone without you all thinking we're sleeping together!"

She stormed out of the mess, leaving her half-eaten breakfast on the table. Caitlin and I looked at each other in shock. I always found those kinds of scenes difficult, because I never knew whether to run after the friend or sit in an awkward silence with everybody else.

We ran after her.

"They just drive me crazy!" Jacoline said when we reached her, spitting out each word. "You know what it's like. You speak to someone for five minutes, and it's on…"

"…like Donkey Kong?" Caitlin finished helpfully. We all laughed. "We know, Jac, it really sucks ass, but there's not much we can do except stay in our rooms every night."

"Yeah, like me," I said, feeling relieved as it meant for once I wasn't the one being targeted by Maria.

"Sorry I wasn't there to back you up, Jac. I was kind of busy with my own private party in Alex's cabin." Caitlin said, almost blushing. "Man, that golf pro can really deliver the goods. Great arm strength, good hands…got one-in-a-hole every time!" She laughed raucously at her own joke. Jacoline and I shook our heads in feigned judgement.

"Do you need me to accidentally let that slip next time I see Gabriel?" Jacoline asked as she opened the door to our cabin.

"Nah, I've got a feeling Alex will take care of that," Caitlin said with an evil grin.

There was a timid knock at the door. Caitlin jumped up to open it, undoing her top button as she went, clearly hoping Alex, or maybe Gabriel, would be behind it. But it was Cooper, looking a bit sheepish.

"Hey, girls," he said, "sorry to interrupt. I was just wondering what I should do today? I haven't seen the new roster or anything."

"Ellie will sort you out," said Jacoline, pushing me towards him. "She was just about to go up to Justin's office anyway."

I knew from her white lie she didn't want to be seen with him again so soon. I wasn't that keen on taking him up to get a roster though, as it meant an unnecessary run-in with Justin.

When we arrived at Justin's office, I knocked on the door timidly. "Knock, knock," I said, tapping on the doorframe.

Justin looked up. He smiled when he saw Cooper. "Hey, Coop," he said, all smiles. "I bet you're here to pick up this?" He handed Cooper the roster.

"Thanks, JR, I sure was," said Cooper, holding it as though it was the Shrine of Turin. Wow, they were on nickname basis already.

"Ellie, don't forget it's 'stores' today," Justin said, finally acknowledging me. "Don't leave it as late as you did last time please." He was referring to the dreaded fortnightly task of collecting photography supplies from the large pallets which were dumped on the St Thomas dock, beside the ship, and so far I'd delayed it as much as possible every time. Just thinking about it was a nightmare. I had to wheel them inside on a trolley and put them away in their various hidey holes. Much harder than it sounded, it normally involved about twenty trips to and from the ship's hull. Since the storage areas were on three different levels, many rides up and down in the freight elevator were required. It always included a lot of sweating and swearing. Stores was the Pic Stop person's thankless job, and nobody ever helped.

"Hey, Ellie, I'll help you," said Cooper, interrupting my self-pity party. "It'll be much faster with two people."

Justin raised his eyebrows, but said nothing.

Walking down to the dock, I was excited by the idea of having assistance with my least-favourite job of the cruise. Still, I thought it would be polite to offer him an out. "Look, thanks so much, Cooper, but you really don't need to help me. Everybody hates stores, and it's my job, really." I smiled, and silently hoped he'd still help me.

"No problem at all, Ellie," he said, smiling. "I'm always a team player. Besides, you seem like an awesome chick, and I haven't been able to spend any time with you this week."

It was hard to know what to say to a declaration like that. "Um, thanks," I managed in response.

It was obvious, as we sorted out the boxes on the dock, Cooper had done this before. He arranged the boxes into piles, according to where they had to be stored. I was embarrassed not to have thought of it myself before. I normally just took a bunch at a time, but they were so mixed up it took forever to sort them out once on board.

We worked in silence, traipsing back and forth onto the ship, and the piles depleted surprisingly quickly.

When we were finished, Cooper sat down on a crate, wiped his brow and cleaned his thick glasses. He motioned for me to sit next to him, suddenly looking very serious.

"You know how I told you about my old job last week?" he said. "Well, I didn't tell you the whole story."

Very intriguing. "Okay," I said slowly. "What do you mean?"

"Well, the real reason I left the police force was that they wouldn't let my fiancée travel with me."

"Fiancée?" I said, a bit confused. I thought he'd left that job because he was tired of all the travelling? It was another thing that didn't add up.

Was I doubting him again for a reason? He seemed

harmless enough, not to mention helpful… Maybe he hadn't been ready to mention her before. Maybe he'd left that life for a multitude of reasons. Still, a series of six month photography contracts at sea hardly constituted a relationship-friendly move. I was intrigued. "Do you find cruise ship work gives you more time together?"

He looked down at his hands. "Amanda—that was her name—died a couple of years ago," he said. "That's when I started working on ships."

Oh, so he'd left his job for her, then she had passed away. That explained it. Lost for words, I stared out at the ocean. I hadn't quite been expecting the mood to turn so dark.

"It's okay, we can talk about it," he added, acknowledging my awkward silence. "I still miss her so much, but I'm learning to move on." He smiled a thin smile, his eyes looking sad.

"I'm so sorry, Cooper," I murmured. "I really don't know what to say. That is just so awful… Such a terrible thing to deal with." Why did my ability to talk nonstop always disappear at the moments I really wanted something to say?

Cooper stared at the ship. "I haven't been with anyone else for three years. I haven't been able to bring myself to find joy in another woman."

I still didn't know what to say, so my idiot alter-ego spoke for me. "Can I ask how she died?" As soon as the words were out of my mouth, I regretted them immediately. I knew there was a reason I didn't normally probe.

He looked down. "She died in a car accident," he whispered. "I think that's another reason I like working on ships. Means I'm not thinking about her every time I get into a car."

I could feel the pain emanating from his every pore.

"Actually, Ellie, sorry, I know I brought it up, but would it be okay if we didn't talk about it anymore?" he said, his face turned away again. He took off his glasses and rubbed his eye with a balled fist.

Did he suddenly look more attractive? *No, Ellie. Don't be daft.* It was probably just a reaction to learning about his tragic loss. I was a sucker for vulnerability. The doubts which had been plaguing me only moments before melted away. Cooper had such charm and found it so easy to get on with everyone, and was so helpful; as Dad had always said, it was important how a bloke got on with other people. Well, Dad had been thinking specifically about boyfriends, but now was an entirely inappropriate time to be having any romantic thoughts about Cooper. Even if there was something special about a man showing his sensitive side.

"Of course," I said. "I'm sorry, Cooper. I hope I didn't upset you." I felt awful for him, and wished I'd known what to say when he told me about his fiancée. Instead I was more like a guppy. Big eyes and open mouth. Nothing of value to contribute. *Nice one, Ellie.*

We both sat silently. The easy-going nature of our earlier conversation had been obliterated with talk of the past.

As a parting thought, Cooper leaned over and wiped his hands on his trousers. "Ellie, I'd appreciate you not mentioning this to the others. I won't be telling anyone else."

"Of course," I said. "No problem." At least I felt confident about that. I was a vault when it came to others' secrets. Certainly when they were really important ones, anyway.

When I returned to the cabin, Caitlin was nowhere to be found. Jacoline poked her head in to see if I wanted to go into town for cocktails, but I declined; I'd promised Jock I'd go to the beach with him and a few of his mates. Glancing at the time, I realised it was later than I'd thought, and dashed around the cabin, throwing things into my beach bag. Jock was waiting for me when I reached the bartenders' corridor, bag on shoulders, sunnies and swimming trunks on.

"Oh, sorry, Ellie, the other guys can't make it," he said. "They've all bailed on me at the last minute. Are you okay to go along anyway?"

Quite honestly, I wasn't at all disappointed the others couldn't join us. It would be nice to spend some time with Jock.

We went through the disembarkation security check, jumped in a taxi, and drove the fifteen minutes to Coki Beach in record time. A tiny beach, it was famous for snorkelling and for the nearby Coral World Ocean Park.

We found a spot on the umbrella-sprinkled beach among a throng of sun worshippers. Not really in the mood for water sports, we decided against snorkelling and rented reclining beach chairs and a huge umbrella. We bought ice cold coconut drinks from a little green caravan and sat in the little patch of shade the brolly created.

Having placed our bags between us, we accidentally grazed hands as we both reached for our sunscreen. "I need to make sure I go home looking like a Greek God, not a spotted lobster," Jock said, and I laughed in agreement. It was nice to meet a guy with the same concerns. Slathering on a generous layer of sunscreen, he said, "I still haven't met the new photog you mentioned."

"Oh, Cooper?" I said.

"Aye, that's him." Jock settled back and closed his eyes. "Had some fancy background taking bullets for the Queen."

I'd never heard him sound so cynical and cutting.

"He was in the Canadian Protective Policing Service," I corrected. "Protecting the Governor General, not the Queen. Although he *would* have looked after the Queen while she was visiting Canada."

"Mhmm," Jock said, doubt dripping from the word. "Of course he did."

"Why are you being weird?" I asked, frustrated. "You haven't even met him yet."

I barely even knew Cooper, while I'd got to know Jock fairly well over the last few weeks; I wasn't really sure why I was defending our new photog. Jock had proven to be both a good guy and a good judge of character, but I was reluctant to hear anything negative said about Cooper, especially after hearing about his fiancée. Maybe Jock was jealous…

"I'm sorry, Ellie," he said, opening his eyes and looking over at me. "I'm just jokin' with you. You got your goat up though, didn't you, lass? Might you fancy the fella a wee bit?"

"Pfffft," I huffed in response. I always seemed to end up trying to avoid talking about my romantic entanglements—or lack thereof—with Jock. I shook my head and changed the topic. "So, what do you want to do with your life? Is bartending a short-term or long-term plan?"

Unperturbed by the abrupt change of subject, Jock said, "Well, I'd really like to open my own bar. Maybe back at home in Edinburgh, or London. It depends how much I can save during the next few contracts, actually. I love bar work. I love the people you meet...but I don't love ships. Too transient for me—I like to put down roots, you know what I mean?"

I did know what he meant. I'd felt like that when I'd moved in with Dan years before. And look how well that had turned out. One minute I was on the verge of marriage and babies, or at least I thought I was, and the next, I was packing my bags and moving in with my parents until I worked out my next move. Not exactly what you expect to happen when you're twenty-eight, engaged, and in a four-year relationship.

"And what about you?" he asked, peering at me over his sunglasses. "Any big dreams?"

"Well, the ultimate dream is to open my own gallery," I said. "Probably in London. Although truth be told, I'd be happy with just getting an exhibition somewhere, so that people could see my work. I'd love a career with *National Geographic*. They do the most amazing stuff." I looked over at him sheepishly. Sometimes when you said your dreams out loud, they sounded foolish, and even though I'd told Cooper, Jock's opinion seemed much more important.

Happily, Jock looked genuinely interested. "That sounds fantastic, lass. You should really go for it. I bet you've loads of talent."

"Thanks," I said quietly. My cheeks burned at the compliment. Dan used to say every wannabe photographer and his dog wanted to work for *National Geographic*. I wondered whether to mention that Cooper had said he might be able to hook me up with a friend who worked for the magazine, but decided against it. I didn't want to make Jock grumpy again.

"Maybe we should open a gallery with a bar," Jock said, interrupting my thought. He grinned. "Join our talents together." He was joking, but I turned the idea over in my head anyway. It was a nice thing to think about. And Jock sounded supportive. More and more I was beginning to think that my dreams might actually be possible.

I glanced at Jock, wondering if I should throw out another topic of conversation, but he'd settled back, his eyes closed, and I didn't want to disturb him. Instead, I smiled; I wasn't sure I'd ever seen him so still, and he looked somehow different. Younger, maybe. Stiller. More peaceful.

Realising I'd been staring at him, even if he hadn't noticed, I dug into my bag for my sunhat. I lay back and put it over my face, letting out my tension with a long breath. The warmth of the sun felt welcome on my skin, and although I was wary about sunburn, I did want to keep working on my gradual tan.

I could feel my breath slowing down; my eyes were comfortably heavy. I was happily drowning in a sea of relaxation, breathing steadily, listening to the sounds of the people nearby. The still, flat water produced tiny waves as it kissed the sand, making a gentle, lapping sound.

With my eyes shrouded in darkness under the cover of my hat, I relaxed further, and my ears started to tune out the finer details of their conversations. Soon, their loud, clear chatter blended into a muted drone.

Floating on a cloud of nonsensical thoughts, I drifted into a comfortable snooze. Did I really get paid to do this every day? I smiled again. I was never going home.

Chapter Eleven

I was sorry when the time came to go back to the ship; it was so peaceful lying on the beach with Jock, both chatting and sharing companionable silences. I wasn't looking forward to manning the shop, but luckily for me the afternoon and evening flew by in a ritual of work, customers, and endless questions.

As soon as I'd locked up, I bolted for the bar. Jock had a glass of white wine waiting for me by the time I reached him, and I'd just settled in when Caitlin arrived, accompanied by the infamous Gabriel.

Despite hearing all the sordid details of their sex life, it was my first time meeting him, and I was surprised to see how handsome he was. Tall, broad, dark brown hair, green eyes, a long, straight nose...he reeked of masculinity and oozed across the floor like syrup. More than one woman sent an admiring glance his way.

Caitlin was grinning, leaning into Gabriel and pawing him like a kitten playing with a ball of wool. They'd quite obviously patched things up.

"Roomie, this is my boyfriend, Gabriel," Caitlin said, stumbling over her words a bit. Looked like they were already a few drinks into the evening. "Gabriel, this is the bestest and most beautiful cabin-mate in the world, Ellie."

"Hi Ellie," he said, leaning over to kiss my cheek. I thought he was going for a hug and leaned in with my arms open. We bumped cheek to shoulder and ended up with a cross between a back pat and air kiss. Ugh. Gabriel just smiled and added, "I've heard so much about you." He almost sounded American, but not quite, and I couldn't place the accent.

"Pleased to meet you," I said. "Where are you from? I can't place your accent."

"Croatia, although we moved to the States when I was twelve," he replied, his hand still on my upper arm.

"Great, great," said Caitlin, pushing her way in between us. She stroked Gabriel's arm and leaned in to nibble his ear. "Babe, can you go and get me a drink, please? I'm so thirsty." She grabbed his bum and squeezed it as he walked away.

Gabriel disappeared into the crowd at the bar, and Caitlin dragged me over to one of the booths. "Oh, roomie, we have had the most awesome day," she said, with her mouth about an inch from my ear. The music hadn't been turned up yet, so the volume of Caitlin's voice made me flinch. She was definitely a little trolleyed.

Obviously feeling affectionate, she draped her arms around me and put her head on my shoulder.

"I see you've made up," I said, stating the obvious.

"Dude, we did more than just make up," she said. "We bumped into this Aussie chick, Jane, from the casino. She's having a fling with another casino guy, Jacob, who Gabriel knows from a previous contract. Jane is so nice, you know, really pretty, black hair, big boobs." She gestured to indicate the size of Jane's bust. "I mean, you know me, no boobs whatsoever." She looked down at her chest, which was, in fact, more or less as flat as an ironing board, and pouted. Then she laughed and shoved me hard with her shoulder.

"Ouch!" I exclaimed, rubbing my arm.

"Haha, sorry, dude, I can kiss it better," she said, leaning in with her lips pursed.

"No, thanks," I replied, swatting her away playfully. I nudged her back. "Continue with the story, woman!"

A quick glance told us that Gabriel was deep in conversation with Jock and showed no signs of imminent return, so Caitlin launched into the story at breakneck feed, unable to get the juicy details out fast enough. "Anyway, I clicked with her straight away. I heard on the grapevine that she likes a bit of girl action sometimes. So she's with Jacob, right, and he is totally hot, too. I mean, together, they're like fucking Ken and Barbie. So we saw her up on deck, and Gabriel invited her to bring Jacob to his cabin for brunch drinks. We started playing this crazy drinking game, and got totally hosed in like an hour."

Caitlin's voice kept getting louder; as she was completely blotto, she completely didn't notice, and just laughed off my attempts to shush her.

"Anyway, so Jane was flirting with Gabriel big time," she continued. "Well, actually, she was flirting with both of us. Then Jacob started paying me compliments, and, well..." She giggled and cast me a sideways glance. "Just me and Jane got it on at first. Fuck, she's hot. She just leant in and kissed me— just like that. Her lips were so soft, and her tongue kept darting in and out, like she was tasting an ice cream... Fuuuuck." Caitlin shuddered.

"I almost felt like I was in a dream, you know? I mean, I've been with girls before, but this felt so much damn better. It was also way dirtier though..." She smiled wickedly before continuing. "The boys had been playing with themselves, watching us, and they were definitely up and ready. They practically pushed us onto the bottom bunk...so we both knelt down, and they were standing behind us...then we'd swap, then they'd swap...it was so bad, but in a good way." Caitlin couldn't stop giggling, her shoulders shaking; she was obviously still high from the experience.

I was completely hooked in, and could feel a familiar little tug of excitement between my upper thighs. I was suddenly finding it hard to remember why I'd sworn off men a few weeks earlier. And actually, if I was honest with myself, I was surprised at my reaction—I'd never had any interest whatsoever in girl-on-girl action, much less group sex, and here I was practically drooling as Caitlin described all of the intimate details. I'd always thought that it would be so peculiar; sex on its own could be embarrassing enough, so imagine the potential embarrassment when you started pulling in more people! But the way Caitlin talked about it, it didn't really seem all that weird at all—just a different way of having fun—more fun than was possible with one partner.

I'd arrived on board keen to experiment, but I'd not expected to find myself wondering what it would be like to tangle limbs with another girl or to experience group sex. Now I was tentatively wondering if maybe I'd been missing out...

As Caitlin continued her blow-by-blow account, I realised I was getting even more turned on. I was pretty sure that if someone had tried to tell me about their sexual experiences— multiple positions (most of which I'd never heard of, much less considered), multiple partners (at the same time!), chair straddling, neck devouring—even six months ago that I'd have been so embarrassed I probably would have fled the room and avoided ever seeing the person again. Now, though... Okay, so I was still shocked by quite a lot of what Caitlin described, but I wasn't feeling any desire to flee. No, the desire I felt was of a very different kind...

It took me ages to find my voice again. "Wow," I managed at last. I licked my lips, hesitated, and then added, "I might go for a threesome, but I'd feel weird swapping juices."

Caitlin looked shocked for a moment, probably at the fact I said I'd be open to a threesome. I was surprised myself; it wasn't something I'd ever thought I'd consider, much less admit to someone else. But Caitlin's story had really turned me on, and now I couldn't help but wonder.

Caitlin's mouth opened and closed, making her look a bit like a fish, and then she took a deep breath and shrugged. "Thinking about it, yeah, I guess it seems pretty wild, but once you're in there, doing it, it doesn't even cross your mind," she said, completely unperturbed. I'd have to take her word for it, as I didn't think I was really quite ready to jump into the deep end just yet. Caitlin smiled happily and added, "Yep, it was a great fucking day."

A great fucking day indeed.

At that moment, Gabriel tapped Caitlin on the shoulder and handed her a tall drink with two straws, an umbrella, and a strawberry on a swizzle stick hanging out the top. Caitlin grabbed the drink, threw the decoration onto the floor, and slammed down the brown liquid. "Ahhhhhhh," she exclaimed, smacking her lips. "What was that?"

"A Long Island Iced Tea, beautiful," he said. "You're supposed to drink them slowly."

Caitlin shrugged, grabbed his hand, and pulled him onto the dance floor. Within moments they were locked in their own little world, oblivious to onlookers; Caitlin twined herself around Gabriel sinuously, reminding me of a cat. He watched her hungrily, his hands roaming over her body, and then, leaving one hand drifting down her back, he captured her face with the other and lowered his mouth to hers. The longer I watched the more intimate they got, until really, my face should have been absolutely flaming in embarrassment.

"Get a room!" someone shouted.

They were like a car accident: you didn't want to see, but couldn't tear your eyes away. In the past, I'd always been so careful to avoid watching people engaging in PDA; Dan had always found it disgusting and I'd picked up the habit of being embarrassed by others' actions from him. Then again, he hadn't even liked to hold my hand in public. He'd have died of horror at the show Caitlin and Gabriel were putting on; I found it exhilarating. I wasn't sure when I'd become such a voyeur, but I mentally filed it away as an interest to pursue later.

I had been so engrossed in Caitlin and Gabriel I hadn't noticed the bar filling up with all the usual suspects. Waitresses flirted with personal trainers and youth staff, while lots of short, skinny Filipino guys sat huddled close together, downing beers and playing cards. Nobody seemed the least bit interested in the show Caitlin and Gabriel were putting on.

Except Maria.

She was standing against the opposite wall, staring at the

two figures passionately entwined in the centre of the room. Her expression was a mixture of sad and stormy, and her hand was frozen in mid-air, clutching a Mexican beer so tightly her knuckles were white. There was something else, though, beneath the sadness and anger—a hint of vulnerability, maybe, though the Brazilian Bitch was the last person I'd have ever expected to feel vulnerable.

Obviously unable to bear watching them anymore, Maria spun around and practically ran to the bar. I stared after her, wondering what she could be thinking. If I were honest, I was hoping Caitlin had managed to spoil Maria's designs on Gabriel, and that now she was jealous and hurt and about to go into a decline. I'd love Caitlin to give Maria her comeuppance. But that look on her face bothered me. It had shown me a side of Maria that I'd have preferred to continue thinking didn't exist.

Somebody tapped me on the shoulder. "Howdy. How're you doing?" a familiar voice said.

I turned to find Cooper standing over me, a big smile on his face, and I wondered how I hadn't noticed before that he had a really lovely smile. "Hey, you," I said.

He looked past me and let out a long whistle. "Wow, that's quite a show they're putting on, hey?"

I followed his gaze. "Yeah," I said. I felt my heart skip a little beat and a smile cross my face, and for a moment I wasn't sure if it had been caused by Caitlin and Gabriel, or by Cooper. It was nice to smile, for any reason; my face had felt like it had been frozen in a dumbfounded expression for the past half an hour. It was surprisingly good to see Cooper, in any case.

"Want a drink?"

I declined, and pretended I wasn't that interested in watching the floor show anymore as he sauntered over to the bar. When he hadn't returned a few minutes later, I glanced at the bar to see that Cooper and Jock were both standing rather stiffly, their jaws set and annoyed looks on their faces. I walked up just in time to hear Jock's question.

"So, they let you into the RMP with those thick glasses,

mate?" he asked, polishing a glass with great force.

"Yeah, of course," said Cooper, shrugging.

"Hmmm," Jock said noncommittally. "That's really interesting, mate. My old cabin mate was Canadian. Thing is, he was rejected from the police force because he wore thick glasses similar to yours." He mirrored Cooper's shrug and added, "Something about a minimum vision requirement...?"

Cooper didn't respond, and I felt myself holding my breath. Then he looked me and smiled broadly. "You know what we need? Better company and a cabin party!"

Jock snorted and moved down to the other end of the bar.

"A cabin party?" I echoed, my eyes following Jock before snapping back to Cooper's face. "Sounds good to me. We can have it in mine."

As Cooper dragged me away to find some people to party with, I wondered what had happened to set Jock and Cooper at odds. Cooper had clearly made many friends in his short time on board; he was practically vying for Most Adored Man. I'd been so sure that he'd get on with Jock; Jock seemed to get along with everybody anyway—well, almost—and I'd thought they'd be fast friends. Apparently I'd been wrong.

As I trailed after Cooper, I glanced back at the dance floor and saw that Caitlin and Gabriel had stopped their groping shuffle. They stood in a little huddle with Maria, their foreheads almost touching. Suddenly, they all threw their heads back, and I saw they were doing shots off a little drinks tray Maria was holding. It was weird to see Caitlin drinking with the Brazilian Bitch...although, that being said, Caitlin had never been one to turn down a free beverage, and the drunker she got the less she cared about where the booze was coming from.

Still, I couldn't understand why Maria had bought rounds for the couple she had been giving the evil eye only moments before. I'd never understand her.

Once we'd rounded up about a dozen people, Cooper ambled over to collect the dance floor trio. Caitlin, always up for a party, whooped and hollered, while Maria slunk away into the darkness. As I was carried out amongst the throng of party-goers, I looked back at the bar and met Jock's gaze; he'd been scowling after us, though his expression lightened when he saw me, and he returned my wave as I disappeared out the door.

Once in the cabin, the party took on a life of its own. It was so easy to throw a great bash on board a cruise ship. No one minded being crammed together in the close quarters of a cabin; people talked and laughed and drank and tried to dance, and I listened as Cooper told stories about passengers he'd met during his time on the ship. We were wedged between the desk and the wall, our legs touching, and though I'd been convinced that Cooper really wasn't attractive, I was incredibly aware of my leg against his.

As he laughed, wrapping up another story, his hand brushed my thigh. A thousand tingles ran down my spine, and the tightening between my thighs I'd felt during Caitlin's story earlier in the night came rushing back like a thunderbolt. My body arched forward, drawn to him like a lodestone.

Then Gabriel grabbed my shoulder, disturbing the moment. "Hey, Ellie," he said, sounding worried, "did you see Caitlin come out of the bathroom? She's been in there for ages. I knocked, but she's not answering." There was fear in his eyes. I ripped myself away from Cooper's magnetic field and pushed through people to the bathroom door. I pulled on the knob, but it was locked.

"Caity!" I called, leaning against the door jamb. No answer. I pounded on the door. "Caity! Are you still in there, gorgeous?"

There was no answer. I banged hard with my open hand and yelled again. Still no answer.

Cooper disappeared for a minute, then reappeared with a Swiss Army Knife. "Here's a little trick I learned on my last ship," he said. He pushed the knife underneath the handle's base, and with a quick flick of the blades, slipped a file into the door crack. The door popped open.

I swung the door open and there she was—slumped down

between the toilet and the wall. Her head was hanging forward, eyes closed, and her feet were splayed far apart on the bathroom floor.

"Caity!" I squished into the small bathroom and grabbed her shoulders. I shook hard and tried again. "Caitlin! Wake up, darling. Come on, wake up!" I could see the rise and fall of her chest, but she didn't open her eyes. My high of moments ago was replaced by sheer panic. I breathed in sharply and slapped her cheek. "Caitlin!" Still no response.

Gabriel shoved me aside and started shaking her. "Sweetheart! Baby! Wake up, come on, wake up!" His voice was hoarse. "PLEASE wake up," he begged.

Cooper put his hands on Gabriel's shoulders. "Here, man," he said calmly. "Try this cold towel. Sprinkle some water on her head." He handed Gabriel a water-soaked hand towel he had grabbed off the rail.

While the boys tried to wake Caitlin up, I went back out into the cabin. Everyone else had quietly filtered out once they'd realised something was wrong. "I'm calling the doctor," I said, reaching for the telephone.

"No!" Gabriel cried out. "She'll get fired for being so drunk."

I knew what I had to do. "I don't give a shit, Gabriel," I said sharply. "I'd rather she was alive!"

Cooper put his arm out to hold Gabriel back and shook his head. "She has to call them, man. You know it."

Gabriel buried his head in his hands. Cooper reached down and scooped Caitlin up into his arms and carried her out of the bathroom. He laid her on her side on our floor of the cabin and checked her mouth for vomit. The doctor arrived with a nurse in tow minutes later. They whisked Caitlin away in a wheelchair; her body slumped over as though she were dead. I ran after them. Cooper and Gabriel ran after me. As we rounded the first corner, we almost slammed into Maria. She stepped back, blocking our path.

"I just saw Caitlin with the doctor," she said, sounding concerned. "She had a lot to drink tonight. I hope she is okay."

I shoved her aside; we didn't need to stand and listen to any more of her bitchiness.

"I hope she does not lose her job for drunkenness," she called after us.

Fucking bitch. She'd been practically pouring shots down Caitlin's throat back in the crew bar. I wanted to say something, but Caitlin came first. I would have to worry about Maria later.

As we caught up with the doctor again, he began to ask questions as we ran through the halls, asking what she'd had to drink, and how much, and if she'd taken any drugs… Gabriel and I answered as best we could. She'd drunk a lot throughout the day, but not really more than she had done on previous occasions. Neither of us thought she'd done any drugs.

Then I remembered the bulimia.

I hesitated at first, unsure if Gabriel knew, and then decided it didn't matter. "Doctor," I said, "she has a history of bulimia…so she may have been throwing up today, and drinking on an empty stomach." I hated being a snitch, but he needed to know what he was dealing with.

The brightly lit medical centre was a stark contrast to the hot, sweaty party we'd so recently been enjoying back in the cabin. The doctor and nurse lifted Caitlin up and swung her onto a bed. As the nurse gathered instruments and equipment to check Caitlin's vitals, the doctor spoke in hushed tones.

He used his thumb to pull her eyelid back and flashed a light into them. "She's not responding," he said. "Pupils aren't contracting." He checked her pulse, and her blood pressure, and recorded her BAC, measured her oxygen…

I could see the worry on his face and felt like I was going to pass out. I felt horrendously guilty; my tendency to blame myself for everything surged to the fore. How could I have let her drink so much? How had I not noticed she'd had more than enough? Why hadn't I followed her into the bathroom? I felt like the worst friend in the world, even though rationally I knew it wasn't my fault, and said a little prayer for Caitlin.

"Please let her be okay," I whispered, and then added, since

I didn't make a habit of praying, "I'll do anything. Just let her be okay."

I stared hard at Caitlin, silently pleading for her to wake up. Her eyes stayed shut and her tiny, delicate body lay limp on the hospital bed. She looked like a child. And at that moment, I knew it might not be okay, my prayers might not do her any good. Maybe this was one of those turning points in life, the kind of thing that changed you forever. I wasn't ready for that. I just wanted my roomie back.

Chapter Twelve

Watching my new best friend lying unconscious was torture.

I closed my eyes, tears threatening to spill out and over. A warm, comforting arm slipped around my shoulders, and I opened my eyes to see Cooper right next to me, tipping his head towards mine. "She'll be right, Ellie. She's in good hands here."

A small whimper escaped my lips.

The doctor picked up a little, metal stick-type thing and pushed it hard under Caitlin's thumbnail, his expression suggesting it was his last chance to get a response.

"FUUCK OFF!" Caitlin screamed, sitting bolt upright and opening her eyes. Then she slumped back down and closed them again.

The corner of the doctor's mouth twitched upwards. "She'll be okay," he said. "She just needs to sleep it off. But just to be safe and ensure she doesn't have any complications, we'll keep an eye on her in here overnight."

We breathed a collective sigh of relief.

"Oh, thank God!" I exclaimed. She was going to be okay! Relief rushed through my body and I felt a moment of weakness. I leaned against Cooper for support.

"Thank you so much, Doctor. We'll leave you in peace now," Gabriel said. "Please let us know when Caitlin wakes up. Thank you again for everything."

I echoed my thanks and reluctantly left Caitlin in that cold, uncomfortable room.

My dad always said you could see people's true colours in

an emergency. Cooper had been amazing—calm and cool, knowledgeable, and reassuring to have around. He put his arm around me as we walked back up to the cabins and I leant into him, feeling completely drained by the evening's drama. Gabriel thanked Cooper with a silent handshake, kissed me on the cheek, and disappeared, no doubt back to a sleepless night in his cabin. His reaction in the medical centre had surprised me, and I wondered if the situation would make him rethink his feelings towards his relationship with Caitlin. As for me...I knew Caitlin drank a lot, but it had never seemed like it was enough that it might be a problem. And now, even though I knew she'd be okay, I was desperately worried about her.

As we neared the photographer's corridor, I began to dread going back into my cabin. I could still see Caitlin sprawled on the bathroom floor and I knew that I'd just sit there and stare and overthink and blame myself.

Cooper seemed to pick up on my tangled emotions and stopped me before I got to my door. "Ellie," he said gently, "just come into my cabin for a while. You shouldn't be alone right now."

I breathed a sigh of relief, grateful he'd realised I didn't want to go back into the cabin I shared with Caitlin after what we'd just witnessed.

We stepped into the stillness of his cabin. For a moment I felt disoriented; the last time I'd been in this particular room had been when it was Seth living here. I'd been rather drunk then, though, so happily for me my recollection was somewhat fuzzy. I pushed the hazy memory to the back of my mind and turned my attention to the cabin's current occupant.

"Take a load off," Cooper said, motioning to the bed. "Want something to eat? I've got plenty of snacks." He opened the fridge to reveal a couple of containers of what looked like home-baked goodies, which was definitely weird. "Oh," he added, seeing my reaction, "I've got a buddy in the kitchen who makes these for me."

Of course he did. I wished I had a buddy in the kitchen who'd make me chocolate chip cookies. I eyed Cooper with renewed interest, wondering if I could convince him to share...

He fished around on his desk and then popped a DVD into the widescreen laptop. I was surprised to see the main menu for *Serendipity*. "I love this movie," he whispered, settling down beside me and taking a bite out of a delicious-looking brownie. "I really believe in fate and destiny."

The sarcastic part of me really wanted to pounce on his girly comment — fate and destiny? Really? — but the romantic part of me appreciated a guy in touch with his feminine emotions. Though I'd probably appreciate it more if he'd offer me some of that brownie...

"I guess I do too," I said, although given my current shite track record with men, I thought maybe it was time to rethink the whole fate thing.

"Hope you're okay after what happened tonight," he asked moments later, looking at me square in the eyes. "It was a really scary experience." He patted my arm reassuringly. My father would have patted my arm in exactly the same manner. Somewhat surprisingly, I found myself thinking that I'd rather not have Cooper treat me quite so platonically...

I answered him truthfully. "I'm fine now that I know Caitlin will be okay. Thanks ever so much for being there. I was a mess. I really appreciated your support."

He just nodded and went back to watching the film. It was quite strange, being there with him in the dark, watching John Cusack and Kate Beckinsale fight over a pair of gloves. I'd felt such electricity between us at the room party before everything got shot to hell, and now I felt nothing coming from him at all. I sneaked a peek at him out of the corner of my eyes, loving how the flickering lights of the screen reflected on his glasses. A lock of hair had fallen down across his forehead, over his eye; I reached out and swept it back, my fingers tingling at the brief contact with his skin. He just smiled at me and kept watching the screen.

It must have been about twenty minutes later that it finally dawned on me he actually wanted to watch the film. In my experience, men invited you to watch a movie and then pounced before the opening credits finished. Cooper apparently wasn't like most men. He was on his third brownie and as far as I could tell was completely engrossed in the story. He showed absolutely no interest in anything else, and to be perfectly honest I was starting to get a little frustrated.

On the bright side, with the second brownie he'd brought out the whole container and plunked it down between us, so at least I was getting my chocolate fix.

I hadn't been sure if I liked him, other than as a generally lovely person, but after the intense events of the evening my emotions were running high. Being alone together, on his bed, watching a romantic movie, was making me more than a little bit frisky. And he seemed oblivious, completely ignoring a perfect opportunity. I reached for a broken piece of brownie, finished it in a few bites, and casually put my hand back down, just touching his. The electricity was back. I smiled to myself and waited for his reaction.

He also reached for another brownie, and then put his hand back down...several inches away from mine. And kept watching the movie.

Arg. A part of me was annoyed, even offended, but the part of me that had recently been royally rogered by two sleazy bed hoppers was actually pretty impressed. I'd started to think that the men on this ship only had one goal, and that was to see how quickly they could get into a girl's pants. Looked like Cooper was one of the good guys...or he wasn't attracted to me. I dismissed that thought immediately. I was in the best shape of my life. A small smile crept across my face; all the time in the sun had finally turned my pasty skin into a pretty golden tan, and before I'd even realised it, the uniform that had started out too tight not only fit perfectly over my slimmed-down hips, but had just reached the point where it was almost too loose. If Seth and Luciano had found me even reasonably attractive weeks and weeks ago, then there was no way Cooper didn't find the new and improved me even a little bit attractive.

While I loved a romantic comedy as much as the next girl,

fatigue was starting to set in; my eyes were starting to droop. I grabbed a pillow and got into a more comfortable position, and the movie gradually started to fade away. I struggled to stay awake, because I didn't really want to be rude and fall asleep in someone else's cabin, but my self-will wasn't a match for the sleep dragging me under. I'd just close my eyes for a few minutes.

When I opened my eyes again, the cabin was illuminated only by the fairy lights, and I was lying properly in bed, with the covers on top of me. Stifling a yawn, I squinted up at the desk, confused. The bright numbers of the digital clock said 06:32. Surely that wasn't right. I pulled my hand out from under the covers and checked the time on my watch. It was right. I had slept there all night!

For a moment, I thought Cooper wasn't even there, until I started to move and realised he was behind me. I twisted around and saw he was fast asleep, too. He'd clearly taken off his glasses to sleep; it was the first time I'd seen him without them, and he had the cutest little boy face. I turned back over and closed my eyes. It was still early; I wanted to get as much sleep as possible before opening the shop.

Then Cooper mumbled something and put his hand on my hip. He moved his thumb in circles; the friction burned me through my clothes. I moved back slightly until my body was millimetres away from his. The energy between us felt hot and intense.

He hadn't shown any interest the night before, but in that moment I knew he was interested. I could feel it. Kind of hard to miss when you've got an aroused man directly behind you; it pressed hard against my bottom, and my stomach lurched in anticipation.

Before I had a chance to second-guess myself, Cooper's arm slid around my waist and pulled me hard against him. I wriggled playfully against him as he kissed my ear, and was rewarded by a hitch in his breathing. My heart raced as warmth pooled between my thighs; Cooper's hand drifted upwards, beneath my shirt, his fingers feather-light over my skin. As he kissed along the curve of my neck, down to my shoulder, his hand worked its way higher, until it cupped around my breast. I swallowed as he found his way into my bra and pinched my already-hard nipple between his fingers. He nibbled on my neck as he played with me, and a soft moan escaped my lips. "Make love to me, Ellie-Belly," he whispered, tugging at me until I rolled over and faced him.

Nobody had ever called me that. It was so cute and intimate, and when he said it I got little butterflies in my stomach. My shirt took up residence on the floor, swiftly followed by my bra; as Cooper kissed his way from my neck to my navel, his right hand stayed busy at my breast while his left found the zipper to my skirt. I would have been happy to return some of the attention, but he seemed entirely focused on me. I couldn't say I objected; I'd recently started to almost expect foreplay. And Cooper was definitely not putting himself first. My skirt and pants joined the rest of my clothes on the floor, and I stopped thinking, far too distracted by the magic his tongue was wielding.

I was glad I wasn't hungover, as I wanted to enjoy and remember every moment. It was hard to believe that when he'd first come aboard I'd not been particularly impressed. And then I'd seen how lovely he was, and how much everyone liked him, and how good he was in a crisis, and had learned about how tragic his romantic life had been... I fancied the pants off him now, and I knew at least part of it was because he was a tragic figure; the tragic, romantic figure was incredibly alluring, and I was deeply affected by the fact that not only had he chosen to share that story with me, he'd also chosen me to help him move on.

Cooper lifted his head, leaving me feeling abruptly bereft, and rolled off the bed. I opened my eyes in time to see him tossing his boxers on top of the rest of his clothes, and couldn't help but stare in surprise.

He was shaved. Not just neatened up, but completely hairless. All off. Totally bald. It might have just been me, but it was a little off-putting. I went in for a wax pretty regularly, and

I knew some of my girlfriends who'd had everything taken off, but I'd always thought the completely hairless look was a little creepy. It looked too much like a little kid. Maybe that was what bothered me about Cooper; he suddenly looked much younger than he had before the boxers came off. And as I stared, a stray thought flitted through my head; if Cooper hadn't even thought about sex for three years because he was so traumatised after the death of his fiancée, why on earth was he still shaved?

Then again, Caitlin was pretty well waxed; she complained it was too hot in the Caribbean otherwise. Maybe it was a Canadian thing.

Cooper returned to the bed, hovering over me on his hands and knees, and leaned down to nuzzle my neck. "Please let me inside you," he groaned, lowering himself until he was just touching me; his skin was so hot he felt like a furnace.

I moaned in reply.

"Oh, by the way, I'm safe," he said, next to my ear. "I was tested years ago, when I was with…her…" he sucked in a big gulp of air, and on the exhale added, "and I haven't had sex since." Then, without waiting for my response, he slid straight in.

I hadn't even thought about safety, which was incredibly unusual for me; normally it was at the front of my mind. His swift movement had surprised me, though; he didn't mess about. I supposed it was only to be expected; he'd been celibate for years. Really, it was amazing—and incredibly thoughtful—that he'd taken as much time on me as he had before turning towards taking care of himself.

He thrust hard, and I arced up to meet him.

"Oh, yeah, you like that?" he asked, biting his own bottom lip with his front teeth. "Uh huh, you like it when I stick it in hard like that?"

I cringed. I'd never gotten into dirty talk, and especially not the way Cooper did it; it was just awkward. I'd tried it out before, with Luciano, and it had been okay, but it would never be high on my list of sexual preferences. Cooper sounded like a terrible, 90s porn star, and very sure of himself for someone who hadn't been with a woman in years.

As soon as I thought it, I felt guilty—here I was judging a lovely guy who'd picked me, of all people, to begin his journey back into intimacy. He was probably nervous and didn't know what to say. I knew how he felt. I was lost for words myself, and anyway we all said embarrassing things—certainly my mouth had got me into trouble more than once.

Reminding myself that Cooper had already focused on making me feel amazing, I pulled myself together; now it was my job to make sure Cooper enjoyed himself. I wanted his first foray back into the world of sex to be one to remember.

With that in mind, I smiled up at him, wound my arms around his neck, and whispered, "I love it."

Chapter Thirteen

Celibacy is overrated.

Really, I didn't know what I'd been thinking when I'd declared myself to be an orgasm-free zone. Surely it wasn't something a sane person would do on a cruise ship. The opportunities for sex were varied and numerous, and to continue denying myself would have been a travesty, really.

I hugged myself in Cooper's bed after he went to have a shower. After a couple of false starts, I had found a man who was more than just a bed buddy and I hadn't even noticed him at first. Maybe that was what made it more real. This time I hadn't been swayed by good looks or a sexy accent. Cooper was just a genuinely nice, good guy, liked by everyone. He was charming, funny, smart, accomplished, and talented. The sex wasn't bad, either. The fact he had waited three years to be with someone and then had chosen me proved he was pretty crazy about me, too. He hadn't even pounced on me at the first opportunity. A gentleman through and through. Definitely a rarity in these parts.

I wondered what the other photographers would say. Caitlin would be ecstatic.

Caitlin. A wave of remorse washed over me for enjoying myself while she was still in hospital. And then I pushed it away. Caitlin was going to be okay, and if there was one thing I knew, it was that she'd want me to be having as much fun as possible. It didn't mean forgetting about her, though; I thought I'd go and see how she was doing later in the morning. If she was doing okay, maybe we could have a rant about the

Brazilian Bitch and her part in landing Caitlin in hospital.

Ugh. The Brazilian Bitch. Just thinking about her made me angry, disrupting my happy buzz about Cooper, and making me angrier still. I blamed her for Caitlin drinking too much; it probably wasn't fair, since Caitlin had had plenty to drink beyond the shots Maria had bought, but it was easier to be cross with Maria than with Caitlin. And she'd even had the nerve to say she was worried about Caitlin! Though if I were fair, I thought Maria had probably been hoping to get Caitlin sacked; I doubted she'd actually intended to send her to hospital. Probably.

The bathroom door opened a crack and I looked up, distracted from my grumpy thoughts. Cooper pushed the door open further and came out into the room, securing a towel around his waist.

"Hey, Ellie," he said, "I've been thinking…" He hesitated. "It's been…" His words trailed off into a heavy silence.

"What?" I stared at him, a sudden knot of anxiety beginning to form in my stomach. His tone of voice made me worried. The optimist in me said that maybe he was just going to say "It's been a pleasure…", but the pessimist told me I was headed for another disappointment.

He looked at the floor. "It's been so long since I lost my fiancée," he said slowly. "I'd almost forgotten what it was like to be intimate with someone."

My heart skipped a little beat. Maybe this wasn't going to be so bad.

"It's just… Well, it just feels strange, that's all." He bit his lip and sighed. "I need to think about things for a while," he said, finally looking up and meeting my eyes. "I'm just a bit confused."

Confused? What did he mean, confused? I stared at him as he shuffled over to the wardrobe and started to dress, wondering if he was just going to ignore me now.

"I've got to do some stuff in the lab," he said over his shoulder. "Can you show yourself out?"

Sure, I could show myself out. It certainly wouldn't be the

first time I'd let myself out of a man's cabin on this ship. Hell, I'd shown myself out of this very cabin before, long before Cooper came aboard. I was a bloody expert at showing myself out of men's cabins.

I slid out of bed, into my now rumpled clothes, and out the door. Cooper never turned around.

I slipped into my cabin and slammed the door behind me; my eyes were starting to burn with tears, and the last thing I wanted was for someone to see me. I think I'd felt like crying more often since starting this supposedly fabulous job than I had done in years. I slumped down onto the bed and closed my eyes. This was fucking ridiculous. How the hell had this happened *again*? He'd jumped me the moment he'd woken up, called me by a pet name, explored every inch of my body...and now he needed to think? Arg. I really wanted to drown myself in alcohol, but with the events of the previous night still vivid in my mind, I thought that might not be the best idea. Anyway, here I was thinking of me when I ought to see how Caitlin was doing.

I searched around on the desk for Gabriel's number and then called to ask if he'd heard from Caitlin.

"She's here, and fast asleep," Gabriel said. "She'll be fine, but the doc said she'd need to rest today."

"Please give her my love," I said, glad that my roomie was okay. I was actually rather surprised Gabriel had shown genuine care for her. I smiled; in spite of the mess I'd just landed myself in with Cooper, at least there was some good news.

I stared at the phone for a while, thinking. Booze wasn't an option. That left me with tea, and as an Englishwoman born and bred, if there was one thing I knew, it was that a cup of tea could solve almost anything. And I also knew of one other person on this ship who almost certainly knew the same— Jock.

I freshened up and changed into shorts and a t-shirt, then navigated my way through the ship to Jock's cabin. As I banged on the door, it occurred to me that maybe I should have called first. He might not be there. Or he might have met a girl and stayed the night in her cabin. Stranger things had happened on the ship; I was certainly proof of that. Worse still, Jock might be *in* there with a girl. That would be horrifically embarrassing. And upsetting, though I wasn't sure why.

Feeling I'd waited long enough, and concerned I might be overstepping the mark, I withdrew my hand and started to creep away from the door.

At that moment, the door flew open to reveal Jock, in a crumpled t-shirt and stripey boxer shorts, hair askew, bleary eyes only half-open. "Ellie?" he said, his voice thick with sleep. "What's up, lass? You okay?" He squinted at me, looked quite worried.

Just the concerned tone of his voice was enough to make me crumble. He caught me as I stumbled forward, and then wrapped his arms around me. "You want to talk about it?" he asked. His hand moved gently up and down my back in a soothing motion; I felt like a little girl again, curled up on my mother's lap while she made whatever was wrong go away. Not that Jock reminded me of my mum, of course. That would be weird. Jock pulled back far enough to look at my face and then let go of me. "Come on in, lass."

"I'm so sorry to wake you up so early, Jock," I said as I walked into the tiny space. My eyes darted about quickly; no visitors, female or otherwise, unless they were hiding in the loo.

A bartender on a cruise ship who actually slept alone. Would wonders never cease.

Jock gestured to his guest chair and I plonked myself down with a loud huff. He flicked on the kettle and sat down on the edge of his bed, watching me patiently.

I took a deep breath. "I... You see... Cooper..." I couldn't get the words out.

"Ah," he said. The corner of his mouth twitched downwards. "I think I can guess the story. Cooper sweet-talk you into sleeping with him, lass?"

I nodded and looked down. Was it that obvious?

The kettle clicked off and Jock stood. "How do you take your tea?" he inquired, setting two mugs on the desk and dropping teabags in.

Oh, excellent. I knew Jock would know to ply me with tea. "Just a splash of milk, please," I said. I watched him prepare the tea; the familiar rhythms immediately made me feel more relaxed. He handed me a cup and sat back down on the bunk. I wrapped my hands around the comforting warmth and breathed in the steam gratefully.

"Ellie," he said, leaning forward, "this is my third contract, and I've seen that face a million times. I know everybody says life on ships moves four times faster than real life, but sometimes I think it's even more." He looked down at his tea and sighed. "People meet. They fall into bed. Sometimes they fall in love. Mostly they fall right back out of both." He met my eyes and smiled crookedly. "That's another reason I mostly just keep to myself these days." An almost imperceptible sigh escaped his lips. Almost. I could hear the wistful sadness, and wondered what heartbreaks he'd endured. I didn't ask. If he wanted to tell me, he would.

We sat in silence for a few minutes. I sipped at my tea and closed my eyes, pretending that everything was okay. Jock was such a comfortable person to be around. He didn't probe or ask too many questions or give too much advice, and though I always got the feeling that he knew exactly what was going on in my life and how much I was screwing up, I never felt like he was judging me. Which was nice. He was just there in case I needed to talk. And talk I did.

"I've been so stupid," I said miserably. "I have the bloody worst taste in men—they're all cheating bastards who suck me into believing they're perfect and lovely and everything I've ever wanted, and then bam! The truth comes out and I end up alone and crying and wondering why I never seem to learn." I paused for breath and peeked at Jock, wondering if he'd realised what he'd got himself into and was preparing to run. Somewhat to my surprise, he seemed genuinely interested in what I was saying, and showed no sign of preparing to bolt—

then again, I'd been wrong about men before, so what did I know?

"I wouldn't say you've been stupid," he said gently. "Maybe a bit naïve. But it's easy to get swept up in ship life."

"It's all Dan's fault," I wailed.

"Dan?" he asked.

"Yes," I said. "My no-good, rotten, cheating ex-fiancé. The one who told me I was fat and boring and responsible for all of the passion going out of our relationship."

An unreadable expression had settled over Jock's face. "I don't think I knew you'd been engaged."

"I didn't want it to be a thing," I explained. "I didn't want to be the girl who'd just been brutally pitched out of a relationship that I thought was heading towards a lifetime of love and happiness and two and a half kids." I looked down into my cup and discovered I was out of tea. "So instead I became the girl everyone thinks is a slag."

Jock flinched slightly and stood up. He plucked my mug from my fingers and flicked the kettle on again. "Sounds to me like you escaped what would have ended up being a bleak and loveless future. I think you were lucky, there."

"I guess," I said. "Except then I just seem to keep sleeping with blokes that I think are going to be amazing, just like I thought Dan was going to be amazing, and then they turn out to be as full of shit as Dan was."

"I think you're punishing yourself for something that wasn't your fault," Jock said, handing me a new cup of tea and sitting back down. "I think you're ending up with blokes who don't respect you because you're afraid of getting into something serious like you did with Dan and then having it all go tits up. And it hurts, but it's easier than trying something with someone who really does respect and love you and always being afraid that they'll do exactly what Dan did in the end, too."

Good grief. Who needed a therapist when you had a bartender?

I gulped down half of my tea and burst out, "But the thing

is, I thought this thing with Cooper was really going to be the real thing! He was so lovely, and he has *such* a tragic past, and everyone likes him—" I hesitated, remembering that Jock had never seemed to like Cooper. Come to think of it, actually, Jock hadn't been all that keen on Seth, either. I couldn't remember what he'd thought of Luciano.

"Ah, yes," Jock said. "*Such* a tragic past. Tragic pasts are like catnip to women."

"What is *that* supposed to mean?"

He hesitated, and then said, "Nothing. Go on—I didn't mean to interrupt you."

"The thing is," I continued, "it's not just that his fiancée died, you know. He's been celibate for three years, because he couldn't bear to just move on and forget about her." I was talking too fast, but I was so hopeful that Jock would understand and would agree with me that I couldn't keep the words from tumbling out of my mouth. "Her name was Amanda, and he loved her so much that he's blocked out all sexual and romantic possibilities since she died. So you see, the fact that he turned to me was so important—he wanted me to help him move on, to begin living again."

"That's a mighty interesting story, lass," Jock said. He swilled the last of his tea around in his mug, his brow furrowed. "'Tis just a pity I've heard variations on it for years."

"What do you mean?"

"Men like Cooper—they know that a sob story is almost guaranteed to catch a woman's attention. Playing hard to get because of that sob story, well, that just makes the woman feel like she's something special when he finally succumbs, instead of feeling like she's been taken advantage of. And she's been taken advantage of."

"Don't be ridiculous," I said, but there wasn't much force behind the words.

He looked at me, his eyes sad. "Ellie, men like Cooper tell the same story over and over and over again because they know that they'll be able to get women to sleep with them. It's an ugly trick used by far too many men. I'm sorry, lass, but you've been taken in."

It all sounded so logical the way Jock put it, but the way I saw it, there was one common denominator in all of these failed relationships, and that was me. There had to be something wrong with *me*. After weeks and weeks aboard the ship, I knew it wasn't my body; I'd shed all of that extra weight that Dan had so disliked and had acquired a pretty tan. All of the time in the sun had lightened my hair, and I *knew* I looked good. So it had to be something else. Maybe I jumped into bed with people too quickly. No, I *knew* I jumped into bed with people too quickly; I never had a chance to really get their measure. And I knew that that was how most people on board lived, but maybe I just wasn't equipped for the moral-free lifestyle.

And maybe I was just too pushy, expecting too much too soon. I thought maybe things had just moved too quickly for Cooper; between his tragic past and the speed with which our relationship had progressed, I wouldn't be surprised if he'd been overwhelmed with emotion. And guilt.

"I should probably just give Cooper some time, right?" I asked Jock.

"I don't know, lass," he said. That unreadable expression was back on his face. "Not sure I'm the best person to ask; I've not been in the dating game for ages." He laughed. "Even when I was, I'm not sure I ever had a clue what I was doing!" He shrugged. "I guess the only thing I can say is that I've always figured you should just be yourself when it comes to dating. I think the right person will love you as you are."

Maybe so, but I still felt like there was something I could have or should have done differently. I looked down at my tea, wishing the answers were at the bottom of the mug. They weren't, but I kept hoping.

Several hours later, I dragged myself out of Jock's cabin and up to the Pic Stop. I could have quite happily stayed with Jock all day; we'd talked about holidays and our families, our favourite books and our favourite movies, and when I'd realised I needed to leave we'd been in the middle of a conversation about food.

My shift was incredibly dull, and by the time I closed up I had a splitting headache. I was looking forward to crawling into bed. Not that it took much to convince me to avoid the crew bar; I wasn't in the mood for playing nice, and the last thing I wanted was to run into Cooper before I figured out what I wanted to do.

When you're feeling rejected and depressed, there's a kind of satisfaction in putting on your granny pyjamas and going to bed early. A brief phone call from Caitlin assured me she was fine and that Gabriel was taking good care of her. I was secretly a little relieved, as I needed the time alone.

"Justin won't put me through disciplinary action, dude," Caitlin said, sounding extremely relieved. "He was actually kind of sweet, like he was actually worried, you know? I told him about the bulimia and everything, and he's going to watch over me more from now on. Not too closely, I hope." She exhaled loudly over the phone.

That was certainly good news. When I hung up, she was on her way to bed with Gabriel; despite everything, it seemed like they were pretty well suited after all.

I, on the other hand, was far from happy. Cooper had seemed so perfect. I went over everything he'd said to me over the past few weeks. There'd been the friendly banter, the genuine conversation, and then the flirty remarks. He'd confided in me about his fiancée, told me about his struggles with moving on...and as our closeness grew, so did the attraction. It had all seemed so perfect, so real.

I had to admit that I'd chosen to ignore the part of me that felt his story might not have been one hundred per cent true. I hated to think it, but maybe Jock was right. I mean, he was a very charismatic guy, so much so that it was almost surprising. He had that nerdy, floppy-haired, unassuming look. Maybe that was how he drew them in?

Even just *thinking* it made me feel bad. Nobody would lie about that sort of thing. Jock had to be wrong. I was just upset about Cooper wanting distance, and regretful that I'd done too much, too soon. Again. I'd read a lot about guys getting freaked out when they fell for someone too quickly, and I was sure that was what had happened here.

I'd just back off and let him come to me. Show him I wasn't pushing things. If you love someone, set them free, and all that. I thought back briefly to the golden canary we'd kept at home for years. He had his wings clipped and all, but still managed to disappear forever the day I let him out of his cage with my bedroom window open. Bad example, I thought with a shudder.

I hadn't known Cooper long enough to really indulge in a good cry, but I still felt sad as I lay on my bunk, thinking back over the past weeks. And stupid. When had everything become so fucked up?

It had all started with Dan, really. Why the hell had we fallen apart so badly? We used to have so much in common. Despite our ups and downs, I'd always felt as though we were best mates. Friends forever. My nan used to say that the best foundation for a happy, lasting marriage was friendship. Sorry, Nan, but that had been complete bollocks. Dan had pretty much rejected me as soon as something more exciting came along, leaving me fragile and vulnerable and wildly insecure. Was it any wonder I'd fallen into Seth's arms, and bed, the moment I arrived on board the ship? And when that failed, that I'd turned to Luciano?

I thought Cooper had been my turning point, but his unexpected rejection was just so deflating, and the things I thought I knew started to get scrambled and I realised I really had no idea what I was thinking anymore. My head started to spin with thoughts of them all, and how much I had failed, and I became more and more depressed. Hot tears welled up in my eyes, and one or two sneakily escaped to slide down my cheek onto the pillow.

I didn't want to be the girl that cried over boys. I wanted to be the one who didn't care and who rolled with the punches. In some ways, I was incredibly jealous of Caitlin. Obviously this recent hospital trip had shown us all that her life wasn't quite as breezy as everyone thought, but all the same, I envied her ability to bounce back from relationship failures. Cruise ships were supposed to be fun, but it was hard to feel joyful when you felt completely rubbish. Deciding I was allowed to wallow, at least a little, I pulled up Coldplay, Adele, and some old school Tracey Chapman on my phone and let my melancholy mood deepen.

The real problem was that however much I wanted to live a carefree life and pursue my love of photography, I knew I didn't want to be alone. And I didn't really want to let Cooper go so quickly. The situation would require careful handling, though, and I fell into a much-needed slumber with thoughts of getting Cooper back by rejecting him.

"That'll do the trick," I mumbled to myself as I drifted off. I was determined to put my own rejection plan into action first thing in the morning.

I was dragged from sleep sometime later by a rap on the door. I opened my eyes and squinted at the clock; I'd been asleep for several hours.

"Ellie-belly," came the distinctive sound of Cooper's voice. I sat up straight, staring at the door. "Please let me in. I have to talk to you." I experienced a brief moment of confusion, unsure if I was awake or dreaming. "Ellie!"

I scrambled out of bed, my legs tangling in the blankets, and stumbled to the door. I had barely opened it when Cooper slid inside, kicked the door shut, and pushed me up against the wall with a rush of energy and passion.

He kissed me fervently, his teeth nipping at my bottom lip. His breathing was so loud that the sound reverberated through my head like a freight train. He reeked of alcohol and was more than a bit unsteady on his feet, something that became very obvious as he tried to lift me up and manoeuvre my legs around his waist. I faltered and landed in an awkward position with one foot up and one foot down. Cooper barely noticed; he just pressed me further against the wall, rubbing himself against me and kissing me with such desperation my lips started to bruise.

"I thought you wanted to think about things?" I whispered into his ear.

"This *is* me thinking about it," he replied. "I still don't know what I want."

His words stopped me cold. Though my body wanted to arch towards him, I stiffened up and turned my head away from his hungry mouth. I placed my hands on his chest and pushed him away.

It was such a confusing moment. I had been wondering how to get him back, wanting him to want me, and now he did. Problem solved, right? Except he was drunk, and I couldn't help but wonder if maybe he didn't actually want me after all, if I was just a convenient body. How could his words say one thing when his body clearly said another? I knew if I was going to fix things, I had to let him know that his uncertainty wasn't going to wash with me.

I took a deep breath and said, "Cooper, I think you should go." I briefly caught his eye and then looked down at the floor. "We can talk about this in the morning." I slid away from the wall and opened the door.

He shot me a sad, sad look that just about did me in; I was a sucker for puppy-dog eyes. As he placed his hand on the door handle, he asked, "Are you sure? I thought this was what you wanted."

"I do. I did. I...don't know." The multitude of smashing one-liners I'd conjured up hours earlier all escaped me in my moment of need.

After Cooper slunk out, I put my ear up to the door to listen to his departure. I waited for his cabin door to open and slam shut, but it didn't. I waited a minute or two to make sure the coast was clear and then opened the door a crack. I peeked through, scoping out the scene. Cooper was nowhere to be seen; the corridor was empty. Probably he'd gone back to the crew bar. I liked to think that he needed to drown his rejection sorrows.

Following Cooper's visit, sleep was impossible. I tossed and turned, wondering if I should just have gone with it, impressed him with my inventive moves, and driven him crazy with my sexy, irresistible, and tigress-like sexual power. Or something. Still, while hindsight was fantastic, it didn't solve any of my problems, and so I resigned myself to a sleepless night listening to further sad music and planning my next course of action.

The morning called for double espresso and a girly-chat with Caitlin, who'd reappeared at the cabin in the early hours. I'd wondered if I should tell her I thought Maria might have purposefully plied her with drinks in an attempt to get her sacked, which was my deduction from her actions on the night in question, but had ultimately decided against it. Caitlin didn't need more things to worry about, and I needed to focus on my plan to get Cooper back. I thought playing hard to get and making him jealous might do the trick.

Caitlin's response to the story was to emphatically declare, "Motherfucker." She settled in for a planning session, adding, "We're going to get him to notice you again. He doesn't know who he's messing with."

I opted not to go ashore with Caitlin in Barbados, deciding instead to catch up on my tanning upstairs in the private, crew-only sunbaking area at the back of the ship. I knew Cooper would be on board for the day; he was on a daytime shift, printing photos, and therefore had no time for onshore frolicking. My theory was simple: if he happened to stroll by the crew sundeck and see me flirting with an officer or two, then so be it. There were always plenty of men around, and with a ridiculously high male-to-female ratio, the very fact of being female was guaranteed to get me some attention.

The smorgasbord of men sunning themselves on the top deck certainly didn't disappoint. It was still early, but mirrored sunglasses, tiny swimwear, and coconut-scented body oil were in plentiful supply, as were washboard stomachs and blonde tufts of chest hair. Testosterone hung heavy in the air. Most of my friends back in the UK would have started hyperventilating at the choices surrounding them, but they were only so much window-dressing to me. I was keeping an eye out for a slightly tubby Canadian.

I found a spot amidst testosterone-filled sailors and set up my deck chair, towel, and iPod. Just before the moment of disrobing to my modest one-piece, I felt a sharp stab of panic about exposing my body to these golden gods, and then remembered that I wasn't the same pasty, fleshy girl I'd been when I first come aboard. No, I was Ellie, golden sex goddess. Or at least I was pretending to be. So, with a deep breath, I shed my excess clothing and settled down on the deck chair. As soon as my bottom hit the chair, it was on. The surreptitious glances I'd noticed when I'd first appeared had become much more blatant stares, and by the time I'd listened to three songs through my headphones, I'd had one guy ask me if he could borrow sunscreen, another offer me a bottle of water, and a third go straight in for the kill, introducing himself as Bernard in a very Americanised Norwegian accent. Without waiting for me to reply in kind, he plunked himself down on the neighbouring deck chair and proceeded to pump me for information: name, rank, serial number... Okay, so it wasn't quite that bad, but I did feel a bit like I was being interrogated.

He seemed pleased when he discovered I'd only been working in the world of cruise lines for a couple of months. With a tell-tale glint in his eyes, he said, "I could show you around."

I restrained myself from laughing in his face. I imagined he could, although I was quite sure it would only involve showing me around his sleeping quarters.

It wasn't at all why I was there, but it was difficult not to feel flattered. I looked around the deck, my eyes falling on pretty, slim, tanned girls everywhere, and I suddenly realised that I was one of them. I sneaked a peek at my body; maybe I wasn't as stunning as some of them, but I could hold my own. And that was a nice realisation.

"Yes, I have two stripes," Bernard said, puffing out his

chest and dragging my attention back to him. As he continued talking about himself, and how important he was on the ship, I stifled a yawn and stole surreptitious glances around the deck for Cooper. Lordy, Bernard was boring.

"So, Ellen…"

"Ellie," I corrected him.

"Right, Ellie," he said, rolling his eyes. I got the impression that my name was really not of much importance, which didn't bode well for any woman he attempted to draw into conversation. As I was really only using him as a jealousy tactic, it didn't matter much to me if he knew my name or not. "As I was saying," he continued, "now it's really difficult to be at home on my vacation, because I don't like doing my own washing and cooking." He looked very sorry for himself. I didn't even feel all that bad for not paying much attention; anyone who bemoans living a normal life has got to be a bit of a douche. Probably he thought all women were good for was cooking, cleaning, and sex. Real catch, this one.

"It sucks to be you," I said. He completely missed the sarcasm in my voice, and launched into the details of his gym routine. I was just contemplating ways to get rid of him when movement caught the corner of my eye and Cooper appeared on the sundeck.

"Hi, Cooper!" called a stunning blonde on a nearby sun-lounger. Well. Cooper's charms were definitely far-reaching.

He ambled over to her group of friends and they all exchanged cheek kisses. A spare chair was produced, a beach towel arranged, and a cold drink thrust into his hand before he'd been there two minutes. I watched in stupefied silence as the girls practically tripped over themselves offering to rub sunscreen on his back. Cooper took it all in stride; he looked happy and seemed unflustered by all the attention.

It wasn't until he was settling back into his sun lounge, about to pull his hat over his eyes, that he finally noticed me. He took a double take and sat up a bit, half-raising his hand in greeting.

I gave him a completely uninterested wave in return,

suppressing the urge to wave wildly and beckon him to come over, and turned back to Bernard. I giggled loudly in response to the workout story he was now telling, and leaned over to touch his arm flirtatiously. He probably thought I was crazy, given I'd been bored out of my mind a minute before, but the sudden show of interest must have been quite the aphrodisiac. He immediately started speaking at a million miles an hour, prattling on about bicep curls and his paleo diet and intermittently showering me with half-baked compliments. Definitely the first time I'd ever been compared to a piece of gym equipment. On the bright side, at least I made his pulse rise? And then, of course, to top off the flirtatious tableau I'd set up, he started throwing in some accidental knee grazes. I tried my best to give him my full attention, despite the fact my interest was pretty much nil, and didn't cast even the tiniest glance at Cooper.

When I eventually peeked in Cooper's direction, he was staring straight at me, his face frozen into an angry mask. What was that terrible expression my father always used? "Treat 'em mean, keep 'em keen," he used to say. Dad had used it to ensure I never got too close to any potential boyfriends, but I thought the tactic would work well here.

I gazed at Bernard, and wondered how mean I could get.

Chapter Fourteen

The fake tête-á-tête with Bernard carried on longer than I'd anticipated, which was unfortunate seeing as I was bored after about five minutes. After an hour of listening to his stories of bravado and then being dragged around his group of friends, I agreed to meet up in the officers' bar after work. I then gratefully escaped, without so much as a backward glance at Cooper, and hid in my cabin until it was time to go to work. For once, I wished work would last forever; I had to go meet up with Bernard once I closed up, and I'd have been much happier if I could have gone back to the cabin and snuggled up with chocolate and a rom-com.

I'd only been to the officers' bar once, weeks earlier with Caitlin, and I was struck by how different the atmosphere was. It was so much quieter than the crew bar; the music wasn't ear-splitting, which meant people weren't trying to shout over the top of it. Since the dance floor was miniscule, there wasn't anyone on it; the bar's occupants were well-supplied with drink, but seemed content to carry on quiet conversation.

Bernard saw me come in and waved me over. I joined him, taking care to stay slightly out of reach; I had a bad feeling that if I seemed at all encouraging that I might spend the entire evening dodging his advances. I went with the classic *I'm English and we don't really do affection* ploy, which seemed to work its magic once I managed to avoid an attempted hug.

"Ellie, I bought you a drink!" he exclaimed loudly, causing more than one head to turn our way. "I hope you like vodka," he added, beaming at me excitedly.

Hooray, vodka. I'd avoided vodka since a particularly drunken night out in second year, when I'd got completely pissed, blacked out, woke up the next morning on my floor, and then spent the entire day hanging my head over the toilet. Vodka had promptly gone on my 'never again' list. Unfortunately for me, my parents had taught me to be gracious, so I smiled at Bernard and sipped gingerly at the shot glass he'd given me.

"Not like that!" he said. He slammed down his own drink. "Skoll!" he said, indicating I should do the same. I stared at the shot glass, pasted a smile on my face, and went for broke. The clear liquid felt like fire in my throat—I squeezed my eyes shut and shook my head vigorously. Ugh. No sooner had I quaffed the shot than Bernard thrust another into my hand. Sensing I was doomed, I knocked it back as well. It went down so quickly, I basically inhaled it, and my eyes started watering.

I had no interest in Bernard, his friends, or the bar; the whole point of going through this stupid rigmarole was the hope that Cooper would turn up, see me having fun with other men, and become insanely jealous.

The thought had just crossed my mind when Cooper appeared at the door, closely followed by Caitlin and Gabriel. A feeling of relief flooded through my body; hooray, backup! And Cooper. Even better. Caitlin skipped across the room and flung her arms around me. Her face buried in my hair, she whispered "Oh, God, roomie, I didn't realise you were with these guys. I fucked two of them in a threesome the other week."

"Do you want to leave?" I asked, even though it would pass over a perfect opportunity to make Cooper jealous.

She tossed her head, grabbed the nearest drink, and threw it back. So much for being bothered either by her former lovers or by her recent near-death experience. It didn't keep me from worrying, though, and when Gabriel appeared with a can of lemonade, I was relieved.

Caitlin rolled her eyes and whispered in my ear, "Doctor's orders. I've got a super sore throat today anyway."

Behind them, Cooper was standing like a bit of a gooseberry, clearly ill at ease and unsure how to break into the group. I fought my instinct to pull him into the festivities and make him feel comfortable. After all, my goal was to make him jealous. I couldn't crumble at the first opportunity.

Caitlin sized up the situation straightaway and immediately introduced Gabriel and Cooper around the group, making a special point of introducing Cooper to Bernard.

"This is the guy who is totally into Ellie," she said, pretending to be completely oblivious.

Cooper's face clouded over with a stormy expression. "Right," he said curtly. "Yeah. Good to meet you, man." He grabbed Bernard's hand so tightly that his knuckles went white.

Bernard smiled cheerfully and withdrew his hand. Slapping Cooper on the back, he said, "Drink up, the vodka is on me." I could almost hear Cooper's teeth grinding.

I did a little mental happy dance; I hadn't expected it to work so quickly. Everything was going according to plan! I swung around to the bar to order drinks for the first drinking game, trying to keep the smile off my face, and came face-to-face with Jock. He did not look happy.

"Good evening, Ellie," he said, his voice flat and clipped. "Enjoying your evening?"

Confused by his presence in the officers' bar, and disturbed by his tone, I stood and stared at him before spluttering and trying to speak. "Jock—is everything okay? What—" I stumbled over my words and then managed, "What are you doing here? I mean, in the officers' bar." I came out with several more unintelligible sounds and finally just shut up, watching Jock worriedly. There was something wrong; his face was completely devoid of the warmth that usually filled it when I talked to him.

"I'm filling in for the usual bartender," he said shortly, picking up a glass from under the counter and starting to polish it.

"But are you okay? You seem…" I tried to find a word and failed. "You don't seem like yourself," I finally said.

Jock shrugged. "Just not sure what game you're playing," he said.

"Game?" I was completely confused.

He jerked his chin in Bernard's direction.

"You said to move on from Cooper," I retorted. "What makes you think that's not what I'm doing?"

He raised an eyebrow. "Guess I'm just a wee bit confused at the way you're going about things," he said. "Thought our conversation today might have given you a few things to think about."

Now I was just completely confused. "It did," I said, "but…"

"Seems to me you're just making the same fool mistakes you've been making all along." His harsh tone cut deep, and I could feel tears pricking at my eyes. Jock was one of the few people on this ship I'd really felt I could count on, who I thought really cared about me, and I'd never thought he would have said anything unkind. And anyway, hadn't he been the one who'd said something about having fun? Not taking things too seriously? Or was it something about being true to myself?

"Look," I said, "it's not at all what it looks like, I promise. It's really just—"

"Tell it to someone else, Ellie," he said, and I noticed that he was still polishing that same damn glass. "I have work to do." He turned away and finally put the glass down, a smile appearing on his face as he addressed an officer further down the bar.

I stood staring at his back, feeling oddly bereft. I wasn't sure I even knew what had just happened, but I suddenly felt like this whole make-Cooper-jealous thing was just a bit silly. But before I had a chance to dwell on that, Caitlin bounded up to the bar to find out what was taking me so long.

"Jock's being weird tonight," I said.

Caitlin's eyes flicked from me to him and back again, and then she leaned against the counter, directing a million-watt smile at the other bartender working that night. "Get us some vodka shots, will you, handsome?" His face turned red and he practically tripped over his own feet to pour the vodka. Grinning, she turned to face me and leaned back, her elbows on the counter. "You gonna stand there, dude, or you gonna get in on that drinking game?" Shrugging, I trotted across the room to join the boys, Caitlin right behind me with the shots. I figured we could work out Jock's problem later. Right now, I had bigger problems: Cooper. Caitlin had bought a shot for everyone at the table, and was ready to play.

She settled down between me and Gabriel and draped her legs over his lap. "Let's play 'I have never…'"

"I'll start," Bernard said eagerly, vodka shot in hand. "I have never…slept with an English girl." He grinned, looking directly at me.

Well. That was…great. Despite my genuine lack of interest in him, I felt my cheeks burn and couldn't help the embarrassed smile that spread across my face. To be fair, actually, the lack of interest probably made the embarrassment worse; if I'd liked him, I might have been able to giggle and play to it. Oh well…

Turned out the group were pretty lacking in the sleeping with English girls department; only a couple of them slammed down a shot, including Caitlin. Somehow that didn't surprise me. I snuck a look at Cooper, in time to see him knock the vodka back; the expression on his face told me he was *not* happy, and as soon as the round had been downed, he got up and stalked towards the bar. I wasn't sure whether to feel worried or victorious. I'd never been good at playing hard to get; my face was always an open book, and I was always so worried about hurting people's feelings.

I glanced over at the bar to see if Cooper was on his way back and saw him in heated conversation with Jock. The two of them looked furious, and I was a little concerned that they might come to blows—but before I could even hope to intervene, Cooper stormed out the door.

My stomach twisted into a thousand knots. I had gone too far. I turned to Caitlin, but she was already looking at the door Cooper had just exited. She smiled broadly and gave me two thumbs up. "It's working, roomie," she said, dropping her head back until it rested on my shoulder. I narrowed my eyes, but she only responded with, "Trust me."

I swallowed hard and took a deep breath. Despite my lifelong aversion to people who asked me to trust them, I knew Caitlin had my best interests at heart. And seeing as she was a hell of a lot more experienced than me at the whole dating thing, I had to believe it would work as planned.

The next half an hour or so crawled by. Bernard brushed up against me constantly and continually bent down to whisper flirtatious statements in my ear; maintaining a pleasant smile when he was breathing stale coffee and vodka fumes in my face was difficult. With Cooper gone, it seemed pointless to continue the charade, but Caitlin wouldn't let me go.

"He'll be back," she said knowingly. "He'll be back…"

I didn't know if she was a genius or psychic, because it wasn't long before Cooper came back through the door…with Maria in tow. Caitlin and I looked at each other in shock. Shit. This wasn't part of the plan. Why Maria, of all people? The only thing I could think of was that he planned to make me jealous in return by using my absolute least favourite person on board.

Cooper got straight to the point: "Bernard, this is my colleague, Maria," he said, shoving Maria towards the tall Norwegian. "I think you two will like each other."

Bernard was drunk, but at least he proved himself slightly less fickle than certain other men I could name; he grabbed me around the waist and pulled me towards him, saying, "Thanks, man, but I am already spoken for."

I plastered a smile on my face and tried to look like my body wasn't stiff in his embrace. I wasn't sure what was happening, exactly; did Cooper bringing Maria in to throw at Bernard mean that he really did like me? Or was it just another layer in the game? Actually, more urgently: had Bernard really just rejected the gorgeous Maria for me? Was he out of his mind? Or was my new look even better than I'd thought? Arg.

I didn't have time to react to the whole situation, though,

because Cooper was already taking the lead…just not the one I wanted.

"I'm tired," he snapped. "See you guys in the morning." He shot me a look of pure venom and spun on his heels, stalking out the door again.

I desperately wanted to run after him, but one look at Caitlin kept me in my seat. Cooper quickly left my mind when I realised that Maria had slid into a seat next to Gabriel and was talking over him to Caitlin, their faces inches apart. Horrified by the idea that Maria might be unleashing her poison on Caitlin directly, I pulled free of Bernard and moved towards them, just in time to hear Maria's words.

"I really did not know you would get so sick, Caitlin," she said, and from what I could hear she sounded genuinely apologetic. "I am so sorry. I thought you might get into trouble from the staff captain, like I did when you and I partied my first week on board…" She breathed in and said, somewhat shakily, "I never thought your life might be in danger. I am so sorry."

Well, damn. Maria was actually being apologetic, which meant I couldn't justifiably give her shit for putting Caitlin in danger. It was so much easier when Maria was just pure evil; I hated to think that she might not be horrible through and through after all.

Unable to hold my tongue, I interrupted, saying, "Well, it was a really stupid thing to do, Maria." Maybe not the greatest thing, since I was probably asking for trouble, but I couldn't let her get off scot-free. Caitlin, however, proved to be far more than forgiving than me.

"Don't worry about it, dude," she said, and then turned a sweet smile on Maria. "Apology accepted. I know how it is." That out of the way, she returned her attention to me and said, "You wanna come up to the cabin with me for a while? My throat is killing me right now."

"Sure," I said, grateful for an excuse to leave at last. "Sorry, Bernard, must go. Caitlin's not feeling well."

We escaped before Bernard had a chance to protest, leaving

Gabriel to console him and drown his sorrows with drinking games. Back in our cabin, Caitlin whined as she searched through cupboards and drawers for a throat cure. "The doctor told me it's tonsillitis and put me on antibiotics, but they're doing fuck-all good. My throat feels like it's lined with sandpaper." She swallowed and winced painfully. "It hurts to swallow." She laughed and added, "Yeah, I know, me not being able to swallow is going to place a massive dent in my love life." We both laughed, and then she groaned. "Oh, it hurts to laugh. Stoppit!"

Knocking on the door interrupted our merry-making, and when Caitlin flung open the door we found Nick on the other side.

"Where have you bitches been?" he demanded. He pushed past Caitlin and flopped down on the bottom bunk. "Have you been avoiding me?" he wailed dramatically. "I've missed you!"

"We are far from avoiding you, my love," I said as Caitlin shut the door and came back in. "We promise you plenty of juicy gossip. Especially about this one," I added, jabbing my thumb in Caitlin's direction.

It was time for a girly pow-wow and a cup of tea. I was wary of introducing alcohol into social situations now that Caitlin was supposed to be off the wagon. Or was it on? I could never remember. Well, bugger it in any case; tea was the drink of the day. I had an excellent stash of tea tucked away, so I flicked on the kettle and set out three mugs.

"Well, I'll start," Nick said, swinging himself into an upright position and sitting cross-legged. "You know how I was basically a shoo-in for that dance captain position? My sneaky, lying, backstabbing roommate only went and fucking got the job himself! He's already moved out of the cabin into his fancy new double bed."

We both gasped in shock.

"What the fuck is that fucking asshole up to?" demanded Caitlin.

"I know, right?" said Nick. His face crumpled. "Without that job, I'll have even less money for New York. I've already missed out on a cheap apartment, and now I'm going to have to beg for my parents' help. It's just getting worse and worse." He buried his face in his hands and added in a muffled voice, "The best I'll be able to afford now is a crack house over an air shaft." He paused, and then lifted his head to look at me with gloomy eyes. "And I don't even like crack."

"Why don't you just ask your parents for the money?" Caitlin asked. "I thought they were super rich?"

"Well, yes," Nick said, "but they don't support my dancing, and are definitely not keen on the New York idea. They've never even seen me dance."

"So invite them on board for a week," she said cheerfully. "Let them see you dance and sweet-talk them into financing your New York dream."

Nick didn't reply, but the expression on his face said he was thinking about it. "But how could I afford to pay for their cruise?" he said at last. "It would be all the money I have. No point in spending everything I've got if I'm not going to get anything out of it."

Caitlin shook her head and waved his protests away. "No, silly, they could stay in your cabin. The cruise line will let them visit for something like 10% of the normal price."

Nick jumped to his feet excitedly, narrowly missing bashing his head on the top bunk. "I'd totally forgotten about that!" he cried. Then, like a balloon on a hot August day, Nick deflated before our eyes and collapsed in a heap on the floor. "I can't bring my parents on board," he said miserably. "They don't know I'm gay. I've never dared bring it up—they'll never accept it. At home I can hide it more easily, but I always get my hair bleached on the way to a contract…"

"They have actually *met* you, haven't they?" asked Caitlin incredulously. "How could they not know?"

I thought about defending Nick's manhood, but that would have been a bit pointless. Seriously, Nick really was the gayest of all gay men.

"I'm really quite masculine at home, you know," he said, dabbing at the corner of his eyes with a lace handkerchief he'd just produced from his pocket. He saw our disbelieving faces and insisted, "I really am! I know you girls won't understand, but this has been one big ordeal my whole life. My parents are, well...traditional. They're Filipino-American and built themselves up from nothing. I was meant to grow up and take over the business, but then I ended up wanting to dance and they were so disappointed in me. We've fought about it *so* many times. They finally let me work on ships, to 'let me get it out of my system'—though by that point I was legally an adult and they could hardly stop me anymore. They've never even seen me dance." He looked desolate. "I've done lessons for years, and practised until my feet bled, and they never turned up to a single performance!"

Caitlin and I both sat in silence. I had no idea what to say, and I didn't think Caitlin did, either. Nick was usually so buoyant and carefree; I'd never seen him so emotional before.

"But Nick, maybe if they saw you dance...?" I thought about my parents; they didn't always fully agree with my decisions, but they always supported me, no matter what. I'd never really thought about how lucky I was.

"I know, Ellie," he said, "but they expect me to work in their business, and take over when they retire. It's what they've always wanted. They don't have a *clue* that I'm gay," he added. "I've never been able to tell them. When Elton John came out of the closet, my parents didn't believe it—I mean, you think *I'm* camp! And when they finally realised it was true, they threw out all his albums!"

Caitlin gasped in shock, her face showing pure horror as she clutched her heart. "They *threw out* Elton? Blasphemy!"

"I know, right?" Nick said, "They don't even believe they know anybody who *is* gay!" He sighed. "They've got blinkers on, and I'm just not sure I want to take them off. At home, I hide everything about me. I wear the clothes my mother picks out for me. I skateboard. I even wear a baseball cap." He shuddered, and I realised I actually liked him in a feather boa.

"I can't destroy their image of me," he said sadly. "It will crush them...and it will crush me. I need them, girls. I'm an only child, you know."

"Me too," I said, nodding.

"Me three!" chirped Caitlin. "We are three lonely only-children together."

There was a moment of silence, which, naturally, Caitlin broke. "So, if they're going to give you money for New York, they'd need to see your talent, *and* you'd need to be straight?" She sounded far more excited than the occasion warranted.

"Well, yes, I think so," Nick answered, sounding confused, "but given the history, I just don't see it happening."

Caitlin jumped up. "No—I've got an awesome idea!" She looked very pleased with herself. "Operation Straight Boy! I'll just *pretend* I'm your girlfriend. Gabriel won't mind."

"Wait, really? You think it will work?"

"Oh, God, parents *love* me," Caitlin said, shrugging. I glanced at her, surprised, as she added, "Really, it will be a pushover."

Nick's face brightened. "I could go to New York, and not be homeless, and my parents would still be happy…" He beamed. "Let's do it."

The moment devolved into a giant cuddle pile, until Nick finally extracted himself.

"I really want to thank you girls for tonight," he said. "I have wanted to get that off my chest for ages, and… I'm really glad I told you everything." He looked at Caitlin. "And thank you for offering to help. I am off to bed to ponder 'Operation Straight Boy'."

"And I'm going to go down to the medical centre again, to see the doc," Caitlin said, dragging herself to her feet. "My throat is still killing me and these drugs aren't making a scrap of difference."

"That's okay," I said. "I'm going to hit the sack. I'm completely knackered."

Left alone in the silence of the cabin, I lay back on my bunk and stared into space. A crack of light appeared at the door, and I realised Caitlin had left the door ajar. I didn't have the energy to get up—my worries were weighing me down. Had I really made the right decision in making Cooper jealous? Or had I gone too far and made him think I was a skanky tart? I sighed. Maybe I just shouldn't think too much. Perhaps it was time just to listen to my own heart, which was telling me to just talk to Cooper about how I felt.

I'd just started thinking about how to start such a conversation with Cooper when the door flew open.

"Forget something, roomie?" I asked without looking. She was always forgetting things.

"It's not Caitlin," said a familiar male voice, in an accent I instantly recognised.

I sat up and swung my legs around, carefully putting my feet on the floor.

"Wait, don't get up," Cooper said. "I need to say this without you looking at me."

"Okay," I said, with some trepidation. That sounded a little ominous, and I wasn't sure I was prepared for any more bad news.

"I'm really sorry I stuffed you around," he said quietly. "I really like you, Ellie, and I've realised I'm ready for a relationship. Let's give it a go."

I sat silently while my brain processed what he'd just said. He wanted to be with me? The jealousy game had actually worked! I wanted to shout it from the pool deck and let everybody know he was finally my man. Success was mine!

Instead, I smiled shyly and stood up to take Cooper's outstretched hand.

"I'm in."

Chapter Fifteen

Puerto Rico is an excellent place to swan around on the arm of a new beau. I wanted to introduce myself to everyone we passed in the historical city of 'Old' San Juan and chirp "Hi, I'm Ellie. This is my boyfriend, Cooper." Puerto Ricans tended to be a friendly lot, so they probably wouldn't have minded, but I rather thought that I might embarrass Cooper if I started showing him off.

"So, babe, what do you want to do?" I purred, nuzzling Cooper's shoulder with my chin. "It's such a beautiful day." I latched onto him tightly, resisting the urge to skip down the cobbled street. Given how little sleep we'd both had after earnestly consummating our 'official' status, I was a little surprised at how bouncy I felt. Sex really does wonders.

When I say 'official', I mean it was official to the two of us. Cooper had asked if we could keep it quiet for a little while, as he was still relatively new to the team. Hearing this news for the third time, I didn't even bat an eyelid. I knew the drill: nobody minds who you sleep with—except your boss.

"Hmmmm, do you wanna go to McDonald's?" he said after a moment, sounding unsure.

McDonald's in Puerto Rico? How boring. I'd read an article in *Cosmo* that said men got really turned on by adventurous women. I was hardly the most adventurous person, but he didn't know that. So instead I said, "How do you feel about street food?"

"Wow, really?" Cooper said, looking down at me with a definite air of newfound appreciation. "You're amazing! Most girls shy away from street food. Worried they'll get food poisoning or something…"

Hooray, success! I sent a silent thank you heavenward to *Cosmo*, the holy book of all relationships. I shrugged nonchalantly and smiled up at Cooper. "I'm always up for something new." I patted the charcoal tablets I'd stashed in my pocket in case of emergencies and secretly hoped we'd find a vendor who didn't cook our food in last week's oil.

We strolled up the street, looking for an irresistible display of mouth-watering delicacies. My camera, slung over my shoulder, knocked against my side, so I picked it up and popped off the lens cap. San Juan was a photographer's paradise; the buildings, like those on most of the other Caribbean islands, were painted in a fruit-inspired palette of yellows, pinks, and blues. Many of them were crumbling away; years of sun and salt air corroded the layers of paint, creating an irresistible canvas of textures just begging to be captured on camera.

I swung around and focused the lens on Cooper's face, and, laughing, tried to prod him into pulling a pose. He stuck out his tongue and crossed his eyes, and proceeded to pose in increasingly ridiculous positions for me.

"You are ridiculous," I informed him, replacing the lens cap and slinging the camera back over my shoulder.

"Oh, I know," he said. He held out his hand and wiggled his fingers. "Shall we?"

I took his hand and we started down the street again.

A few minutes later, we passed an open-air theatre where a small crowd had gathered to watch a band playing drums in a thumping, rhythmic beat; a sweating dance troupe was jumping around to the music in what I would have described as jungle-inspired dance steps. A sign announced 'Bomba Dance & Drum Show—Daily'.

"Did you know Puerto Rico has American, European and African influences?" Cooper said, startling me. I looked up at him as he nodded at the dancers. Adopting an encyclopaedic voice, he continued, "Puerto Ricans love this African-inspired

Bomba dance, which is a battle between dancer and drums, but they also claim to have invented salsa. Do you know how to salsa?"

"No, not really," I answered, blocking out visions of my first night on board, when Seth and I salsa'd our way into the sack. "I'd love for you to teach me."

In response, he grabbed me around the waist and gave me a squeeze. "Maybe later," he whispered.

We wandered the city's narrow streets, dodging out of the way of oncoming cars and peering into the shops we passed. Even now, after having been on and off at each port of call more than once, I was still surprised by how many high-end shops there were. Never underestimate how much tourists are willing to buy.

We settled upon a street food vendor who had just cooked up a fresh batch of garlicky, spicy chicken on kebab sticks. I inspected them as subtly as I could for tell-tale signs of poor hygiene.

"*Hola Señor, cuatro por favor,*" Cooper said, the Spanish rolling off his tongue. I hadn't known he spoke Spanish, and I wondered what other unexpected talents he possessed. I was imagining all of the things he might be able to do with his mouth when he nudged me towards a couple of plastic crates.

We sat down and he handed me a plate. After a few minutes of silence as we ate, I looked up to find Cooper watching me, a smile on his face.

"You've got a little thing...here..." he said, wiping the corner of my mouth. His hand lingered, and then he leaned forward and licked the corner of my mouth. Warmth surged downwards and I started to feel tingly; if we hadn't been sitting out in the open I'd probably have jumped him right then. Then I remembered that I was supposed to be trying to be a bit less available; playing hard to get had worked so well thus far that it seemed a shame to toss it aside so soon.

"Let's go play pool," I said, jumping up and smoothing down the back of my shorts. "Nick told me there's a great bar near here, where all the crew go."

Cooper groaned with mock exasperation, but got to his feet and followed me down the street.

The bar was tricky to find; after we'd been searching for a while with no luck, Cooper wanted to give up, but I insisted we keep looking. We found it eventually, and when we walked inside, I was glad we'd made the effort. It was long and narrow, with dark paint on the walls; it smelled of stale beer and spicy potato wedges. Atmospheric, one might say. I'd been expecting to find it full of crew, but it was completely deserted. I was completely fine with that, because it meant I could drape myself all over Cooper.

He racked up the balls and offered me a break, the smile on his face telling me that he expected me to have no idea what I was doing. I concealed my own smile; my dad had started teaching me to play pool from about the age of four, and although I rarely defeated him or his pool-hall mates, I generally wiped the floor with my friends. Being the daughter of a pool champ has its advantages. It had been years since anyone had even invited me to play; they'd all got tired of losing. Even Dan, who'd fancied himself a bit of a pool shark, had always avoided playing against me.

But this wasn't Dan, or my dad; it was Cooper, and the last thing I wanted was to embarrass him. Male pride is such a funny thing. So I erred on the side of caution and tried not to sink too many balls on the break. I did sink one, but admittedly, it looked like a fluke. The sight of Cooper concentrating hard on the balls, secretly willing me not to pocket anything, was so cute I was a little distracted.

"Oooh, lucky," he said, leaning on his cue and shaking his head adorably. He gave me a kiss on the forehead and grinned. "Let me show you how it's done." He proceeded to make a big display of announcing the desired pocket and lining up the ball with great fanfare, explaining things to me carefully. He pointed out his stance and hand technique.

And then missed.

Red cheeks declared his embarrassment, and I felt awkward for him; he'd wanted so badly to show off for me, and it had backfired. It was one of those times you *want* to have your arse kicked.

When I'd come home for Christmas my first year at uni, I'd massively fancied this bloke who didn't seem to realise I existed, and I'd wailed about it to my mother as we cleaned up after Christmas dinner. Dad and the rest of the family were watching *Elf* on telly, so Mum and I sat down in the dining room and talked about men and relationships.

"Ellie, men are simple," she'd said. "They just like to be bigger, better, cleverer, and more talented at everything than we are."

She'd pulled down an old photo album and flicked through it to pictures of her and Dad before they'd had me. "See how happy he looks, Ellie?" she'd said. "It's because I always made him feel like a man. You just need to cajole and caress their egos at every opportunity, love."

I knew my mother was brilliant at a lot of things, but you'd never have known. My whole life, she'd let Dad be the one who was right, let him be the one who always won.

I had always found their straightforward, light-hearted relationship inspiring. They were always laughing, and Mum was ever the vulnerable female. I knew it was a bit 50s, but I quite liked the simplicity. It had always seemed a bit unfair to keep Mum's talents hidden, but their marriage was so solid, it seemed like it was worth following my mum's lead.

With that in mind, I soothed Cooper's ruffled ego, assuring him he was brilliant and sexy and every other positive term that came to mind. I purposefully missed my next shot, which seemed to perk Cooper up quite a bit; he consoled me in much the same way as I had him, and then successfully potted his next ball. "You make me so happy," he said, leaning on his cue stick and holding my hand in his. Smiling, he added, "I'm the happiest I've been in years. Thank you."

Mum was right; men really were simple.

We played three more games, and I managed to lose each one worse than the last; by the final game, I was trying to see how badly I could miss my shots. Cooper made sympathetic clucking noises and, while beaming after winning his fourth straight game, suggested we ought to head back before he thrashed me again. Which was fine by me; don't get me wrong, I loved spending the time with Cooper, and I was pleased about helping to make him happy and boost his ego, but there's only so long you can pretend to be bad at something before you get bored.

Cooper dropped me back at my cabin after lunch; I'd hardly been there for five minutes before Caitlin ran in the door, arms flailing, dress askew, hair flying, puffing like she'd run a marathon.

"Thank fuck you're here, roomie!" she said, almost tackling me with a hug. She buried her face in my shoulder. "You are not going to believe this..."

This did not sound promising. "So you know I went back to the doctor last night to get more stuff from my throat?" she asked, flopping down on the bottom bunk. I nodded mutely, wondering where this was going. "He was worried the antibiotics weren't working, and called the senior doctor. *He* looked in my throat and said, 'That's not tonsillitis. It's herpes of the throat.' Oh, my fucking God, roomie, can you believe that?! So fucking gross."

I stood speechless for a moment. On the bright side, she wasn't pregnant and there wasn't any further alcohol or Gabriel-related drama. On the other hand...ew. She was right, it *was* disgusting. "Eeeeewwwwwwwwwwww," I said.

"I know. I'm so hideous," she said, sitting up. "I thought Gabriel would be a bit more sympathetic, since he obviously gave it to me, but he was actually a bit offended when I suggested it was him!"

I grimaced. "Not that it matters, I suppose, but is there any chance it wasn't?" I was thinking about her foursome story. I loved Caitlin, but I knew she wasn't always as careful as she could be, and so it was entirely possible it hadn't been Gabriel after all. One look at Caitlin's face, though, told me it wasn't the right time to bring it up.

"Well, yeah, we've both fucked around lots," she admitted.

"But it was almost definitely him. I have always been okay with using protection, but Gabriel never does. He gets tested a lot and he thinks it's the same thing." She rolled her eyes and pushed her hair back. I stayed quiet. "On the up side, the doc gave me some antivirals. He said they should work pretty quickly, so I'll feel good as new in a couple of days." She smiled weakly, looking strained and tired. "And until then, I'm so not giving him head," she added. She definitely had her priorities in order, this one.

Later, after a loved-up day with Cooper, I practically floated to the crew bar after work. He'd promised he'd meet up with me later on; in anticipation of the off-chance he let me stay the night in his cabin, I'd even done a little DIY bikini wax.

Jock was behind the bar when I drifted up to it. He looked in rather a better mood than the last time I'd spoken to him, so I thought maybe he'd forgiven me for whatever I'd inadvertently done.

"Hi," I said. Ellie Green, master of the stunning conversation opener.

"Eh, well, hello there, lass," Jock said. His eyes darkened to a deep blue-grey; the colour made him look rather melancholy. Somewhere deep down, something was still troubling him, and I still had no idea what it was. He looked down and then, avoiding my gaze, said, "Sorry about the other day. I was being a right bastard for no reason."

"It's okay," I said cautiously. "It was probably my fault." I hesitated, and then added, "I've missed you."

He laughed. "You can't miss someone in a day or two!"

I shook my head. "You were so cross with me that I was afraid maybe I'd completely buggered up our friendship."

"I'm harder to get rid of than that, lass," he said. "Now, what are you having?"

"Can I get a wine please?" I said. I scanned the room. No Cooper. "I'm just waiting for Cooper." I leaned against the bar. Jock's expression didn't change, so I added, "We're all sorted now." Cooper wanted to keep things quiet, but Jock already knew basically everything about my escapades on the ship, so I hardly thought revealing the secret would be problematic.

"Ah," Jock said noncommittally, measuring out a large glass of wine. "I see. Excellent."

That flat tone had come back again, and this time I knew it had something to do with Cooper. I wished Jock could see how wonderful Cooper was, like I could, but sometimes men could be so ridiculously stubborn that there wasn't really much point in trying to convince him.

I wanted to stick around, try to keep repairing my friendship with Jock, but I knew Cooper would arrive any moment, and the last thing I wanted was another confrontation between the two. "It was good to see you," I said, picking up my wine. As I walked away, I took a sneaky look back. He was so lovely with his floppy hair and expressive eyes, and I really hoped our friendship would be okay. Jock meant a lot to me—maybe more than I was willing to admit. I didn't want to drive him away.

As I crossed the room, I spotted Maria in the booths, sitting with a guy I'd never seen before. She was wearing a short white skirt that barely covered her knickers and was laughing and flirting like her life depended on it. The really odd bit was that despite the skirt, her flirting lacked the sexy edge it usually had; she was oddly sweet, and for a moment I wondered if I'd accidentally stumbled into a parallel universe— a feeling only amplified when she spotted me and called out in a warm, friendly voice,

"Oh, my God, Ellie! Hi! How are you?" I stared at her, wondering if there was another girl named Ellie who happened to be right behind me, but when I glanced around, I was the only one in the area. And then she called out again, in the same sickly sweet voice, "Ellie! Hi! Come and meet my darling boyfriend, Luiz!"

There was absolutely nothing I would have liked to do less, but since she'd singled me out I couldn't exactly ignore her. Gripping my wine glass like a shield, I crept closer, just waiting for the claws to come flying out to rip me to shreds.

The guy sitting next to her smiled at me as I approached, but unlike the sweet smile on Maria's face, it looked genuine. He was quite large in the body, and had a very round, soft face. His curly black hair stuck to his forehead with sweat, and one of his hands was placed almost gingerly on Maria's thigh. He reminded me of the stereotypical computer geek: chubby, pasty white, awkward—he was only missing the glasses. This must have been the boyfriend. Wealthy polo family, if I remembered Caitlin correctly. Caitlin had described him as a sad, overweight loser, which I thought was a bit harsh—though I could see why Maria was looking to trade up. He looked sweet, if about as far from Maria's type as you could possibly get.

I switched my wine into my left hand and greeted Luiz with a handshake, ignoring Maria's creepy Stepford Wives act. "Welcome aboard," I said, with the warmest smile I could muster.

The smile he gave me in return was affable and genuine, and I found myself warming to him immediately. How the poor bastard had ended up with a bitch like Maria was beyond me. He certainly seemed decent enough; you'd think he could have found someone less psychotic.

"Ellie, sit down, please, please," Maria said earnestly, patting the space next to them. Right. Great. Things were getting even creepier. She'd never been this nice to anyone. Quite frankly, I'd thought it beyond her ability.

I sat down, with great reluctance, and as Maria reached over to put her hand on my knee, I had a sudden fear that she wanted to ask me to participate in a scary threesome. Eek. Where was Caitlin when I needed her? I looked around the room hopefully, but saw no sign of either Caitlin or Cooper. Great. I was on my own.

"So, Ellie," Luiz said, pulling my attention back to him, "Maria tells me you are from England. I've been there many times. Such a beautiful country."

I nodded, wondering how long it would be before I could escape, but before I could answer, Maria was on her feet. "You two have so much in common," she said, and as I watched her, the tiny anxious movements she made, she reminded me of a trapped animal. Which was bizarre. I mean, Luiz didn't exactly look exciting, but he was hardly scary, either. As I stared at her, a stray thought popped into my mind: what if Maria wasn't as confident and secure as she always seemed? What if she was stuck in a life she didn't want, throwing herself at every man who came along in a desperate attempt to forget that eventually, what waited for her at home was the round-faced, fleshy Luiz? It didn't make her any less of a bitch, but it would make the reason for her bitchiness a little clearer.

As I pondered that, Maria said, "I have just remembered something I must do, but I am so happy Ellie is here as you will be able to talk to each other while I am away!" Before Luiz or I could so much as think of saying anything to protest, she darted across the room and out the door.

"Erm. Sorry," I said to Luiz, fighting the urge to grimace. I was embarrassed; I'd no idea what Luiz did or didn't know about Maria's behaviour on board ship, and so I'd no idea what to say to him.

"Don't worry," Luiz said kindly. "I'm sure it's nothing." His eyes told me that was a lie; he was concerned, but I couldn't tell exactly what it was that was bothering him. "Maria told me what a great friend you are," he added. "She's been so excited for us to meet."

Maria had clearly spun some kind of story for Luiz about her life on board the ship, and I didn't really feel like it was my place to crush that fantasy. My parents had always told me to smile and nod when I didn't know what to say, so I smiled. And nodded. And smiled. "Mmmmm," I said.

On the bright side, Luiz turned out to actually be a lovely guy, and a wonderful conversationalist to boot. We soon discovered that despite our different backgrounds—he'd grown up on acreage, in a mansion, raising thoroughbred polo horses and travelling the world—we liked the same books, the same music, and the same movies. Even our family values were surprisingly similar. His English was impeccable, which made conversation far easier than I'd anticipated.

Despite how easily we'd kept up the conversation, I was quite relieved when Cooper arrived with Caitlin and Gabriel. I introduced Luiz, and the three of them slid into the booth with us. Cooper managed to claim the spot next to me without trying; his thigh was hard up against mine on the cosy booth seat.

Caitlin and Gabriel took over the conversation, and I felt myself relax. I hadn't realised how stressful I had found it to keep talking with Maria conspicuously absent.

With everyone's attention elsewhere, Cooper leaned closer to me and whispered, "Sorry I'm late, Ellie-belly. Had heaps of shit to do in the lab." His little finger found mine and rubbed it suggestively. "Let's have a drink and get out of here."

I conveyed my agreement with a smile and immediately offered to buy the first round. Luiz, very sweetly, insisted on buying. Cooper and Gabriel followed him to the bar, though whether it was from some odd man sense that told them that Caitlin and I needed a girly moment together or because they wanted to find out how he'd managed to snag Maria as a girlfriend, I couldn't tell.

As soon as Caitlin and I were on our own, she said, "What the fuck is with Maria's boyfriend? How did you get stuck with him?"

"Oh, Caitlin," I said, "he's actually really, really nice."

She shrugged. "Yeah, okay, whatever, dude. But while he's here with you, Maria is off fucking some other bloke."

"What!" I knew Maria was a bitch, but this was just cruel. "How can she do that to him?"

"She's only holding on to him until she finds someone who's as wealthy as he is...but more attractive," she said.

"Wow," I said, stunned. "What a fucking cow."

"You're preaching to the choir," snorted Caitlin. "I ran into her earlier, and I swear she was so friendly that it was like she'd got a complete personality transplant. And then it all came out: we met this fucking gorgeous guy today while shooting embarkations, and she was determined to get him in the sack. Only reason she'd been sweet-talking me was because she knew Luiz was coming on board and she needed someone to keep him busy while she fucks the brains out of this other dude." Caitlin hissed angrily. "I told her to fuck off, you know? Told her to grow up and deal with her own shit. But I saw her on her way to meet the guy, and realised she must've left Luiz alone." She sighed. "What can I say? I'm a fucking softie. I didn't want the poor guy to be alone hours after he'd got here."

Well, that was all properly depressing. I was grateful I had Cooper; maybe no one else knew we were together, but I knew it, and that was the important thing. And I knew he'd never treat me like Maria was treating Luiz.

Almost as if she were reading my mind, Caitlin checked to see the boys weren't yet returning and grabbed my arm. "So, roomie, what's the goss with you and Cooper?" Her eyes were bright with excitement. "We didn't get a chance to talk about it this morning... Did the jealousy thing work? He sure looked pissed when he left the officers' bar last night." She giggled and bit her lip in anticipation.

"Well..." I said, drawing out the suspense until Caitlin looked ready to explode from anticipation, "we shagged... And now we're officially together!" Okay, so I'm rubbish at keeping secrets. But if I'd already let Jock know, I could hardly keep Caitlin out of the loop.

She whooped and high-fived me before I shushed her, worried that someone might hear.

"Oh, Ellie, that's such great news," she said, more quietly. "Actually, I've got news, too." I could have sworn she patted her tummy subconsciously, and for a minute I was terrified that she *was* actually pregnant. "Gabriel wants to get serious," she said, putting to rest my fears of her impending motherhood. "He said he really loves me and doesn't want either of us to be with anybody else."

I squealed in excitement, but before I could offer my own congratulations, the guys came back laden with drinks. Cooper edged his way between Caitlin and me; Gabriel slid in on Caitlin's other side and threw his arm around her shoulder affectionately. Luiz looked hopefully towards the door. No sign of Maria.

It was the first time since I'd arrived that Caitlin and I were both seriously involved with someone special, and there was no drama in sight. Would wonders never cease?

I should have known better than to celebrate so soon, as Luiz's crestfallen face suddenly lit up like a Christmas tree. I followed his gaze to find Maria, sashaying back into the crew bar; her fluorescent pink bra was particularly noticeable through her white vest in the UV light. Nothing says classy like a bright bra under a white top.

She sashayed up to our booth and plonked herself down next to Luiz.

"Did you know that the new passenger we met today is gay?" she demanded, looking at Caitlin.

Caitlin and I both stifled a giggle. Luiz looked confused. Poor man.

Maria looked displeased and snuggled into Luiz's side, stroking his chest. Her face was out of his line of sight, which let her safely raise a questioning brow in Caitlin's direction.

"Nothing," Caitlin managed, nudging me in the ribs. I poked her back and giggles escaped both of us. Maria did not look impressed. This was going to be interesting.

Chapter Sixteen

"So," I said, moving my thumb in circles in the centre of Cooper's palm, "we're finally alone." We had finally escaped the crew bar for some quality time in my cabin.

But things weren't off to a great start. Cooper wanted to talk about Maria, which kind of ruined the mood. After everything she had said and done to her female colleagues, I couldn't stand Maria. My abrupt insight earlier in the evening had suggested that she might actually be human after all—but that didn't make me like her. She was still an exotically beautiful libertine and a massive bitch. Happily for her, and unhappily for the rest of us, her personality wasn't what attracted men to her. They were more interested in her DD-cup and willingness to do anything a man wanted.

And now my boyfriend wanted to spend the evening discussing her. Hooray.

"I feel sorry for her boyfriend. He seems like a great guy," Cooper said. "I hope she doesn't hurt him too much." He looked down sadly. "Women have a way of breaking our hearts, you know…"

I nodded in agreement. Cooper's fiancée had died, rather than cheated, but I understood what he meant. I loved his sensitivity.

That being said, I was eager to move on from discussing Maria and Luiz to thinking about us. It was rare for us to have time alone and I wanted to make the most of it. "Shall I put on some music?" I asked.

Cooper nodded, and I skimmed through my phone until I

found some old-school Sadé, created a quick playlist, and flicked on my Bluetooth pod. As 'By Your Side' spilled through the tiny speakers, I slid across the bed and reached out to pull Cooper off his chair. It would only be a tiny lie to say I'd had fantasies about snogging to that song since Samantha and Richard at that rooftop pool in *Sex and the City*.

Before we could so much as get close enough to kiss, though, the sound of angry voices filtered through the walls. It was pretty obvious after a minute that they weren't speaking English, and by process of elimination I quickly deduced that it was Maria and Luiz. Well, mostly Maria; her fiancé's voice was lower—calmer.

Cooper and I sat, frozen in place by the increasing volume of Maria's voice, until a shriek echoed through the halls.

"Right, I'm gonna go help," said Cooper, standing up. "You stay here. I'll be back shortly."

I watched through a crack in the door as he slipped across the hall and knocked loudly on their door. Maria opened it a tiny crack, and once she saw it was Cooper, let him in without a word. He was absolutely a hero.

Figuring Cooper would be back soon, I flopped down on my bed and listened to the romantic playlist alone. I wanted to look dreamy and tantalising when he returned, stretched across my bed like a seductive maiden.

Eight songs later, I could no longer fake a 'come hither' look. The short visit to resolve what was, at its root, a domestic, had become uncomfortably long, and I was getting frustrated. Where the hell was my boyfriend? This was not at all how I'd envisioned the evening going when I'd left work earlier.

I stormed out the door and across the hall to listen at Maria's door. Everything was quiet, and since I didn't really want to deal with Maria again, I slunk back to my cabin and resumed my position on the bed. It was late and I was tired. I wished I knew if Cooper was still in the cabin across the hall. For all I knew, they'd all gone off somewhere. Or one of them had buggered off and Cooper was talking quietly to the other.

How was I supposed to know?

I really hated waiting, particularly when I'd been looking forward to some alone time with Cooper.

Over an hour later, Cooper still hadn't reappeared. I'd dozed off and awoken several times, kept checking the clock and putting my ear to the wall of Cooper's cabin next door. No noises, no call, no signs of life.

I hated being a worrier, because really, on a ship, how far could someone go? I did feel justified in my concern, though; really, if your boyfriend goes off to help settle a dispute but then doesn't come back, surely something must have happened... Had something bad happened to Maria and Luiz? Did he not want to come back to my cabin? Had he bumped into some other friends and gone to a cabin party? Had Justin asked him to work? If he had just poked his head back in and let me know what was going on, I could have rested easy, but not knowing was incredibly frustrating.

I eventually paged him; we weren't meant to use it for personal reasons, but I was getting worried. Except then I heard it beep through the wall, and realised he must have left the pager in his cabin.

I lay on my bed and stared at the ceiling. Where the fuck was he?

I slept badly, drifting off for anywhere from a few minutes to an hour and then jolting awake again, thinking I'd heard him come in. When he finally returned in the early hours of the morning, I opened my eyes and registered the sound of his door opening and promptly stormed over to confront him.

"Where the hell have you been?" I demanded, my hands placed firmly on my hips. Me plus lack of sleep plus frustration and worry was not a pretty picture. And I had a bad feeling my hair was a mess, which was undoubtedly adding to the crazy look.

Cooper looked at me as if I was mad. "I had a drink with Luiz to calm things down," he said. The expression on his face told me that he didn't understand why I was making such a fuss.

"Oh, really?" I said, not even bothering to keep the accusatory tone out of my voice. "Where were you having a drink? You know we're not allowed out past 1.30."

He rolled his eyes and stepped into his cabin. Before closing the door, he turned around and said, in a low, exasperated tone, "Ellie, I'm tired. I've been sorting out their relationship issues for hours, and I just want to sleep. I can't deal with your insecurities right now. See you in the morning." He closed the door.

Damn, I'd fucked that up. He'd told me he was going to sort them out, and I'd turned into a complete and totally insecure bitch. I thought about trying to remedy things right then, but realised that we were both exhausted and it would be better to wait until the morning to try to apologise. Sometimes it's better to go to sleep angry.

Cooper had been right; I'd been jealous. I trudged back to my cabin with my head hanging. Honestly, when had I got so barmy? Or did I have a reason to be worried? I thought back to my friends with the problem boyfriends. When the men had been dishonest and cheating, they'd always managed to make it look like their girlfriend's fault for being paranoid and picky. Was I in that relationship now?

I thought about it as I crawled back into bed and pulled the blankets up to my chest. No, I wasn't, I decided, staring at the underside of Caitlin's bunk. We'd had a minor blip when he freaked out after our first night together, but he'd never given me another reason to doubt him. I'd just had a bad run, that was all; of course I was anxious. But Cooper didn't deserve that.

Lying in the dark, with a sick feeling of regret in the pit of my stomach, I knew I'd overreacted. My low self-esteem had made me feel angry and suspicious, which in turn made me sad; I thought I'd been doing so well with improving my self-esteem. I was much happier with the way I looked. I sighed. I was just being silly, and I needed to not take out my frustrations with myself on Cooper. No. Tomorrow, I simply had to apologise and smooth things over.

I fell asleep trying to compose a suitable apology, and when I woke up a few hours later I felt ratty and pathetic. Not a good start to the day.

When we docked in St Thomas, I went to go make up with Cooper, only to discover that he'd already left his cabin. When I got up to the mess, rehearsing my apology on the way in anticipation of finding him there, I found I'd missed him there, too. Feeling miserable, I hunched over my breakfast and ate in silence, avoiding eye contact with anyone who might have been interested in striking up a conversation.

When I finished, I checked back at the cabin to see if Cooper had returned, but he wasn't there. Feeling depressed, I headed up to do stores, looking forward to it even less than usual. On the bright side, it kept me busy. On the other hand, rushing around and moving boxes in the humid St Thomas heat made me feel disgusting and unattractive and dragged my mood down even more. I resented having to do the work; all I wanted to do was go and find Cooper so I could apologise. The delay was gnawing at my nerves and making me anxious and jittery.

I finally finished and headed back to the cabin, beads of sweat clinging to my forehead and damp patches under my arms. I'd just opened the door when Cooper turned the corner.

"Ellie!" he exclaimed. "Hey! I was looking for you this morning." He trotted down the hall and hugged me from behind, dropping a kiss on my neck before turning me to face him.

"Really?" I felt a warm rush of reassurance flood through my body. I knew I'd been overreacting. "You'd gone by the time I got up. And then I had to go do stores."

"Oh, shit," he said, looking upset, "I was totally going to offer to help you with that! I completely forgot."

"It's okay," I said, already feeling better knowing that he'd wanted to help.

"I knocked this morning but you didn't answer, so I figured you were asleep." He paused and looked me over, taking in the sweat and my damp clothes and my bedraggled hair, and then said, "I've got to get the lab ready for some printing, but…" He grinned at me. "Wanna ditch those clothes and invite me in for a shower?"

"Absolutely!" I said enthusiastically. The idea of getting clean and possibly getting in a shag was definitely in the top five best ideas I'd heard all year. As I shucked my sweat-soaked clothes, Cooper turned on the shower and heated it to the perfect temperature. By the time I joined him, his hair was already wet and slicked back, and he was waiting for me with Caitlin's loofah and body wash. She usually didn't let anyone else use her things, but I had a feeling that once I told her exactly what we'd been up to, she wouldn't mind.

Shagging in the shower is never easy at the best of times. Cruise ship showers have a little moulded shelf, just below knee height—perfect for getting yourself into just the right position during a vertical shag-fest. Unfortunately, cruise ship showers are tiny, and anyone who's ever encountered soft, plastic shower curtains knows that they're a bloody nightmare. They stick to you in all the wrong places even during a normal shower, and just at the moment, it was being a damned nuisance.

I clung to Cooper like a limpet, trying to keep my balance; not exactly ideal, really, given that he kept slipping and banging his head against the wall. Showers are seriously not designed for having sex. Everything was too damn slippery.

Not that it stopped us from trying. Cooper was getting into the spirit, and the passion more than made up for the awkward position I had ended up standing in. "Oh, Ellie-belly," he murmured, "you're so sexy. So confident." He tangled one hand in my hair and slid the other along my side, down to my thigh. You just go for it in the shower. It just makes it so much better. Most girls are so self-conscious about being naked in bright light."

The compliment was nice, but… "Most girls?" I asked, trying not to sound jealous. Or paranoid.

He looked embarrassed. "It's been years since I've been with someone," he said, "but I remember Amanda worrying about that. And, well, you know…" He smiled sheepishly. "And I kind of remember what it was like before I met Amanda. It was a long time ago…"

"Oh, I'm so sorry," I said. I didn't want to take him down that road again, so I changed the subject, like a pro. "Um…there's an 80s night in the crew bar tonight. Do you want to go?" I loved 80s music.

"Sure." he said. "I'll come after I finish work. Might be a late one though." He met my eyes and grinned. "Now, however, I need to do something about that mouth of yours. Too much talking, not enough moaning."

True to his word, very shortly I was unable to continue the conversation, and rightfully so. The rest of the shower passed in a blur of wet skin, hot water, and soft moans. After several minutes to recover, I slipped out of Cooper's grasp. A few days earlier I'd slipped the cabin steward five dollars in exchange for extra towels; at the time I hadn't been thinking about having one for Cooper—I just liked the luxury of wrapping one around my hair, and one around my body. Today, I tossed one fluffy white towel to Cooper and left my wet locks drip on the floor.

Cooper came up behind me as I was drying my legs and kissed the back of my neck hungrily. His body was still damp, his skin soft but the erection pressing against me was anything but soft. Lordy, I thought. Not that I was complaining, but he had a hell of a fast recharge. And then as his hands drifted down my body, I stopped thinking altogether.

By the time I got to the Pic Stop that night, my legs were feeling kind of weak and shaky, but in the best way possible. Cooper had ended up being late for work; his phone went off every few minutes on the other side of the thin cabin wall. With a kiss and a promise to watch me at karaoke, he left me to recover before work.

All night, I found myself smiling like a crazy person. Things were definitely going better than I'd expected. I was on an all-round high, and even the night's few obnoxious passengers couldn't dampen my spirits.

The crew bar was pumping with neon-clad revellers when I arrived. Nick wasn't there yet, as he was still doing the second show, but Caitlin and Gabriel were there, snogging in the corner for a change.

When she came up for air, I took advantage of the moment to tap her on the shoulder. She spun around and laughed. Loudly. "How the fuck are ya, roomie?" she said. "Did you hear?"

"Hear what?" Between stores and Cooper, I hadn't heard a thing all day.

"Maria's fiancé left. Family emergency."

"No shit?" I was surprised. He'd been on board such a short time. "You don't suppose he broke it off, do you?"

"She's not pretending to be nearly miserable enough for that." Caitlin glanced over my shoulder. "Cooper coming?"

"He'll be here later…"

Three drinks and several sweaty dances later, I was eyeing the crowd anxiously. Cooper hadn't arrived yet. I couldn't remember what time he said he'd finish work, but knew it had to be soon as nearly everyone else had already arrived. Even knowing that, though, I couldn't keep my eyes from continually drifting towards the door. Where was he?

"Dude, are you looking for Cooper?" Caitlin asked finally, noticing I was distracted. There was an odd look in her eyes—sadness, maybe. Or pity. Though I wasn't sure why she'd be feeling either.

"Mmmm, maybe," I said, unable to lie. "He said he'd come up when he finished."

"We had a pirate shoot in the dining room tonight, Ellie. He's probably still printing the photos," she said sympathetically.

An hour and a half later, I finally got tired of waiting. Caitlin had reassured me more than once that Cooper was bound to be by soon, but I was frustrated and suspected he wouldn't be making an appearance that evening.

Without saying goodbye to anyone, I disappeared out the

door. Caitlin and Gabriel were having a fantastic evening, and I didn't want to ruin it for them, but I couldn't concentrate on having fun once I suspected Cooper wasn't going to be around anytime soon.

I went back to the photographers' cabins and saw no one; I stopped off to change into my uniform and then headed up to the officers' bar. No luck there, so I worked my way through the ship, from the Spring Fling in the passenger area to the 24-hour buffet to the crew mess, finally resorting to checking the laundry. Striking out everywhere I went, I crept into the nightclub, Diamonds in the Rough.

I saw Cooper's friend Mikhail, but didn't see Cooper. I thought about asking him, but, feeling terribly cynical, figured that even if he knew he might not want to tell me. Instead, I walked around the club, my eyes moving from person to person without really taking anything in. Until my eyes came to rest on the back of someone's head and I stopped short. I couldn't see the man's face, but there was something about him that had caught my eye. His hair curled over the back of his collar, and he was wearing a white shirt and grey trousers—the photography standard issue. He was deep in conversation with a girl with platinum blonde hair and a deep tan; careful not to make any sudden movements that might attract either of their attention, I slowly moved closer, and just as I got within earshot, he laughed and turned enough that I could see his profile.

It was Cooper.

I took a deep breath. What the hell was he doing here? And who the fuck was the girl? She reminded me of Jessica Simpson circa 'Daisy Duke'.

I walked up and tapped him on the shoulder. "Hi," I said. I figured I'd start with simple, and go from there.

Cooper's eyes widened and the smile dropped right off his face for a moment before reappearing as a stiffer version. "Oh, hey, Ellie," he said casually, apparently oblivious to my mood. "This is Cassie. She's cruising with us this week from Portland, Oregon." Cool as a cucumber.

"Hi. Nice to meet you," I said, without looking at her. "Cooper, can I talk to you for a minute?"

I dragged him over to stand under a towering plant in the corner.

"Ellie, before you start," he said before I opened my mouth, "she's just a friend. We got talking earlier tonight, and she mentioned that her grandfather died just before she came here." He turned those sad puppy-dog eyes on me; my instincts told me to cuddle and comfort, anything to take the look off his face, but I resisted. When I didn't say anything, he added, "I know a bit about grief and loss, you know. I just thought she could use the support of someone who understands what she's going through."

"Uh huh. Right," was all I could manage. I glanced back at Cassie; she was the happiest-looking person-in-mourning I'd ever seen.

I felt like that insecure moron again, second-guessing every move and every word, and I hated that I was doing it. I hated this woman I seemed to be becoming; I didn't *want* to be jealous or overreact or suspicious, but... It was just that he'd said he was going to come to the crew bar after work to spend time together. I *was* his girlfriend. And I just thought it was a little weird that he was here instead. If he'd really wanted to talk to Cassie, surely he could have snuck her into the crew bar and talked there.

Cooper interrupted my thoughts, saying, "Look, can I just finish my conversation with her?" His tone was half pleading and half frustrated. "She is pretty upset, and I don't want to leave mid-discussion."

I looked at Cassie again. She was studying her manicure. Yeah, she really looked upset. "Sure," I said flatly. "Carry on." Words escaped me, and despite my attempt to tell myself that it was fine, that I was overreacting, that I was just jealous, I could feel the anger bubbling up inside. It just...didn't feel right.

Cooper left without saying anything and returned to Cassie, who greeted him with a smile. He bent his head close to her and I heard him apologising. She flicked her hair, clearly unperturbed. And clearly not upset.

I stood still for a few minutes, gathering my fractured thoughts and trying to calm down. As I headed for the door, Mikhail started after me and caught my arm.

"Hey, Ellie, are you okay?" he asked. "You look upset."

"Apparently I'm the only one," I muttered.

Mikhail's eyes flicked past me and then came back to rest on my face. "If you're upset about Cooper," he said gently, "you really have nothing to worry about. He adores you. He wouldn't do anything to jeopardise that."

I hadn't realised Mikhail knew about us, and I felt better about telling Caitlin and Jock.

I looked at the floor. "He said her grandfather just died," I said to my shoe. "That he's just trying to comfort her."

Mikhail smiled. "He mentioned that," he said. "He's a good guy, you know? Always trying to help others."

I mentally chastised myself. Of course he was trying to help Cassie. He was a lovely, genuine guy, just as Mikhail had reminded me. Whatever Cassie's motivations were, it didn't matter; Cooper wouldn't let anything happen, no matter what she wanted.

Feeling slightly more cheerful than when I'd arrived at the club, I thanked Mikhail for his concern and left. I stood in the hall for a while, debating the merits of going back to the crew bar and trying to get some time to discuss things with Caitlin versus going back to the cabin and trying to get some sleep. The latter won. We'd had so many late nights that I was starting to feel a bit like a zombie.

When I got back to my cabin, Jock was waiting outside, which was a first, not to mention a nice surprise.

"Hey!" I said, pleased to see him. By the way his face lit up when I arrived, he was clearly happy to see me too. "How are you? Come on in."

He followed me into the cabin and took a seat on the desk. I flicked the kettle on and curled up on my bed.

"What's wrong?" he asked, his eyes dark and serious.

"Oh, not much. Just me and Cooper," I said, shrugging my shoulders. "You know we're together now, and things have been going really well, but…"

"But what? You can tell me, lass," Jock said. The kettle flicked off, and before I could move he'd already pulled out the mugs and teabags and was pouring the water. As he handed me a cup of tea, he said, "We're mates, right?"

I wrapped my hands around the mug and stared down at the steam curling up from the liquid. "I found him up in the disco, chatting to some blonde girl I've never seen before," I said, finally feeling the anger rising again. "He had this completely reasonable explanation—her grandfather just died, and what with his fiancée he knows what it's like to lose someone you love, so he was trying to give her some support. It's just…"

"Just what, lass?" he asked kindly. "There's surely something bothering you." "

I hesitated. Jock was always so warm and friendly; he was supportive, and non-judgemental, and aside from when I managed to make him shut down and his voice go flat, he was always the perfect person to talk to about anything. My parents would have loved him; he ticked just about every box on the 'perfect boyfriend' list. If he'd ever shown the slightest bit of romantic interest in me… Well. That was neither here nor there, and anyway, I was with Cooper. Hence this conversation.

I looked up at Jock, who was still watching me, and then let loose all of my worries and fears and jealousies. I talked and talked and talked, and it was only when I happened to glance up mid-sentence that I realised that despite his best efforts, Jock's eyes had glazed over.

"Oops," I said, abruptly ending the story about Cooper and Cassie. "I'm boring you."

"It's not that," he said. He was silent for a moment, clearly having some kind of internal battle, and finally he blurted out, "Ellie, I'm sorry, but this guy is a complete twat." I stared at him, completely taken aback. "He's a fraud, too," Jock continued, an angry look I'd never seen before on his face. "All that bullshit about the police and his dead fiancée? Christ, Ellie, he's just spinning you a line. Men do it all the time. Why the fuck are you putting up with him?" He took a deep breath and then added, more calmly, "You deserve better."

I stared at him in shock, completely at a loss for words. This wasn't the Jock I knew.

"You should never let a man treat you the way Cooper's been treating you," he said suddenly, and a whole series of emotions crossed his face and then disappeared again, leaving behind a completely unreadable expression and stony eyes. "Just finish with him, lass. Do yourself a favour."

And with that, he stood up and walked out of the cabin.

Still shocked, I just stood there, silently, trying to work out what had just happened. I had a feeling that there'd been a whole bunch of other things going on besides the Cooper thing, but at the moment I couldn't deal with trying to work them out. Instead, I bolted to my feet and out the door, intending to chase Jock down and—I don't know, demand an explanation or try to work things out. Something. Anything.

I didn't get very far. I'd just got out my door when I saw something that stopped me in my tracks: Maria. The fact that she was with someone who wasn't her boyfriend wasn't a surprise; Luiz might have left unexpectedly, but we were all accustomed to seeing her draped around a new man every night. No, the problem was that the man she was currently snuggled up against was someone I knew—and someone who was already well and truly spoken for.

It was Gabriel.

Chapter Seventeen

There's no easy way to tell your best friend that their boyfriend is a lying, cheating arsehole. If that wasn't bad enough, the other woman was the Brazilian Bitch; revealing that bit of bad news was going to be almost impossible. Like almost everyone else on board, Caitlin hated Maria. And I knew that she thought Gabriel might be The One. I was worried the news might destroy her.

Rather selfishly, I was also worried that Caitlin might take out her anger and hurt on me. No one likes to hear their significant other is cheating, and sometimes it's easier to turn against the bearer of bad news than actually confront the cheater. And I hated to think that me telling Caitlin about Maria and Gabriel might permanently damage our friendship. Although Caitlin and Gabriel's laissez-faire attitude towards love and commitment might convince almost everyone else that something like this wouldn't bother her, I knew she'd be crushed. She was all loved up and excited because he had just told her he wanted to get serious. I was guessing that his idea of serious and Caitlin's idea of serious weren't quite the same.

But I was willing to take the risk, because Caitlin deserved better. I waited until she got back to the cabin and we were alone. I closed the door quietly and leant against it, watching as she stomped around the cabin.

"For fuck's sake, roomie," she said, stripping off her clothes and tossing them to the floor, "he just disappeared. We made all these plans and everything for tonight."

"Caity," I said, before she could say anything else. I stared at the floor. "I know where Gabriel is."

"Great!" she said, her voice muffled by the pyjama top she'd just dropped over her head. "Where is he?" she asked. Her head popped through the t-shirt and she caught sight of my expression. "What is it, Ellie?"

"He's with Maria." The words rushed out of my mouth like a gust of wind and I flinched, anticipating her reaction.

"He's fucking *what*?" she yelped. "You have to be fucking *kidding* me." She stood there for a minute, looking absolutely furious, and then abruptly deflated and flopped down in the desk chair. "Of course he is," she said drearily. "Everyone ends up with Maria sooner or later. She's like fucking catnip for men."

"Do you want to go over there and confront them?" I asked. Personally, I didn't, since avoiding Maria was at the top of my list of priorities, but as Caitlin's best friend it was my job to back her up.

"No, thanks, beautiful," Caitlin said, slumped back in the chair like a rag doll. "I just can't face it right now." She sighed. "I should have tried harder, been more like Mom said…fitter, slimmer, quieter, more feminine…"

"Caity, no way!" I protested. "None of that stuff matters to the right guy." I said it with such confidence, I almost believed it myself.

Caitlin didn't reply. When I glanced over at her, I saw a fat tear rolling down her cheek. Her bottom lip was quivering and her eyes were dark and sad.

"Oh, sweetie," I said, hugging her. "I'm so sorry. Should I not have told you?"

"No, it's okay," she said, sniffling. "I'd rather know now."

As I stood there, gently stroking her hair, I realised that my problems with Cooper had been thrust almost completely out of my mind. Normally I'd have been obsessing and fretting and pouring out the whole story so that Caitlin and I could pick everything to bits, but at the moment Caitlin's problems far eclipsed mine.

Caitlin and I sat up for a while longer talking, but the

conversation kept going in circles. I finally tucked Caitlin into bed, and while I didn't at all begrudge sitting up with her, I was grateful to be able to crawl into bed myself. Unfortunately for me, without Caitlin's cheating boyfriend to focus on, my mind went right back to Cooper. I tossed and turned most of the night, replaying the day in my head, second-guessing everything I'd said and done and re-examining everything *he'd* said and done. I came to no conclusions other than that I'd probably been needy and suspicious, and finally drifted off.

When morning came, I needed a bit of air. Caitlin had the morning off, so I left her curled up in the bottom bunk, a cup of tea beside her in case she woke up.

I grabbed my phone and headed out for a stroll along the top deck until I had to open the Pic Stop before docking in Martinique. It was early enough that there weren't many people around; it was just me, my music, and a beautiful sunrise. I leaned against the rail and stared out across the ocean; it was going to be another gorgeous day.

The promise of another perfect day in paradise didn't lighten my mood much, though. Yesterday had really taken it out of me; first everything had gone wrong with Cooper, and then Jock had walked out on me, and then poor Caitlin... I paused the music and pulled out my headphones to take in the moment. As I closed my eyes, the salt-heavy breeze washed across my face and I felt a moment of peace. I breathed in, and out, and in again, and slowly I began to feel a bit better, like I might be able to go below again and face the day.

"Ellie!" called a voice behind me. "What are you doing?"

I turned in time to see Cooper bolting across the deck towards me. He grabbed me around the waist and hauled me away from the railing.

"What the hell are you doing?" he demanded. "You should never lean over a ship's railing!"

Well, he sounded worried. It was nice to be the object of concern instead of the concerned party for once. "I wasn't about to jump or anything," I said, laughing a little. "How did you know I was here?"

"Didn't you hear me calling you when you left the cabin?" he asked, still looking worried.

I waved my phone at him. "Sorry about that," I said, shrugging. I wrapped my headphones around my phone and stuffed it in my pocket, waiting for him to continue.

"I'm really sorry about the last couple of nights," he said apologetically. "I'm just really sensitive about being questioned, you know? And no one likes being accused of something they haven't done."

I didn't really feel as though I'd actually accused him of anything so much as wanted an explanation, but seeing as he clearly wanted to smooth things over, I didn't really want to make a big deal of it. "That's okay," I said, smiling. "I understand. I'm sorry I chased you around like a crazy person."

He caught my hand in his and pressed his lips to my palm, sending tingles along my fingers. He was so sweet, and it was lovely to make up so easily. I wanted to stay topside and just enjoy Cooper's company, but duty called. My morning passed much more quickly and calmly knowing Cooper and I were okay again, though, and it was easy to keep a smile on my face. Everything was once again right in the world; I was determined to curb my daft, paranoid behaviour and never let it be a problem again.

After the shop closed at lunchtime, I sauntered down to the crew internet room. Cooper was working in the lab all afternoon, and in any case I'd promised Nick I'd help him plan 'Operation Straight Boy'. First things first, though. I sent off a quick email to Mum and Dad to let them know I was still alive and promised a lengthy email later—I'd get to it eventually. I pulled up the news with good intentions, but gave up after the first three headlines were incredibly depressing.

I'd reached that age where it seemed like every time I checked Facebook, someone else had got engaged or married or had a baby. When I'd been engaged to Dan, it hadn't been a problem; I'd been secure in the knowledge that one day it would be my wedding plastered all over everyone's newsfeeds.

In the aftermath of Dan, and then Seth and Luciano, I'd hated checking Facebook as it reminded me of my own romantic failures. Now, however, I happily liked photos of my school friends' children, knowing I had Cooper. Not that I was thinking about having children with him, of course... Maybe just a bit of practising.

I'd just about run out of things to like and share when a notification popped up. Luiz Martinez had added me as a friend. I checked out his profile, and realised pretty quickly that he was Maria's Luiz.

I wasn't one of those people who friended every person I met, so I hesitated before accepting Luiz's request. As soon as I did, a new chat window popped up. We exchanged pleasantries, and then he asked me how his beautiful girl was doing. Maria. I'd been hoping he wouldn't want to talk about her.

I was really glad he couldn't see my face as I typed a response telling him that Maria was great. I didn't feel like it was my responsibility to tell him that Maria was so great that she was probably still wrapped in the arms of another man. I got the feeling he'd have liked to talk for a while, but as I didn't really feel like dodging Maria-related questions, I soon apologised and logged out.

I found Caitlin awake and staring into her empty teacup when I returned to the cabin.

"Hey, roomie," she said, sounding as miserable as she looked. She hesitated, and then said, "I just wanna say something, and I don't want you to get upset."

"Mmmmmmmm?" I hoped she wasn't upset I had blabbed about Gabriel and the Brazilian Bitch.

She ran her finger around the edge of the mug. "Look," she said, sounding less confident than I'd ever heard her, "you just need to be really careful of Cooper." I stared at her. That hadn't been what I was expecting. She caught my eye and added, "I don't want you to get your heart broken, too. Take a good look at what happened to me. I never thought I'd want to get serious, and as soon as I did... BAM!"

"But you said he was this awesome, trustworthy guy and I should go for it!" I said, my voice squeaky.

Caitlin winced. "I know, but, you know…" She sighed and drew patterns on the carpet with her toe. "Look, anyone who's that genuine, experienced, charming, and perfect usually isn't. At least in my experience." She looked up at me and then added, "I'm sorry. I don't want to upset you—I'm just trying to look out for you, you know?"

My emotions felt like they were in a tumble dryer, spinning around and around and around without making any sense. Okay, so Cooper and I had been through a couple of misunderstandings, but that was hardly enough to warrant concern. It was just my insecurity getting the better of me. I'd never been so clingy before, certainly not with Dan and never before that, either. My confidence had just been damaged, that was all. Now I was like cling film fresh out of the microwave, but I was sure that that would go away in time.

A tiny voice in my head asked me why, if everything was as perfect as I thought it was and the blame was all on my side, both Caitlin and Jock were concerned about my relationship with Cooper. I briefly considered the tiny voice, and then shoved it into the back of my mind and concentrated on ignoring it.

Caitlin hopped up and set her empty cup on the desk. "I'll be here for you no matter what, roomie," she said, and then hugged me, snuggling into my side. "And thanks for last night. And for the tea."

I had wanted to catch up with Jock, to try to talk about what had happened, but Nick wanted me to meet him in his cabin for our afternoon of planning, and by the time Caitlin was ready to go, I'd run out of time to find Jock. I should have gone to see him instead of checking Facebook. Oh well, I'd find him later.

Once comfortably ensconced in Nick's cabin, Caitlin and I filled him in on everything that had been happening with our respective boyfriends. He didn't say much about Cooper, but when we got to Gabriel's betrayal, Nick behaved as any good friend should.

"Oh, my God, what a fucking tart," he said, flipping his feather boa over his shoulder. "I bet he's come crawling back with a grovelling apology."

"Actually, I haven't spoken to him," Caitlin replied, sounding flat. "He knocked at the door this morning and begged for me to let him in, but I'm not interested."

"Good," Nick said firmly. "He can just go fuck himself. He doesn't deserve you, gorgeous." He hugged Caitlin and gave her a loud, sloppy kiss on the cheek. Caitlin managed a smile, but she still looked far from her usual cheerful self.

I waited for the moment to pass and then said, "Okay, guys, so what's the plan for the parents' arrival?"

Nick sat down, smoothed his hair and flipped his boa over the other shoulder. He reached over to grab his iPad and said, "I've been thinking about how to approach things with Mom and Dad when they arrive on Sunday." He pulled up what looked like notes on the iPad and continued, "It's not going to be easy. They don't miss a thing and can sometimes be quite judgemental. I think the best plan is to have Caitlin pose as my girlfriend. We can tell Mom and Dad that she's planning on moving with me to New York, and if we happened to mention something about getting married, they'd probably be pretty pleased."

I looked at Nick and then at Caitlin. He was a platinum blonde Filipino bloke who wore a feather boa. She was a spunky, loud-mouthed Canadian. This was never going to work.

Nick wasn't finished. "We just need to convince them we're mad about each other." He reached over and squeezed Caitlin's boob. She shrieked and jumped off the bed, into his lap. Nick tilted her backwards, leant down, and kissed her. In fact, he nearly swallowed her whole. Caitlin responded by wrapping her arms around his neck and letting out a heartfelt moan.

Well, this was uncomfortable. They were actually quite convincing in their faux-passion. Perhaps this crazy plan had a chance after all.

I cleared my throat. "Were you planning on snogging her to death in front of your parents? Because I'm not sure they're going to want to see that."

As quickly as the moment started, it ended. Caitlin slid off Nick's lap and wiped her mouth. "Okay!" she yelped. "I get the picture!" Then she smiled and playfully punched him in the arm. "Count me in, motherfucker."

We spent another hour working out where he ought to take his parents during the cruise and smoothing out all of the little wrinkles in the plan. Caitlin was excited—having a project would keep her mind off Gabriel, at least temporarily.

"Well, girls, I need to get to a rehearsal," Nick piped up. "Thanks so much for this. I don't want to sound dramatic, but my whole future depends on how this turns out. A straight son who is settling down with a serious girlfriend is a much better investment for their money than a feather boa-wearing fairy." He smiled wryly. "It means a lot you're willing to help me out with this."

On my way out, I glanced around the cabin. With the promotion to dance captain, Nick's cabin mate had been relocated, leaving the whole cabin subject to Nick's bright and campy interior decorating skills.

"Can I make a suggestion?" I asked, halfway out the door. "You might want to pare things down a little." I gestured around the room. "Just, you know, to make things more convincing…"

Nick threw a pillow at me. "Out!"

I laughed and trotted down the hall to catch up with Caitlin. Next cruise certainly wouldn't be boring.

Cooper was amazing the whole week. When we were in the staff mess at the same time, he played footsie with me under the table. He held my hand when I visited him in the lab, and he kissed me in our hallway, despite the fact anybody could have seen us.

Now that Caitlin was single again, she was back in our

cabin every night; I no longer had the luxury of spending my nights alone, or indeed, sharing them with someone else. Luckily, Cooper did have his own cabin, and I was able to pop in for a couple of quickies. He even let me sleep over one night, when we were sure Justin wouldn't find out.

Then Sunday came—the day Nick's parents arrived. Caitlin had somehow convinced Justin to take embarkation photos in her place so she could do her best girlfriend impersonation. She got all dressed up in a feminine pink skirt suit, and Nick donned a bland pair of khaki pants and a Ralph Lauren t-shirt he'd borrowed for the occasion. A more natural hair colour would have helped, but Nick was determined not to let himself go completely.

"I can't change my hair colour mid-contract," he protested. "I'll just tell them it was needed for the show."

His parents were a diminutive, well-dressed couple; they held hands as they walked the passenger gangplank onto the ship. Nick enveloped them both in a big hug. His dad wiped away a tear as he held onto his son, and his mum clung to his arm and kept asking if he was getting enough to eat. "Your hair!" were the first words out of her mouth. "I am grateful your grandfather is no longer alive to see this. You look like an albino cockatiel!"

Instead of responding, Nick grabbed Caitlin by the wrist and shoved her in front of his parents. "This is Caitlin," he said, a smile plastered on his face. "The beautiful girl who has captured my heart." He turned the smile on Caitlin and brushed a strand of hair off her forehead. "These are my parents, Maricel and Teodoro—but you can call him Teo."

"Oh, so nice to meet you," Caitlin said, bestowing her sweetest smile on the two of them. I'd seen the half-second where she'd thought about going in for a kiss and hug, and thought it was probably a good idea that she hadn't. I'd done that the first time I'd met Dan's parents, and his mother had ended up never liking me. There might have been other reasons, but I'd always figured that it had started with that first meeting. Much better to let the parents decide how much physical contact they wanted.

Nick's mother took Caitlin's hands in her own and held her at arm's distance, her eyes searching the younger woman's face. "You are certainly very pretty," she said at last. "I am so happy that Nicholas has found a nice girl at last. We had hoped perhaps he might one day meet a nice Filipina and settle down, but now I am just so happy he has found someone who makes him happy."

Caitlin stood for a moment without saying anything, and from the look on her face I was guessing that she wasn't quite sure how to respond to that. If she'd actually been Nick's girlfriend, I suspected she'd have been rather offended.

"Well," she said at last. "I'm very glad I make your son so happy."

I stifled a laugh, glad I wasn't the one playing girlfriend. Caitlin was a much better actor than I was.

Nick had asked me to be there, even though I had no connections, real or contrived, to the family, and thus far I'd been standing off to the side, trying to stay out of the way. Eager to turn his mother's scrutiny away from Caitlin, Nick turned and beckoned to me.

"This is our best friend, Ellie," he said. "She's Caitlin's roommate."

Nick's mum looked me up and down and then smiled. Apparently I didn't warrant the same kind of scrutiny as Caitlin, for which I was grateful.

"I imagine you know all the things about these two that they do not want to tell us," said Nick's father, but from his tone I was guessing he was teasing rather than interrogating.

"Oh, Teo," said his wife, knitting her brows at him in disapproval. "Let's not talk about that. I'm sure they are very well behaved and respectful."

I agreed. The situation was weird enough without thinking about the kinds of things that kids don't like to tell their parents. And while, as it happened, I did know quite a lot about both Caitlin and Nick's sex lives, it felt oddly wrong to think about them having a sex life together. Ew.

Nick, on the other hand, looked pleased. His parents hadn't started an argument and they seemed willing to like Caitlin, so all in all, it was a great start to his plan.

We showed them Nick's cabin, which had been carefully stripped of its campy splendour, and then did a quick tour of the ship. They oohed and aahed at the ship and asked questions constantly about everything from eating, to friends, to the islands we would visit.

"Mom, Dad, you haven't asked me anything about my show yet," Nick said, sounding hurt. "I'm performing tonight, you know."

"Well, we're both a bit tired after the trip," said his dad, looking away. "I don't know if we'll make it."

Nick opened his mouth, but no sound came out. He closed it again. The resigned look on his face told me this was not the first time he'd had such a brush-off.

"Oh, do come," Caitlin piped up. "Nick has so been looking forward to showing you how talented he is. I promise, you won't be disappointed."

"Mom, it would really mean a lot to me if you could make it," Nick said, pressing home the advantage. He turned to his mum and blinked with small boy sadness. She seemed torn between following her husband's lead and pleasing her only son. "Please, Mommy?"

The last plea sealed the deal. "Of course, darling," she said at last. She turned a meaningful look on her husband. "We'll just have a coffee and something to eat, and we'll be fine to see the show."

"It's not going to be full of those drag queens and guys running around in white tights, is it?" asked his father, looking worried.

"No, Dad, it's a rock and roll show," Nick said, laughing awkwardly. "You'll really enjoy it. Lots of music you'll recognise."

His father didn't look convinced, but his mother pulled him along and had a quick, quiet word in his ear as we headed back to the cabins.

We'd arranged to meet in the Spring Fling after we'd all finished work, because we agreed the crew bar probably wasn't the best place to take a couple of conservative fifty-year-olds. Although I'd been at work, and had not seen Nick's show or his parent's reaction, the scene I saw when I entered the bar told me everything I needed to know. His mother was sipping champagne like it was water; the alcohol was clearly having an effect, as she looked a lot more relaxed than she had earlier and was chatting excitedly to Caitlin. Nick was talking to his father, who was speaking with true excitement. He kept bending down to scribble on a napkin and showing Nick what he'd written.

"And if you eventually employed some other teachers, you could make a passive income!" he was saying as I sat down next to him.

"Hi, Ellie," Nick said, with more enthusiasm than I'd heard in weeks. "Mom and Dad really loved the show. They want to support me in going to Broadway!" His cheeks were flushed, and his eyes were sparkling. It really was the happy ending to his years of dreaming and hard work.

"That's brilliant," I said, leaning over to give him a hug. I turned to his father. "You enjoyed the performance, Mr Canlas?"

"The show was just incredible. I can't believe it took us so long to watch him dance. I actually feel very ashamed. We really had no idea how talented our boy is." He beamed at his wife, then smiled at Nick. "Nick and I have just been discussing the possibility of opening a dance studio as a secondary income. I hear Broadway bucks aren't so big these days."

This was Nick's moment, and he was revelling in every second of it. Caitlin had clearly made an impression; Nick's mum was already working out the wedding details, and when the conversation came around to where they would live in New York, Caitlin smiled sweetly and said, "Of course, we'll have to get a two-bedroom apartment if we're going to have a baby in the next couple of years."

Mention of a future grandchild was the icing on the cake. Nick's mother almost fell off the couch.

Although I was pleased for Nick, and happy everything was going so well, I also felt bad for his parents. His mum was going to be absolutely crushed when it turned out that there wasn't going to be a wedding after all, and that there would be no grandchildren on the way. Still, for the moment everything was smooth sailing, so it was silly to worry now.

Nick and Caitlin laughed and made plans; she snuggled into his side and he draped his arm around her. From my point of view, as the slightly awkward outsider, they looked like the lovers they were pretending to be. I was just grateful that most of the conversation didn't require me to talk; I occasionally commented on Nick's talent and his future career, but otherwise stayed quiet, watching.

Then Maria walked in.

On a ship of over 3,000 people, she had somehow managed to find the three people who probably despised her the most. Why now? After Maria and Gabriel had slept together, Caitlin had managed to avoid her all week; having their first meeting now heightened the potential for disaster.

As I watched her, I realised she hadn't come looking for us. She hadn't even noticed us; she stood in the doorway for a moment without drawing any attention to herself, scanning the room. It was clear she was looking for someone, and equally clear from the expression on her face that she didn't see whoever it was. A fleeting look passed over her face—sadness? Vulnerability? I wasn't sure, but it wasn't something I was familiar with seeing, not when it came to Maria.

And then her eyes landed on our little group. She stared at us for a moment, expressionless, before the more familiar calculating look appeared. There was the Maria I recognised. And when she started towards us, I got worried. Word had spread quickly that Nick's parents were coming on board—the fact that they were filthy rich only made the whole thing that much more interesting. While most people had been content to whisper and avoid interfering directly, I doubted that Maria was coming over to play nice.

She swept up to us and smiled. "Good evening," she said dramatically. "I am Maria. You must be Nick's parents. I can see where he gets his good looks." She batted her eyelashes at Teo and added, "You have raised such a lovely boy. He is a credit to you."

Maricel and Teo both beamed with pride.

"We are so pleased to meet another of Nicholas's friends," said Teo, with genuine warmth. "Nicholas's fiancée was just raising our hopes about finally getting a grandchild."

"His fiancée?" Maria looked confused.

"Oh, I'm sorry," Teo said. "I'm getting carried away. They're not engaged yet." He turned to Nick and said, "Sorry, son, we're just so excited."

Maria's eyes narrowed infinitesimally. "This is a joke, yes?" she said, her voice suddenly deadpan.

"Maria, now is not the time," I said, standing up in the hopes of being able to stop the inevitable. "You know, I'd actually really like to talk to you, if you don't mind…"

She ignored me, her gaze zeroing in on Nick. He looked like a deer caught in headlights, afraid to move and unable to speak.

"Oh dear, I hope it wasn't a secret…" said Maricel, who'd gone from positively radiant to looking confused and worried. "I thought everyone knew about Nicholas and Caitlin. We're helping them move to New York."

Maria switched her attention to Maricel, a confused smile on her face. "Everyone knows about Nicholas and Caitlin?" she repeated. "You mean that they are a couple?" The confused smile lightened into a knowing one. "Ah, now I understand. You are all having a joke with me." She laughed a little. "I am afraid you cannot fool me, since *everyone* knows Nick is gay…"

Shit. I closed my eyes and pressed my fingers against my left temple, just like my father did when he heard bad news. When I opened them, Maricel and Teo had thunderstruck looks on their faces. Nick's mouth was hanging open and he looked stunned, rather like a beached trout taking its last breath. Maybe that's what he *was* doing.

Maria was now looking at Nick's parents with pity, adding, "But you must know! It is simply so obvious. Ricky Martin is...is *masculine* by comparison!" She turned to Nick and Caitlin, asking, "What are you two doing, lying to Nick's lovely parents like that?"

Our whole group sat frozen; no one seemed to know quite what to say. Maricel's beaming face had dropped; she looked crestfallen. Teo, on the other hand, was expressionless. He picked up the napkin on which he'd been scribbling his dance studio plans for Nick. He carefully folded it and tucked it away into his pocket, then stood up and took his wife's hand.

"Goodnight, everyone," he said simply, and turned to leave.

"Dad, wait!" Nick got up and put a hand on his father's arm. "Look—I—Let me try to explain."

Maricel and Teo looked at Nick expectantly, and he dropped his eyes to the floor. "I'm sorry," he said. "I didn't want to lie to you, but I was afraid that if I told you that you wouldn't be able to love me. So Caitlin said she'd help me, and we concocted this whole ridiculous charade to convince you that I could be the perfect son." He took a deep breath. "The thing is, I'm not the perfect son. I never will be." He lifted his head proudly and met his mother's gaze; I suspected she was easier for him to face than his father. "I am gay," he said. "I'm still a good person. I still love you both with all my heart." His voice breaking, he continued, "I really need your love. I was just so afraid—I didn't want to disappoint you."

His parents hadn't moved or reacted in any way, but Nick continued regardless. "It's just that I'm realising I can't be anything other than what I am. If you can't support me emotionally or financially, that's okay, because I *will* make my dreams happen. I can just go it alone." He hesitated, and then added, "I really hope you can love me the way I am. But if not...I get it."

Caitlin stood up and grabbed Nick's hand in support. The

air was thick with tension, and as I stood there, breathless, I realised I had no idea how this whole thing was going to end. Nick's parents stood there for what felt like ages, looking at him with blank faces. Then Teo turned to Caitlin and me, nodded, and said, "Goodnight. This has been a long day." They walked away, Teo supporting Maricel with his arm across her back. She looked back over her shoulder and caught Nick's eye. She hesitated, as though she was about to say something, and then looked away again. She kept walking and didn't look back again.

Nick looked relieved, worried, and sad, all at the same time. The relief of finally telling his parents must have been immense, but the fear of having them reject him... I edged closer and took his other hand, leaning my head against his shoulder as tears welled up in his eyes.

Maria looked pleased with the mess she'd created. "Oops," she said, an innocent look on her face. "Did I say something wrong?"

I wondered how much trouble I'd get in if I punched her square in the face, and for a moment I was tempted. I felt awful for Nick, and violence was a tempting immediate retaliation. But it wouldn't get us anywhere; we needed to plan. It was time for the Brazilian Bitch to pay.

Chapter Eighteen

"Right," I said, "time to go."

I dragged a stunned Nick and Caitlin out of the Spring Fling, leaving Maria behind and heading for the relative safety of the crew bar. I settled the two of them into a booth and went for drinks. No sign of Jock, which was too bad, but I'd catch him later. Nick was my more immediate concern.

I set down the drinks and slid into the booth. I'd expected Nick to be in pieces, but he was surprisingly calm.

"I'm just so glad I told them the truth," he said. "When I was a teenager, their non-acceptance might have killed me, but now I think I'll be okay, even if they don't come around. I'm probably in shock, I know, but my overwhelming feeling right now is relief!"

We sat in silence for a few minutes before Caitlin's head came up.

"But what about New York?"

Nick's face told us he'd completely forgotten. His parents had been his last chance to get the money he needed to pursue his Broadway dreams; with his secret out, those dreams were unlikely to ever come true. It was a devastating blow.

Nick looked lost for words. "I just haven't thought that far ahead yet," he said finally. He folded his arms and sighed. "Lots of people move to New York without money or a plan, you know... I just never thought I'd be one of them."

"Can we do anything to help?" I asked.

"No, but thanks, Princess," he said. "It'll be fine. They're my parents, anyway. I'll have to deal with this eventually." He sighed again, looking exhausted. "Do you guys mind if I go back to my cabin now? I need to rest. I have a lot to think about." He got up slowly, kissed us both goodbye, and dragged his feet out the door.

Caitlin and I had both finished our drinks, and as I was hoping to talk to Jock, I hopped up to get the next round. I hadn't been in the crew bar all week as I'd been spending so much time with Cooper, and I really wanted to talk to Jock about what had happened, and make amends. I hated being at odds with him. Again.

When I reached the bar, Jock was still nowhere in sight; the bloke who'd served me before was serving another customer. I waited for him to finish, then beckoned him over. "Where's Jock tonight?" I asked. "Is he up in the officers' bar again?"

"Jock? No. He's gone to the *Triton*," he said. "Or was it the *Goddess*? I can't remember. Anyway, can I get you something?"

"Sorry, what? He's gone where?" I asked. On such a large ship, it was hard to remember all the bar names

The bartender looked at me as if I was a bit simple. "He got trans-shipped," he said. "Left this morning. Halfway to his new ship by now, no doubt. Now, what can I get you?" I stared at him blankly, stunned, and finally he said, "Look, that's all I know. I'm sorry. You gonna order, or what?"

I waved him away, my mind elsewhere, and slipped out of the crew bar without saying goodbye to Caitlin. I didn't really feel like talking to her or anyone else; it had come as such a shock that all I wanted to do was get back to the cabin and try to sort out my tangled emotions.

Jock was gone.

As I entered my cabin, my foot kicked against something that had been slipped under the door. I flicked on the light and bent to pick it up; it was an envelope, with my name written neatly on the front. My stomach fluttered as I turned it over and slid my finger under the flap; maybe Cooper had written me a love letter!

Hey Lass,

I tried to tell you this in person the other night, but things went a bit sour and I didn't quite manage it. I'm being trans-shipped. I've been offered a managerial position on another ship, which also does my favourite run. The current manager broke his contract, so they want me to start right away.

I have to be honest and say I think it's best that I leave anyway... I don't know if you noticed, but I'm head over heels for you. I thought we really clicked, from the first moment we met, and I kept hoping to make a go of it, but you never seemed interested. I can't say I wasn't disappointed, but in the end my friendship with you was more important, if maybe not in my best interests. Anyway, based on the guys you've been picking, I don't think I'm your type anyway—I guess I never really had a chance.

The thing is, Ellie, I couldn't bear to see you with Cooper. The man is an absolute wanker, and I just couldn't do it anymore. I tried so hard to be there for you every time you had your heart broken, but it got to be too much. You couldn't see the kind of man Cooper was, and I couldn't stand around and watch you get hurt again.

Cooper doesn't deserve you. I've long since given up any hope that you might want to be with me—all I want is for you to realise that you deserve better. You deserve someone who can give you the world—not just a cruise.

Be good.

Jock

x

I read the note three times in quick succession, then sank down on the bed, feeling dizzy. If I'd thought my emotions were in turmoil before, it was nothing compared to how I felt now. I was grateful that Caitlin was still in the crew bar; I needed to sort out how I felt about the note. And about Jock.

Jock was an attractive man; I'd thought it more than once. But I'd never seen this coming, because I'd never allowed myself to think of him as anything other than a mate. As far as I'd been able to tell, he'd only ever shown me brotherly concern. Okay, so he'd never much liked any of the men I'd been interested in, but I'd always seen that as a big brother kind of thing, keeping an eye out to make sure I didn't get hurt. I'd never even caught so much as a whiff of romantic interest. If I had... Well. I wasn't really sure what I would have done. My emotions had been all over the map since even before I came aboard, and every time I thought things were finally settling out, something else happened to upset them.

I thought back over all of the conversations I'd had with Jock and felt both embarrassed and guilty. I'd talked to him so much about my relationships—he'd never seemed to mind, had even seemed to want to listen, but now that I knew how he'd felt, I realised that listening to me talk about Seth and Luciano and Cooper must have been incredibly painful for him. I knew he'd not liked them—that much had been obvious. And yet somehow I'd never really clocked that it was less that he disliked *them*, and more that he liked *me*. He'd given me advice on other men, he'd taken me to the beach, he'd made me tea when I was upset, he'd got proper het up when he thought I wasn't being treated right...

Maybe I'd been so invested in keeping Jock as a friend that I'd never really let myself consider other possibilities. Maybe I'd been careful not to recognise any romantic vibes because I was afraid. Being friends was safe. It meant no anxieties about things ending, or risking losing an important relationship if things went wrong. And there was no doubt that Jock had been important to me.

This left me in an uncomfortable place. Things with Cooper seemed to be going okay again, and despite warnings from both Caitlin and Jock, I was still convinced that he was a good guy and that our relationship was a positive one. But...could I imagine myself with Jock? That was the big question.

Jock was lovely. He was kind, he was fun, he was easy to talk to, he was reliable... He was attractive and he certainly seemed to care about me. And as far as I knew, he wasn't a skirt-chasing lunatic.

Had I missed an opportunity? Made a huge mistake?

I stared down at the letter in my hand and then crumpled it. Dammit. He should have told me in person. And he shouldn't have waited so long. Now it was too late; I was with Cooper, and thinking about what could have been was pointless.

So, that was settled then.

I lay back on my bed and ran back through all of the conversations I'd had with Jock. I thought about the day on the beach, and imagined a different ending to that day, one where he kissed me and…

I shook my head and sat up. I was with Cooper. It didn't matter that I'd been able to see myself kissing Jock easily, that in my head it seemed right; I had no right imagining myself with someone else. Cooper deserved better. I wouldn't be happy if he were lying on his bed, dreaming about another woman, and I couldn't have different standards for myself than for him.

I wished Cooper wasn't working. It would have been nice to go snuggle up to him and feel like everything was okay. But he was working, so instead I changed into party clothes and headed back to the crew bar. Caitlin was still sitting where I'd left her, and I felt a wave of guilt crash over me for her leaving so abruptly. As I passed the bar, I spotted Nick at the bar; he must have come back after I'd left. He looked up and saw me; he waved and indicated he'd get me a drink.

I slid into the booth beside Caitlin, and moments later Nick appeared with three Long Island Iced Teas.

"You're back," I said to him.

"So are you," Caitlin said, smiling.

"My cabin was too quiet," Nick said, pushing the drinks across the table towards us. I downed half of mine before Nick got settled, and looked up to find both of them staring at me.

"Okay, something's up," Nick said.

"What's wrong, beautiful?" Caitlin asked. "You kind of vanished without warning. Are you okay?"

I hesitated. I desperately wanted to talk, but both of them had their own problems and I didn't really want to burden them with mine. Again. But they were watching me expectantly, so finally I said, "Well...yes. No." I winced. "Not really." I took a deep breath. "Jock's been trans-shipped. But before he left, he put a note under the door of our cabin. Telling me how much he fancies me."

"Oh, my God!" Caitlin squealed, plonking her drink down on the table. "I can't believe it! I hoped you two would get together! I can't believe the motherfucker left it so late—and then went and got himself trans-shipped before you could find out!"

"Wait, what?" I said. "What do you mean, you hoped we'd get together? Why didn't you tell me this before?"

"You were all loved up with Cooper," she said, "and I didn't want to pressure you or try to sway you, because I *hate it* when people do that to me..." She paused, waiting for my reaction, but I was so stunned that I was speechless. "I just thought you two would make such a cute couple, and god, it was obvious he wanted you."

"Yeah, totally," Nick added.

Well, that was just great. Apparently I was more oblivious than I'd thought.

"Who fancied you?" enquired a voice from behind us.

"Cooper! Hi!" I yelped, coming to my feet and throwing my arms around my boyfriend, adding, "Nobody—they're just being silly." I shot my friends a death glare over my shoulder. It wasn't my fault Jock had feelings for me; god knew *I* hadn't encouraged him. No point in stirring things up by telling Cooper.

"Okay, whatever," he said, shrugging his shoulders, unperturbed. "I saw Maria and Jacoline on the other side of the bar when I came in." He looked down at me. "Want to join them?"

"NO!" Caitlin and Nick said together. I stayed silent.

Cooper rolled his eyes at them and said, "You two are welcome to stay here. Ellie?" I hesitated, and he sighed. "Come on, Ellie, I've only got twenty minutes before I've got to leave again. I promised them I'd have a drink tonight. Please?"

I didn't want to talk to Maria right now, or ever, actually, but I didn't want my boyfriend drinking with her, either. And I'd been wanting to spend time with him all evening, so it would have been stupid for me to pass up on the chance. Admitting defeat, I mumbled, "Okay," and trailed after Cooper. "See you guys soon," I said, looking back at Nick and Caitlin. I gave them a sad little wave goodbye as I walked away. I didn't like the feeling that I'd chosen a man over my friends, but really, I hadn't had a choice. My time with Cooper was precious, and I got to see Nick and Caitlin much more often. They'd forgive me.

Jacoline and Maria were huddled together at a table; when they saw us coming they moved around to let us in. When she saw me, Maria looked away and sipped her drink.

Don't worry, bitch, I'm just as unhappy to see you. "Hiya," I said aloud.

"Don't let us interrupt," Cooper said, slouching down and putting his hands behind his head.

"Maria was just telling me about a passenger she met," Jacoline said, sounding excited.

Maria looked far less excited. "I met him on the first night of the cruise and he told me he loved hunting. He said that his family never worries about money. So I thought he was rich, you know, like Luiz's family. *They* never worry about money, either."

Oh, hooray. Insight into Maria's love life. Normally I wouldn't care, but I was curious if this mysterious passenger might have been the person she'd intended to meet in the Spring Fling. In any event, I'd brought my drink with me and felt no compulsion whatsoever to enter into the conversation. So instead, I listened and absorbed so I could take the conversation back to my friends later.

"I was supposed to meet him in the Spring Fling earlier," she said, "but he never showed."

"Oh no," Jacoline said, looking concerned.

I bit my lip and looked down. It was incredibly tempting to make a snide comment, but I resisted. *Be better than Maria*, I told myself.

Maria flicked her hair over her shoulder and said, "I know. I cannot imagine why he would stand me up." That look—the one I'd seen when she'd been standing in the doorway to the Spring Fling, after realising she'd been stood up—flickered across her face again and then was gone. Jeez, this was starting to get annoying. If it carried on, I might actually start thinking Maria had a soul. That was a terrifying thought.

"Anyway," she continued, ignoring me, "I was naturally upset, so I went for a walk, and then I ran into him on his way to meet me. He had got his times wrong." She looked smug, but only for a moment. "So we went back to the Spring Fling for a drink. And it was all going so nicely, until I asked him about his family. I asked how and where they made their money…and he just laughed at me."

"What? Why?" Jacoline exclaimed.

"He is not rich!" Maria replied hotly. Jacoline gasped in horror. "They never worry about money, because they accept they will never have any! They hunt pigs—to eat them!" She paused, fuming. "I wasted so much time with him, thinking he was someone he was not. He works at Walmart and lives in a caravan! He saved for four years to come on this cruise!" By the end, she was nearly hysterical; her voice had gone up with every sentence, until she was registering pitches that were nearly inaudible. And she also looked like she might burst into tears.

"Maria…" Cooper said, leaning forward and putting his hand on hers, "I'm sorry, but you're barking up the wrong tree. None of the passengers on this ship are wealthy. I mean, maybe one or two, but generally, it's a pretty middle class cruise line." He looked at her pityingly. "Come on. Everyone knows the swanky ones travel with Crystal or Regent Cruises."

Maria looked even more distressed, if that was possible. "Why did no one tell me?" she wailed. "My mother has been telling me to come here for a long time for this exact reason.

Now I will have to marry my fat, loser boyfriend." She stared down into her drink, looking miserable. "Maybe I can get a job with one of the other cruise lines."

Cooper checked his watch and sighed. "Sorry, ladies, but I've got to get back to the lab to do some printing." He stood up, his fingers trailing briefly across my shoulder. "I'll see you all later."

The last thing I wanted to do was stay for drinks with Maria, so I quickly excused myself and slipped away. Caitlin and Nick had disappeared, so I made my way slowly back to the cabin. This whole evening had been a shambles; I was looking forward to bed. Maybe tomorrow would be a better day.

Caitlin was already snoring on her bunk when I opened the door, her arms protectively wrapped around the teddy bear she dragged out on days she was feeling low. I pulled up the covers and tucked her in, like my mum had done when I was little. And when I'd come home after ending things with Dan. Apparently I'd inherited my mother's need to take care of other people.

I changed into my pyjamas and crawled into bed. As I lay there, staring up into the darkness, I wondered if it was possible to like two blokes at once. It had never happened to me before; I'd always been a one-man kind of girl. And now I was just confused. Cooper was charming, and his traumatic past just made him that much more alluring, because what girl doesn't want to be the one to heal a broken man? Okay, so I'd questioned his behaviour a few times, but really it was only that I'd got super anxious and had overreacted to a few things because I was insecure. He just wanted to take things slow, and who could blame him?

And then there was Jock. He was so lovely, and while he'd had shit in his past, he hadn't let it affect him. He was sweet and strong and such a good listener...and, oh, who was I kidding, he was really sexy with that floppy hair and gorgeous blue eyes.

Arg. I rolled over and buried my face in my pillow. I was

going around in circles.

After a fitful night's sleep, the cabin phone woke me up. I lay in the dark for a moment, still groggy, and then slipped out of bed. I'd been here long enough that I could navigate in the dark; I tripped over a pile of Caitlin's clothes, but otherwise made it to the phone relatively unscathed.

"Hello?" I said chirpily. Good morning, this is Ellie, no, of course you haven't woken me up!

"Ellie, it's Nick!" He sounded excited, and some of my bad mood washed away. Yay for calls from friends. "Can you and that gorgeous bitch meet me for breakfast on the pool deck? I've got good news!"

"Let me get her out of bed," I said, flicking on the light and the kettle, "and we'll be there."

By the time I had tea ready, Caitlin had woken up and was stretching. She'd managed another morning off from shooting passenger photos on the St Thomas gangway. Lucky her.

"What's going on?" she asked.

I handed her a mug. "Nick has good news."

She downed the tea and bounded out of bed. As soon as we'd dressed, we headed up to the pool deck, where we spotted Nick sitting with his parents at a long table near the pool bar. Things looked a lot less tense than they had the night before.

"Come join us," Nick called when he saw us. As we sat down, he said, "I've got good news and bad news. Which do you want first?"

My father often started conversations in this way. "The bad news," I replied. Caitlin nodded in agreement.

"I hoped you'd say that," Nick said, grabbing his mother's hand. "The bad news… I'm leaving the ship." He grinned. "But the good news is that I'm going to New York!"

"Yaaaayyyy!" Caitlin and I leapt on Nick, smothering him with hugs. His parents were startled at first; I'd got the impression the night before that they weren't real big on physical contact. But they seemed pleased, which was nice, both for Nick and for their family. I was so glad his parents had come around.

"Girls, I wanted to apologise for last night," Nick's father said once we quieted down. He hesitated, and then said, "I believe it would be safe to say that Nicholas's mother and I were…surprised. I imagine he has told you that we are, in many respects, quite a traditional family?" Caitlin and I both nodded. "That has not changed, and while Nicholas might be…" He stopped, his mouth twisting. "Well. We are working on that." Maricel took his hand and squeezed it, her eyes on her son. "Maricel and I talked it over last night," Teo continued, "and asked God for His guidance. In the end, Nicholas is our son. We cannot expect him to be perfect—to follow our ideal. It is not fair of us to try to change him." He looked at Nick and his face softened. "We love our boy. We want to help him."

"They came and found me last night," Nick said. "We were up really late talking. And I think it's all going to be okay."

"I'm sorry we lied to you, Mr and Mrs Canlas," Caitlin said awkwardly. "We just wanted to help Nick."

The conversation settled into the topic of New York. Nick, clearly pleased he no longer had to hide who he was, talked excitedly of where he'd live in New York, the shows he wanted to audition for, the places he wanted to visit…

"Don't forget," Caitlin interrupted, "if I get into Parsons, I'm coming too!"

Nick cheered. And then, as though they'd planned it, they both turned to look at me.

"Now we just need to find a way to get you to New York, too, Princess," he said. "We're incomplete without you!"

"You definitely need to come," Caitlin said.

I laughed. "What would I do in New York?"

"Be a totally f—" Caitlin caught herself and glanced guiltily at Nick's parents. "Be a totally fantastic photographer. Open your own gallery!"

I wasn't convinced. "Maybe in a few years," I said, more to appease them than anything else.

"Babe, everybody fakes it in New York," Nick said reassuringly. "We'll find the space, the finance, and all you need is to take a few fabulous photos."

"Well, I'll think about it," I said. It was a nice dream, but I had a feeling that making it into reality would take more than I had to give at the moment.

Maricel stood and kissed Nick on the head. "We see you three have much to discuss. We will see you later, Nicholas."

With the parents gone, we headed for the internet room; Nick and Caitlin were keen to start looking at places to live in New York. I just wanted to check Facebook.

I was tired, so I almost missed it as I scrolled past the inevitable baby pictures and happy couples, and then realised what I'd just seen and frantically scrolled back up. There it was: Luiz Martinez is Engaged. Well, bollocks.

I checked to see if he was online and then sent him a message.

I see that congratulations are in order.

Oh yes. ☺ We're so happy.

When did it happen?

I wanted to ask when I was on your ship, but when I was called away so soon I wasn't certain it was the right thing. But last night Maria Skyped me to say she missed me so much, and wished I was there, and she hoped we could be together forever. I was inspired to ask her to marry me in that moment, and she said yes! So I know it was the right thing to do.

Wow.

There wasn't much more to say. I didn't think it was the right time to tell Luiz his new fiancée was a lying, cheating, inconsiderate whorebag...so I opted on the side of caution and removed myself from the conversation once again, silently regretting my decision to accept his friend request. Way too awkward.

The news pulled Caitlin and Nick away from flat-hunting.

"What are we going to do about it, guys?" asked Caitlin. "We can't let Maria marry that poor guy." Nick and I both nodded in agreement, and then as we headed back to our cabin, Nick and Caitlin began to plot Maria's downfall. It made me a little uncomfortable; I didn't like her, but I also didn't want to destroy her life, either. My parents had always said it was better to keep the moral high ground—that way, if things went wrong you were secure in the knowledge that at least you've behaved appropriately. I tried to say this to Nick and Caitlin, but they were having none of it; both were absolutely determined to get their revenge on the Brazilian Bitch.

I'd given up trying to persuade them otherwise by the time we reached the cabin. As I started to open the door, I realised that another note addressed to me was stuck in the doorjamb. It was a phone message from the communications officer.

Ellie, please call Rachel from Celestial Cruise Line head office. +1 305-222-3456

"That's strange," I said. "Why would she be calling me?" The others shrugged as they read the note over my shoulder.

Caitlin and Nick crowded into the cabin behind me and insisted I call her back right away. When I finally willed up the courage to call, I wasn't expecting it to be Rachel's direct line, and when she answered, I nearly hung up in shock.

"Ellie, great to hear from you," she exclaimed after I introduced myself. "I am part of the team who recruited you, and I need to tell you that the girl whose job you are currently doing has recovered from her appendix operation, and will be coming back to the ship."

Oh, shit.

"Oh," I squeaked.

"Of course, we don't want to lose you," she continued, "So we're going to trans-ship you and put you in a proper photography position."

"Oh!" I said in a much happier squeak. Despite my problematic personal life, I'd managed to impress them with my professional skills! Hooray! I suddenly realised she must be wondering if I could say anything other than my name and 'oh', so I added, "Right, yes, that would be wonderful. Erm, thanks so much."

Nick and Caitlin were staring at me eagerly, waiting for me to drop some crumb of information that would let them know what the conversation was about. I turned my back on them; they were way too distracting!

"We're not quite sure yet," Rachel was saying, "but I think we're sending you to Hawaii. Might be Alaska, though. I'm just waiting on a few things."

She relayed a few more things to me, promised to ring as soon as details had been sorted, and then ended the call.

I stared at the wall, dazed, and then excitedly filled Nick and Caitlin in on the call.

Pros: I'd actually be closer to my real dream job, and somewhere as spectacular as Hawaii or Alaska.

Cons: I'd have to leave Cooper, so soon in our relationship. I bit my lip.

"Dump him, babe," was Caitlin's response when I asked for their opinions. "Seriously, people come and go all the time, and you've just got to go with the flow. Do what is best for you."

"Yes, and that could be coming to New York," Nick chimed in eagerly.

I smiled at them both, but inside I was a bundle of nerves

Why was everything so hard?

Chapter Nineteen

I invited Cooper to our cabin for drinks after work, to tell him about the position. I knew I had to take it for my career, but had spent the afternoon dreaming about a long-distance relationship—or, if possible, maybe he could even trans-ship with me!

At about 11.30pm, he turned up, his mate Mikhail tagging along after him; Mikhail knew Caitlin was single and had been after her throughout his whole contract. Sadly, for him, Caitlin had completely sworn off men. Gabriel was the closest thing she'd come to meeting The One, and his betrayal had left her cold.

"I just feel dead inside," she whispered, having dragged me into the bathroom while the boys were making music selections. "I know I thought he was just for fun, but something just changed, and everything got serious. Maybe I scared him away?"

"I don't think so, sweetie. You're amazing. He's just a man. They're weak, dick-led fuckwits—we both know that. What is it Bridget Jones says? No more of this fuckwittage!"

Look at me, giving tough advice. I'd never have said something like that when I'd first come aboard. I looked at Caitlin hopefully; she looked sad and nestled up against me for a moment.

"You're a good friend," she said into my top. Then she pulled away and added, "Right, motherfucker, stop being a big sap. It's time to get out there and entertain those boys!" She gave me an exaggerated wink and flashed her trademark smile.

To anyone else, she'd have seemed the same Caitlin as always; I knew better, and I knew just how fragile that façade was.

We rejoined the boys, and had just cracked the beers and opened a bag of salt and vinegar crisps when Caitlin spoke.

"So, Cooper," she said, "has Ellie told you her fabulous news?"

"Um, no," Cooper said, raising his eyebrows at me. "What?"

"Someone from head office called to say I'm being trans-shipped," I said. "The girl from the Pic Stop is coming back. I only just heard about it today and was just about to tell you." I swallowed nervously. "They're not sure where yet, but maybe Hawaii or Alaska. It's a proper photography position."

I waited for Cooper to react and beg me not to leave him.

"Wow," he said, "that is big news." He popped a crisp into his mouth. "When do you leave?"

His emotionless tone and unconcerned body language took me by surprise. Did he really not care if I left? No, I thought, he was probably just trying to be supportive and didn't want to seem like he was holding me back. Maybe he didn't want to appear vulnerable, especially in front of his mate. Men were like that.

A small part of my heart, and the sudden aching pit in my stomach, told me he actually might not be bothered, that maybe Caitlin and Jock had been right, and that I'd been trying to make this into something it wasn't. I instantly became nervous. We'd had our share of ups and downs; maybe if I could bring back the fun and romance, it would liven things up again. I slurped down my beer and opened another.

I sidled over to Cooper and slid onto his lap, which was a bit tricky, since he was perched on the end of my bed. "So if I moved to another ship, you wouldn't miss me?" I asked, draping my arms around his neck and using a husky, Scarlett Johansson-inspired voice.

I'm a seductive sex kitten. Want me already, dammit.

"Ellie, you're squashing me!"

He pushed me off his lap, and I felt the fear inside rising.

Why was he acting so peculiar again? I downed another beer, already feeling the rush of swirly tingles from the previous bottle.

Cooper reached over and removed the beer from my hand. "Ellie, people get trans-shipped all the time, and sometimes you can't avoid going it alone." He sighed. "But I'll tell you what—obviously I don't want you going away without me, so I'll look into getting trans-shipped, too."

I looked up at him, hope crashing through me. "Really?" I squeaked. "Oh, Cooper!" I flung my arms around him and then quickly let go. "Sorry," I said.

"So why don't you go," he said, "and then, as soon as I'm able, I'll see about joining you. And it doesn't have to be in the photo team, I've got heaps of experience outside this you know. I've been in the casino, bartending, cruise staff...so I could take almost anything. Let's not talk about it now, but I'll sort something out."

I wondered briefly if maybe he was just trying to brush me off, and then mentally scolded himself. My little scare had been brief and unfounded; he was just trying to find a way to keep us together, which was what I *wanted*. I smiled happily; maybe I'd end up having everything, after all.

Caitlin was a bit quiet in her corner, and I suspected it was because I'd just quashed the idea of coming to live in New York. I still thought New York might be in my future, but not right now. It seemed a stroke of incredible luck and fate that the original job I'd been given wasn't in line with my career goals, but now they had one that was. Maybe Cooper and I could do a contract on the new ship, and then join my friends in NYC? I couldn't keep the smile off my face; the tipsier I became, the more fabulous were my ideas.

Between the booze and Cooper's promise, I was feeling upbeat, so the timing was perfect for a spot of dancing around the cramped cabin. Caitlin joined me; the boys' focus on us abruptly became more intense, and, knowing that, we jokingly turned it on for them. At first, it was just for fun; I'd been riveted by Caitlin's stories, of course, but just as I'd never imagined actually doing anything she'd described, I would never have actually followed through with any of the suggestive moves. But as the guys played increasingly sexy music and the beer flowed, I felt myself getting more than a little bit turned on. Caitlin was dancing behind me, and with my back to her, I was playfully gyrating my bottom against her stomach. She ran her fingers delicately up my sides from behind. I instinctively raised my arms into the air, and she continued the line up my arms, and then entwined her fingers in mine.

Then she lowered our hands together and crossed them across my chest in a spoon-like embrace. Caitlin was breathing hard behind me and kept darting the end of her tongue to lick my earlobes. The room was spinning and I was absorbed in her sensual moves. She released her hands and caressed my breasts briefly before slipping her hands into my shirt. A pleasurable pain pierced my groin and I groaned. My legs felt weak beneath me, and I felt the urge to lie down. I made my way to the bed and collapsed onto it, face first. Caitlin continued to explore, her hands drifting over my skin until I felt like I was on fire.

She turned me over roughly and pinned my arms down. As she brought her face close to mine, I became acutely aware of how heavily we were breathing. Caitlin leaned in to kiss my neck, her hands making their way much lower. She traced a line around my belly button, then walked her fingers down to my skirt. Without looking for a zipper or button, she slid her hand straight underneath the hem and into my pants. When she reached what she was looking for, I breathed in sharply, my eyes rolling back in my head.

Just as I felt ready to explode, Cooper let out a moan. I had forgotten they were even there. He grabbed my hair, then leant in to kiss me hard on the mouth. Caitlin wiggled down to the floor and pushed my skirt up around my waist. I briefly caught sight of my pants as Caitlin tossed them to the floor and, just as Cooper stuck his tongue deep down my throat, I felt Caitlin's tongue exploring somewhere else entirely.

So this is a threesome. I stifled a laugh. How was this even happening? With my roommate and boyfriend? Cruise ships definitely weren't for the faint hearted—it seemed like anything you wanted to try was entirely possible. Cooper was completely into it, and my eyes searched for Mikhail and found him hovering over us, virtually salivating. I only needed to flick my eyes towards Caitlin to encourage him to join us. *And then there were four...*

Mikhail got busy somewhere up Caitlin's skirt; she, meanwhile, was still occupied with me. She responded to Mikhail's overtures by withdrawing from me and pulling him up onto the top bunk, where I could no longer see them.

"Let's catch up to them," I whispered hoarsely in Cooper's ear, and he soon filled the breach, making me moan as loudly as Caitlin was above me. If the cabin had had windows, they would have been steamed up—and I could do a very *Titanic*-esque hand on the glass—although I suspected that actually only happened in movies. Our windows would be clear and I'd probably pull a muscle.

Moments later, as I was struggling to get my breath back, an uncomfortable sense of guilt and shame washed over me. What had I just done? Having sex with my boyfriend was fine, but getting it on with Caitlin and then being intimate with Cooper in the same room as Caitlin and Mikhail? I never would have imagined myself in this situation when I'd first arrived only a couple of months earlier. Though, to be fair, it wasn't exactly something I'd not thought about; Caitlin's stories always turned me on, and I'd realised, watching Caitlin and Gabriel on the dance floor, that I enjoyed observing.

I suddenly felt awkward, and naturally couldn't let the moment go unnoticed. "So... is it just me, or is this anybody else's first time having group sex?" I said to nobody in particular, cringing at having to say the word 'sex' out loud.

"Don't worry, roomie, it's not group sex until there's at least five people," Caitlin said, popping her head over the side. "So you're practically a virgin." Well, that was a relief. "Let's go up to the crew bar for a drink, shall we, guys?" she added.

Grateful for the distraction, I got up and straightened out my clothes and hair. I thought it would be better to just ignore the fallout of what we'd just done, so I buzzed around the cabin, chatting inanely about a bizarre passenger I'd encountered in the Pic Stop. I caught Cooper looking at me sideways a couple of times, but I couldn't quite read him, so I just kept talking. My motor-mouth had made a stunning return, and I couldn't seem to shut up.

As we were preparing for the crew bar, Cooper headed for the door. "I'm really tired," he said, smiling as he stifled a yawn. "Let's catch up tomorrow to talk about the new job, okay?" He kissed my cheek and disappeared to his cabin. I was disappointed; I'd wanted to talk things through—both the job and the sex, if I were honest. But in light of my vow to be bright, breezy, and super-sexy, I just returned his kiss and said goodnight.

Caitlin pointed at the top bunk. "He's asleep!" she said, laughing. "Let's just leave him there."

Apparently the men had been rather more tired by our exertions than Caitlin and I.

On our walk to the crew bar, I had a profound thought—or at least one that felt profound in that moment. I suddenly understood why ships were known for so much salacious behaviour. So many emotions—excitement, disappointment, and anticipation—fuelled by plenty of alcohol, and combined with living in such close quarters, were a recipe for disaster. And the fact that people moved on so quickly meant that no-strings-attached sex was easy and even encouraged.

The crew bar was pumping as usual, despite the late hour, and I wondered if anybody ever performed their job with a full quota of sleep. Maria and a hoard of her admirers were in the corner near the jukebox, and before she saw us, she grabbed the guy nearest to her and kissed him deeply. I recognised him as a waiter from the pool deck buffet.

"She's clearly enjoying life as an almost-wed woman," I said to Caitlin dryly. "Poor Luiz. He really has no idea what he's gotten himself into."

"Mmmmmm," Caitlin said. "We really should enlighten him."

I frowned at her. "What are you thinking?"

Without a word, Caitlin whipped out her phone and snapped a few photos of Maria tangling tongues with the handsome blond waiter.

"Right, roomie," she said, looking at me with a satisfied smile, "let's get back to our cabin and see if Mikhail is awake. I think I'm in the mood to party again!"

We crept quietly into the cabin, but Mikhail had mysteriously disappeared. Caitlin shrugged and said, "Truthfully, roomie, I'm not worried. I still hate men after what Gabriel did. I'm just trying not to focus on being so sad." The cheery façade had fallen, and her eyes were sad.

I hugged her. "I know, Caity. Just do what you need to do."

The night had taken its toll, and soon we both settled in to sleep.

"Ellie?" Caitlin whispered from her bunk. "I'm glad we're okay after the thing that happened here before…"

"Of course we're okay," I said. We were, mostly. It was a little weird, though. I'd never thought of myself as bisexual, but I had to admit it was the best tongue-work I'd ever had. I laughed quietly; maybe she could give Cooper some pointers… On the other hand, while it had been exciting, I didn't think I'd be likely to seek a reprise of the night's action, and although she liked a bit of girl-on-girl action from time to time, I knew she'd respect my limits.

I decided to start locking the bathroom door, just in case.

The next morning was Martinique, so I opened the shop for the required few hours.

It was a boring morning, so I was grateful to finally be able to close up. I'd originally thought I'd head back to bed for a nap once we'd docked, but I realised I hadn't emailed my parents lately and instead detoured to the internet room.

Sitting at the computer, waiting for it to boot up, I stifled a yawn and tapped my fingers impatiently on the table. As I wrote a carefully edited email to my parents, I thought about the night before; I needed to track Cooper down today so we could talk. I was so distracted it took me a while to realise that I'd accidentally typed everything I was thinking into the email to my parents. Oops. I deleted it; they definitely didn't need to know all of the details about last night.

With the email sent off, I brought up Facebook—and immediately wished I hadn't. There, at the top of my newsfeed, were the pictures that Caitlin had taken of Maria last night...and worse, she'd actually tagged Maria in them. It suddenly dawned on me that Caitlin was doing to Maria exactly what Maria had allegedly done to the other girl on her previous ship. I checked the time; Caitlin had posted these not long after I'd opened the Pic Stop, which meant they'd been up for several hours now. Luiz wasn't online, which I was grateful for, as I'd no idea what I would have said to him. And then I realised that he was no longer listed as engaged to Maria, but as single.

Shit, shit, shit.

I'd felt bad for Luiz, and I thought he deserved much better than Maria, but I didn't really feel like this had been the right way to go about it. But then, Maria had hurt Caitlin much more than she had me. She'd been cruel and cutting to me, but I'd been the one who'd slept with men she'd previously been with, not the other way around, so I could at least understand why she might have hated me. Caitlin, though, she'd destroyed by sleeping with Gabriel, and I knew Caitlin had never really recovered.

Before I had a chance to think about what I wanted to do, if anything, the door banged open and Maria appeared, looking frantic. She spotted me and stormed over.

"You!" she shrieked. "Where is that fucking bitch?"

I stared at her, speechless. She looked like she was about to cry, and I realised that the vulnerability I'd been seeing in her face was probably a symptom of a much bigger problem.

Her eyes darted past me to the computer, which was not

only still open to Facebook but had those damn photos plastered across the top of the page, and she wailed, sinking down into the chair at the computer next to me.

"He called me," she said, her voice wavering. "This morning. He saw I was tagged and looked at the photos expecting to see something nice and then saw—that." She gestured weakly at my computer. Her lower lip trembled. "He ended our relationship. And hung up on me. And now he will not answer the phone."

I sat there, completely flabbergasted. What the hell was I supposed to do? Caitlin would kill me if I comforted the Brazilian Bitch, but...

"Do you want me to message him for you?" I asked hesitantly.

Maria burst into tears. "Why are you being nice to me?" she demanded. "You do not like me."

True. "You're right, I don't," I said bluntly. "But you're upset, and I like to think I'm a nice person. And for the record, I didn't know Caitlin was going to post those photos."

By now she was sobbing, great shuddering sobs that shook her small frame until I was afraid she might completely fly to pieces.

"You do not understand," she said, sounding hysterical. "I *have* to marry money. I *have* to. I have to marry someone with money because otherwise, how am I supposed to look after my family?" She dragged her sleeve across her face. "It is not fair...no. I am beautiful. I know I am. But no one wants me!"

I blinked in surprise. "Erm," I said, "really? From where I'm sitting, everyone wants you..."

She lifted her head, a miserable expression on her face. Her eyes were puffy, her skin blotchy, and part of me was pleased to see that she wasn't one of those women who managed to look beautiful when crying. "But they do not want to keep me," she said.

I waited for further explanation, but when none was forthcoming, I said, "I'm sorry, you've lost me."

"They meet me. They like me. They sleep with me, and for

a little time I feel better about myself. I feel beautiful again. And then, a day or a week or a month later, they toss me aside like so much garbage." She took a deep breath. "Seth no longer wanted me, and he went to you. I was not important enough to Luciano for him to only want me."

"Well, I hate to break it to you," I interrupted, "but Seth and I didn't work out, either, and it's not like Luciano wanted to be exclusive with me, either."

"But they still wanted you!" she wailed. "I have to marry money, and Luiz has been the only man I could find with money who was willing to stick with me—because he is so fat and dull that he thought a beautiful wife was too good to be true. And now even he has cast me aside."

I hesitated, turning words over in my mind, and then said, "Look, Maria, I'm not trying to be a bitch, but if you wanted to make sure Luiz didn't end things, you probably shouldn't have been sticking your tongue down other guys' throats, much less sleeping with them."

"But I do not want Luiz," she said miserably. "I am so unhappy with him. He is so...nice...and boring. I keep trying and trying to find someone I can be happy with and who has the money to help me take care of my family, and it just goes wrong every time."

The weird thing was that a lot of what she was saying made her sound a lot like Caitlin. Both seemed to bolster their self-image by sleeping around, except that for Caitlin it wasn't nearly as destructive as it seemed to be for Maria. It seemed to me that Maria felt trapped in her relationship with Luiz—or *had* felt trapped—because she didn't want to be with him, but also didn't feel like she could really get out of it because she wanted, or needed, the money. Based on what I was hearing, she'd ended up hating herself because despite her many charms—personality not being one of them—she couldn't catch an attractive rich man. Luiz was the only one she was able to catch and keep hold of, and so she'd ended up feeling angry and bitter, choosing to sleep with any man who crossed her path to remind herself that she was still attractive and *could* get any man she wanted…even if she couldn't hold on to him.

It was incredibly sad, really, to realise why Maria behaved the way she did. She lashed out at other women and was ugly and cruel because it helped her forget, for a little while at least, her own shortcomings.

Unfortunately, none of this insight helped me figure out what I ought to do about her right now.

Finally, I said, "I'm really sorry, Maria. I didn't know. Look, do you want me to help you find Caitlin? Maybe the two of you can figure it out."

"Why are you helping me?" she asked again.

I snorted. "Because generally speaking, I'm a nice person, and I have issues being mean to someone who's crying. And also because I'm much better at dealing with other people's problems than I am with my own."

She sniffled and dragged her sleeve across her face. "If you *ever* tell anyone about any of this…"

"Don't worry, I have no desire to be associated with you." I logged out of Facebook and stood up. "Come on. Let's go find Caitlin."

We found Caitlin back in our cabin, her head bent over a book. When the door opened, she said, without looking around. "Hey, roomie, I've got some news to tell you!"

I cleared my throat, feeling awkward. "Erm, Caity…"

She closed the book and turned around. Her eyes narrowed to little slits when she spotted Maria.

"What the fuck is that bitch doing here?" she demanded.

"Yes, of course, I am always the bitch," Maria snapped. "The Brazilian Bitch, yes? I hear things."

"It's certainly an apt descriptor," Caitlin retorted.

Great start, Ellie.

"Guys," I said, hoping to get a handle on things before they go really ugly. "Caity, Maria was really upset by the pictures you posted, and I thought maybe if you talked to each other, you might be able to resolve things?"

She laughed bitterly. "Oh yeah, we'll just kiss and make up, is that it?" Glaring at Maria, she added, "I guess now you know how it feels to have someone taken away from you. You slept with Gabriel. Luiz dumped you. I'd say we're even."

Maria looked furious. "How do I know you will not hurt me further in the future?"

"I quite frankly don't give a shit what happens to you from here on out," Caitlin said bluntly. "My only interest was making you understand what it feels like when someone tramples on your heart." She turned her back and opened the book again. "I broke your heart because you broke mine. Now get out of my cabin."

Maria and I exchanged glances, and I shrugged. The corner of her mouth twisted, then she left, slamming the door closed behind her.

"Caity, I'm sorry—" I began, but she cut me off.

"Roomie, I don't give a fuck about Gabriel or Maria or anything else on this whole fucking awful ship." She turned around and stared at me. "I got into Parsons."

"Oh, Caity!" I exclaimed, hugging her. "I'm so glad!"

"Me too," she said, leaning her head against me. "Means I can leave this damn ship asap instead of just slogging on. Nick and I can just go to New York as soon as we possibly can." She checked the time and then stood. "I promised him I'd meet him in the internet room to look for apartments and to discuss what we're going to do when we get there. Want to come?"

I trailed after Caitlin, back to the internet room, and then hovered as she and Nick dove straight into planning. Finally, I interrupted, saying,

"When are you going to go?"

"I'm only here as a fill-in, so I'm out-skis as soon as possible," Nick said cheerfully, tossing his feather boa over his shoulder. "I'm thinking...five days."

"Don't they need something like a month to replace dancers?" I asked. I felt like I'd been socked in the stomach; I hadn't expected him to want to leave quite so soon.

"Oh, really?" asked Nick. "I guess when I book my flights, I might forget all about that."

Caitlin was quiet for a moment, and then she said, "Fuck it. I'm going to leave on Friday. I've got a friend in St Martin, and I can hook up with him for a few days, then fly up to New York when you're there next week!" She looked at Nick expectantly. "What do you think?"

"I think it's a goddamn super idea!" Nick shrieked, taking off his boa and swinging it around his head. "Let's blow this joint, biatch!"

They seemed to forget me as they dove back into apartment hunting. I stood behind them for a while, trying to adjust to the fact that my best friends were leaving in less than a week. Although I was getting trans-shipped, which was of course exciting, I'd imagined we'd have had a few more weeks together before I left.

I had Cooper, but he worked longer hours than me…and besides, your best mates are different. They're the ones you talk to *about* your boyfriend, and I was losing both of mine within days. In that moment, I also admitted to myself that I felt a little jealous. Caitlin and Nick were running off to New York together, and I was going to be on a new ship, without my friends or boyfriend, and where I didn't know anybody.

"Don't forget me," I whispered, but they didn't hear me.

Chapter Twenty

By the time I had to go open the Pic Stop, I was beginning to get pretty irritated; I'd been looking for Cooper for what felt like hours during our afternoon in Martinique, but it was like he'd disappeared. Frustrations with Cooper, fears about trans-shipping without him, and sadness at Caitlin and Nick's pending departure all built up inside until I felt about ready to explode.

After closing time, I went to our cabin, but Caitlin wasn't there. She'd left a note: *Hangin' out with Mikhail xx.* I went to Cooper's cabin and banged on the door. No answer. I went by the crew bar. He wasn't there. I popped down to the lab. One of his colleagues told me he thought Cooper was up at a party on the crew sundeck, so I headed in that direction.

By the time I had stormed halfway up to the crew deck, I was seething. If there was a party, why hadn't Cooper invited me? What kind of relationship would we have if he kept avoiding social situations together? Granted, we were still somewhat 'secret', but he partied with people all the time. It would hardly ring alarm bells for him to include me on occasion, especially if I was leaving soon.

Just before I opened the door to the windy top deck, I stopped and took a deep breath. "Ellie, arriving angry and ready for a fight won't achieve anything," I muttered to myself.

After I had composed myself, I pushed open the door and stepped outside. I couldn't see Cooper anywhere, but right in front of me were Caitlin and Mikhail. They didn't look happy. In fact, they both looked angry

"Hey guys," I said, "what's happening?"

Caitlin took a deep breath and enfolded me in a hug. "Dude," she said into my hair, "I have to tell you something bad. I'm sorry..." She stepped away and met my eyes.

"What is it?" I asked, worried that something had happened.

"It's Cooper," she said softly. "Mikhail said he was in the spa with some girl, but they disappeared five minutes ago, just before I got here." She studied my face and added, "I'm sorry, roomie."

I stood there blankly for a moment, only vaguely aware of my surroundings. Maybe Mikhail had been wrong, and it hadn't been Cooper. Except... I thought about the time I'd come across Cooper and the girl in the nightclub. Mikhail had defended Cooper then.

"Mikhail," I said, and was pleased to hear that my voice was steady. "That time Cooper was talking to the girl at Diamonds..."

"I'm sorry, Ellie," he said. "He is a great guy, but he's not a good boyfriend."

I was reminded of Luciano apologising for Seth. "What else don't I know?" I asked.

"Well... I don't think that girl had a dead grandfather," he said quietly. "And I think Cooper spent the night with her. More than once." He sighed. "I'm sorry I lied to you, Ellie."

I took Caitlin's arm and tugged her back towards the door I'd come through. I was grateful to Mikhail for his honesty, but I had no words. A large part of me hoped he was very, very wrong, but the heavy feeling in my gut told me he was right. All those times I'd told myself not to be silly, not to overreact, not to be so sensitive...

I felt sick thinking about Cooper with somebody else. And I was so confused; he'd talked about trans-shipping together, and I'd thought... Well, I'd thought we were happy. I thought we were serious. Had everything he'd ever said to me been complete bollocks?

Before I'd even raised my hand to bang on his door, I

heard them. A woman giggled and said something, and then Cooper's voice hushed her.

My heart almost stopped, and for a moment the hall spun around me.

I took a deep breath. I didn't actually have a plan. I'd been hoping that there was some misunderstanding and he was alone. Clearly, that wasn't the case. I wanted to confront him, but I didn't want to do so while I was still so shaky. So I did what any self-respecting woman would do in this situation: I slipped into our cabin to listen through the wall, dragging Caitlin behind me.

Annoyingly, the cabin walls were thin enough to identify individual voices and their genders, but they weren't thin enough to actually pick out the words. We could hear a lot of giggling, a bit of shushing, a fair amount of shuffling, and a faint hint of music.

I fished around the mess on our desk and found a glass; people in the movies were always holding glasses to walls to magnify the sound. I couldn't actually remember which way to hold it, though, and eventually tossed it aside in disgust.

Things got very quiet for a moment, and the pangs in my stomach became so strong I wanted to vomit. That absolute bastard. I lived right next door, and he had to know that it was possible I'd be here. And yet he'd openly brought someone back with him. How had I not noticed?

Or maybe he wanted me to hear. It was a sickening thought. Was this just his way of breaking it off with me? I sank down onto my bed and dropped my head into my hands. How could I have been so wrong about him? I was such a pathetic loser. I'd fallen for three arseholes in a row, each time thinking I'd learned something and determined not to make the same mistake again. I thought I'd worked out how to distinguish the good guys from the bastards, when in reality the only good guy I knew had given up on me and left. God, I was an idiot.

Caitlin was fed up of waiting. "Wait here," she said, standing up. "I'm going next door." She marched out the door and stomped over to Cooper's. I hid inside with my heart pounding as Caitlin banged on Cooper's door and shouted "Open the door, motherfucker!" As I heard it click, I remembered the broken lock. *It sucks to be you, arsehole.*

I heard Caitlin shriek, "How could you?! You knew how much Ellie likes him!", but the reply was too quiet for me to make out.

Who the fuck was in there?

I closed my eyes and took a deep breath. Without thinking about it any further, I got up, went out the door, and turned to face Cooper's cabin. I peered past Caitlin and found myself staring at Ruby, curled up on the bed with the sheet clutched in front of her.

"You," I whispered. "You fucking bitch."

I suddenly understood how Maria had felt about me sleeping with Seth and Luciano—if I'd replaced Maria in their lives, Ruby had done the same to me with Seth and Cooper. The only difference was that I was actually still in a relationship with Cooper...not that the rest of the ship knew it.

I turned my venom on Cooper, who was standing against the wall, his hands clasped in front of him. "And you! You fucking bastard! You said you'd trans-ship with me! Why the fuck didn't you just *tell* me?"

Before Cooper had a chance to defend himself, Ruby said, "Look, Ellie, I'm sorry you found out like this, but you must have known that Cooper was just having fun with you, right? Things are really serious between us." She sighed and then said, "I promised I wouldn't say anything, but the thing is, Cooper had a fiancée who died, so tragically, and when we worked together before the *Galene*, we just got really close. When he got posted here, we just rekindled those emotions." Since she was looking at me, she hadn't noticed the expression on Cooper's face, and continued, "Ellie, I'm sorry if you got hurt, but I'm the first person Cooper's been ready to be serious with, and—"

I started to laugh. It was better than crying. "Wow," I said. "Just...wow." I shook my head. I thought about the girl in the disco, all the times that he'd disappeared, and every night he'd not wanted to stay the night. It seemed pretty clear that he'd been playing me all along, and if Ruby was any indication, he'd been using the same ruse on more than one girl. It occurred to me that we'd had unprotected sex; he'd said he'd been celibate for three years, and I'd believed him. Now I rather suspected he'd been sleeping with other girls the whole time. Shit. I filed that away to deal with later. If that wasn't bad enough, I was pretty sure Jock had been right—Cooper had been using the sob story about his dead fiancée to lure in women. It was perfect: no woman is going to push too hard for details about a dead girl, so the odds he got caught were low.

I shook my head. "I really ought to be thanking you, Ruby, for saving me." I laughed again, feeling slightly hysterical. "You're welcome to him. Him and his lies about Amanda and his tragic past, and his moving story about only now finding The One to enter into a serious relationship with." Something shifted in Ruby's expression, and I added, "Yeah, he suckered me in too. Good luck with that."

Cooper leapt into the breach, giving Ruby a reassuring look and then turning his big sad eyes on me. "Look, Ellie, I'm sorry. I didn't mean for this to happen. I mean, you're a nice girl and all, but, well, Ruby and I are just really well suited. I mean, you're getting trans-shipped…"

"Oh, shut the fuck up," I said, suddenly incredibly tired. All the wind had gone out of me. "I'm tired of listening to your bullshit." Feeling deflated and destroyed, I said as I headed out the door, "Believe him or don't, Ruby, but don't expect to be the only woman in his bed."

Caitlin followed me back to the cabin, made me tea, and then disappeared again. I lay down on my bed, put on my headphones, and turned up the music. I didn't want to hear the activity next door; I didn't want to hear my own thoughts.

Cooper had given me so many small signs, but I'd just ignored them. Every time I'd worried that maybe something was wrong, he'd made me think I was crazy, that I was overreacting, that I was too sensitive—that things were my fault, not his. I'd felt like it was my own paranoia that made me not trust him; I'd thought I was just too insecure to recognise a good thing when I had it. It turned out my instincts had been bang on target; I just hadn't trusted myself. Well, that was a lesson for the future: if your gut tells you something, bloody well listen to it.

I sighed and turned over, pulling the sheets up to my chin. I didn't think I'd sleep, but I was so tired and worn out that I soon started to drift off to my favourite Coldplay song.

Hurts like Heaven, indeed.

Chapter Twenty-One

Despite having drifted off so quickly, I woke up less than an hour later and couldn't get back to sleep, so I lay in bed and thought instead.

I was grateful I'd found out the truth about Cooper before things progressed any further. It didn't mean I wasn't a wreck, though. Did I love him? I wasn't sure. There had been moments when I'd been able to imagine our future together, but...

I sighed. I didn't think I was unlovable. And after months on this boat, I was in the best physical shape of my life; I certainly wasn't unattractive. It was weird, but for once it felt like Maria was the one person on board I most understood—it was a terrible feeling, thinking that you were only ever a temporary shag until someone better came along.

Just because someone desires you, it doesn't mean that they value you.

I had read that once, and it was so, so, heartbreakingly true. Seth, Luciano and Cooper had all been involved with other women, without a moment's thought for how I might feel about it.

The worst part, really, was knowing that I'd just been a bit stupid. I'd gone home to my parents after leaving Dan, but truthfully, I'd never really left the rebound stage. I'd rebounded from Dan to Seth, from Seth to Luciano, and from Luciano to Cooper. I'd put myself out there too much, too soon. Nick had warned me to take it slow, and so had my mother, and I just hadn't listened—I'd wanted so much for my life to change that

I'd tried to do everything at once.

The night before I'd left, my mother had said, "Ellie, don't you behave like a floozy in a jacuzzi on that boat."

"Your mother's right, kiddo," my father had added. "Men don't want to buy the cow when they can get the milk for free."

I'd cringed, and then reminded Mum, for about the eighth time, "It's a ship, not a boat. And I'm not planning on behaving anything *like* a floozy."

How wrong I'd been.

I should have listened to my parents, to Nick, to my own instincts. The thing was, as much as I wanted to hate myself for my behaviour, what upset me most was feeling like I was the one to blame. I wasn't the one who'd cheated, or lied—that had always been them. Maybe I'd acted like a trollop, but they'd behaved much worse, with absolutely no consequences. It was stupid to be cross at myself for behaving the way I had, given that in each instance I'd thought things were going well. I sighed. I'd always had a bad habit of blaming myself whenever anything went to hell, even when—as now—I knew that I wasn't the one in the wrong.

That being said, I didn't really want to go on as I'd begun. I'd decided that there was no point in bashing myself over the head with regret when really I'd done nothing wrong, but that didn't mean I had to keep behaving the way I'd been doing. No, from now on I needed to focus on *me*. I needed to do what was best for me, not try to make myself into someone else so that a man would want me. Before things had gone to shit, I *had* had fun with Seth, and Luciano, and Cooper...but with each of them, I'd put them at the top of my list of priorities. Whatever they wanted to do, whatever their schedules were, I'd put that first. The things I wanted—to do, to have—I'd kept putting last. Wherever I ended up next, I decided, I wasn't going to let that happen again. Maybe I'd find another man, maybe I wouldn't, but I didn't want to lose sight of what was important to me in the process.

As I was thinking this, the door opened and Caitlin slipped

back inside. "Roomie?" she whispered into the darkness. "Are you still awake?"

"Yes," I said quietly. "Hello, lovely."

She flicked on the lamp and came to sit on the edge of my bed. "I'm really sorry about Cooper," she said, squeezing my hand. "I know how much you liked him."

"That's okay," I replied, "We sure know how to pick them, don't we?" I managed a wry smile at the fact we'd both been duped by charming bastards.

"Yup," she said with a sigh. "Sure do." She jumped up onto her bunk, snuggled down under the covers, and whispered, "Night, Ellie."

It was nice to have her sleeping back in our cabin again. Especially when I was feeling so rejected and alone.

By the time Caitlin's alarm pierced the silence the next morning with its awful, shrill ring, I felt as if I hadn't slept a wink. In fairness, I had probably managed only a few hours of sleep, having tossed and turned and fretted for hours.

I dragged myself out of bed and went with Caitlin up to breakfast. Given my recent heartbreak, I was expecting not to be hungry, but I was absolutely starving.

"You better hope Maria doesn't see you," Caitlin said, eyeing my plate. It was piled high with food. "She'll say something cutting about eating your feelings."

"Mmph," I said, sitting down at a table. "Well, she can say whatever she wants, but I'm hungry." I sighed, and then said, "You know, I don't really want to see Cooper, except…"

Caitlin filched a hash brown from my plate. "Yeah, I get it," she said.

I wasn't quite sure *why* I wanted to see Cooper, though. Did I want him to apologise? Beg my forgiveness? If so, then it would be a cold day in Hell before that happened. No, it would be better if he were embarrassed and small, ashamed of his behaviour. I sighed and popped a piece of bacon into my mouth; that was also highly unlikely.

As I was contemplating this, a group entered the mess, and

as I looked up, I caught Cooper's eye. I managed not to choke on the bacon and quickly looked back down.

"Ellie!" he called out.

"Don't say anything," Caitlin murmured. I was glad to have her support.

I nibbled on a few things before sneaking another glance towards the door. Cooper was still standing there, staring my way, looking red and flustered. That was certainly unlike Mr Cool, Calm, and Collected.

Looking annoyed, he marched over to Caitlin and me. "Ellie," he said as he approached our table.

"Just go away, Cooper," said Caitlin, putting down her cutlery. "Leave Ellie alone. You've done enough."

My mouth opened, but no words came out. My heart was thumping so hard, I could feel it in the back of my throat.

"Fuck off, Caitlin. This is between Ellie and me," Cooper said, folding his arms and facing me, trying to edge Caitlin out of the conversation. "Ellie, please, listen to me," he said, kneeling down next to my chair. "I'm so sorry about last night; you've got to believe that nothing actually happened." He was looking at me with his puppy dog eyes. Oh, how I loved those eyes.

No, wait, hang on a minute. I wasn't going to get dragged back in by a pair of sad eyes. I'd been proud of myself for taking a stand last night, and I wasn't going to let that get brushed under the table, no matter how strong Cooper's magnetic aura was.

"Cooper," I said gently, "if you think you're going to convince me of that, you're batty. Or have you just managed to rewrite yesterday's events for yourself?"

"Ellie, honestly, with that whole display you and Caitlin put on the other night, I didn't think you were very serious about me." Oh, for fuck's sake. I could *feel* Caitlin seething beside me, but she stayed quiet. "And I was so upset that you were leaving me for another ship," Cooper continued, "I acted out. I had drinks with Ruby in the jacuzzi because we're old friends, and I did take her to my cabin... To punish you for hurting me.

Things did start to progress a little, but I stopped them before anything serious happened. I know I said that stuff about her and I being well suited, but it was just to stop her from acting crazy after I'd just rejected her. You know how I feel about you."

"Cooper," I said, "I told you that I wanted you to trans-ship with me. You said you'd try to do so. Regardless of whatever happened afterwards, that at least was made clear. You don't get to suddenly claim that I hurt you because I'm taking the offer to trans-ship, and you especially don't get to use that as an excuse for cheating on me."

"Ellie—" he began

"No," I said. I knew the truth. I deserved better. "You know, I never should have trusted you. You were too good to be true, and any time I had doubts, you threw them back in my face. You started to make me feel like I was going crazy, like there was something wrong with *me*, when we both know that you were the real problem." I shook my head, trying to ignore the fact that our conversation had attracted the attention of a number of people around us. "I shouldn't have trusted you before, and I'm not going to make that mistake again. Now, if you don't mind, piss off, because I'm hungry." I picked up my knife and fork again and carefully ignored him.

Cooper's demeanour changed, like the flick of a switch. He got up, saying, "Fine, Ellie. If you can find someone else to put up with your clingy bullshit and paranoia, then go right ahead. Just don't come crying to me when you end up alone." Then he turned and walked away, past the table of photographers, and towards the door.

"Oh, Cooper," I called after him. He stopped and looked around, apparently ready to deliver another insult. I smiled sweetly. "I know you said something about shaving 'down there' because of the heat, but I know the real reason." I held up my fork, on which I'd speared a small link sausage. "I hate to break it to you, but three inches is three inches, no matter which way you shave it."

Cooper's face turned bright red, and laughter burst out at

several tables. He slammed the door behind him as he left the mess, and I sank down into my seat, letting my fork clatter to my plate.

"Well," I said after a moment, "that was...fun." I felt a bit ill.

"Sweetie, let's eat something quick and go," Caitlin said, placing her hand on mine. "Yeah?"

I wasn't very hungry anymore, so I finished my hash browns and followed Caitlin out of the mess. As we reached the table right before the door, a girl I didn't recognise reached out to stop us.

"Good on you, girl," she said, smiling supportively. "He screwed me his first week on board, and then never spoke to me again." She shook her head in disgust.

Ah, and there was my confirmation that Cooper's lies had gone beyond me and Ruby. It was depressing to realise that not only was he a serial liar and manwhore, but that I hadn't suspected anything. Ugh, the things I'd said to him... The things we'd done! I knew she'd only been trying to be supportive, but at that moment I just needed to get away, so without saying anything I bolted for the door, and headed back to the cabin to hide under the covers until I could leave the ship.

Hiding in the cabin except for when I had to work ensured that I didn't run into Cooper again. Hooray for small favours. The week passed incredibly quickly, and in no time at all, it was Friday. St Martin day. The day Caitlin was leaving.

She had to report to the crew purser first thing in the morning, so we were up extremely early. "Dude," Caitlin said, "I know you're supposed to be trans-shipping, but you really need to come to New York. Nick and I won't be the same without you...and we will have SO much fun!"

"What about a visa?" I asked, thinking of the horror stories I'd heard about the American government.

"Come on a visitor visa, and we'll work something out," Caitlin said, waving away my worries. "I've heard people do it all the time."

"I'll think about it, Caity," I said. "It's just… After everything with Cooper, I don't want to hang around here anymore for a moment longer."

"I totally understand," she said. "I can't wait to get out of here either. I still want to poke Gabriel's fucking eyes out."

Nick joined us for the sombre walk down to the purser's office. He'd spent most of his free time during the week with the two of us; he'd felt awful about not being around for the Cooper fiasco, but he'd more than made up for it in the days that had followed.

He helped with Caitlin's bags while I held her hand tightly. I hated goodbyes.

"Well, you can at least come to visit, you silly goose," Caitlin said, pulling me into a hug. "I'll send you a text as soon as we get an apartment and find out the lay of the land. There's a lot of partying to be done in New York, you know."

"We're going to New York, biatch!" Nick hollered, as though Caitlin wasn't standing right next to him.

After Caitlin left, I wiped away my tears, and Nick put his arm around me for the walk back to my cabin. I wasn't really in the mood for St Martin. "I think I'm going to lie down for a while," I told him, now feeling lower than I did already.

"Ellie…" Nick stopped in front of my cabin and turned me to face him. "I know you feel like shit right now, but you know the problem, don't you?" I nodded. "And before you say anything, it's not for the reason you think… You're measuring yourself by the value Dan showed for you when he started treating you like dirt. He said you were fat and boring and not worth shagging, and you wanted to prove him wrong. This is coming from someone who knows from personal experience." He smiled sadly.

This was quite a revelation—Nick had never showed that kind of vulnerability when it came to men. "Really?" I asked, surprised. "You never talk about that stuff."

"Let's just say that lessons have been learned, Princess," he said, still sounding uncharacteristically serious. "I guess it's why I'm so flippant with everything these days…" He took a deep breath and said, "Anyway, you are worth so much more, and I hope you realise that."

Just when you least expected it, the boy with the feather boa came out with a pearl of wisdom.

"But don't feel bad, Princess," he added, sounding more like himself. "Someday you'll be as wise as me." He winked. "I'll come get you for an early dinner at four," he said, hugging me tightly.

Inside the cabin, I flicked on my bed light and lay down to think. I had come aboard to have fun and further my career. I thought back over the last few months. I'd had a lot of fun, made a lot of mistakes, and while I'd amassed a decent number of photographs, including a few good enough for my portfolio, I hadn't taken nearly as many as I should have.

Why had that happened? The more I thought about it, the more I realised that I'd kept letting the men get in the way of my passion for photography. And that was something important to take away with me: I defaulted into making myself into the woman I thought a man wanted, instead of being myself and waiting for a man who loved me for me. I thought of Jock, and realised I actually felt worse about hurting him, about losing him, than I did about Cooper cheating on me. They were different feelings, but I really regretted not valuing Jock enough. Cooper and Ruby, though…well, they'd done me a favour.

Right. I gave a decisive nod. Enough moping. It was time to get properly excited about my new move. I was actually going to work as a photographer! Yes, it was still gangway photos and restaurants, but I could officially write 'photographer' on my CV. I'd wanted this since I was a kid— and now it was finally here.

Damn it, I was going to be trans-shipped and enjoy it. I'd avoid men, go to bed early, save some money, and work on my craft. For real, this time. I needed to focus on me and my dreams—it had just taken me a while to realise it.

That settled, I bounced out of bed and tracked Nick down in his cabin, eager to celebrate. He pulled out the bottle of Kahlua Caitlin had left in his cabin and banged down two shot glasses.

"To Ellie," he said dramatically, handing me one, "and her fantastic, new, exciting life!"

I raised the shot to Nick. "And to you and Caitlin—I *promise* I'll come visit you in New York!"

We both downed our shots, and as Nick poured another, I said thoughtfully, "Now, I wonder where they're going to send me?"

Epilogue

The cold hit me like a bucket of fresh snow as I exited Vancouver International Airport. *Why on earth would a cruise to somewhere so warm start out somewhere so damn freezing?* I thought back to the coldness of England and decided Vancouver wasn't that bad—but after months in the Caribbean, it definitely *felt* cold.

As I got onto the cruise line's mini bus, I looked down at the letter they'd faxed me, containing the details of my new posting.

Position:	Photographer – Level Two
Contract length:	Six months
Ship:	Triton
Departure dock:	Cruise Ship Terminal,
	Canada Place, 100 The Pointe,
	999 Canada Place
	Vancouver, BC V6C 3T4

I was going to be doing a weekly run to Hawaii! Having dreamt of attending a luau since I was a child, I couldn't be more excited. Visiting so many naturally beautiful locations also meant I could work on building my portfolio. I would be knocking on *National Geographic*'s door before long. And I wouldn't even need Cooper's probably fake friend to do it.

After a half hour trip, I stepped off the bus and walked towards the gangway with my fellow newbies, glad to feel a bit more at ease than last time. Now I was a seasoned pro, or at least I pretended to be, nodding and smiling at the people I passed. The sea of crew milling about in front of me seemed to part, and I found myself looking directly into a pair of beautiful blue eyes. I squinted a little as I registered the familiar face, wondering if I was seeing things.

What the...?

Was this a setup? Had my trans-shipping been secretly arranged so that I'd be sent to this particular ship?

A big smile spread across my face because I actually didn't care how I'd ended up here. At least I was here.

And so was he.

"Well, hello there, lass," said Jock, opening his arms for a hug. "I'm glad you finally made it."

I sank into his arms and breathed in his familiar, comforting smell. It was the absolute perfect ending and beginning, all at the same time. Fate had taken care of everything, after all.

– The End –

Author's Note

I hope you enjoyed the book as much as I enjoyed writing it.

Okay, so that's partially a lie. I nearly died from exhaustion writing this book while working full-time and looking after my beautiful baby, who loved to wake me up for a feed just as my head hit the pillow around midnight, then woke up again for the new day at 5am with an absurd amount of energy.

The thing which kept me going was the thought that one day I might make a living from writing books. If everything went to plan (combined with a few prayers and a whole lot of luck), I could quit my day job and do something I loved—something I finally worked out I'm reasonably good at. And with all the crazy shit I've done to inspire me, I've got loads more books in me…

But I need your help. Books—especially ones by debut authors—are usually noticed because of the number of reviews they receive on bookseller websites, Goodreads, etc. If you could write a review, even a couple of sentences, I would greatly appreciate it. Just be honest, and simply write what you'd tell your best friend.

And please go to **www.cathrynchapman.net/readers** to join my Readers' Group. I'll have someone to tell about my latest books, and you'll have the opportunity to be a Beta Reader and win some groovy giveaways. I'll occasionally get around to telling you my latest news, and I promise I won't sell your details.

I'd love to hear from you. Please contact me via Facebook, Twitter, or through the website, to give me feedback or have a chat.

Thanks again. The fact you even read this far totally rocks.

Cath xx

Love, Drugs, and New York

Sailing around the Hawaiian Islands on her new cruise ship, Ellie is happy to have finally found her place in the world. She's pursing her dream of being a photographer and is in a relationship with the greatest guy she's ever known—and even better, he's the marrying kind, so she knows he won't break her heart like every other man she's been with.

The only downside to this perfect life is that Ellie's two best friends are living in New York, having the time of their lives. They desperately want Ellie to join them in their adventures, and even find her an opportunity for her photography to be shown in a prestigious gallery. It's a great chance to take her career to the next level — but it means that Ellie would have to leave the ship, and her boyfriend, behind.

Like so many women in their twenties, Ellie has a hard decision to make between her career and her love life. Should she let go of her perfect boyfriend and pursue her career, following lifelong dreams? Or should she let such a perfect opportunity slip away so she can stay with the only man who has ever truly loved and respected her?

Torn between the two, Ellie must make an almost impossible decision and, in the process, set her life on a path to the future. Whichever way she chooses, she knows that she'll be making a major sacrifice — and realise that sometimes it's impossible to have everything you've ever wanted. Not everybody will be happy with her decision…even Ellie herself.

LOVE, DRUGS, AND NEW YORK is scheduled for release in October 2015. Join Cathryn's Readers' Group at **www.cathrynchapman.net/readers** to find out when it's finished and Cathryn is looking for Beta Readers, and also to receive special member discounts.

Acknowledgments

Without my mentor, James Parsons, this book would never have been finished. Let's be honest, I had absolutely no idea what I was doing, and Jim guided me through the whole thing from planning to completion.

The day I was introduced to Makenzi Crouch completely changed my life. Editor extraordinaire and all-round amazing woman, Mac completely understood my vision, and even when she returned my chapters with enough tracked changes and comments to take my breath away, she was still my favourite person on the planet. Mac made my little story so much better, and I can't imagine ever working with another editor.

I also need to thank Joel, Kathryn, and especially Kristy – my old cruise ship buddies – who helped my story by sharing their thoughts and experiences. Also, my amazing designer friend, Jo Kuipers, for creating the fab cover, and the lovely Wasfi Hfaidhia for photo editing... I would have been lost without my beta readers who gave me immeasurable helpful feedback: Ann, Scotty, Angie, Claudine, Karyn, Jo, Juli and Carmen... and particularly Brinsley, who convinced me it really was worth publishing, even when I was sick of the sight of it.

Finally, to my wonderful husband Andrés, and my Mum, Rose. Without your love, and support in looking after our angel, I would never have been able to spend hundreds of hours locked away in my writing room, convincing you I'd one day sell a million copies, and keep you in the lifestyle to which you'd like to become accustomed. I love you.

Lightning Source UK Ltd.
Milton Keynes UK
UKOW04f1900150715

255274UK00001B/33/P